ANTHOLOGY
Year Three

DISTANT DYING EMBER

Edited by Tim Deal

Four Horsemen
Somersworth, NH

The Four Horsemen Present ...

Anthology: Year Three
Distant Dying Ember

First Print Edition: June, 2015

Copyright © 2015 The Four Horsemen
All Stories and Artwork © their Respective Creators
All Rights Reserved

ISBN: 978-0-9858925-2-4

Editor: Tim Deal
Book Design, Interior Layout, and Line Editing by Tim Deal
Cover by Bob Ford

www.anthocon.com

We, the authors, editors, artists, and friends of AnthoCon, dedicate this book to Tracie Orsi. She, like so many others, fought bravely against such overwhelming odds. We wish peace and light to her and her family.

"Let go. Let love."

CONTENTS

Contents

Contents

Contents

Introduction

LEAVING THE ANTHOLOGY CONFERENCE (ANTHOCON), AND I'm watching the lights from Portsmouth grow smaller in my rear-view mirror. My head feels thick — that last swig of celebratory scotch was probably not a good idea, but hell, it's tradition.

My trunk is full of books and art, a couple of cases of beer leftover from the conference sponsor, and whatever clothing I was too lazy to pack back up before leaving the hotel.

My mind, on the other hand, is filled with images from the weekend. There's the arrival and the excitement of seeing old friends, and the nerve-wracking conference set-up. There's the first conference mixer, which invariably blurs into a string of room parties and a stop in the con suite. There's the morning after where I have to somehow intelligibly, if not eloquently, introduce the keynote speaker. Then the panels, readings, and workshops followed by a dinner party and jam session in the hotel restaurant.

At the end of the conference, I collect my thoughts with the other Four Horsemen (conference organizers Johnny, Mark, and — at the time — Danny), and try to figure out if the whole damn thing was a success. We measure success in a variety of ways (did it break even?), but perhaps most importantly by the level of connection, friendship, and fellowship that the con was instrumental in facilitating. By that metric, the con has been successful *every* time.

And as I drive away from Portsmouth — a simple act that has since 2011 become more poignant and symbolic — I am already looking forward to the next conference and the images, scenes, and stories that will be born from it.

In this anthology, the third of its kind, you'll find a wide variety of stories, poetry, and art from the talented hands of AnthoCon attendees who shared in our vision over the past few years.

Within these pages are terrifying tales of scientific experimentation, apparitions on lonely highways, and death in the cold isolation of the Maine woods; there are space epics, Norse/Cthulu mythos crossovers, and medieval fantasy in verse; there is mystery, apocalypse, and the extreme. *Anthology: Year Three, Distant Dying Ember* is a collection of work that represents the wide range of genres that our guests create.

I think you're going to like this.

— Tim Deal, 2015
Jeddah, KSA

"…And I collected up the song and cheer,
And all I could remember.
Then watched the shrinking harbor lights,
Like distant dying embers…"

— Olga Slivovich, "Blind by the Second Set."

KNOCK AT THE DOOR
Jacob Haddon

"What else did you get?"

I flipped through the newly acquired collection of CDs.

"Jimmy Eat World."

"Who?" Jeff asked.

"You know, that song, It just takes some time, nanananaa…"

Jeff just looked at me.

"Whatever. What else?"

As I flipped to the next one, there was a knock on the door. I displayed the cover to Jeff as Mike pulled himself from whatever stupor he was in to answer it.

"Fuckin' Guns n Roses, dude, put that in," Jeff said. I tossed him the broken CD case, and he went over to the makeshift collection of electronics we called the stereo.

Mike pulled up the bar and dragged the junked car transmission we used as a doorstop out enough to look outside. Sunlight poured in joining the artificial light of our windowless house.

"Who the fuck would be here at this time of day?" I asked.

Jeff, his back to me as he played with the CD player, just shrugged.

"Hey guys!" a voice said. Jeff and I turned to the door.

"Nick, you fuck, what the hell are you doing? Don't you know what time it is?" I said.

The transmission was too damn heavy for Mike. He couldn't pull it all the way back, so Nick had to squeeze through the gap. He had a hose in one hand.

"Hey guys, you mind if I get some gas from one of your cars? It's for the bike so it won't take much."

Welcome to the Jungle started playing on the stereo. Jeff gave me a thumbs-up and came back over to the table.

I looked over at the door.

"Mike! The fuckin' door man!" I yelled.

Mike jumped up and went to the door, pulling down the bar and sliding the doorstop back into place.

Nick glanced around the room with a confused look. He then started nodding his head to the music, a shit grin appearing on his face.

"I haven't heard this in years, man. This shit is awesome," Nick said.

"Where you going?" Jeff asked.

I got up and went to the fridge.

"Beer?"

"San Francisco," Nick answered. He then shook his head, waving the hand with the hose in the air. "I'm gonna be on the road, just need some gas."

"Bring me one," Jeff said. "Nothing fucking imported either. I still can't believe you buy that shit."

"It ain't my fault that you don't like a real beer. Just wish they still made Guinness. That was a real beer."

"Well, Ireland would have to still be around for that," Mike mumbled, lighting up another cigarette.

Nick eyed the door, then us.

"Guys, gas?"

I looked over at my two useless roommates.

"You can get some from the truck. The tank was filled not too long ago," I said, sitting down and giving Jeff his beer. Jeff dealt out the cards for a game of poker.

"Righteous," Nick said. I always hated it when Nick talked like that. Some things I wished hadn't lasted. Survivors hold onto the weirdest things though.

"Ok, well, I'm gonna head out. Check you guys in a few months," Nick said.

"The fuck you are," I said, looking up from my cards. "Your ass is sitting down; you know what time it is."

Nick looked more confused.

"Come on guys, Steve and Bryan are outside waiting for me."

Jeff looked up from his cards, at me, who looked at him. We both turned to Nick.

"You have no idea, do you," Jeff said.

"Fuck, guys, what the hell is wrong with you?"

There was a sound from outside like something heavy being thrown.

"Nick is from the city, remember?" Mike said, fading back into his drug-induced state. "He ain't no country boy like us."

I shook my head and looked back at my cards: an ace, two fours, a three and a deuce. I think Jeff said deuces are wild, but fuck if I was gonna ask and give away what I had.

"Two," I said, taking the chance that the ace wouldn't do me any good.

There was another loud noise from outside. Nick turned nervously to the door.

"What is going on out there?"

Someone outside screamed. I'd never met Bryan or Steve, so I had no idea what they looked like, much less sounded like screaming in pain.

"Dealer takes three," Jeff said.

Another sound, more screaming. Nick moved to the door and started fumbling with the lock.

"Get the fuck away from that door, Nick," I said, still watching Jeff. He had a twitch in his left eye when he was bluffing; it was subtle, but there if you knew where to look.

"What the fuck? Steve! Bryan!" Nick yelled through the door.

Something heavy slammed against the side of the house.

"Harley," I whispered. "Raise you two."

"No, sounds foreign, like one of those big fucking Hondas," Jeff said. The sound was repeated.

"Yeah, hear that? Too much fuckin' plastic. Harley's are all metal."

Nick was in a near panic now. Fucker was stronger than I picked him for too. He lifted up the bar and yanked at the door handle.

Thank Christ for that doorstop. Nick got the door open about two feet in his first pull. By then, the back of the transmission had jammed pretty hard in the space under the door and refused to move any more.

Mike actually looked up.

"Nick, what are you doin' man?"

I looked at the door. Nick was peeking his head out. I put the cards down on the table and ran.

"Bryan! Steve!" he yelled. "HOLY SHIT WHAT THE FUCK IS THAT?"

Nick tried to back away. Something reached in and grabbed him and with one swift motion it broke his body as he was pulled through the door space.

I slammed into the back of the door. The door slammed into something hard on the other side. Less than a second later, Jeff slammed next to me.

"Mike get off your fuckin' ass!" he yelled.

Mike was playing air guitar to Mr. Brownstone and looked up at us. "Oh fuck!"

It took almost three attempts to get the bar down, even with all of us on the door. Mike inched the transmission forward as we went, making sure that fucker stayed out there.

The bar down, the three of us backed away from the door. I bent over to catch my breath.

"Your friends suck," I said, looking up at Jeff.

"Fuck they do. I thought Nick was your friend," Jeff said.

I made my way back to the table and sat down. I had seen that twitch in Jeff's eye right before Nick had opened the door, and I wasn't about to let him get out of this.

Jacob Haddon is an engineer by day, editor by night and a Viking in his sleep. He can be found online at jacobhaddon.com

OZARK
Scott Christian Carr

WILDEST THING I EVER SAW COMING at me, a bear—big one, I'll tell ya what.

Me, I'm no expert. But I'll say he was a brown bear, maybe a grizzly. Crazy thing, he must've been nine feet tall on two legs—six on four. Three tons, if he was an ounce. Claws out, teeth barred, bristling fur, yellow fangs, all growling throat and drool. And when I say he could run—brother, I tell you, he was *fast*.

Here's me, after a good year runnin' into nothing bigger than a raccoon with an ornery streak or a tree-rat with a bad disposition—here's me, after nothing more difficult than a high flying bird to challenge me, and I have no problem telling you that when I say he was scary—brother that bear was *fierce*. And fierce ain't the half of it, ferocious to boot.

Straight up, I'll tell you what: I've no trouble admitting that for second there I panicked. Me, my fight or flight kicked in and tangled up and I was only focused on not soiling my workpants. Me, I'll tell ya—for a second or twelve, I couldn't remember if the Fence was on or off. Him coming right at me and all. But the *Ozark WSC*, they don't put you through six years of intensive border training for you to panic at the first sign of a riled up grizzly barreling outta your neck o' the woods (extinct though they're supposed to be). They don't pay you to forget to keep the Fence turned on.

Gathered my wits and I checked my controls and sure enough, that little green light told me, yeah, it was on. So I relaxed. And when I say relaxed, brother I folded my hands behind my neck and leaned back in my booth and pried my eyes for the show!

The bear's about fifteen yards from the razor's edge line where the wildgrass meets the tarmac, and I do some quick calculating in my head: *Size of bear. Speed of bear. Weight of bear. Inertia.*

I gave him twelve feet. Thirteen on a fluke.

Another second, he hit the line. Hit the line and everything in his face just sort of froze. And when I say froze—brother I mean *dead*.

Then his forepaws are through, and they freeze up, too.

Thinking it back in slow motion, I tell you—to see half of a dead bear coming over the line like that, eyes all glazed over, mouth frozen open an' drooling—it's quite the rush! And all the while, his back legs, they're still tensed and pushing—brother, he was strong!

Well, I'll tell ya what—I'll swear if he didn't slide a good *fourteen feet* over the line, if he slid fourteen inches! Not for nothing, though—any way you cut it, now I had a situation.

See, usually how it is with the smaller animals, I'll gather them all up in the afternoon, and make a pile. End of the day, I'd throw all them little chucks, birds, squirrels, and whatnots back through the Fence and into the tall grass and woods on the other side. Me, I'm supposed to turn the Fence off to do this, but between you and me—I usually leave it on. I get a charge out of the *ZAP!* noise they make when I chuck 'em through.

At night, I have to leave the Fence on when my shift ends, and by morning, usually there's enough dead little critters lying about to start a small pile. Sometimes, though, on really slow days, or when I'm really bored, I'll turn off the Fence, step over the line (something I'm *never* supposed to do) and go in there and find me a big ole' stick. I try to find one that's long and hard, with no branches sticking out of it. Then I go back and turn the Fence back on, and I stick the end of that stick over the line just to hear the little *ZAP!* dragged out into a prolonged *BZZZZZ* and watch the end of that stick turn all gray and dead.

The stick, I'll pull it out and stick it back in, again. And again. Faster and faster. Just laughing, listening to the steady *ZAP! ZAP! BZZT!* Watching it turn grayer and grayer. And brother, I'll go on like this until I'm sure that stick is good and dead.

I'll tell you another thing, though. The air sure is a lot cleaner on the other side of the Fence. On the rare occasion I do find myself over there (like I said, I'm never supposed to go over there), I like to take a good, deep breath. So... *refreshing*, I guess is the word for it. Don't smell nearly as bad as it used to.

Used to be, the smell was so bad along the line, that we'd need to have someone come in once a year just to dig it up and clean it out. Seems that all the bugs and the insects and other little critters trying to come across would start piling up and stinking. That's the price, I guess, that you pay for a sterile city. But that was all years and years ago. It doesn't happen any more. The bugs, for the most part they keep their distance. I tell you, it's like *they know.*

And not just the bugs—I swear that the critter piles I make in the mornings are getting smaller and smaller all the time, too.

I guess the only real problem we ever have is with the high flying birds.

When the birds fly through and die, they usually get pretty far before they come to earth. But that ain't the problem—I've got a radar GPS device in my booth to track wherever they come down, and I can usually send someone right over to pick 'em up. No, the problem is with the really *high flying* birds.

See, the Fence, it ain't so strong way high up. And it doesn't always kill them. Now, nine hundred and ninety nine times outta ten, they'll be stunned and hit the ground before they ever come to. But every once in a while you get a bird that wakes up—and the only way I know it is when the little falling dot on my screen suddenly goes all crazy. I'm lucky, that little bird will be so disoriented he flies back into the Fence and gets himself fried on the other side. But he doesn't, well all I can do then is call to it in. They've got guys to take care of that—I don't know quite how, but they do. I imagine that they shoot them down, somehow.

See, all it takes is for one mamma bird to get through and lay a bunch of eggs somewhere. Birds are incestuous, you know. Before you could say *tweet tweet* we could have a real problem on our hands.

And now I've got another sort of problem, namely a bear. A bear that's too big for me to just push him through the Fence, toss him back into the woods. Brother, I couldn't roll him in. So me, for a while I just sit there in my booth. Looking at him.

My funny little booth—always reminds me of a brave little kid running ahead of the parent buildings behind him. Escaping the mob. My stainless steel little booth, sitting almost exactly between the city and the woods. And me in my booth, I'm just sitting there, watching the carcass of the bear. And brother, let me tell you, I didn't know *what* to do.

After a bit, I noticed that there were a lot of dead flies starting to build up in a circle around the bear. The same thing happened around my piles of critters, on sunny days. Hungry little bloodsuckers, buzzing outta the grass and through the Fence. One more clean-up to deal with.

So, next day and I'm still trying to figure out what to do. Sitting in my booth, looking over my manual for any bear suggestions I might've somehow missed, when brother, I saw something so strange that for a second I forgot all about my bear problems. And when I say weird—I mean I ain't *never* seen the likes. And not coming out of the woods, neither. Coming out of the city.

A man and a woman, all haggard looking, scruffy and whatnot. The man, he's got himself a scraggly old beard, and brother, I'm not one to talk, but it just didn't look clean. On his back, he's got a backpack the size of I don't know what. And don't ask me what it could have been filled with.

Their clothes, they're all faded and worn out (me, I always made sure my groundskeeper's uniformed was neatly pressed every morning, my *Ozark WSC* badge proudly displayed). And the woman, she's got a little ole' baby all cuddled up in her arms.

Believe me when I tell you, I jumped up and out of my booth and ran on over to see what was what! Mind you, I didn't want them getting no wrong impressions about that bear. You see, there are certain things that ordinary people just shouldn't have to see. Don't get me wrong, not that there are actual *laws* to such an affect—I wouldn't get in no trouble or anything, at least not too much. But there's a certain decorum—a *Code* that we at *Wildlife Sanitation and Control* like to follow. That is, that there's just some things that ordinary citizens shouldn't have to see—dead bears being one of 'em.

Brother, that hot Sun, it's beating down on my big ole' grizzly, and I have to laugh when I picture myself standing between them and the bear. Like I had any chance in hell of keeping them from seeing it. And brother, when I say *seeing* it, I mean that baby started to cry, and the woman started gagging on the smell that was coming off the thing. And the man, well his eyes, they just got wider and wider—all glassy and staring and whatnot. I mean, that bear was *ripe*.

"Help you folks?" I kept my hands in my pockets, trying to assume an unassuming position between them and you know who.

"The hell is that?" the man, he's eyeing up my grizzly. "A bear?" Me, I just nodded. "You killed it?" he asked.

"No," I said, suddenly feeling defensive. "But he's too big for me to roll back into the woods."

"Maybe you should call someone to help," he's looking at the badge on the sleeve of my uniform.

"That's what I was just about to do," I stammered, "when I saw you folks coming down the street. How can I help you?"

"Were just heading out," said the man.

"Out where?" I had no idea what he was talking about.

Him, he just nods towards the forest. "Out of the city. Into the woods."

"You're going over the line?" I couldn't believe what I was hearing. "I don't think that that's allowed. Pretty sure it ain't. You'll wanna talk to someone in *Population Allocation*, or *Housing Research and Development*."

"Don't think so," still not taking his eyes off the bear. His wife, she just keeps looking down at her feet, whispering to the baby not to cry and whatnot.

"WSC," he says. "Your job is keeping the animals out?" Still looking at the bear, not me. Talking all quiet.

"Yep," I said.

"Not keeping people in."

"Well, not technically, I guess…" I don't know why, but I'm unable to meet his piercing eyes.

After what seems like forever, "That's sure a big bear, isn't it?" he says. "Such a shame. I'd hate to think what the *Green Police* or *God's Gardeners* might have to say about it." Him, frowning. Me, just staring at him, then the bear, then my muddy boots. Me, I didn't know *what* to say. Him just glaring right back at me and all, and after a while I figured I'd better say *something*.

"I'd still have to report it," I said. "If you went over the line."

The man, he just keeps staring at that dead ole' bear and after a while he says, "Ozark's a big place. Three days is all we'd need." He never even looked at me. "Three days," he said.

For a little bit, all of us just stared at the bear. All you could hear was that baby crying and the occasional *ZAP!* of a fly coming over the line. Breathing in the reek of it all. Finally, 'cause I couldn't think of nothing else, I said, "I suppose I could wait until the end of the week before I file my report."

And then, I don't know what came over me, but when I say came over me—brother, I guess I just didn't want any trouble. I said, "Maybe if you waited until I wasn't looking, then I wouldn't have anything to report at all."

And him, he just kept staring at the bear. His wife shifting the baby in her arms, and I'm not sure, but I'm pretty sure, that he nodded.

So I turned around went back into my booth. I watched the woods in the other direction for a while. Twiddled my thumbs. Looked the other way. Then I picked up the phone to call a man about a bear.

Dialed the number and the extension, and when I heard the click I suddenly got this sinking feeling in the pit of my stomach. And when I heard my man say hello, that sinking feeling just squeezed itself into a hot, tight little ball. I clenched shut my eyes, my temples starting to throb. Sweat broke out in my armpits, ran down my sides.

I was afraid to turn around. Afraid even to open my eyes, because brother—I couldn't for the life of me remember if I'd left that Fence off or on.

Scott Christian Carr has been a radio talk show host, editor of a flying saucer magazine, fishmonger, spelunker, psychonaut, journalist, award winning poet, TV producer, and author. He is a Bram Stoker Award nominee, Scriptapalooza 1st Place Winner for Best Original TV Pilot, and in 1999, he was awarded The Hunter S. Thompson Award for Outstanding Journalism. Visit him at: www.scottchristiancarr. com

THREE LITTLE WORDS
Michele Mixell

SAM GLANCED AROUND THE COFFEE HOUSE, looking for an open table. The place was crowded for a weekday morning, and he considered just tucking his newspaper under his arm and returning to his sister's apartment. The four block walk had left a slight stiffness in his back, though, so when he caught sight of the empty booth in the back, he headed straight for it.

He made it as far as setting his tall paper cup on the table before he realized the booth was, in fact, occupied. A dark-haired woman, leaning over a paperback so that she was a few inches shorter than the high back of the bench, looked up at him. Her startled green eyes were wide behind a pair of dark rimmed glasses.

"Oh, excuse me," he said, trying not to stammer. "I didn't see you there."

"That's okay. Please, go ahead." She motioned to the empty seat across from her. "It's pretty much standing room only in here otherwise."

Sam thanked her and slid into the booth, wincing slightly at the twinge in his right side as he did so. He was relieved to be off of the pain medication that had often left him nauseated and clouded his head, but today he missed the sweet numbness they had afforded him.

The woman — barely more than a girl, he realized now — had turned her face back down to her book, but was watching him curiously over the top of her glasses.

"Are you alright?" she asked.

"Oh, I'm fine," he replied. "Recovering from a back injury, is all."

She hesitated a moment, then said, "I'm sorry to stare, but you look so familiar."

"I've been coming in every day for the last two weeks."

The young woman shook her head and closed her book, laying it aside. "This is actually my first time here. No, I've seen you somewhere, but I don't think it was in person." She leaned closer, propping her chin up on her fist and chewing at her bottom lip as her eyes examined his face. "I think you were on the news."

Sam felt a flush in his cheeks. It seemed his fifteen minutes weren't quite over yet.

"Well, yes, I suppose I was." He looked, almost sheepishly, down at his coffee cup, waiting her out without offering a hint. He found he was still a little uncomfortable with the attention his story had attracted.

"Oh!" she exclaimed suddenly, snapping her fingers. "I remember now! The fire on George Street last month. You're the guy. You pulled your whole family out of that burning house."

He nodded. "Yes, my wife and daughter."

"I'm afraid I can't recall your name…"

"Sam," he said, offering his hand.

"Ellie," she replied, accepting with a shake. Her hand was pleasantly warm in his, and he thought he could still feel a little of that heat linger on his skin when she pulled away. "I hadn't expected to have coffee with a genuine hero this morning."

"That word," he sighed. "I really didn't do anything all that extraordinary."

"You saved your family's lives. That's a big deal."

"Anybody would've done the same for people they love."

"You're a humble guy, Sam," Ellie said, a slight lilt in her voice that made him suddenly wonder if she wasn't hitting on him just a little. She could be no more than twenty-five, and was the sort of pretty that could gain the favor of any man half his forty-eight years. Still, even a slight touch of fame could be pretty impressive to younger women. At least, so he'd heard.

"The news said you had to carry your wife, huh?"

"Martha passed out," he said. "From the smoke. Jenna, our daughter, was able to follow us out on her own."

"Tough kid. How old is she?"

"Twelve."

"How are they now?"

"They're both fine," he said. "Thank God."

"Well," Ellie said, one corner of her mouth rising into a smirk. "Thank *someone.*"

Sam opened his own mouth, then paused. The hairs on his arm had begun to stand up. "I, um, I'm afraid I don't follow."

Ellie leaned forward, and asked, in a conspiratorial whisper, "Did you pray, Sam?"

"*What?*"

"That night, with your eyes stinging and the smoke flooding your lungs, and Jenna's hand clasped so desperately onto the back of your shirt. When you felt your foot slip off the top stair, in that instant when Martha's limp body shifted and the pain ripped through your back, and you knew — just *knew* — you were going to fall. You were going to drop your wife and tumble down the stairs after her, dragging your little girl along and leaving all three of you to die in your own burning home. In that split second of absolute certainty that you were about to lose not only your own life, but those of the two people you love most in this world, *did you pray?*"

Sam was stunned into paralysis, his mouth hanging open, his knuckles white as he clasped the table's edge.

"How?" he started in a hoarse voice, and paused to clear his throat. "How could you know —"

"*Sam.*" Her tone was sharp, and something dark passed behind her eyes. "Yes or no."

"I… Yes, yes I think I did. I'm sure I did." The words rushed out of him in a single breath. "I haven't since I was a child but I prayed then, I prayed for God to help me hold on, to give me the strength to save my girls."

"Now, we both know that's not precisely true."

From the bench beside her, Ellie produced a black briefcase. She sat it on the table, and opened it facing away from him so he could not see inside. She took out a small notepad, leafing through a few pages before focusing on one in particular.

For the first time, Sam noticed she had not ordered a coffee.

"Ah, here we are. Your exact words that night were simply 'Please help me.' Does that sound right to you?"

He tried suddenly to stand, to walk, no, *run*, straight to the door and back to the clear reality of the world outside. At the same time, her hand shot across the table to lock over his, the movement so fast it was barely more than a blur. Her touch was no longer merely warm, but scorching against his skin. The shadowy darkness flickered behind her eyes again.

"You don't want to do that, Sam."

He stared at her, the noise and bustle of the shop fading into the background as a bead of sweat slid down his temple.

"Who *are* you?"

Ellie smiled. "A duly appointed representative."

"Of who?" he barely managed to whisper.

"I think you know who by now." And she winked at him.

Sam slumped against the hardwood back of the booth. "No," he muttered. "That can't be. I never asked —"

"You never specified. It's a bit of a loophole, yes, but you should be glad for that."

Sam swallowed a hard lump in his throat, and took a deep, slow breath, trying to control his pounding heart. Her hand was still clutching his, the burning heat of her touch growing almost unbearable.

"What do you want?" he asked finally.

Ellie appeared pleased, relaxing her posture and lightening her tone, though not yet releasing his hand.

"My employer provided you with a very valuable service," she said. "A service, I'll point out, that our competition does not go around handing out to just anyone who bends the preverbal knee. Do you think if you had directed that panicked request of yours upward that you would be here today? That Jenna would be in school right now, or Martha at breakfast with your sister?"

Sam did not reply. Hearing the names of his loved ones coming from the mouth of *whatever* it truly was he was sitting across from made every muscle in his body clench.

"All three of you would have burned to death at the bottom of that staircase," she continued. "Do not doubt it."

He shook his head slowly. "I don't believe you." He looked her straight in the eye. "And I don't believe this. *Any* of this. This is some sort of dream, or a hallucination. A reaction to the pain medicine, maybe."

"Doctor Bennet took you off the meds three days ago, Sam," she said, matter-of-factly. "Now, shall we discuss the terms of payment?"

"*Payment?*" he gaped.

"Of course. You walked away from certain death with your life, Sam, and with the lives you hold most dear. Did you really think that would come without a price?"

He frowned. "Whatever it is, I won't —"

"But you will, because it's never too late for our services to be *revoked.*"

Her hand tightened its grip, the heat shooting up his arm and flooding the rest of his body. He inhaled sharply, and his lungs suddenly stung with a hideous flood of searing smoke. Sweat ran into his eyes, and he squeezed them shut. When he opened them again, what little breath he had managed to inhale was trapped in his chest.

Sam was back at the top of the stairs, surrounded once more by the flames as they devoured his home.

He was back, and he knew that it wasn't a memory or a dream. It was real, it was that night happening again, now, and his foot was once more sliding off the step as Martha shifted unexpectedly in his arms. He was twisting to the side again as pain tore through his back, and this time the words did not come.

They didn't have time to come, as his wife of twenty years rolled from his grasp, dropping into smoke-filled space, and he was following her, feeling only a momentary tug of Jenna's hand on the back of his shirt, her grip too frightened to let go, and he was falling, dragging her after him, and he reached out his arms to brace himself...

And was pulled back. Not a physical pull, but as if someone had hit a rewind button. The pain retreated and he was upright again, his arms tightening back around Martha's body, the step returned solidly under his feet.

Fearing he was about to relive the scene again, madness momentarily fluttered at the edge of Sam's mind. He opened his mouth to scream, and began to cough.

He gasped, and the blessedly clean, aroma-rich air of the coffee shop greeted him. His body jerked, and he looked around, startled. Ellie had finally released him, and sat watching with a look of smug satisfaction.

"You understand, don't you?" she said. "What just happened?"

Sam nodded. He had to clasp his hands together to keep them from shaking, and there were tears in the corners of his eyes. His posture had become that of a praying man, but the words were lost to him.

"Let me hear you say it."

"Yes," he whispered. "I understand. That was real. This is real. All of it."

"Good."

From inside her briefcase she produced a photograph, sliding it across the table to him. Sam couldn't bring himself to touch it, only looking down into the smiling faces of a pair of girls he did not recognize. One was a blonde, the other a brunette, both dressed in casual hiking gear and NYU sweatshirts. It appeared as though the blonde had held the camera to take the photo at arm's length. A pine tree-laden forest spread out behind them.

"Who are they?" Sam asked.

She raised an eyebrow. "Are you sure you want to know?"

He felt something in his stomach turn over, and a dark idea occurred to him.

Ellie shook her head. "I wouldn't recommend it."

"What?"

"Killing yourself. It would be cheating, and my employer does NOT go easy on cheaters. It wouldn't save them anyway. *Your* family, I mean. He'd make you go through it all again, the fire, the fall. Only this time, you'd live. Just you. You would have to watch your family burn, and see what's leftover be buried in the ground, and you would remember why."

She placed another item next to the photo of the two girls. It was a folded map, and he could see "MOUNT DESERT ISLAND" printed at the top. Below was an expanse of green labeled "ACADIA NATIONAL PARK," and an area circled in red pen. Beside the circle were a set of numbers he recognized as coordinates.

"This isn't right," Sam said. "I'm a good person. My wife, our daughter, we don't deserve this."

"So?"

"So… Why?"

Ellie shrugged, taking a third item from the briefcase. The object was nearly ten inches long, and wrapped in a red handkerchief. It made a heavy clunking sound when she sat it on the map.

"I suppose it's mostly because you're a good person. There's no challenge otherwise."

He finally pried his fingers apart, reaching out and running them over the item. Through the thin fabric, he could feel the distinct edge of a hunting knife blade.

He looked up into her eyes.

"I don't have a choice in this, do I?"

"Of course you have a choice, Sam." Ellie favored him with one last, sweet smile. "It's simply between what you can live with, and what you can't live without."

Michele Mixell is an author, photographer, artist, & dinosaur wrangler from Central Pennsylvania. Her short fiction has appeared in Apokrupha's LampLight Magazine and Dark Bits. Her novella "End of the Night" can be found in their collection FOUR SLEEPLESS NIGHTS.

RASPBERRY SUMMER
Diana Catt

"JUST LOOK AT THESE WOUNDS, YOUNG man," Cora McCardle said, rolling up the sleeve of her bathrobe and pulling off the bandage. "You'll never believe what happened." She was hard of hearing and compensated by speaking loudly. I smiled, nodded encouragement, and adjusted my glasses for a closer look at my patient.

Cora launched into her tale. "It was like a scene from that old Hitchcock movie about the birds. You must know it. Except these weren't psycho seagulls. They were crows. Psycho crows."

Cora McCardle is my oldest patient, coming in at just under ninety-eight. That's both age and weight. I've been her physician, seeing her once a month on average, ever since she moved to Pleasant Vista Estate ten years ago.

"I must admit," Cora continued, as I lifted her arm to examine several deep scratches, adjacent puncture wounds and surrounding bruises, "I never could watch it to the end. The short story, however, was captivating."

The shapes of her wounds were definitely unusual. Punctures of varying depths, some with jagged edges. The facility nurse had done a good job cleaning them, but one required stitches. I started to explain my treatment plan, but Cora continued her rambling.

"Guess I prefer writing horror, or reading it, to watching it on a little screen. I wish I'd watched that movie from start to finish, though. In Daphne's story, the birds' behavior was never completely explained. Did Hitchcock provide a reason in the movie? Maybe it'd help me understand what's going on in this crazy world. Right now, I'm living the horror."

Cora is also, by far, my most famous and dramatic patient. She was a celebrated writer in her heyday. Knew all the old timers. Dropped names like crazy, but I'm sure this time it's for real. Daphne du Maurier reviewed one of Cora's novels. I know because the review is in a frame on her wall and was one of the first things Cora showed me when I entered her life.

"Remember what I told you last time you were here?" she continued.

I didn't remember, but it didn't matter. Cora reminded me.

"Things are changing in a weird way. I still have that funny feeling and it's not from insomnia like you thought. I know what happened to me yesterday and just because I'm old doesn't give those damn nurses the right to accuse me of anything."

"Calm down, Cora," I said, watching her face to confirm that she was listening. "Tell me what happened."

She closed her eyes for a moment, took a deep breath, and let out a sigh. "Yesterday was the first day of summer. There, you see? I'm still well-oriented in my mind as to time and place, for God's sake. Those nurses...."

"Cora..."

"All right, I won't complain about them. But it's significant, I think, that this happened on the first day of summer. The influence of planetary alignment may not be bullshit after all. I used that in my third novel, I think, but I can't rightly recollect the details. Anyway, I took my usual morning walk down by the woods over there. You can see them from here if you kind of lean way over to your left. Dorene says Marjorie went with me, but I doubt it. I'm sure I'd remember her whining. Besides, Marjorie doesn't like to walk very far."

She glanced at me and I nodded, so she continued.

"Yesterday was a cool, drizzly day. Felt like a storm brewing. Not a promising start for summer. I can remember when summer was always hot. Hot and dry and endless. So much to do in the summer, isn't there? My brother and I would play outdoors for hours before Mom would call us in."

A smile materialized on Cora's face from beneath the deep wrinkles, making her look twenty years younger. Her pale blue eyes twinkled at a bygone memory.

"What happened yesterday, Cora?" I asked, trying to refocus her thoughts.

The smile vanished as quickly as it had appeared. "I'm telling you if you'll listen. I just wanted to emphasize that it wasn't your typical summer day. My mind is not wandering. If you want to hear this, you'll have to let me tell you in my own way."

My turn to sigh. I waved my hand for her to continue, catching a glimpse of the time on my watch.

"Okay, then," she said. "I'd noticed the wild raspberries were ripening so I took a small bucket along. I love raspberries, heated in syrup, on a stack of steaming pancakes. Such a special summertime treat!"

My attention wandered for a minute while Cora rambled on about cooking.

"Are you listening?" she asked.

"Of course, Cora," I lied.

"I said it's fun and excitement that make life worth living. Don't forget it, young man. You really seem too serious for your own good. Are you still in your twenties?"

"I'm over forty, Cora. You know that." I scribbled a description of her wounds in the chart.

"Lord-y, I'm way off," she laughed. "Well, I hope you didn't waste those years and had yourself some fun."

When I didn't reply she returned to her narrative. "Now, yesterday was exciting, I'll grant you that. But, I wouldn't exactly call it fun. Some of the berries were ripe, as I expected. Black raspberries, plump and juicy. Did you know Daddy Long Leg spiders like to eat raspberries? I find that fascinating. Imagine being that tiny spider, with that strange circle of a body controlling those outrageous legs and discovering a luscious ball of sweet juice. Then imagine being brutally dashed aside by a giant human hand which steals your personal piece of heaven. I don't suppose they think about it though."

I put my finger to my lips for quiet while I listened to her breathing, checked her pulse and heart rate.

"*Revenge of the Spiders*," she said when I put my stethoscope in my pocket. "That's a good title. Write that down so's I'll remember it after my nap."

I humored her and jotted down her title idea after I entered her vitals in the chart.

"My bucket was nearly full when I noticed the birds," she continued. "Actually, the first was a catbird. Do you know it?" I shook my head. "No? You should get outdoors more, young man. Learn a few things. Take time to relax. The catbird's mostly all gray, with a speck of red. A little smaller than a robin. Surely you know the robin?" She looked relieved when I nodded.

"Anyway, I know this particular bird. He's always in the area around the wood's edge. I hear his call nearly every morning and see him sometimes, though my eyesight's worse than my hearing."

I could debate that point, but I chose a different tactic.

"So, when did Marjorie join you?" I asked.

"Marjorie who?"

"Come on, Cora. You know Marjorie Moore – from across the hall?" Was it fear flashing momentarily in Cora's eyes? I'd seen that look in elderly patients when they realize they should be able to remember something but cannot. Dementia strikes fear into the stoutest heart. I'd also seen the same look in the eyes of the guilty. Which was Cora?

"I didn't know you meant Marjorie Moore. She's never joined me on a walk. Can she still even walk? I never see her anymore."

I patted Cora's hand. "Dorene says you and Marjorie had a fight. That you two hadn't spoken in weeks, and then yesterday you asked Marjorie to help you pick berries."

"Don't believe a word of it. Dorene hates me, the little shrew. Can't mind her own business."

"So you didn't see Marjorie yesterday?"

Cora stared at me for so long I was afraid she'd lost track of our conversation. "Marjorie wasn't with me," she said finally, then returned to her account.

"I upset the poor little catbird. It didn't like me picking the berries, I guess. I'm more of an adversary than those small spiders. Competitors for the same food source and all. Or, maybe it wanted to eat the spiders and not the berries? I just thought of that.

"Either way, the little thing was overly agitated. It started coming closer to me, calling out its song quite insistently, following me from briar to briar all along the tree line. Getting closer and closer to my arms and head each time it flew by. He was becoming a pest, but not frightening. It happened right over there. See. If you lean out just a little more you can see it from here. Yes, there."

She pointed out the window. I leaned forward in my chair and craned my neck in order to view the area. The woods from the adjacent farm grew right up to the property line. Briars, still bearing their white blooms, were thick along the edge of Pleasant Vista Estate's boundary. The deep ditch separating the two properties was not obvious from this viewpoint. The crime scene tape could be seen though. "Tell me what happened next. How did you end up hurting your arm?"

Cora shivered. "I may not walk down there ever again," she said. "Without warning, I was surrounded by birds. I noticed the blue jay's arrival. And the cardinal's. Then the crows joined in. A murder of them.

Maybe if I had watched that movie to the end I would have recognized the catbird's behavior as a warning and been prepared for the attack."

"You mean that's how you got these wounds? From birds?" I couldn't keep the astonishment out of my voice. Cora's imagination was insufferable at times.

"Yes. It was an onslaught. I was defenseless. Well, I had the bucket, of course, which I swung rather wildly. See it, sitting there in the corner. I'm sure I hit a few crows. Cost me every damn berry I picked. I'm going to change that title to *Revenge of the Birds*. I've got enough material to do a sequel to Daphne's. We're ruining their habitat and the little buggers want revenge."

She looked defiant now, waiting for me to challenge her storyline.

"And then you fell into the briars?"

"Exactly," she said, triumphantly. "Those damn nurses just laughed, but this is a serious situation."

"Yes, I agree. Is that what happened to Marjorie, too?"

"I told you Marjorie wasn't with me. I don't know as anything's happened to her." She looked at me suspiciously then. "Has something's happened to Marjorie? Is that the real reason you're here?"

"Yes. I'm sorry, Cora. Marjorie's body was found today in the ditch beyond the briars. Right near where you fell yesterday, from what you're saying."

Cora flew up out of the rocker and stood staring wide-eyed at me. "Someone must be notified. The game warden or… an ornithologist. Someone. I was nearly killed by that vicious community of birds. And now they've murdered Marjorie. They're organized, you can be damn sure of that. They've killed my best friend." Her voice lost its bravado. "What can we do?"

I put my arms around Cora's frail shoulders and could feel her body quake. I guided her over to her bed. "I'm going to give you something to help you relax, Cora. It's time for your nap, anyway."

"I don't need anything to calm me down," she said. "What I need are shots for rabies. Look at these arms. Surely you can tell the difference between briar scratches and bird pecks. Doctor, please believe me. I saw it, I tell you. They were mad. The whole world has gone mad."

The shot took effect quickly. She's a tiny woman, after all. Too tiny to have inflicted the damage that Marjorie sustained. The medical examiner told me Marjorie died from a blow to the back of the head; possibly hit a rock when she fell. I walked over to the corner of the room and picked up Cora's bucket. There were feathers sticking to the berry juice on the outside of it, not hair. The medical examiner had also described puncture wounds on Marjorie's body which were of different depths and of unknown origin. That was eerily similar to Cora's wounds.

According to Cora, her injuries were the result of a massive bird attack. A crow's beak would certainly poke a bigger hole in the flesh than the smaller catbird's, and could account for the different depths of the wounds, but whoever heard of an organized bird attack? Other than Daphne du Maurier and fans.

As I left the assisted living facility, I had a sudden impulse to wander down to the briar patch where Cora experienced her bird misadventure and where Marjorie fell to her death. Today certainly met Cora's requirements for a typical summer day and I didn't walk far before I felt sweat trickling down the back of my shirt. The heat was diffused momentarily when I passed through the shade of a sprawling oak. A flier was stapled to its huge, gnarled trunk. It read, "Beware – Birds in this area may attack." The Pleasant Vista Estate letterhead suggested someone at the facility took Cora's story seriously.

I stepped out of the shade and continued toward the edge of the raspberry bushes. I stood still in the bright sunlight, arms akimbo, inspecting the briars, careful not to step into the area the police partitioned off. I suppose I expected obvious bird activity around secluded nests, or excessive amounts of bird droppings, or at least a loud, raucous chatter from perturbed bird inhabitants. But all was quiet. I began to regret this whim. I'd barely have time to run home and change into a fresh shirt and tie before my afternoon clinic.

Still, I felt a bit uneasy. I had lost one patient at this location and a second was wounded and confused. When a small gray bird suddenly flew across my field of view I jumped back with a start. But, it merely flew by. I felt foolish at my response.

However, the longer I stood there the more activity I observed. In fact, I witnessed several birds plucking berries off the bush, and another was single-mindedly pursuing the spiders that seemed to be everywhere. I decided to try an experiment. I stepped, as quietly and as unobtrusively as I could, toward a briar bush occupied by several small birds. I spotted a cluster of black raspberries deep within the center and thrust my arm into the dense thicket of jumbled briar branches. Thorns snagged at my shirt and I cursed as sharp pricks found the back of my hand. My fingers curled around the fruit and I withdrew my arm slowly to avoid further damage.

Suddenly, a mass of birds rose as one from the nearby brush, screeching into the quiet countryside. My heart pounded in my chest and I ducked to avoid the mêlée. I turned and ran back toward the parking lot and the safety of my car.

I sat in my car and took inventory. I was basically unharmed and no birds were chasing me. Then I started to laugh. I was a mess. The squished berries left purple streaks all over my fingers and palm. The back of my hand bled from numerous tiny scratches and my shirtsleeve was torn. Worst of all, I had lost all dignity by fleeing from tiny woodland creatures.

I contemplated what I'd learned from the fiasco as I drove away. The two women had most likely had similar experiences: startled some nesting or feeding birds while leaning in to pick the raspberries, lost their precarious balance and then pitched into the briars and down into the ditch. I was sure that if the police looked hard enough they'd locate the rock Marjorie hit her head on while tumbling down the embankment. It made sense to me. Cora's unique mind had woven a story to fill the blank spots in her memory. I decided to keep my little excursion to myself and not add fuel to Cora's imagination.

Later that evening I returned to Pleasant Vista Estate, eager to check on my patient. As was my habit, I first stopped by the nurse's office to see if anyone needed urgent attention. The evening shift nurse mentioned her shock at losing Marjorie so suddenly, and how Marjorie had intended to surprise Cora with the freshly picked berries.

"You mean Marjorie wasn't with Cora when the accident happened?" I asked.

"No. It's odd, isn't it, that both were injured at the same spot? I've already suggested to management that we fence off the area so no one else tumbles into that death-trap of a ditch."

"Did Cora say anything about birds?" I asked.

The nurse laughed. "That's all she's been talking about. Why, I'm surprised Marjorie was brave enough to go berry picking alone this morning after listening to Cora's terrifying tale. Mr. Moore pooh-poohed the idea of a bird problem, of course, and that made Cora a little mad. I think Marjorie hoped the berries would restore peace between them. It's so sad she fell like that."

"Mr. Moore? Is that Marjorie's son?"

"Nephew. Buck visits three times every week, regular as clockwork."

I mulled this over, wondering if Cora had any regular visitors. I asked the nurse.

"Oh, yes. Occasional fan letters still reach her and lately a college student's been interviewing her for a project. Got her all fired up, ready to write again. I'm sure she'll tell you all about it, as soon as this 'bird attack' thing dies down."

I found Cora sitting at her writing desk.

"Glad to see you, Dr. Walsh," she said, swiveling around to face me.

"How are you feeling this evening, Cora?"

"Fine." She stuck out her bandaged arm. "One of the nicer nurses changed the bandage after dinner."

"Good," I said, "but I'll just take a peek, as long as I'm here." She was quiet as I examined the bandage and then took her blood pressure. When I finished she grabbed my arm with more strength than I thought possible for someone her age.

"Don't go out there, Doc," she said in her brash voice. "They're waiting. I watched a dark cloud move in today. It separated into thousands of birds when it reached the woods. They've gathered and are just waiting for a victim. Best to stay indoors."

"Thanks for your concern, Cora, but I'll be fine."

"I've remembered something," she said, whispering now. "About Marjorie." She looked significantly toward the open door and nodded when I shut it.

"What have you remembered?" I asked.

"I spoke to Marjorie after that gold digger, Dorene, cleaned me up yesterday." She met my gaze, unwavering. "I think Marjorie went out there alone this morning to pick raspberries for me. She knew how much I looked forward to them every summer."

"It wasn't your fault, Cora," I said.

"Hell no, it wasn't my fault," she said. "That's not where I'm going with this. I think someone tried to cover up murder by making it look like a bird attack. I understood Marjorie very well – better than most. She'd never have reached very far into the briars to get the berries, even to please me. Afraid of the thorns."

"What do you mean?"

"It's the berries, don't you see?" Cora sighed dramatically. "Marjorie would've only picked the ones within easy reach. Think about it. She'd never have stirred up the birds like I did. She'd never stretch so far into the briars that she'd lose her balance and fall into that ditch, either. Someone pushed her."

"But who would want to hurt Marjorie?"

"How the hell would I know? For God's sake man, if I can figure out the 'how' while sitting in my room, surely you and the police can figure out the 'who' and the 'why.' Follow the money trail, as they say."

Cora's pale blue eyes held a fierce determination. There was no point in arguing with her. Her logic was hard to dispute and I agreed to give the problem some serious thought. She said she'd give me a chance, but then she'd still call the police herself first thing in the morning. I thanked Cora for her vote of confidence and continued my scheduled rounds.

Marjorie's unfortunate fall was the major topic of conversation among the residents, and I couldn't help but give Cora's observations some credence. Marjorie had always struck me as a timid woman. If Cora was right and Marjorie was too afraid of the thorns to reach in after the berries, how had she managed to tumble into the ditch? Maybe she the heat made her dizzy? Maybe the terrain was uneven causing her to stumble? Maybe she was pushed? Although the sun was low on the horizon, I decided to take another look at the site of Marjorie's death before heading home.

This time I viewed the scene with a different frame of mind. Someone could easily park and walk down there without being seen from the facility. And the gnarled oak tree with the flier posted to it was near the ditch and large enough to conceal someone from a berry-picker's view.

Of course, I was thinking about the nephew, Buck Moore. Who else had ties to Marjorie? And he could have known of her berry-picking plans. I imagined a middle-aged man, probably overweight and balding, holding a large stone in his left hand – no, make it his right hand – looming over his oblivious aunt. Had she turned at the last moment and recognized her assailant? No, she'd received a blow to the back of her head, according to the medical examiner. She never knew what hit her.

Then the man would've only had to make sure Marjorie fell through the briars to the bottom of the embankment.

I scanned the ground around the top of the ditch where police tape marked the scene. I didn't know what I was looking for. Blood maybe? My imagined rock-weapon? Signs of a body being dragged across the ground? I came up empty.

I walked toward the big tree I'd chosen as the killer's hiding place, feeling a little out of my element. I'd never be able to compete with Cora, the Plot Queen. Beyond the sound of dried leaves crunching under my feet, I noticed birds singing. I paused a moment and listened closely, amazed at how I could distinguish different patterns in their calls. Maybe Cora had a point. I didn't get out enough.

I reached the tree and circled its base, eye to the ground. When I moved to the side of the tree opposite the ditch, a sense of horror engulfed me. Three discarded cigarette butts suggested someone had been standing there, waiting. My imagined scenario could have happened.

I called Police Chief Gordon Knoblett on my cell phone and explained what I had found and what I thought it meant. I waited at the tree until he arrived, then I waited some more in my office at Pleasant Vista Estate while he called in the forensic team to conduct a more extensive search of the area. I was curious to see what they would turn up, so I hung around and spent the time updating my patient records.

Many of the residents were gathering in the activity room to socialize or play games when I heard the front door open and the security guard greet visitors.

"Evening, Mr. Moore. Sorry about your aunt. She was a nice lady. And Dorene, I didn't expect to see you tonight. Have you changed shifts?"

"No, I'm still on mornings. I came to help my fiancé collect his Aunt's things."

"You know the drill," the security guard said.

I peeked out my office door and watched Dorene, dressed for a night on the town, and a tall, middle-aged man sign the visitor's book. My imagination had let me down when it came to Buck Moore. He was definitely not overweight and had a full head of hair. I vowed to stick to what I knew and leave the story-telling to Cora.

About ten minutes later, Chief Knoblett stopped in.

"Dr. Walsh? I want to thank you for calling me with your tip. Did you happen to touch the flier or the cigarette butts by any chance?"

"No," I said. "I walked around the area quite a bit though. Hope I didn't disturb any evidence."

"Ah, well, that remains to be seen."

"Did you find the rock Marjorie hit when she fell?"

"Maybe. We found a rock with blood and hair on it. Trouble is, it wasn't in a spot where Mrs. Moore would've hit it when she fell."

I swallowed hard. My God, Cora was right. It was murder.

"You know, Chief," I said. "Marjorie's nephew is here at the moment and I was thinking about asking him some questions about Marjorie's fall."

Police Chief Knoblett raised his eyebrows. "Well, now, Dr. Walsh, I appreciate your input so far, but please, leave the rest to me and my team."

I nodded. He was right, of course. Still, I couldn't resist the role of interested observer.

"Can I show you to Marjorie's room and introduce the nephew?"

"See that's all you do," he said.

He followed me down the north corridor to the third unit on the right. The door was ajar and I smelled cigarette smoke. My knock pushed the door open further. Many of Marjorie's belongings were piled onto her bed. Buck Moore and Dorene were busy emptying the top dresser drawer. They stopped and eyed us.

"Mr. Moore?" I asked. "I'm Dr. Walsh, your aunt's physician. I wanted to pay my respects." I shook his hand, nodded to the nurse, and then introduced Chief Knoblett.

"My condolences on your loss," the chief said. "I'd like to ask you a couple of questions, Mr. Moore."

"Sure, I guess."

"Where were you yesterday morning between seven and nine?"

Buck Moore's eyes narrowed. "That's when Aunt Marjorie fell, isn't it? Why would I need an alibi?"

"We're still investigating the circumstances surrounding her death," the chief said. "New evidence has come to light suggesting foul play."

Buck paled. "Are you saying that Aunt Marjorie was murdered? I can't believe it."

I stared at the smoldering cigarette in the ashtray on the dresser. "We found cigarette butts at the scene," I blurted out. "DNA evidence will prove you were there."

"Dr. Walsh, please," Chief Knoblett said. "Why don't you wait in your office?"

I guess I'd overstepped my bounds.

"Listen, Buck," Dorene said, "I'd probably better leave, too. Call me later, okay?" She blew a kiss in his general direction and left, her high heels clomping across the linoleum floor.

I was slowly heading for the door when Buck responded, "I don't even smoke and I was at work when she fell. I can prove it."

I whirled around to face him. "Then whose is that?" I pointed to the smoldering cigarette.

"It's Dorene's," Buck said. "Good God. You don't think she's involved, do you?"

I had let her waltz past me, pretty as can be. I ran toward the front entry and caught a glimpse of her as she passed through the door.

"Dorene, wait," I yelled. "Were you smoking in the room?"

She didn't stop. Instead, she broke into an awkward run toward the parking lot. I didn't have any trouble catching her though; her heels proved to be my ally.

Buck and the police chief were not far behind me.

"Dorene?" Buck asked. "Is it true? Did you cause Aunt Marjorie to fall?"

She was a wreck; broken shoe, open purse with contents spilled all around, mascara streaked down her tear-stained cheeks.

"Aw, Buck," she said. "You know I wouldn't do something like that.

Just like I know you wouldn't. The birds frightened Marjorie, like they did Cora. It was the same, I swear. Buck, Honey, your Aunt Marjorie just fell and hit her head. I found her is all." She turned pleading eyes my way. "It was the birds."

Buck stared at her for a moment before turning a troubled gaze on the police chief.

Just then, Cora appeared on the front steps of Pleasant Vista Estate and called sharply to me. She held out a crumpled paper in her extended hand. I smoothed out the notepaper. It was a handwritten version of the message stapled to the gnarled oak tree.

"It's the girl's handwriting," Cora said.

"Don't worry," I told her. "We've got Dorene in custody."

"Not Dorene," she said with a huff. "The girl. The uppity one from the college that's been interviewing me." She pulled another paper out of her pocket. "I found these story ideas in the trash. That little golddigger's trying to cash in on my name, create a sensational mystery by killing my best friend."

It took the residents weeks to get over the shock of the murder of one of their own. Dorene quit working at the facility and married Buck Moore. He forgave her for thinking he killed his aunt and she promised to quit smoking. Cora went on to write her version of the story and called it *Murder Most Fowl*. It appeared in a prestigious magazine and she's in the limelight once again. She presented me with an autographed copy and announced she's turning it into a serial set in an assisted living facility with a bumbling physician as the hero. Which, of course, is not based on me.

Diana Catt is a writer from Indiana. She has eight short story credits to date and has several novels underway. She's a married microbiologist with three kids and little time for housework - which is perfect, actually.

THE MILLER'S TASK
Jonathan Dubey

He ascends the tall steps to castle gate,
Exhausted from the trials that are his fate.
When he sees her smile he's more at ease,
Her rosy face, her lips that tease.

She gives him strength with her eyes,
To avoid her gaze he fails, but tries.
For her loving father is the King,
And he hasn't gold to buy her ring.

He is but a simple Miller's son
No station, no power, to be her one.
The King is old, and ill, and weak.
But fortnight ago they did speak.

He's here to do what he can,
To make the land prosper again.
Three tasks the king gave,
The first difficult, the second grave.

For the third he would have no clue,
Until completion of the first two.
That very day he began the first.
Ignoring fright, ignoring thirst.

The neighboring lands grew hungrier by the day,
War would come, they fear it may.
He gave the grain from his fathers mill.
He took nothing in return, an empty till.

The second task, held more danger.
For to combat, he was a stranger.
He had to best the greatest lord,
of the next land, he had no sword.

With no horse, he walked nine days.
Racking his mind, thinking of ways.
He was beaten and thrashed, but each time would
stand and offer words, it was all he could.

In the end that lord did not fall,
but with his actions, surprised them all.
He was sent home on his nine day walk,
with a treaty on parchment stalk.

"If all your people are as strong as he,
then we must have peace, it has to be."
He could hardly stand, he could barely bow,
He straightened tattered clothes, lifted his brow.

He asked to be given the third trial,
Knowing he could well be dead in a short while.
The king looked him over, covered in mud.
"Powerful men are clean, not caked in their own blood."

But the princess knew now, that this was a man,
who asked for nothing, and gave what he can.
"You've saved our Kingdom, the people I adore,
from death by starvation, from bloodshed and war."

She ran to him, she held him tight.
She kissed his lips, she set him right.
"Winning me, was your third task.
If you want my heart, dear one, just ask."

Though born in Saint Johnsbury Vermont, Jonathan Dubey has lived his entire life (so far) in the greater Berlin, NH area. Jonathan works full time as a Paramedic and is very involved with local arts, specifically community theater.

NORTHERN LIGHTS
Rob Smales

"AHOY THE CABIN!"

BEN'S TRADITIONAL GREETING was something of a joke, but he shouted the same phrase each time he called on folks out here during spring thaw. People who hadn't seen another soul for the better part of three months sometimes entered spring with funny ideas in their heads.

"Mr. Hesston? Harold? It's Ranger Biddlestrom. Hello?"

The snow, two feet deep in places despite the coming spring, swallowed Ben's voice: thick silence returned. Empty windows stared at him, dark in the afternoon sun.

The sudden squawk from the radio at his hip nearly stopped his heart.

"Ben? You up the Hesston place yet, or did you drive that big tank of yours into a ditch?"

He snatched the hand-held from his belt. "Yeah, Del, I just pulled up. S'matter, you miss me?"

"Not hardly. Chief wanted me to remind you we ain't even had radio contact from Hesston in near seventy-five days. Good chance you're walking in on a corpse, is all. You copy that?"

"I copy that. Thanks, Del. Biddlestrom out."

He thrust the radio back on its clip. Snow crunched under his boots as he rounded the Suburban.

I hate checking the hermits.

There was quite a bit of solitude to be found in the mountains of Maine, and every year some city folks decided they wanted some of it. Maybe they were on the run from something; maybe they wanted to just get away from people; and maybe they were looking for someplace to get some work done. Hesston was one of those last — a man writing the next Great American Novel who just wanted peace and quiet to work in.

What many city folks don't realize, no matter how often they're told, is people die up there alone. Once the snows come and shut down the roads, there's no one to rely on but themselves: by the time they figure out they're not up to the task, it's sometimes too late. Ben had thought Hesston would be one of the ones to make it. There's no cell coverage up there, so the radio is damn important. When the man had stopped making regular radio checks a few weeks ago, Ben had hoped it was some technical problem. As he approached the cabin, however, his hopes shriveled.

The snow in front of the cabin was undisturbed. The last snowfall had been more than two weeks ago, but from what Ben could see no one had forced the door open, there were no tracks leading to the woodpile, and the scent of woodsmoke was noticeably absent. Still, you couldn't play it too safe; he continued to call out as he neared the door.

"Hesston? You in there?"

Then he saw the window.

The window next to the cabin door was smashed, shards left in the frame like a mouth full of broken teeth. Though he'd seen no sign of life, Ben drew his gun and moved through the snow toward the open hole in the cabin's side.

"Hesston," he called through the gap. "Are you in—"

Harold Hesston lay on the cabin floor, framed by the square of sunlight spilling in through the broken window. He lay on his back, legs splayed, one hand resting on his chest while the other thrust straight out to the side, fingers even now curved into claws that gripped the floorboards with splintered nails.

His abdomen was torn wide open, like something out of a Hollywood horror movie.

"Aw, dammit!"

Ben turned from the window, raising the hand-held to his mouth.

"Del, this is Ben."

"Go ahead, Ben."

"You were right, Hesston's gone, and he's in bad shape. Looks like some animals had a field day with the carcass. I may be here awhile. It's a mess."

"You want some help out there?"

Ben looked at the sun, riding low in the afternoon sky.

"No, not yet. They wouldn't get here before dark, not with the roads the way they are. I'll secure the scene and we'll send a team tomorrow."

"Copy that."

Ben went back to the Suburban for a shovel, then set about excavating the cabin door.

Squatting over the remains, Ben shook his head.

"It doesn't make any sense."

Harold Hesston's body had been torn apart, splayed open like a frog pinned to a high-school dissection tray, but from what Ben could see, it was, well... whole. Or near enough to make no difference. He was no doctor, or coroner, but he hunted quite a bit, and after dressing game for so long he had a pretty fair notion as to what all the parts looked like. Though it appeared at first that some wildlife had gotten into the cabin and partially eaten the body, Ben didn't think so once had taken a closer look. Heart, lungs, liver, the large muscle of the diaphragm, all were present and accounted for, as far as he could make out. And though the intestines were spread about, they looked to be mostly unbroken. There were no gnaw-marks he could see, not on the exposed guts nor on the flesh of the arms or face... and the open eyes were intact; an oddity in and of itself

Ben shook himself and stood.

Well, this is one for the books, I guess, he thought. *This looks more like he just, I don't know, exploded, than anything used him for food. Hmm... MythBusters ever done anything on "exploding humans?"*

He looked about the cabin. Clothing everywhere, sink full of dishes, books and notebooks scattered about. Ben remembered Hesston as a fastidious man— on his last visit, the cabin had been immaculate. He frowned. This whole thing looked wrong. He glanced down at Hesston, seeing again the hand clutching the floor in what looked like agony, the other flung across the chest.

Heart attack?

A notebook lay just inches from that claw of a hand. Inches from that, a pen. Ben surveyed the mess. Books and notebooks were everywhere: the desk, the counter, spread across the table. But there was only one book on the floor, and it was right next to the body. Ben donned some latex gloves from his belt and scooped up the book, opening it to the first page.

10-12-2011

Arrived at the cabin today. Everything looks perfect. The local Rangers have warned me about the dangers of staying up here through the winter, but I know what I'm doing…

His diary, Ben thought. *This might help me figure out what the hell happened here.*

He flipped along, pausing every couple of pages to skim a few words, looking for indications of a problem. He flipped and paused, flipped and paused… and his eyes widened.

This looks promising…

11-23-2011

Something strange happened tonight. The day was uneventful — I worked on the book and did my chores in what has become my routine. The woodbin by the fireplace was getting low, so after dinner (Canned beef and some bread that *almost* tasted like bread. I may be getting the hang of baking up here!) I went out to the woodpile to fetch more.

I had gathered a good armload when I thought I heard something; maybe a voice. I stepped to the edge of the roof overhang and peered out into the darkness. Without a flashlight, my eyes still used to the cabin's lamps, I could barely see the trees edging the clearing; but there, amongst trunks that were nothing more than dark shapes against the snow, I saw a light.

Not a bright, direct light, like a flashlight, but more an indirect glow, like a lantern, or maybe a flashlight with low batteries. The voice, if it was a voice, had been familiar to me, though at the time I couldn't place it. It was more a feeling of familiarity than certain knowledge. It might have been that feeling of familiarity — now that I think about it, it must have been — but I was strangely unafraid to see a light in the night outside my cabin in the middle of nowhere. I stepped forward, my armload of wood carried but forgotten, and called out "Hello? Who's there?"

The light faded, as if the lantern bearer moved silently away. I waited to see if they would return, but I had only intended to scoop up the wood and go right back in, so I was without coat or hat; before long the cold drove me back inside, where I filled the woodbox and stoked the fire.

As I've written this entry, it seems part of my mind has been trying to place that voice, that familiarity, though all that keeps coming up is an impossibility.

I keep thinking of Julie.

Lights? A voice in the dark?
Ben's brows drew down in thought.

Hallucinations? Cabin Fever? Was he starting to crack as early as November?

When they'd met in the fall, Hesston had seemed strong-willed, one of those "type-A" guys. He'd seemed capable.

You never know how isolation's going to affect a person, but it was only November! The road wasn't close to closed yet back then. Not to that 4X4 he has under the carport. It just doesn't make sense.

Ben studied the body again, looking for signs of animal activity, but still found none. Why? From the natural point of view this was meat, lying here for the taking, right during the time when other food was scarce. The broken window would allow both the scent of blood out, and those who smelled it in, but as far as he could tell no tooth had touched the carcass.

He looked at the jagged glass still stuck in the window frame, then moved closer. His eyes went to the floor, trying to avoid the broken glass... but there was none. The floor beneath the window was icy from snow blowing in, but there was no glass anywhere.

Did Hesston clean up? Did someone else?

For the first time it struck Ben that he might be at a murder scene. Lights in the night, the place a mess, maybe even searched, someone cleaning up the glass—

No. Why would they go to the trouble of cleaning the glass, then leave the rest of the place a mess?

Ben opened the door, leaned out, and took up the shovel he'd left outside. He reversed it and began rooting around in the snow beneath the window, poking here and there with the handle, sweeping sideways as much as he could. He heard a muffled *clink*.

*Well, there's the glass. On the outside. Like something went **out** through the window, not **in**. But that still doesn't explain why nothing climbed in to have at the free food once Hesston was dead.*

The radio on Ben's hip burped, causing him to jump again. Del's voice filled the silent room.

"Ben? What's your status? Do I need to schedule a crew to come up there tomorrow?"

The big man inhaled, then blew out a breath, annoyed at his own jumpiness.

"I'm not sure, Del. Don't schedule a crew yet, we might have to have the Staties up here to take a look. There's something weird here, and I'm trying to figure it out a bit before I head back down. I'm not sure what killed him, but I don't think animals were involved. I'll let you know what I think when I get in the truck, okay?"

"Copy that, Ben. Anything we have to worry about? You in any danger?"

Ben looked around, his eyes avoiding the corpse this time.

"No, nothing's here now. Whatever happened, it was probably weeks ago. I saw no sign of movement or tracks in the snow. I should be good. I'll get back to you in a while. Copy that?"

"I hear you. Base out."

He finally looked directly at Hesston again: the wide open eyes, mouth frozen in a scream. He looked down at the journal in his hand then held it toward the body, giving it a little shake.

"They say dead men tell no tales, but you just might prove them wrong. You put anything useful in here?"

Hesston wasn't answering.

Ben noticed an easy chair by the fireplace, strode over and took a seat. He shifted about, then removed the gun and radio from his belt, putting them on a low magazine table. He opened the journal to November 23rd and started paging toward the back of the book, looking for more interesting entries. He flipped his way past days of chopping wood, a little hunting, writing progress…

11-29-2011

It happened again. I went out for wood after supper and saw light out there, just past the trees. Dim, almost flickering, accompanied by what sounded like a low murmur. Maybe one voice, maybe more, too faint to tell. I've made sure to wear my coat when going for wood since that first time — it's been almost a week, I was starting to think I'd imagined the whole thing. It's interfered with my writing, wondering if I was already starting to lose it up here, and the winter not even really started yet.

Remembering how it faded away the first time, I put down the wood and started across the clearing as quietly as I could. Spending all week pondering that first time, I'd felt nervous— afraid retroactively; however, as I crossed the clearing it felt just the same as the first time. No fear, just… curiosity. Urged by curiosity, I moved too quickly, my boots crunching through the snow. I made too much noise. The light and sounds began to fade, but more slowly than before. I ran to catch them, whoever they were, crashing through the treeline with thunderous noise in the sudden silence. I yanked a flashlight from my pocket, the beam slicing wildly through the night as I shone it this way and that.

I found nothing. Not a face, not a track in the snow, not a broken twig. I listened, but heard only the rasp of my own breath. It was dark beneath the trees, not even starlight to assist my search, and I'm no experienced tracker. I turned back toward my cabin, intending to return in the morning, hoping daylight might show me some mark or sign that was hidden in the dark. It was as I re-crossed the treeline that I heard it, faint, and riding to me on the wind.

My name.

Someone called my name, from what sounded like very far away. Just "Harold", long and drawn out. I stopped, spun, and called back. I shouted and yelled, heard no response, then yelled again. I stood there for more than five minutes, past the point where the cold hurt my throat and the shouting made it raw, but didn't hear anything. Nothing but the wind in the trees and my own voice echoing faintly from the mountain behind me. Eventually I gave up and came in here to write it down while it was still fresh in my mind. That last voice, calling my name...

I could swear it was Julie.

Follow up note

It's the next morning, 11-30-2011. I just followed my tracks through the snow to the treeline and beyond. Made a full circuit of the cabin, spiraled out quite a ways — past where any visible lights could have been last night. There was nothing; no tracks that I could find, not a mark in the snow other than my own.

In the light of day, I am afraid again.

12-5-2011

Things may have taken a turn for the worse. I'm writing this in the morning rather than the evening as I usually do. I didn't write anything last night — I never got the chance. I'm trying to get it down now, while it's in my head, but it's fading, like a dream seen by morning's light. I've lost some parts already. Some parts I may never have known.

The light returned last night, earlier than I'd seen it before; after dark, but before dinner. I saw it through the window this time. I was working on the book and thought I heard a noise. A voice. I went to the front window, and there it was. Light, just past the trees, this time over by the road. I pressed my face to the glass to get a better look — I hoped if I didn't go out and frighten whatever it was, it might feel more confident, maybe come out of the trees where I could see it.

Close to the glass, however, I heard it more clearly. Maybe it actually got louder, I'm not sure. The murmur became more audible than ever, even than when I'd been outside with it. A rising hubbub, close to becoming individual voices. Some part of me was *sure* that if I just listened a little harder it would sort itself out and make sense to me. I left off trying to see and pressed my ear to the cold glass, listening with every fiber of my being, and suddenly one voice did emerge from the crowd.

One word came to me clearly through the dark.

My name.

The voice was Julie's.

Now, in the light of day, I know this was impossible. I had to have imagined it. I hadn't heard Julie's voice since the final divorce hearing nearly a year ago, and there was no way she was traipsing about through the woods of Maine, in the dark and snow and cold.

No way.

I know this now. I'll know it tomorrow. I knew it yesterday. But last night it just seemed to make sense, her voice calling to me from the night, just as it made sense that I should go to her.

No, it didn't just make sense; I *had* to go. I was compelled. At the time, like I said, it seemed quite natural: Julie was calling, so I would answer. But remembering it now, foggy as some of it is, I could barely restrain myself from running right out the door in my shirtsleeves and stocking feet. I managed to pause long enough to thrust my feet into boots, but I can't remember tying them. I shrugged into my parka, but I seem to recall it flapping open, unzipped, as I ran through the night. I clearly remember running for all I was worth, across the clearing and into the underbrush beneath the trees. I can't remember thinking anything was unusual — Julie wanted me, needed me, and I had to go to her.

When I got to where I had seen the lights, the forest was empty. I looked about and found no signs in the snow, not a track, not a mark... but the light was not completely gone. The light, the sounds, had simply withdrawn a ways. I could see the light, hear the murmuring, back beneath the trees. They seemed to be beckoning to me, friendly, not threatening at all, though thinking of it now I am terrified. I moved forward cautiously, trying not to frighten it away again, whatever it was.

Then Julie called me, distant but clear, and I was off and running again.

From then on my memories are hazy at best. I ran, stumbling, through the trees and underbrush. Small branches and saplings lashed my face in the dark, threatening to put out my eyes, but I didn't slow. Couldn't slow. I simply crossed my arms before my face and ran on, cheeks bloodied, whipping branches now scratching my gloveless hands. Indeed, my hands are now so cut and swollen it is all I can do to hold the pen with which I write this account.

I remember thinking I was going to catch it, whatever it was, that it was just out of reach, and all I had to do was run faster to catch it for sure. I never did. I don't think I ever managed a good look at it. In describing it now I am reminded of the stories I used to read when I was a boy, about the Will-O-the Wisp, the ghost-light that would lead travelers astray — sometimes to their doom. That's what this all puts me in mind of, except for the end of my story. The end is different than anything I've ever heard, and I'm actually afraid I haven't reached it yet.

That's the last thing I remember: running through the pines, lungs working fit to burst, stumbling through the snow and unable to stop. Unable to slow down. I remember running… and then nothing. My memory just gets more and more hazy until there's nothing left. Until this morning, when I woke in my own bed, hands and face filthy, scratched and bloody.

I was also stark naked, with no idea how I got there.

So much of what happened feels like a dream. I woke in a panic, but once I got my wits about me and realized my memory had this gap, I checked myself out as best I could. I don't recall striking my head, and I've poked about and can't find any lumps or bumps on my skull anywhere. My feet are scratched, but nothing like the abuse my face and hands suffered.

Thinking it through as I chronicle these events has not dimmed my fear at all. Either something happened to me that I can't recall, which is scary enough, or I simply lost my mind for a while and ran about naked, which may be more terrifying. Hard winter is coming, and if I can't rely on myself for the season I'll never make it to spring alive. Not up here. I've checked the whole cabin, and the clothes I wore last night are not here— including my boots and parka; two things it would be good to have in any Maine winter.

I wanted to get down all I could remember before it faded entirely, and I've done that, I think. Now I'm putting on my sweater, a couple of sweatshirts, and my galoshes over my sneakers, and going out to follow the tracks I made in the snow last night. I'll see where I went, and hopefully find my coat, at least.

I don't want to go.

I'm afraid of what I might find, what might happen.

I have to go.

Follow Up Note
The good news is I found my parka and boots.

The bad news is I'm more afraid than ever.

I followed my tracks through the snow easily; apparently I make quite a trail when I'm running out of control. My tracks ran in almost a straight line, which made it even easier. Whatever I had followed had led me north. My trail went through all kinds of brush, some places where the undergrowth was so thick I couldn't see a way through, and have no idea how I did it at night, though that probably explains the bruising and lacerations to my face and hands. I cut around and easily picked up my trail on the other side of these obstructions.

My parka was about a mile from the cabin, caught on a low bush just to the side of my tracks, as if I'd casually cast it aside mid-stride. There was no sign I'd stopped, no difference in the footprints there than anywhere else. I picked it up and kept following. The boots were about a half-mile farther, the first right in my tracks, like it had come off by accident, the other fifteen yards beyond and a little to the side, almost as if I took it off myself when one boot made running awkward. The trail continued, as I'd run on, bootless, through the snow.

Eventually I came into a clearing atop the cliff about two miles north of here. It was there that I'd stopped running. It was also there that things got even stranger.

As I've said, I'm not an experienced tracker, but even I could see that I'd walked about the clearing some. I couldn't tell what I'd been doing as I meandered, except I found more of my clothes. Pants, shirt, one sock. The rest may have been there somewhere, but I was distracted by the end of my trail, which was easy to spot — it looked like I'd started to make a snow angel and just lost control.

There was a flattened place in the snow, where my bare back had lain. The snow was churned up, pushed and flung about as if I'd been thrashing like mad. I could tell just how far snow had been thrown, because the snow I threw was pink. The entire nest-like hole I had gouged into the snow was tinted pink and red.

Blood.

I stood, transfixed with horror, about two yards from this bloody wound in the white world, and wracked my brain trying to remember something, *anything*, from that night. I stood, staring at all that blood, *my* blood, much more than can be accounted for by my battered face and hands, wondering how it had gotten there and coming up blank. With a sudden painful spasm, I fell to my knees and vomited into the snow. I threw up again and again, until all that came up was that yellow, egg-like bile that is your body's way of telling you you're empty. I was dizzy and exhausted, tears of pain and fear blurring my eyes as I picked up my bundle of parka and boots and began to retrace my steps toward home.

I was almost halfway back to the cabin when a question occurred to me: how had I gotten home? I had clearly seen my footprints leading straight to that bloody hole in the snow... but that was where the trail ended. No footprints lead *away* from the mess. I almost went back to check, but I had no desire to see that awful red scar in the snow again. Indeed, I could picture it well enough in my mind that I stooped, dry-heaving just from the thought. No, I had no need to go back to verify, I can remember it all quite clearly even now: there were no tracks leading away from that place.

How had I gotten home?

And where had all that blood come from? Aside from my hands, what happened? Did I have a nosebleed? Would have needed a hell of a gusher to stain that much snow. And where was the blood when I woke? No blood stained my pillow, my face, not even the cuts and scratches on my cheeks and forehead. My hands were the same way — there was dirt in the cuts, I had to pick bits of tree bark from my skin, but there was no blood to wash off.

Something happened to me out there I can't explain, can't even remember, and I'm scared. This will be my last entry from this place. I'm too exhausted to try it now, but first thing in the morning I'm getting the hell out of here. I'll pack a few things, then go to bed with my head under the pillow. If I hear any voices, or think that I do, I have to ignore them. I've had enough.

I'm going home.

Holy crap, thought Ben. He held his place with a forefinger as he flipped the book over to look at the cover. *If the whole beginning of this journal wasn't filled with regular old diary entries and day-to-day stuff, I'd say this was the book he was up here working on.*

He flipped back to that last paragraph. The last three words: "I'm going home." He glanced toward the corpse lying across the room.

I can see he didn't make it, but why? He sounds pretty determined in this entry, so… wait, December fifth? Wasn't there…?

He turned the page, scanned the next entry, then nodded.

Yeah, I thought so.

12-6-2011

Somewhere, God is laughing at me.

Exhausted from yesterday's ordeal, I slept the clock around. I woke twelve hours later to realize I had been so wrapped up in what was going on around here, worrying about my sanity, I hadn't paid attention to weather reports. It started snowing about two hours after I fell asleep, and it's still going strong. More than strong. According to the radio, this is the season's first blizzard. I can barely see out my windows in the white-out, and the roads are already closed.

Unless I call the Rangers to snowmobile me out, I'm here for the duration.

Ben shook his head. *Poor bastard. That blizzard locked this whole area down tight in a matter of hours. I don't understand, though: why didn't he just radio for help? That storm kept us hopping, helping some of the older folks around, and there were a few emergencies — there always are, in a big storm like that — but we would have eventually gotten him out of here. Why didn't he call?*

12-11-2011

I'm trying to follow my normal routine, the plan I laid out for getting through the winter up here. I should have radioed for help, called for rescue by the Ranger Service, but I haven't yet. I'm not sure if it was stubborn masculine pride, or if I was embarrassed about what happened to me... or maybe it was that I really have no idea *what* happened. I don't know. But since I didn't do it right away, the longer I wait, the more silly I'll feel actually doing it. I mean, what could I say and not sound at least a little stupid? I couldn't even show them what I found in the clearing, since everything's covered with about eighteen inches of new snow.

I can't really seem to do *anything* but try to remember what happened to me out there. I've tried to work on the book, but I keep coming back to this, and the book has ground to a halt. Nothing's gone on here at all since the blizzard, just normal day-to-day stuff.

Except for the dreams.

It took me four days to realize I was having a recurring dream. I could only recall snatches— though I woke the same way every morning: soaked with sweat, terrified and sometimes crying out. All I could remember was running through the night forest, faster and faster through the snow. I assumed I was reliving the night before the blizzard, remembering bits in my sleep. The day I realized I was having the same dream again and again, I actually hoped my subconscious was working on it as I slept, trying to remember, though even the thought of remembering frightened me.

Then I woke yesterday and could remember more. This morning even more, and I don't know what to be more afraid about: what happened to me out there, or what's happening inside my own head.

In the dream I ran, like before, and I got all the way to the clearing this time. Maybe I always made it, and just forgot. Anyway, I got to the clearing, sure I had caught up with whatever I was chasing, but I got to that big, open expanse, and there was nothing there. No tracks, just... nothing. Like I was chasing shadows the whole time. Despair filled me, as if everything, my whole life, was like this chase through the dark: all running and striving for nothing. I turned back toward the forest, toward the cabin, and despair turned to fear. Something was out there, in the dark, in the trees, watching me. Stalking me.

All that time I was running *after* something, I should have been running *away*.

I dashed about the clearing, trying for the cover of trees, but whichever way I ran I sensed something in the forest before me, the way you sometimes just know stuff in dreams. Whatever it was, it was there, silently waiting. A twig snapped then, and I knew it was coming. I turned to run though I had no idea where, and slipped, tripped in one of my own footprints, and fell headlong in the snow. I scrambled but slid, and couldn't seem to get to my feet.

More twigs snapped, the snow crunching as something moved closer. I flipped onto my back, determined even in my terror to meet this thing face to face, not to die scrabbling like a worm on the frozen earth. Something caught my eye among the trees, a shadow moving amid the shadows. It slid into the clearing, tall and white in the moonlight. Breath caught in my throat and my eyes bulged with terror, unable to believe what I saw, moving toward me with an easy, predatory grace.

It was me.

12-15-11

I'm losing it up here.

The weather hasn't changed — it's been cold and clear, and all the snow dumped by the blizzard last week is still here. I've tried to maintain my routine, but it just isn't happening. I'm not sure *what's* happening.

I can't focus to write any more. I can't think. It's taking everything I have, and a long, long time, just to write this. I feel sleep deprived, though I've been sleeping more now than ever in my life. I'm *sleeping*, I'm just not *resting*. I'll fall asleep right after dinner, sometimes before, and sleep for eight, nine, ten hours. It seems I'm sleeping a little more each night — Jesus, can someone actually sleep themselves to death? — and when I finally wake I'm *exhausted*. I can barely drag myself to the bathroom on legs trembling with fatigue, though I was just lying down for nearly half a day.

There's no sign of fever, no nausea, nothing like that. In fact, my appetite has been up for the past few days. Sometimes it seems like all I do between waking and sleeping is rummage through the cupboard and chew. I'm too fuzzy-headed to to the math, but I think if I keep eating this way my stores will run out long before the winter breaks.

Especially if I stay this shaky. I can't go hunting in this condition, and I never learned the way of setting snares. I've never really hunted for sustenance, just for sport.

I'm getting on the radio now. I need help. I'm sick, no matter what my thermometer and appetite say. I'll call the Rangers and see if they can come get me in the morning.

12-16-11

I can't explain it. I've wracked my brain, trying to remember what the hell happened, and I can't.

I wonder what *else* I can't remember?

The last thing I recall is putting this journal aside, with every intention of getting on the radio with the Ranger Station. The next thing I knew, I woke in the chair almost ten hours later. Like every morning lately, I was fuzzy in the head and weak in the legs. Even fuzzy-headed I worried about falling asleep so fast I never even made it to my feet.

Narcolepsy? Something neurological?

I staggered into the kitchen where the radio was supposed to be sitting on its shelf, but it wasn't there. It lay smashed on the floor, bits thrown or kicked about the room.

The shock blew the fog from my mind, and I reeled back from the mess in horror. There's no way I can fix it — not even if I knew how, which I don't — it's smashed so well. Wires torn loose, circuit boards ripped out — some snapped in half. I don't even know if all the parts are *here*, never mind knowing how to put it all back together, no matter how Mickey Moused.

I must have done it. There's no one else to blame, I *must* have done it... but I didn't. Unless I was sleepwalking. That's all I can think of. I woke up right where I fell asleep — at least I think— but I can't think *why* I would do such a thing, even in my sleep, unless I have some secret death wish. If I do, it's a secret even to me. All I know is I'm snowed in, and I'm not leaving.

Oh, and I'm apparently losing my mind. Almost forgot to point out *that* little detail.

I've tried to remember my dreams, see if I had a dream about smashing or beating something, but it's all a blank again. When I try to remember I don't get any images. I just have this weird sense that I'm stalking something.

And I'm hungry.

12-25-11

I'm running out of food.

I can't remember eating it all, but it must be me. I wake up, and I'm tired, and there are empty cans on the floor, and empty boxes, and I can't remember eating it all. I *must* be sleepwalking, no, sleep*eating*, and I'm eating way too much. Should be making myself sick, but I'm not. I remember my dreams all the time now. I'm hunting in them. Hunting. All the time. Can't remember if I'm chasing a light or something else, but I'm chasing something in my dreams and I'm so hungry. It follows me when I wake up. I go looking in the larder, and there's less and less there. I think I'm eating it, but I can't remember.

The dreams — and this is weird, it feels almost impossible to explain — somehow they don't feel like my own.

My dreams don't feel like my own. Does that make *any* sense?

I wish there were someone to keep an eye on me, someone to talk to. No phone, no radio. I'm all alone.

I'm so alone.

Merry Christmas. Kind of lost track, but I think it's Christmas.

Merry Christmas to me.

12-30?-2011

Sleeping nearly all the time now. I'm hunting in my sleep, hunting all the time. Always hungry. Stores almost gone nearly 2 months early — maybe more, maybe less, I'm not sure of the date anymore. Not sure at all. Sleeping too much.

In my dreams I run low through the snow, much faster than I should, especially now. Exhausted. Legs fatigued though I barely use them. But in my dreams I run. I hunt. Rabbits, weasels, things that I'm not sure what they are. Once a small deer, and I was pouncing. Biting. Blood filling my mouth, salty and hot; gnawing as they lay dying. Not quite dead. I never knew blood was so salty. Is it salty? Did I make that up?

Did someone else?

I'm so tired. And hungry. I'm going to go check out the larder again. I should be rationing, but I can't help myself.

P.S. Can't button my pants. Can barely get them on. All this sleeping and eating and I'm finally gaining weight. Building up fat so I can hibernate? Go to sleep and wake up in springtime?

God that sounds good.

1-?-2012

The dreams aren't dreams. Or not my dreams. Or something. Been about a week since I last wrote here. I think. Something like a week. The dreams have gotten worse. More vivid. More real. Too real.

Rabbit on the floor when I woke this afternoon. Not the whole rabbit, just half. It looked, well... chewed. Chewed and torn. The sight of it made me sick, and I dragged myself off to the bathroom. While I was in there, trying not to vomit, I realized there was a taste in my mouth. The back of my throat tasted vile, acidic from the rising sickness, but my mouth— teeth and tongue— tasted metallic. Salty. Like the blood in the dream. I checked my face in the mirror, but there wasn't anything to see.

Until I opened my mouth.

My teeth and gums were stained red. I leaned in to look close, and there were bits of... stuff... stuck in my teeth. Meat, red and bloody and raw. And hair. Short, like fur. Stuck between my teeth. I vomited then. Puked in the sink, in the toilet, on the floor. On the floor was the worst part. I could see the stuff clearly on the floor. Hunks of meat and some... I don't know... some kind of tissue? Half-digested, lying in this bloody froth I sicked up. Some of the stuff still had fur attached, some was strips of just skin and fur, and I was puking it up. Up from inside me.

It was while I was bent over puking that I noticed my stomach. Big and round, like a basketball. Like I'm pregnant. That's not possible. *It isn't.*

2 days later? 2012

Not five minutes ago, my belly moved. Something in there squirmed. I felt it, with my insides as well as my hands: something flexing. Shifting position. Pushing against the confines of my skin.

Like a baby kicking.

Something's inside me. Something's making me hungry, and have strange cravings, and sleepwalk, sleepeat, sleephunt. I can't be pregnant. A parasite? What could do this? I think the new dreams come from this thing, but what can *do* that? I feel stronger, a little more clear. I think I'm eating better (eating for two?) but I don't remember. The stores have been gone for days, I think. I should be dead. I must be hunting at night... although I sleep most of the day now, too. I try to stay awake, to stay in control, but I think this thing inside me puts me to sleep. Keeps me worn out so I do sleep, and while I dream it drives me like a puppet that it rides... does that make sense? Am I making sense? I can't tell. I feel more clear, but...

(Undated Entry)

Something's happening. Or will. Soon. I know it. Hard to tell if it's day or night now, can't tell without going right to the window to check.

Still chases it away, when I get close. It doesn't go far, never far any more. It's back just as soon as I leave the window. Might be more than one. Hard to tell, I move so slowly. If it's waching as I creep about, it has time to get from window to windo before I get there. I have to crawl, legs so tired and sore, cramping all the time. I crawl about or I sleep, and it watches from the windows.

The light. After all this time the light is bac. Interested in me.

Or what's inside me.

Came back a few days ago. I think. Lost track of days. Sleeping a lot. Long sleeps, short awakes, but the light came back. It was night, then the window lit up like daylight. I went to look, and the light faded, like before, and it *was* night.

I've looked out there in real day, looked out the windows and door. Checked the snow. No tracks around the cabin except footsprints at the front door. Footsprints there, going in and out. Lots.

Me. Sleephunting. Has to be. Food stores have been gone for a while. Maybe quite a while. Can't remember. Found other animal prts, like First Rabbit. In the kitchen. Always gone next time I wake

Maybe it's the light. Whatever makes the light. It's here all night now, all the time, at every window, watching me. Watching what's going n inside me.

Whatever's in me is biger than ever.

And growing.

It keeps moving.

(Undated Entry)

Think its night. Light at windos al time, not running anymore

Inside the light. Wings. Things. Faries with teth. All looking in. At me. At me and my

Thing inside me growing so fast, mving all the tim hurts every move hurts

Light at the window, little faces with teeth big teth such little

Better to eat yuo with

Happning soon maybe now dont know think maybe born being born tonight

PARENTS at the window godam PARENTS watching throgh the glass smiling with teeth big teeth hapy im gonna have

Spit up blood shit blood coming its comng now I think now

God hel—

Ben flipped pages, but found no entries beyond that bizarre last message. He closed his eyes for a moment, considering the condition of the body, looking, yes, burst open rather than eaten. The window that was broken out, rather than in — as if something had escaped from the cabin after escaping from Hesston himself.

*I'd say this was just something he was writing, maybe a delusion he was having, but… I can't argue with **that**.*

He opened his eyes to look at what was left of Hesston again.

I mean, something definitely hap—

He stopped, mid-thought, looking at the light coming in through that broken window. Or, more accurately, that *wasn't*.

Dammit! I must have lost track of time!

He *had* been caught up in the journal, whether it was real or just the fevered imaginings of a sick man. It had been some slow going toward the end, trying to decipher Hesston's deteriorating handwriting, but he'd been too focused on the story to realize he was running out of daylight. This cabin, being on the eastern slope of the mountain, didn't even have until official sundown; once the sun dropped below the ridge to the west this whole area would plunge into darkness.

He dropped the journal as he crossed to the door to check the sky. He thrust his head out just in time to see the red ball of the sun drop behind the mountain, and as he watched, night claimed the land.

"Son of a bitch!"

There was a flashlight in the Suburban, a big mag in the glove box. He'd need that to secure the scene — something he should have been doing rather than reading that damned book. He had to secure the scene as best he could before starting down the mountain. Trying to navigate that mountain road in the dark, barely opened after the harsh winter they'd had, was not something he looked forward to, but there was no way he was spending the night in that cabin with an eviscerated corpse.

Especially not after that journal.

He started toward his truck, stepping in his earlier footprints rather than stumbling through fresh snow. Halfway there, he saw a light.

The road was bright, just beyond the bend. The source was screened by trees, but Ben thought it had been just coming to a stop as he noticed it.

Goddamnit! I told Del to hold off on sending a crew up here! There's nothing they can do until the Staties take their look anyhow… and why the hell did they stop way down there?

He started toward the headlights, stepping into his own tire tracks to follow the road back. As he approached the bend he realized the vehicle was actually stopped quite a bit farther down the road than he'd thought. The headlights reflecting off the snow had fooled him, making them seem closer than they actually were. His sigh plumed the air, the temperature dropping rapidly with the loss of the sun.

What the hell are they doing way down—

A sound came to him from the headlights. A voice.

Dell? What in the hell is Dell doing up here? That old bastard gets stuck in the snow in town! He has no business being on these roads!

That explained the vehicle stopping so far from the cabin. Dell had simply lost the road a little, once darkness came, and had gotten stuck. Ben shook his head.

There's a reason the Chief keeps you on dispatch, Dell, you old fool...

He started forward, jogging a little now, balancing in his old tire track. Running toward the light, to help his friend.

In the darkened cabin, on the small table next to the chair, a forgotten radio handset burped to life. The small red LED that flashed on to indicate it was receiving would have revealed the forgotten pistol, if there had been anyone there to see.

Anyone besides Harold Hesston.

Dell's voice filled the room.

"Ben? Ben you copy? Chief wants to know if you're coming back here any time soon. I told him you must be on your way, what with sundown and all.

Ben? Ben Biddlestrom, you hear me?

Ben?"

A native of Salem, Massachusetts, Rob enjoys writing ghost stories, one of which was nominated for a Pushcart Prize in 2012. His first book, Dead of Winter, was named a Superior Achievement in Dark Fiction by Firbolg Publishing's Gothic Library.

THE ROAD HOME
Sheldon Higdon

CRACKED PAVEMENT ROLLED BENEATH THE TIRES of her battered Buick. The thumping of rubber against the old highway drummed against her ears as if it were the drive's official soundtrack. Monotonous and repetitive. Off in the distance, the sun hid halfway behind the mountains, its amber rays extended upwards, piercing the darkening sky. Those mountains—just like everything else—were miles away.

She'd written the word "home" on a note and tacked it to her steering wheel as a reminder. Now it just seemed to mock her. It was so hard to remember.

"Why don't you try the radio again," said a man's voice from the passenger seat.

With her tired eyes on the road, Martha said, "Nothing but static."

"Remember the song we danced to at our wedding?" said the voice. "I could sing that."

Martha gazed into the rearview. Not to look for other cars, because there weren't any, but to look into her faded browns. To *will* herself to remember. Her sparse gray eyebrows narrowed on her sun-beaten face. A scattershot of partial images burst through her mind, but nothing of significance remained behind.

Through the driver's side window she watched the plains pass by. She cracked it open and let in the cool air.

"It's okay if you can't remember."

"Sorry," said Martha. "I tried but…."

She refused to look over at her passenger. Not because he was a stranger—she knew him quite well—but because she was afraid she'd....

"You want me to sing it?" said the voice.

"Please."

"*Our Day Will Come.*"

The words crackled in her ears like cellophane. Martha wanted to close her eyes and go back to that special day, but she couldn't because that day was lost to her. She smiled anyway and listened as if it were her first time hearing it.

"*And we'll have everything.*"

Tears welled in her eyes.

"Remember?" said the voice.

She thumbed them away.

"I need to pull over. Stretch my legs."

"You don't, do you?"

Without flipping the turn signal on, she pulled along the side of the road and came to a stop, put the old car into park, and sat there in silence for a few moments.

"No," she said.

"You remember me?"

"You're hard to forget." She smiled. "Can't forget the man who made me happy all those years."

"Then why can't you look at me?"

"I'm afraid of what will happen if I do."

Martha opened her door and stepped out into the scenery she'd been driving in for what seemed forever. There was a chill in the breezy air.

From within the cab the voice said, "What about the appointment? What did the doctor say?"

She shut the driver's door and leaned back against it. She had forgotten all about the visit. The prescription Doctor Farris gave her sat in her purse, unfilled. It'd been a month since he prescribed the medication. He explained that she was in its early stages. That they would help her in the long run. Martha would have none of it though. If she refused to take the pills then it wasn't really happening.

She rubbed her wedding ring.

"I've lived a simple life. Nothing fancy. Haven't asked for much."

She glanced down the highway and then back in the opposite direction. The breeze picked up and she hunched her shoulders in response as she walked out toward the middle of the road, and stopped on its broken center line.

At the moment, she knew the highway. Understood its nature. Lonely. Her memory broken into segments just like those dashes that led to nowhere.

Or *home*, wherever it is.

"So why take my mind? You can take anything else but not my memories. Please."

The sun slipped below the mountains. The sky bruised dark purple.

Back in the Buick, Martha sat behind the wheel and stared at the Post-it note that had the word 'home' written on it. She grabbed it from the wheel, crumpled it, and tossed it into the backseat.

"You're not going, are you?" said the voice. "It's where we spent our lives together. Made memories."

"Which are disappearing!" said Martha as she rummaged through her purse. After a few moments she found what she was looking for and pulled her hand out, holding the item loosely in her balled hand.

"Please. Fill the prescription and take the pills. They'll help. In some small way."

A flash flood of tears burst from Martha. "If I take the pills, it wins. I can't give myself to this." She wiped them away, leaned back into her seat, and released a long, slow breath. "What's the use?" she muttered, not expecting an answer.

"You were always bullheaded," said the voice. "One of your endearing characteristics I loved so much."

Out her window—in the night sky—thousands of stars grinned. Each one seemingly a bright pill smiling down at her. The half-moon shone bright on the plains that surrounded her and spilled into the cab of the Buick.

In the blade of pale light that cut across her lap, a silvery hand held hers on her leg. "I'll be here waiting," said the voice.

"I know, Dale" she said.

Over at the passenger side, it was dark. Nothing. No one sat there.

Back at her leg, only her hand lay there, holding the razor blade.

"Our day will come," she sang, and closed her eyes. *"And we'll have everything..."*

Sheldon Higdon's work has appeared in Rue Morgue Magazine, Shock Totem, The Portland Magazine, and Shroud Magazine, among many others. He is also an award-winning screenwriter. You can visit his website at www.sheldonhigdon.com. Or follow him on Twitter @sheldonhigdon.

BATTLE OF WILLS
Tracie Orsi

TRISH SHUFFLED INTO THE BATHROOM. SHE pulled her hair back in a ponytail and stared into the mirror. Her shoulders drooped. She closed her puffy eyes as she dragged the cotton pad across the creases on her forehead. If she saw me watching her, she didn't let on.

I'd met her the summer after high school. She had bounced into Marty's garage in a swishy skirt, her wild hair flying around her face. Her eyes gleamed as she sat on the ground watching us play. I'd had big dreams for our band. We called ourselves The Shades. Once we got discovered, we were going to tour the world.

Trish had the hots for Marty but he was too shy to ask her out. He was just the drummer and not a superstar like me. I played the guitar like nobody's business. I would have been bigger than Jimi Hendrix and Kurt Cobain put together if Marty hadn't destroyed his drum kit.

If Trish hadn't gotten pregnant.

One night, Marty's dad let us play in his bar. I smoked it up on that stage. After the gig, I took Trish by the hand and led her to my car. Marty watched us leave and said nothing.

We hung out for a while. When she told me she missed her period, I pushed her down and told her she ruined my life. She broke up the band. My chance to be a star was smashed to pieces.

Trish pursed her lips in a kiss as she smeared the blood red lipstick across her mouth, twisting her face like she tasted something sour. I wanted to kiss her more than ever, wanted to smear the red all over her face.

"Where you going?" I said.

"I'm going to the bar, where else?"

"You should be home with your family."

"Lizzie's at my mother's. We go through this every night."

"I don't want you to go. Stay with me tonight. I don't want you to be with him."

"I'm not going to be with anyone, Billy. I have to go. We need the money."

"I'm your husband. I don't want you to go."

She put the lipstick on the sink and looked at me. "What's wrong, now?"

"Nothing. Nothing's wrong, Trish. You look beautiful." I put my arms around her, but she pushed me away.

"Billy, stop."

I followed her into the bedroom and plopped myself down on the bed.

"Lay down with me."

She shook her head.

"Remember our first night together?" I said.

Trish walked to the closet. She pulled a sweater over her head, and looked me dead in the face.

"I'll see you later, Billy."

I wanted to grab her, but I didn't dare.

When I heard the back door slam, I rolled over, putting a pillow between my legs. I swirled my hips, pretending my wife was beneath me.

Fuck her then. How does she expect me to do anything when she treats me like that?

Trish came home stinking of cigarettes and booze. She put money in the box on her dresser and walked into the bathroom. I followed her.

"It's 2:30 in the fucking morning, Trish. Where were you?"

"Billy, you know where I was. How much did you drink tonight?" Shit. I forgot to put the empty bottle in the trash out back.

"Was Marty there?"

Trish rolled her eyes at me. She undressed and I wanted her bad. Still a hot body.

"Of course Marty was there. He's always there. He owns the bar. He has to be there. If you had a job, you'd understand."

I grabbed her arm. She drew back and turned on the shower.

"Marty had to toss a few guys who started trouble over the pool table. They were fighting over a girl."

I knew she was trying to lighten things up. Too little, too late.

"It's always over a girl, isn't it Trish?"

"She wasn't worth it, if you ask me. But who knows what goes on in a man's head when it's full of beer and whiskey. Right, Billy?"

She slammed the shower door in my face. Her back arched as she lifted her face to the shower head. Water and soapsuds spilled over her shoulders and breasts.

I clenched my fists, walked back into the living room, and picked up my guitar.

All I wanted to do was play. I didn't want to work at Sam's Guitar shop. The guys down there knew nothing about making music. They sat around, plucked strings, and shot the shit about Maroon Five.

One day I'd be a star. I knew it. All I needed was a break. Maybe things would've been different if we hadn't hooked up. When me and Trish left that night, Marty kicked his drums off the stage, smashed a few tables and chairs, and walked out the door. Marty's father beat him for wrecking the bar. He didn't come to school for a week.

When Marty's dad died, we all went to the funeral. Marty and I made up, but it wasn't like it used to be. He let us rent his father's old house and gave Trish a job because we needed the money. Marty lived above the bar. I wondered what would have happened to the band if he had ended up with Trish.

I jammed out some Hendrix. A string snapped. I put down the guitar and went to bed.

I swore I'd put something together the next day. I'd write a song about two friends who fight over a girl. The song would be a hit and Trish would stop nagging me.

Before Trish left to get Lizzie from her mother's, she held my face in her hands. "I have a good feeling about today, Billy. Talk to Sam. He'd love to have you at his shop. I have faith in you." She kissed my forehead and bounced out the door.

The car pulled out of the driveway. I picked up my guitar. I had forgotten about the busted string, but it didn't matter. I played anyway.

I laughed at myself in the mirror. I'm right-handed. My reflection played lefty.

Hendrix and Cobain were left-handed.

As I reached for another beer, I saw a man's face looking at me through the kitchen window, grinning like a lunatic. I didn't know him, but he looked familiar.

He stood in my wife's rose garden. She'd be pissed if her flowers were trampled. Trish loved her garden.

I grabbed a knife from the drain board. Not that I'd ever stab the guy. I needed something to make me feel safe.

Funny thing was, I hated that knife. Trish used it to cut chicken for frying. I'd cringe. The crunch of blade hitting bone. I'd have to leave the room.

The doorbell sobered me. My heart pounded, my neck flushed as I laid the knife on the counter.

I saw the man through the side window and opened the door.

"Billy Boy!" The man embraced me like a long lost brother. "So good to see you again!"

Again? I wondered. I'd never met this man in my life.

"Don't you remember me, Billy? We use to be good pals. We played together in the band. Don't you remember? We rocked the house, you and me."

The room grew cold. I felt woozy. The walls closed in on me. Like I was in a dream. I tried to place myself on stage with this guy. Marty and I were The Shades.

"Well, well. Maybe you do, maybe you don't. No worries there. We use to tour back in the day. It's been a long time, hasn't it? The name's William Standish. In case you forgot." He held out his hand and shook mine with such enthusiasm I had to invite him in.

"We toured together?"

"Oh my, you don't remember. How could you forget the clubs and big stages we played across the state? Remember all the girls?" I shook my head.

"You look confused, Billy Boy. Here. Go fetch us some beers and we'll catch up." He looked no older than me, but had a worldly air about him. I liked him immediately. I took two beers from the refrigerator and, having a good feeling about the man, grabbed a bottle of whiskey I had stashed behind the washing machine. Someone to share the afternoon with stories of the glory days. Before Lizzie. Before the fights with Trish.

"I've come to bring you back into the loop, Billy! Remember the song you wrote about your father? Truly touching stuff I must say. Truly touching stuff."

I didn't remember writing any song. Why, I wondered, would I write a song about my dad who killed himself when I was ten years old? He shot himself in the head. His brains splattered over my face.

Nobody would ever write a song like that. Would they?

"Ho ho, Billy Boy. It's payday, my friend. A huge payday! This is your big break!"

I shook my head, clueless as to what he meant.

"You and me are gonna be rich!"

I smiled. In a matter of moments, I'd become the key player in the gig I've been waiting for all my life. I was determined to play this one out, no matter what. Nothing could stop me this time. Not Trish. No baby. No stupid drummer. I'm going to do this on my own. Me and this strange man who showed up out of thin air. I felt a connection with him, like he knew me. He was about to save my life.

After another shot, William's glass slipped and shattered on the kitchen tile. I picked up the pieces and had to get on my hands and knees to retrieve a shard that skirted beneath the dishwasher. I didn't want my wife to know I'd broken another glass while drinking in the afternoon. God forbid little Lizzie cut her sweet soft fingers while she played on the kitchen floor.

He apologized. I assured him it was no problem.

Yes. I liked this guy. He was exactly what I was waiting for. This had been my dream since Trish bought me my first guitar.

"William Standish, I do remember you now. You helped me when I was down and out. When I tried to get gigs for the band, you helped me."

"There you go now, Billy Boy. Now you're on to it! I'm a producer now and I'm going to make you a star!"

William picked up a picture of my wife and daughter. I was embarrassed I wasn't in it. In fact, as I looked around, I wasn't in any of the pictures.

"That's my wife, Trish there, and my daughter, Lizzie." I wanted to show off for this man, show him I was a family man. Not a slackard.

"Beautiful, Billy. Both of them, so beautiful. Just the way we like 'em. Ain't that right, Billy Boy?"

"That's right, Will. Always beautiful." I wasn't going to let them come between me and my dream.

"No boys then, Billy?"

"Nope. Just the three of us."

"Ah, surrounded by babes I see. Just like the old days."

I didn't remember that. I remembered Trish in her mini-skirts and those cute little tops she wore when she came to see us play.

"Say Billy! How 'bout another shot? Sorry about the glass. But don't you worry. Trish won't be bothered with that old Dollar Store deal. She'll be drinking milk out of Waterford where you're going!"

I poured two more shots and looked at my new friend.

"We could put a band together, you and me, right, Will? Is that why you're here? You need a lead for your band, isn't that right?"

"Sure thing, Billy that's the spirit! People use to think of us as brothers!

Joined at the hip, we were. They thought we looked alike then! Wheweee. Look at us now."

He had his arm draped over my shoulder.

I slugged down the rest of my beer and threw back the shot.

"What do you say we go downtown and buy that Stratocaster you've been pining for, yes?" Will said.

"Trish would kill me. We don't have the money. We're saving for a place of our own."

"I tell you, there's money in your account as we speak. I put it there this morning. Let's go. I'll show you."

I followed him into the bedroom.

I couldn't believe it. Will was right. Trish made tips every night. The box was filled with cash.

"It's all yours, Billy. The first of many deposits on account of that song you wrote."

"I don't remember writing a song."

"Don't worry about that, son. There'll be more where that came from. I know it like I know my own soul."

What the hell. I couldn't imagine why he'd lie to me. And there were thousands of dollars to my name! I took the money and told Will we were going shopping.

"That's the spirit, old Boy."

We went to the guitar store. I picked up the Fender I'd wanted all my life. A real left-hander. I shook when I held it against me as if I was holding the most beautiful thing in the world.

"What's the catch, Will?"

"No catch, Billy. Every breath you take, there'll be more money."

I snickered, thinking about The Police.

We walked to a pub to celebrate. Will and I ordered the biggest steaks on the menu. We both order beers and a shot.

"Down the hatch!"

"To our success!"

"To Elysium!"

"Here, here!"

"I'm ready, Will. I'm so ready to go on tour with you, it hurts."

"What about Trish and Lizzie? Are you going to tell them?"

"Aw, Will. Why'd you have to go and ruin everything?"

"Didn't mean to bring you back to reality, man, but it's something to think about. You're a family man, right?"

"Right Will, you're right. But listen... She won't be so hot when I send her all that money. She'll be happy I got a job. She'll be happy I'm finally getting what I always wanted."

It grew dark and I was hungry. Whiskey bottle empty and no more beer in the refrigerator.

I wanted my wife and child home, now. Where were there? She and Lizzie should have been home hours ago. Probably not at her mother's at all. Probably with that deadbeat, Marty, where she's wanted to be all along. Damn them! They can have each other.

The car pulled into the driveway. Trish took bags out of the back seat. Lizzie slid out of the car and looked at the house. I waved to her. She waved back. Trish looked at me and pushed Lizzie into the car. Lizzie's hands and face pressed against the window, staring at me. I wanted to tell her everything would be okay.

Daddy loved his little girl.

I stood in the kitchen holding the guitar when Trish stomped through the back door.

"Billy, what is that?"

I grinned like a banshee. "I got the guitar, Trish. I went and got the guitar."

"Did you steal it, Billy? Jesus."

"It's all good, Trish. My friend Will came by today. He sold my song for a lot of money. We're gonna be rich, baby! I'm going on the road. I'm touring with the band!"

Trish looked past me into the living room.

"Billy, there's no one here. Who's Will?"

"My friend, Will. Remember, from high school? He played in the band with us. Now he's a big shot producer."

Trish stared at me.

"There was no guy named Will in your band, Billy. Only you and Marty playing in the garage. There was no band."

But there was.

"Remember? We played at the bar."

Trish's face turned red. "Billy, you and Marty went into his dad's bar and destroyed the house band's equipment. You got drunk and busted up the place. Marty's dad beat him up for it. Remember?"

"No, Trish. Marty quit the band when me and you hooked up."

Trish shook her head. "There was no band, Billy."

"We were called The Shades. You heard us play."

I heard the whining in my voice and didn't like it one bit.

"You pretended to play, Billy. You played air guitar and jumped around like you were rock stars. There was no band."

I followed her into the living room. She looked at the beer cans and empty whiskey bottle. She picked up my old guitar. Trish had found it at a yard sale and told me I would be a star one day if I ever learned to play. I watched the horror on her face as she grabbed the empty box I had thrown on the floor.

Will watched from the mirror and nodded.

"This is your dream," he said. Will had the strength I needed. He was the power behind me. Yet I could never do what he proposed.

"Billy, you must. We must go now. You have no choice. This was our deal."

I shook my head at my reflection.

"You're going to be a star."

"It's not that easy, Will."

"If it were easy, Billy Boy, everyone would be doing it. This is a killer deal. Do it. A huge record deal. Do it."

I closed my eyes hoping he would go away. There was a pulsing in my ears. I felt my head and heart burst. I opened my eyes and saw Trish's face in the mirror. I wanted to pull her ponytail hard to make her understand.

I didn't recognize myself in the mirror.

I questioned my reality.

William Standish sneered. "You are not real, Billy."

I stood a few feet from my wife. I stared into the eyes of my reflection, of what should have been a perfect picture of me. My vision fogged. I faded away. The image grew darker, disappearing into the mercurial surface, and vanished.

I watched Will pace the room, rambling like a crazy man. His gestures reminded me of a drowning man, arms flailing in desperation.

In watching him, I felt I might pull out my own hair in sheer frustration, getting drawn into his whirlpool of madness.

"You must break the fourth wall, Billy Boy," I heard him say. "Show the world your talent. The audience needs you now. The world needs you more than ever."

I watched as Will raised the guitar above his head. He came down on Trish over and over.

Her bloody mouth screamed my name. I could do nothing to stop the demon. His will was stronger.

He never liked Trish to begin with. He wanted her because everyone else did. He couldn't lose to someone like me.

When Trish had gone silent, I looked into the mirror. The face grinned at me. It shook with a satisfaction that terrified me. The reflection of my eyes didn't match what was in my heart. I drew back from the sight and walked into the kitchen. The blood trickling from Trish's beautiful body reminded me of her trampled roses.

"Daddy?"

I froze.

I'd sold my soul to the Devil, and he came for my wife. When he wanted my little girl, I had to take my stand against him.

He picked up the knife and raised it over my sweet child. I threw myself at him knocking the weapon to the ground.

The power of the assault and my determination caused him to drop the knife and flee. I thought he ran out the back door left open by my daughter when she came in to witness what had been done to her poor mother.

Will had dissolved into thin air, leaving me alone with my cowering child.

My shivering little girl.

I looked around the room for my wicked twin. My eyes fell on the knife that had skid under the kitchen table. I remembered the broken glass.

My daughter whimpered in the corner.

"No, Daddy, please," she pleaded between sobs.

Her tears streamed down her cherry cheeks. My heart burst like the day I walked into the room and saw my father standing with a gun to his head.

"Walk out of the room, son," is all he had said.

I disobeyed him.

"Go outside, Lizzie."

She sat on the kitchen floor, shaking.

My eyes scoped the room. I saw the reflection of myself with the knife in my hand.

The image in the mirror was not me, but my tormentor. He urged me to finish the job, willed me to carry out his wicked deed.

My own tears burned my face. Will's power over me was too much to handle. Unheeding the pleas of my child, I raised the knife high.

Looking at my reflection, the truth became clear—I was the one hiding behind the glass like a coward and not the demon I chased away. I stood helplessly trapped behind the shimmering glass, screaming for my daughter to run for her life.

She looked into the eyes of the Devil as he raised the gleaming metal. It thrashed through the air like a shooting star.

The horrible screams inside my head played a cacophony, the light searing behind my eyes. I heard it, blade on bone.

Blade on bone.

I saw myself as I truly was. I put my hand on the cold glass. The man in the mirror drew back, his horror greater than my own. I raised the blade to the glass and shattered it into a million pieces.

Tracie Orsi had owned and operated Ragin' Cajun Restaurant in Belmar, New Jersey since 1992. She wrote dark fiction, but enjoyed a good light-hearted tale. She said, "life is meant to be hard. But it sure can be funny sometimes."

THE ELEVATION OF OLIVER BLACK

Errick Nunnally

OLIVER SWAM BACK TO CONSCIOUSNESS, FIRST becoming aware of a light bathing his face. When he tried to bring a hand up to shade his eyes, the arm would not obey. He tested his other arm, twisting the muscles in his body, unable to lift even a shoulder. *Nothing*. Squinting, he tried to turn his head, but couldn't. He felt a buzzing tingle at the base of his skull and his fingers and toes were cold, verging on numb.

His eyes adjusted painfully while he flexed his fingers for warmth and soon he could see beyond the periphery of the white light. He was laying on his back. He listened. The hum of power. Machines, more lights. A soft beeping. Dancing across the noise was an erratic chatter, the sounds of channels being tuned, switched, and tuned again. Television or radio or both. Various voices, male and female, mentioning Hyperman, Max Speed, and other superheroes those otherworldly beings associated with. Heroes that Oliver desperately wished, for once, would burst through the ceiling right now and free him from this nightmare, wherever he was.

An irregular, scuffing sound met his ears. Footsteps. He strained his eyes to the right and then the left, trying to track the source of the noise. A man shuffled into his periphery, jaw slack, eyes unfocused. Never once glancing at Oliver. The fellow wore simple green coveralls and—it was difficult to tell in this position—an odd, metallic cap clung to the crown of his head, enveloping his pate nearly down to his ears. A canister appeared to be jutting from the back of the thing on the man's head.

The figure sorted through a few materials on a worktable nearby, chose something and began to shuffle away.

"Wha—" Oliver's voice was dry and ragged. He swallowed hard, working some lubrication into his throat. The last thing he remembered was getting on the train with his overnight bag for a college tour. "What's going on, where am I?" The sound of his own voice triggered a tremulous pain in his forehead, an electric strike of pain between the eyes.

Oliver's only answer was the soft shuffling of feet as the figure left what he could only assume was a gigantic room, based on the sound of the space. A soft chiming began, a gentle alarm like hospital equipment. Footsteps followed. Strong steps—nothing like the odd man's shuffle— and the sound of something sliding on a rail, the whirr of electronic gears, all coming closer.

The whirr ended and he heard the flick of a few switches and a shuffling of papers.

"Hello? Please, where am I, what's happened to me?"

A face drifted into his sight. Pale skin on a long face from forehead to chin, a straight aquiline nose and deep, green eyes beneath a prominent brow. None of which was of particular note to Oliver, because above that short expanse of forehead, a length of circuitry began, embedded in the man's skin, deep into his skull, it seemed, spreading backwards over his pate, to the back of his head. Beneath that head and neck, a simple grey, one-piece suit.

"Oh my God, you...you're Machinehe—"

Two strong fingers pressed into his throat, cutting his voice off. After a few seconds of the digits jabbed deep into his carotid, he was released to blink spots out of his eyes and breathe deeply.

"My name is Dr. Martin T. Vesk. You may refer to me as 'Dr. Vesk'— not that ridiculous sobriquet the news media has dubbed me with or there will be immediate consequences. Understood?"

Oliver struggled to nod, eyes drifting upward to the array of wires and cables affixed to the back of Vesk's head, stretching up to a device set on a complex network of rails, a robotized hard connection to... something. They were enveloped in the kind of tech Oliver had only dreamed about.

Vesk's cold fingers clamped around Oliver's jaw and squeezed. "You are immobilized for a reason, Oliver, your mouth is free that you may provide answers when questioned. Use it. 'Doctor. Vesk.' Are we clear?"

"Yes," Oliver answered in a breath of fear-tinged air.

"Yes, what?" Vesk squeezed harder.

"Yesh, Dr. Veshk!"

"Excellent. Then we may begin."

Oliver coughed, blinking the pain from his neck and spoke in a jumble. "I—I'm just a high school kid! What d'you want from me, how do you know my name?"

Dr. Vesk tilted the table up at a more comfortable angle for conversation before answering. "I've been watching you for a significant amount of time, Oliver Godfrey Black. You are on your way to college, beyond high school."

He tried to wrap his head around what one of the most dangerous men on the planet was saying, how he could have been watching him and why. Nothing came to mind along with a deficit of ideas to regain his freedom, but he did consider his penchant for technology and information. Every failsafe and contingency built into hard drives humming in hidden spaces at his mother's house, every secret plan he'd concocted to slip the grasp of authority had been nullified by this unpredicted captivity. Oliver grunted involuntarily when a pinprick of pain tore his attention away from his thoughts. He needed more information about *this* situation. Now.

Vesk looked pleased and turned to one of the many instrument panels surrounding them in the makeshift room. Oliver could see now that they were in a very large space and that all the machines around them delineated this area from the rest of the building—an abandoned factory of some sort. Here and there, between banks of lab equipment, he could make out other shuffling figures going about tasks he couldn't imagine. More tables and equipment fading into the distance and gloomy walls where it all ended.

"The process is proceeding quite well, nano-wires are taking root as we speak. We are near a turning point, Oliver, I require your attention."

Taking root? Oliver thought wildly, *In what?* He'd read about the concept of microscopic devices building connective wires on command, but had never observed or imagined he'd have access to such technology. Not until he managed manipulate his way into a research university or lab, he was only partway through his research in cracking top-secret clearances.

The voice of Dr. Vesk had a dead quality that made him sound like he was speaking through a pipe. It gave Oliver chills, but he remained calm, confident. With his history of slipping the noose of authority, this might be considered his greatest challenge yet. As Oliver maintained an internal discipline, he settled on an immediate plan of outward terror. It was easier than he expected. "Wh—why me? What's going on?"

Vesk's smile reminded Oliver of the incidentally upturned mouth of a reptile. A creature devoid of human emotion. "'Why me?' I had somewhat higher hopes for you. 'Why me' is such a mundane question, devoid of any significant self-awareness. 'Why' you, indeed. Some philosophies might ask in return: 'why not you?' Of course, I find such nonsense the height of ignorance. There is a particular reason for everything, whether it has been grasped or not. You, Oliver, you I have watched and your destiny has reached a turning point in my plans."

Oliver clenched his teeth and trembled as cold washed down his limbs. The ambitions he'd harbored, vague plans and desires, were in dire jeopardy. In order to save himself, he needed Vesk to be distracted; there had to be a way out of this, a way to save his own hide. It was obvious his captor liked to talk. He suppressed a shiver and struggled to keep his teeth from chattering, then managed to grind a single question out between clenched jaw. "Turning…point?"

"Yes, Oliver, a turning point. The data is largely inconclusive as to your fate. Where do you fit into my plans, how do you affect the outcomes in the master stroke?"

Oliver forced himself to think, to dig in and consider as many angles as possible. He saw a glimmer of hope in Vesk's response. There was a way to be forged here, an opportunity to be plucked from the seeming hopelessness of the situation. Despite Oliver's immobilization, Vesk had not taken his thoughts or his ability to speak. His mind, he reminded himself, was his greatest weapon. "What brought you to me?"

"A slightly better question. Here is the answer: you have an above average intelligence, yet you are petty and vindictive with it; you have few acquaintances and fewer morals. Clearly you have sociopathic tendencies, willing to do whatever it is that pleases you and you alone. You have a predilection for treating your mind as a bludgeon instead of the elegant weapon it was meant to be—I find that disappointing. You struggle with your existence."

"I haven't done anything!"

"But you will. I have seen you wrestle with the banal societal constraints of the cretins around you."

"You don't kn—" Vesk turned a knob and a shock to his spine cut him off.

"The process is somewhat slow for a reason, Oliver. We can continue at this pace or I can accelerate it. I suggest you refrain from telling me what I do or do not know. We are not so different, you and I."

Oliver, shaken, managed to respond. "Okay."

"For example, you developed two plans when your English teacher gave you a mark you felt unworthy: one, hack into the school's computer system at the end of the semester and change your cumulative grade—possibly your entire transcript—or, two, punish your English teacher by means both technical and sadistic. Identity theft. Self-destructing software. A scenario designed to humiliate and destroy a man who's only crime was judging you unworthy of a perfect grade. You developed an elegant piece of software coded with the subtlety of an atomic explosion. Neither of your plans would have been traceable to you. In fact, considering your petty scope, I'm sure you would have executed both plans, in due time, with multiple targets. The entire matter was small-minded and vindictive, but the latter plan was brilliant in it's simplicity and understanding of the actionable environment. Clearly, you have not been appropriately challenged."

Oliver's mind tumbled over the possibilities, struggling to understand how Vesk had infiltrated his private systems. A network unconnected to the Internet, isolated from the world. The impossibility of the act and his subsequent vulnerability forced the words of a weaker person out of his mouth. "I *didn't* do anything!"

"Irrelevant. You had the foresight to make such plans and revise them, but not the immediate will to execute them; there are still external moral constraints holding you back. This will change over time as you alienate even those who profess to love you."

With the speed of a dream, Oliver's mind reviewed the incident in question. It had been late in the semester when Mr. Buncy altered the established curriculum. They had been pouring through the Iliad when Buncy assigned a short, Roman text for the students to analyze and determine how it was influenced by Homer's writing.

Buncy disgusted Oliver, there was nothing about the teacher he could find to appreciate. Unkempt, with odd physical tics, balding and sporting a horrific pornstache, Buncy struck Oliver as a failed hippie, flotsam from the 1960s. The final insult was that Oliver had to take this man's classes, to meander through insipid and insignificant reading assignments. None of it had any bearing on Oliver's interests. The assignment, a purely subjective exercise, infuriated Oliver. Yet, he put in the effort required, committing his opinion to paper. For nothing. It had been the first and last time Oliver confronted Buncy.

"This grade doesn't make any sense! This was an entirely subjective exercise, I did the work and, besides, the Roman text was outside the published curriculum we've been working from. How does this affect our final grade?"

"You did the work, Oliver, that's right." Even Buncy's voice grated with it's unending lilt of platitude. He paused to spastically adjust his collar. "But the curriculum is not my ultimate responsibility, your education is. I determined that this text was relevant for your own learning experience.

Your grade reflects that and, yes, this assignment bears as much weight as any other."

More than half the class groaned and Oliver had sat down without replying, without threats or any other outward indication of hostility. He'd learned long ago not to telegraph his intentions. A plan of retaliation had been mapped out by the end of class. Balance would be reestablished.

And now he was strapped to a table, being confronted by a man who'd traded blows with Hyperman, a man who appeared to have his mind wired into a network of some sort, using technology Oliver could barely discern. "You can't know these things."

"Even now you resist simple instructions." Disappointment crossed Vesk's face before he turned turned the knob again, briefly sending a jolt through Oliver. "*Tsk.* I do know, Oliver. I *know* you already have the equivalent of a Bachelor's degree in computer sciences as well as significant skills in physics, biology, and robotics—aptitudes that you have learned to conceal. I *know* these abilities have been used to create a duplicate of your mother's ATM card, that you know her personal identification number, that you've calculated how much money to siphon and not draw attention. I *know* your plans for expanding this little experiment that you have begun with your mother, ruined your absent father with, harassed your stepfather. I *know* that you have no goals yet, but understand the need to be free from funding constraints."

Incredulous, Oliver's eyes watered and threatened to bulge from his head. "How do—"

"Immaterial. You have met Twelve?"

"I…who?"

The shambling, sallow man stepped into the room and handed Vesk a small stack of packages. He stood waiting, like a service animal sucked dry of the loving purpose they seemed to have, he was a thing without the critical higher functions to make him useful. His profile was marred by the bizarre canister jutting from the back of his skull.

"This is Twelve; he was something like you. Intelligent, self-important; a potential problem."

"A p-problem, how?" *Keep Vesk talking, keep working the angles, guide him to the outcome that is most favorable to you*, Oliver thought.

"This one would have developed into a deluded, would-be hero. One more factor to accommodate. Better to redirect such energies to suit my own purposes rather than suffer the need to manipulate him later in life. Why allow their ranks to expand? Cull is my long-term policy."

Oliver's head spun at both Dr. Vesk's verbosity and his oblique responses. "Your purposes?"

"The complete elevation of the human race." Vesk laid a hand gently on Oliver's shoulder and withdrew it just as quickly.

Oliver swallowed, disbelieving of the villain's absurd, stated purpose and that brief touch. He couldn't recall how many times Machinehead had been taken down by Hyperman or some other hero—ostensibly during some mad task: threatening the city's water supply, taking over the state's National Guard armory, robbing a bank. "Hyperman always stops you."

"Of course; it placates the masses watching. And, of course, Hyperman is a buffoon. He is incapable of understanding how his own powers work. I deduced the source of his abilities years ago, I will wipe him off the face of the Earth at the appropriate time."

"I don't understand."

"Of course not. Not yet. You have not been elevated as I have, you see only with your eyes, with the kind of mind I left behind years ago, a mind very much like yours. Hyperman exists in the present, like you, like me before lifting myself. While he is busy saving kittens from trees and posing for photographs, I have moved beyond. I exist in the past, present, and future. It is a worldview that is necessary, Oliver, a view that includes the elusive fourth dimension. It is an outlook ignored by the plebeian authorities. Hyperman sees only what I allow him to see, what I wish him to know. My plans continue regardless of where I am. Prison is meaningless to me; information can not be incarcerated; the future is already mine, but for the details."

"Wh-what about the others?"

"The Dark Detective, Ultrazon, Max Speed, others like them, you mean?"

Oliver knew Machinehead had tangled with all of them and lost. "Yeah."

"A bed-wetting deviant, dominance-obsessed man-hater, and slower than he thinks. Pawns, all of them. I know their home addresses, what their favorite foods are, the names and locations of their families, their businesses. They have no secrets from me. You have seen what I wish the world to see. You, of all people, Oliver, should see more—could see more, in time."

Oliver never expected to be in an adversarial position with any of the world's so-called heroes. "You...you've got it all figured out, huh?"

"To the finest detail. It is a marathon, not a sprint."

"So you're, what, looking to supplant God?"

"Don't be shortsighted. I am far more effective than any imaginary friend concocted by historically insignificant, bigoted megalomaniacs."

Twelve stood and watched the proceeding with soulless eyes, awaiting a command from his master. Another prickle at the back of Oliver's immobilized skull came with a drowning realization. A now familiar and definitive chill shocked Oliver's body. He both wished and did not wish that he could see the apparatus working on him. The image of his skull split open and his brain spread wide across the top of the table was difficult to ignore. "Are you attaching one of those things to my head?"

Real panic began to color the edge of Oliver's world, the former confidence in his own intelligence and abilities and his self-appointed superiority began to melt like an ice cube in a frying pan, sliding to liquid panic.

"What is being done to you is far beyond that." Vesk waved vaguely in Twelve's direction. "It is also irreversible and immaterial to you, a moot question. What we have at hand here is a question of...permanence. Degrees of commitment."

Oliver swallowed thickly, the numbness having spread further up his limbs. If he'd discerned Dr. Vesk's plans and motivations so far, if he'd read the signs correctly, then the villain was looking for a partner. Or a sidekick. Someone to be on Team Machinehead and push the agenda forward. He had no doubt that he was being "enhanced" according to the garrulous Dr. Vesk's standards. *Something* was working its way into his cortex. The thought sent a different kind of numbness down his back, a deadening he had trouble believing were phantoms.

"This procedure, It'll make me...like you?"

"Somewhat. It is a...flexible process, the depth of which, I must admit, has yet to be determined."

"What will I gain, in return for this?"

Vesk's soulless smile slithered across his face for a moment. "You will gain the ability to think and experience at the quantum level, discerning the minutia that escapes the rest of the dolts infesting this planet. Your mind will be open to all the information available on every computer in the world—as much as has been recorded. More, in time."

Oliver chewed his lip, considering as many angles as he could.

Vesk continued, seeing Oliver's interest piqued. "You will age at a considerably slower rate, your reflexes and strength will be increased beyond that of the most efficient human being."

He'd heard enough. What Vesk was offering was near immortality and guaranteed superiority over every dipshit who'd ever crossed his path. There was no need to develop plans to ensure a victorious outcome for himself, everything he wanted was being offered on an unexpected platter. He'd be a fool not to accept. Whatever Vesk had in mind for him to do would be worth the price of admission to become one of the world's super-powered elite. And to likely gain the power to supplant Vesk himself, one day.

"Creating people like Twelve to assist you seems inefficient, Dr. Vesk. Does anyone cooperate with you?"

"I believed you might, Oliver."

This was it, Oliver paced himself accordingly, timing his response to assuage any concerns for hysterics. "I believe you were correct, Dr. Vesk."

Vesk inclined his head quizzically towards Oliver.

"Yes, I agree, *Dr. Vesk.*"

"Undoubtedly, Oliver."

"There wasn't much of a choice, after all."

Vesk pinched his lips and swallowed before answering. "Correct again. The transformation is nearly complete. Your ascendance is at hand." He turned to a series of controls and began typing on a keyboard, fingers moving at a blurring speed.

Oliver could feel energy coursing through him, his brain lit up, he had access to every memory, facts and figures obscured by time. Technical details flooded the pathways of his thoughts, unimaginable connections began to be made. The course of his revenge on the idiots he'd suffered this past decade began to plot itself in his mind. Then a creeping darkness edged in at the corners of his vision, color leached out of his view leaving desaturated and lifeless surroundings that were already dreary to begin with.

"Dr. Vesk? My eyes...they're..."

"It's all part of the process, Oliver. I am subverting your higher functions, slaving them to my control centers. You'll experience a certain deficiency in sensory perception as my overrides fall into place."

Vesk's fingers tapping across the keys became an urgent cacophony to Oliver's ears punctuating the acute concern invading what was left of his mind. Despite the new strength surging through his body, he still could not move, could only swivel his eyes in Vesk's direction.

"I believe you would have cooperated with me, Oliver. For a time. Without question, left to your own devices, your machinations may have rivaled mine—despite your lack of vision. The potential for mischief was high in your future as it intersected with my plans, unfortunately.

"As of this moment, your penultimate deficiency is that you lack imagination and I am truly sorry for that. A peer of some sort to... commiserate with would have pleased me. Your responses in this conversation, however, your disappointing attempts at manipulating me, spoke clearly and left me with no other choice. With no equals, I fear what I must have is me."

A jolt forced Oliver's body to tremble and a lurch followed by a sickening surge of vertigo caused him to dry heave. The spasm ended in uncontrollable coughing as his consciousness slid like mercury on glass and the final controls of higher functions began to fall away.

"Your final failure, of course, is that you are not me. That is being corrected."

Oliver wanted to explain, to make his case and convince the doctor otherwise. He opened his mouth and Vesk closed it with a thought.

Errick Nunnally was raised in Boston, Massachusetts, left for the Marine Corps, and returned for art school. He has one novel, BLOOD FOR THE SUN, and short stories in several anthologies; two lovely children and one beautiful wife.

SPACE STATION OVER THE NORTH ATLANTIC

Esther M. Leiper-Estabrooks

Above the clouds, proud astronauts
— Well past the stratosphere—
Stay tethered to their mother ship
With cables tautly sheer.

Below the pair, a milky globe,
Our marbled sphere spins round
And does not spill its seven seas
Plus scarcely makes a sound —

Save for crackling words come through
From Mission's Ground Control
While the men, attached to lifelines,
Dance weightless toward their goal.

It makes them giddy to look down;
To glance where heaving seas
Are tossing, glossing somnolent
— So deceptively at ease.

There miles below, beneath the salt,
Sailor on sailor lies:

Though water's black and motionless
Wan ghost shapes drift and rise,

While passengers are specters now,
Who lost their lives one night
To another apparition —
Ghastly iceberg draped in white.

The band plays on, plays on and on,
With instruments brine-wet.
Shades amidst shades still waltz away;
Years gone and they're waltzing yet!

To view such restless revelers
Would make the strongest weep
At those drowned Titanic dancers
In the ballroom of the deep,

While space walkers, if eyes are drawn
To search **that** stretch of sea
Feel something clutching in their gut
Like the touch of eternity:

Twirling nerveless on brief lifelines,
With stomachs clenched aghast,
Stare helpless at the horror
Till that grave-less grave whirls past!

Esther M. Leiper-Estabrooks has published since college; wrote a column in Writers' Journal for thirty years, and has sold fiction, poetry, and essays in various genres ever since. Most recently, she has appeared in Canopic Jars and Cellar Door.

THE SUN STRUCK
Gregory L. Norris

THE TWO COMETS CHASED ONE ANOTHER on the final approach to Sol. The first, a bulky, inelegant mass of dust and ice, exuded a dirty tail for a hundred thousand-plus kilometers in its wake. The second was sleek and symmetrical in design, its hull a polished platinum color, the massive V-light engines powering it forward expelling a pale blue contrail nowhere near as long. Solar shields cut through the intense and growing sunlight and channeled nearly a third of the energy back through the second comet's light vitrification collectors. At present capacity, the Nor-Hem lightship *Constellation* could run to the Oort Cloud and back to the inner solar system on her present energy stores.

Norberto Krishnard faced the bright, bloated orb visible through the direct-vision windows. As they neared Mercury flight space, the glare shields compensated.

"We're on track within our estimated arrival time to Heliopolis, twelve hundred hours," Lieutenant Howard said.

Captain Alysson Fanning wandered from the crescent of control boards to the space windows. "So far, so good."

"So far," Krishnard said. "For thousands of years, ancient cultures like our good friends the Chinese used to believe comets were bad omens, blamed them for deaths, blights, war."

"It sounds like you've had enough of dogging space debris, Captain."

Krishnard faced the woman. "*Captain* only until our arrival to Heliopolis. And yes, I've seen enough of the sights. Any time you're ready."

Fanning assumed the military parade rest posture and turned toward the four officers in charge of the lightship's helm. "Prepare to alter course."

Lieutenant Brantly responded with a sharp, "Aye, Captain."

"Take us in along the direct route."

"Adjusting course."

"Captain Krishnard. *Commander*," said another member of his former crew. Gillis, the comm officer. "You have an incoming call from Heliopolis on secured channel. I can patch it through for you at Terminal E."

Krishnard shook his head. "Send it along to my quarters. I'll take it there."

"Yes, Sir," Gillis said, tapping the appropriate sequence of buttons.

Krishnard marched out of the *Constellation's* bridge and down the throat of the lightship, a walk he'd taken hundreds of times. Somehow, this time seemed the longest.

Sunlight streamed through the set of space windows in his quarters. The radio chimed, letting him know there was a voice, a face, waiting for him to answer.

Krishnard tapped a button on the terminal and the space windows darkened by half. The illusion of a sunset fell over the captain's quarters. For an instant, Krishnard imagined that he was home in Bangladesh, standing in his loft apartment within the Nor-Hem base, taking in the incredible view.

The suitcases neatly stacked in one corner of the main room and the chimes from the radio soon shattered the illusion. Krishnard activated the link to Heliopolis. The 3-D signal formed cleanly, sharply. A man not much younger than Krishnard's thirty-eight years materialized in the room with him, looking solid enough to touch. Or embrace, which Krishnard wanted nothing more than to do. The two men faced off.

Krishnard studied the caller's chestnut hair, military short, and the way his blue medical division uniform fit his body in a way that should have been criminal.

"Commander," the man said.

Krishnard choked down a dry swallow and nodded. "Doctor Bendewald. I had hoped it would be you."

Bendewald smiled, a curl of the lips that was crooked on one side. "I understand you'll be arriving to the city within the next three hours."

"Unless Sol tosses an unexpected prominence at us, yes."

"Good. I know this is a secured channel..."

"But there's no telling who might be out there between Earth and Mercury listening in, especially now."

"Would you report to Central Medical once you're off the *Constellation* and gotten your bearings? I'd very much like to discuss mission status with you, face to face."

Krishnard smiled, too, in response. "Face to face, one on one. Expect me the moment I disembark and am briefed by Commander Ronson, Doctor."

"I look forward to catching up."

"Me, too," Krishnard said.

Their eyes met and held. In that bottled gaze, everything they hadn't said, hadn't dared, passed between them without the need for words, a rare moment of telepathy shared nearly ninety million miles, almost an entire Astronomical Unit, from the planet Earth.

Krishnard reached toward the 3-D representation of Darren Bendewald. Instead of touching warm male skin, photons crackled around his fingertips. Bendewald straightened, then the image evaporated as the signal cut out. Krishnard closed his eyes, aware of his galloping heartbeat as well as the ship's, courtesy of *Connie's* V-light engines, feeling it through the deck plates, his boots, his bones.

The interstellar lightship readying to launch at Mercury dwarfed *Constellation* and all of her sister ships in the Nor-Hem fleet. With the threat of war looming, Krishnard would give the order to launch soon after setting foot on Heliopolis, and Darren would board the *Messenger* and feel its massive heartbeat and, he hoped more than he prayed, miss him equally as much as the commander already missed the city's Chief Medical Officer.

Heliopolis, the City of the Sun, rose ahead, growing more distinct by the second. The telltale jeweled glow of the satellite construct announced its presence well before the actual details of its Christmas bulb superstructure pulled free of the glare. The network of solar collectors and shields cast a kaleidoscopic wash of color visible even through the sun's brilliance.

Two solar tankers, the *Zhivago* and the *Sequoia*, circled the satellite, guarded over by the lightship *Nimbus*. The *Constellation* slowed her approach, matching the insane wobble of the city-sized satellite, itself coordinated and in synch with the smallest planet in the solar system's wobbling orbit around the sun.

"Heliopolis Command welcomes you, *Constellation*," a crisp female voice declared, British. "You are cleared to assume orbital path at reference 3-11."

Krishnard faced Fanning. *"Connie's* all yours now."

"I'll take good care of her, Commander," Fanning said. Then she saluted.

Krishnard returned the salute. "You'd better."

He picked his duffel bag from the top of his cases and marched the distance to the hanger, where the light-shuttle waited.

Over the past three years, Krishnard and the *Constellation* had made the run between Earth or Moon City and Heliopolis numerous times, mostly to escort light-tankers safely between the Nor-Hem territories. Islamosphere galleons had taken more than a few potshots at the tankers over the years, usually in the Venus corridor. Lately, it was the Chinese testing their defenses. But it had been some time since he'd actually stood in the city proper.

Krishnard disembarked from the light-shuttle and entered the Arboretum. Fresh air infused with a sweet green fragrance embraced him. Situated at the top level of the satellite, the Arboretum sat beneath three sections of transparent dome. Glare shields tempered the intense sunlight to the perfect consistency. An entire tropical forest thrived beneath the cascade, and colorful birds sang and soared between the branches. The grand glass fountain, a symbol of the light vitrification technology that had led to the building of the city and Nor-Hem's space fleet, launched crystal-clear water several meters up into the air from the center of the courtyard.

Commander Ronson's delegation met him near the fountain. Krishnard noted the absence of Doctor Bendewald among the station's former commander, lieutenant commander, and operations manager, as well as the somber looks on the faces of those assembled.

"Commander Krishnard, welcome to Heliopolis," Ronson said.

Krishnard shifted his duffel from one shoulder to the other and extended his hand. He and Ronson shook. "I'm happy to be back, Commander. I only wish it was under better circumstances."

"I agree." Ronson introduced the others, though it was merely a formality, as Krishnard already knew the woman and the other man from his mission briefing as well as through his earlier runs onboard the lightship. "Commander Keidi, Chief Ukiah," he said, shaking their hands as well.

"This makes it official," Ronson said. "Heliopolis has its new commander."

Krishnard glanced around, drinking in the details. Not much had changed, though the trees looked taller and the green space denser since his last visit. It might have been an illusion, he agreed; the result of too much time spent onboard *Constellation*. "I understand you've got a lightship to command."

Ronson nodded and they began their brisk walk past the fountain and green space, into the inner workings of Nor-Hem's most vital instillation throughout the inner planets. "The *Light Brigade*. She's presently one of two keeping watch over *Messenger*, along with the *Effulgence*. It will be nice to be in motion again, after too long being stationary. Not that Heliopolis nor Mercury are."

"I know what you mean, though for me it's been the exact opposite. Too much time racing forward, and not enough looking back."

Curiously on the heels of the statement, Ukiah said, "Your CMO's replacement in Central Medical is due in on the NLS *Radiant* in two week's time. In the meanwhile, Doctor Bendewald is dividing his duties between us and *Messenger*."

Krishnard didn't comment. On the approach to the network of maglev carriages connecting the space station's decks and destinations, Keidi said, "I wish you had more time to settle in and get reacquainted with the city, Sir, but there are several pressing matters that need your attention. Nor-Hem briefing is at one-hundred thirty hours. Also, though the Chinese ambassador cleared out last week onboard the lightship *Brilliunt*, the I-Sphere representative is still here and has requested a meeting with you as soon as possible to discuss the present crisis."

Krishnard drew in a deep breath. The scent of the green space was gone, replaced by the antiseptic ozone smell of the maglev carriage. "Fine, but I'll deal with the sheik—"

"It's *Imam*, Commander."

"I'll deal with him later. First…"

Krishnard boarded the maglev and sent it gliding at top speed into the heart of the city. He had another meeting to keep and time was short enough, and growing shorter.

He took a wrong turn.

Signs pointing toward the Central Medical section led Krishnard to the next maglev station. He doubled back, trying not to think of the missed connection as representative of a bigger picture or problem. There had been plenty of wrong turns between Earth and Moon City, the *Constellation*, and Heliopolis. And soon, Darren would be leaving on the Messenger, headed toward Planet Gamma in Proxima Centauri, and the distance between them would grow from millions of kilometers to whole light years.

A receptionist greeted him at the welcome area, her uniform a bright pop of blue in an otherwise white expanse. "Congratulations, Commander, on your new assignment to Heliopolis. We're excited to have you in charge."

Krishnard thanked her as another cobalt-blue uniformed body entered the scene, and the butterflies in his stomach took flight.

Like the comet, the waterfall in Darren Benewald's office seemed an ominous omen, an endless cascade of tears.

"So," Darren said, arms folded.

Krishnard caught his own reflection in the waterfall's glass: neat, dark hair going silver above the ears, chocolate eyes, strong jaw, his Indian heritage clear, sharpened by his charcoal Nor-Hem uniform and flat top. "So," he responded in like.

"It's great to see you again."

Krishnard moved closer. Darren matched him. They met at the center of the office in an embrace, arms winding tightly around one another.

"Reconsider," Krishnard whispered at the other man's ear. "I'm here. We're together. Stay and we can finally pick things up and put them in the order where they should have been all along."

"We've been over this."

"Then let's go over it one more time."

"It's too late. *Messenger's* leaving in two weeks. Given what's happening out there, it's more important than ever that we reach our objective."

Put man on Planet Gamma, the admiral had reminded Krishnard during the briefing. No one knew their duties and what was expected of them more than he, the commander silently mused. "Send the backup. What's her name? Elizabeth Campbell."

"Campbell wasn't chosen first out of the Nor-Hem medical division pool to go to Planet Gamma. I was, and I am."

Krishnard seized Darren's face between his hands and gently thumbed his cheeks. "This isn't what I wanted. I know I should have done something more to be closer. You and me…"

"Norberto, let's not waste the little time we have left together."

"Together," Krishnard parroted before crushing his mouth over the doctor's, briefly silencing the old argument.

Heliopolis Command fanned out beneath his new office. 3-D images rose up from the staggered crescent of duty stations: a live feed of the satellite and the four behemoth vessels in orbit; another displaying

Heliopolis' wobble-course around Mercury; one transmitted from Moon City's powerful Landau Telescope showing the distant green dot of Planet Gamma; and one from the Caloris Basin, the largest impact crater on Mercury where the *Messenger* hovered as final preparations were made to launch.

Krishnard moved around the observation balcony outside of the office, his eyes settling on that final image. The intergalactic lightship was nearly four times the scope of the pair of Nor-Hem military vessels flanking her. A vast network of solar collectors were charging the giant's V-light engines—six enormous pods, each considerably larger than the size of the four on *Light Brigade* and *Effulgence*. A pull-down window in the 3-D image noted that the fueling and power-up process was thirty-nine percent completed, enough to reach Planet Gamma one way or the Earth a few thousand times.

Darren would soon walk onto that ship, and wouldn't walk off it again until he and four dozen other mission specialists became the first human beings to set foot on a planet outside Sol's solar system.

Light mining. Sun and glare shield readings. Lightship and light-tanker arrival and departure schedules. With *Sequoia's* and *Zhivago's* V-light conductor holds nearly at fullest charge, two more would soon arrive, assuming their place in orbit around Heliopolis — the *Chaparral* and *Acropolis*, he remembered from the briefing reports. More promising data from Proxima Centauri streamed in from the long range unmanned probe in orbit around Gamma. A hundred other equations and demands, everything from water recycling, oxygen scrubbers, and the tense political situation back on Earth ricocheted around Heliopolis Command.

"Sir, Imam Zaher is asking to speak with you," his new comm officer, Ahearn, said, making it a hundred and one.

Krishnard again faced the screen displaying the *Messenger*. "Tell Imam Zaher I can meet him at the I-Sphere embassy in…" He glanced at the clock among the readings being broadcast from the Caloris Basin. "In twenty-five minutes."

"Sir, he's requesting to join you in your office in five."

Krishnard's expression hardened. "Lieutenant, I said twenty-five, at the I-Sphere embassy."

"Yes, sir."

Captain Fanning would be onboard *Constellation*, sitting in his former chair in command of his former ship, pride of the Nor-Hem fleet. Ronson had by now taken the reigns of *Light Brigade*. And here he was, running a city with an office and a nerve center twice the scope of what he had known, but in a way, he was static, stranded. They'd fed him a line about being the man who'd see to it that the intergalactic lightship got safely on her way, only they'd trapped him in a position where the greatest threat wasn't sneak attack by massing Chinese fleets or I-Sphere Galleons, but being buried under a ton of red tape.

One last look at the vessel that would lead Nor-Hem to another solar system and also take the man that mattered most from him, and then Krishnard exited the nerve center, headed for the maglev and Level 7. At the last second, instead of boarding the carriage, he kept on walking, opting to take the long way to the I-Sphere embassy.

Ibraham Zaher was a tall man who smiled from the moment they met until the two men parted company. Behind the smile, Krishnard sensed motives, the obvious and the hidden.

"Commander Krishnard," the man said, extending a well-manicured hand.

Krishnard studied the gesture and hesitated from accepting it long enough that Zaher eventually withdrew the offer, which suited him fine. "You wanted to see me?"

Zaher's eyes narrowed. "You're Hindu, are you not? If I may be so bold as to inquire."

"I'm the new commander of Heliopolis and a Nor-Hem officer. Whatever personal religious views I may or may not uphold are irrelevant to this conversation."

Zaher's smile inched wider. "I see. If you'd like—" He extended his denied shake toward a sitting area set beneath a row of space windows that looked out on a desolate stretch of the void. "You'll excuse the lackluster view. Part of the wobble maneuver, I am told, though I think it has more to do with the political situation than anything scientific."

Krishnard followed. "We wouldn't want I-Sphere looking down on Mercury and growing jealous, would we?"

"Direct and without unnecessary platitudes. I like that, Krishnard. You know, I'm used to taking meetings in the commander's office, and Ronson never kept me waiting."

"I'm not Ronson."

Zaher's eyes swept him up and down. "No, you're not."

Zaher sat. Krishnard stood.

"What do you want, Zaher?"

"It's *Imam*," the other man barked, showing as Krishnard already sensed that there were plenty of teeth behind that smile.

Still, he wasn't intimidated. "I have a lot on my desk, and I just arrived, so if you have a point to make, please make it."

Zaher's smile again covered his teeth. "I'm sure, so I'll return you the honor of directness in the face of the present unease. You have nothing to fear from our people or our military. We share your concerns as well as your hope. Our greatest concern centers around Mercury—specifically that impressive juggernaut being fueled and readied for launch in the Caloris Basin. We would like for Allah to be onboard your *Messenger* lightship when it leaves for Planet Gamma."

Krishnard flashed a smile of his own in response, though a cold one. "Allah is more than welcome to join the mission and crew, as are Jehovah, the Catholic Saints, the Buddha, and Brahman," he answered lightly. "But as far as I-Sphere is concerned, I'm afraid you could all hold your collective breaths until you turned blue and met your Allah, and you'd still never see *one* of your people headed aboard a Nor-Hem lightship for Planet Gamma, so I suggest you not waste any more of my time."

Zaher settled back in his seat, the stars and, somewhere out there, Earth to his back. "You are as formidable as I have heard. Is it any wonder your government put you here at this auspicious point in human history?"

"I'll take that as a compliment."

"It was meant as one."

A woman dressed in heavy, boxy black garb appeared, carrying a serving tray that bore fruit, honey confections, water in a pitcher, and a pair of empty goblets. Krishnard was about to declare his disinterest when Zaher held up a hand and waved the woman away.

"Never mind, I know you'll refuse my offer of refreshments as clearly as my handshake—or to join me in the seated position."

"I'm not hungry or thirsty, but thank you."

Zaher reclined and crossed his feet. For the first time, Krishnard noticed that beneath the tailored cuffs of the man's slacks, Zaher was barefoot. The notion struck him as so odd, so funny—bare feet in a wobbling, city-sized instillation in orbit around Mercury—that he worried he might laugh. Somehow, Krishnard contained the outburst fully.

"What do you have against us, Commander?"

At that prompt, Krishnard decided to sit. He assumed the same jaunty pose as the Imam and stared out into space for a second or two before meeting the other man's dark gaze. "Since you asked, on the *Constellation*, along a section of the dorsal fin that houses the secondary sunshield generators, there used to be a hole about this big."

He mimed the size with both hands, forming an 'O'.

"It's from one of several hits we took from a squadron of your snipes. Snipes, that's what we call them. We sustained the stings in that skirmish last year on the final approach to Moon City after our tankers came under heavy fire above the Mare Imbrium."

"An unfortunate misunderstanding, that lunar incident."

"Yes, it was. Especially for your ships. There are still plenty of pieces floating around up there, maybe even a few bodies."

"Need I remind you that you and your fleet have had just as many run-ins with the Chinese in recent weeks."

"I don't trust the Eight-Stars any more than I do I-Sphere or you, Zaher."

"One would think, given the need for diplomacy now more than ever..."

"I know all about your strides toward diplomacy—with the Chinese, who offered to share their inferior version of V-light tech with I-Sphere. That jagged black scar across the part of the globe where Jakarta used to be is so clear from Earth orbit."

Zaher's smile hovered on his lips, threatening to waver. It did not. "And you certainly have an excellent view from up there."

"Best seats in the house."

"Nor-Hem and its mighty fleet of lightships. I admire your ingenuity, as well as the whimsy in which you've named all of your heavy cruisers after sunlight definitions. The *Illuminant*. The *Prismatic*. The *Quasar* and the *Brilliant*. Very clever, Krishnard."

"Thanks, but I didn't come up with the naming rights to the light-fleet. Now, how about you take some advice from me."

Zaher made a slight motion with the fingers of one hand, welcoming the offer.

"Since Peak Oil and V-Light breakthrough, you no longer hold the rest of the world in a headlock."

Zaher snorted a humorless laugh. "Not that tired old chestnut, Commander."

Krishnard rose. "Nor-Hem will not longer tolerate potshots at its fleet, its citizens, or its instillations, Zaher. You want us to develop some sort of true diplomatic relationship, you can start by keeping a very low profile until *Messenger's* on her way to Planet Gamma and itchy trigger fingers are off the red buttons. If you're really sincere about us and I-Sphere getting all buddy-buddy, show it in actions, not empty words."

When Krishnard marched away, Zaher was still smiling. Satisfied that he'd played the situation correctly, the new commander of Heliopolis boarded the closest maglev and rode it to the junction outside his quarters, where he began to unpack.

He lie in the darkness, the glare shields at the space windows turned up to their maximum setting. An eclipse shrouded the room, a strange room, with only the glow from the communications terminal and the galley's digital clock piercing the shadows.

Krishnard was exhausted but actual sleep eluded him. The most he managed was to drift in and out of a fog. During the last memorable spell before the doorbell chimed, he replayed Zaher's comment about the light-fleet and mentally attempted to name all thirty-six battleships in alphabetical order, starting with the *Apex* and ending with the *Zenith*. He got as far as the *Perihelion* before the bell shattered his train of thought. He jumped up, naked except for a pair of charcoal-colored BDU mid-length briefs, and reached for the radio terminal.

"Who is it?" he asked, activating the voice but not the visual controls. For the first time, he realized he didn't know where his bathrobe was, or if he'd even brought one with him from the *Constellation*. *Note to self, contact the station's quartermaster.*

"It's me," Darren said.

A smile broke on the commander's lips. Krishnard activated the door switch. He stood up from the terminal, instantly erect. In the dark, there was no longer a need for bathrobes or facades.

"Come on in," he said.

Darren entered. The door trundled shut behind him. No words were spoken as they met. Krishnard walked the other man backward toward the bed and its mess of sheets, and the last of the commander's clothes dropped, along with his inhibitions.

"I love you," Darren whispered.

Krishnard's fingers walked down the doctor's spine. He felt the other man tense, shudder. A warm moan teased his ear. "I love you, too."

They fell upon the bed awkwardly, but in the shadows neither took notice for there were other, more pressing matters to attend to.

Darren slipped free of the covers at 0400 hours and change.

"Where are you going?" Krishnard asked in a sleepy voice.

"To my quarters to shower. I'm due on the *Messenger* at zero-six hundred."

Krishnard grabbed hold of a wrist and hauled him back. "Stay for five more minutes."

Darren patted a length of muscled thigh and kissed Krishnard's cheek.

Their lips sought one another out in the darkness. "Can't. Five will end up being ten."

"What's wrong with that?"

"The five more that will follow, which will end up being twenty."

Krishnard exhaled. Darren pulled away. The moment they broke contact, Darren Bendewald already seemed 4.22 light years distant.

The light-shuttle departed Heliopolis, entered the wobble, and raced past the newly arrived *Chaparral* and her escort, the *Luminous*, before dropping toward Mercury's pitted face and the Caloris Basin.

Krishnard tracked its descent and estimated arrival figures on the 3-D image levitating above one of the terminals. His morning cup of Kona coffee, light on the cream, probably a bit too heavy on the sugar by most people's standards, went down well, but his stomach knotted at the reality that this new morning in orbit around Mercury was one closer to the behemoth's departure, perhaps one closer to war.

"We caught three I-Sphere Galleons lurking near Venus," Captain Eskridge said from another of the screens. "We warned them off with several light-salvos that went far wide of their position."

"Their Imam here tells me they've been keeping a low profile, trying to stay out of this looming turf war between Nor-Hem and the Chinese."

"Either he's getting bad intel from the Middle East, or we're being chased and threatened by ghosts."

"Galleons, you're sure?"

A handsome woman, Eskridge fixed Krishnard with a good-natured look that was half smile, the rest scowl. "Yes, Commander. Remember the Mare Imbrium? *Luminous* was there, as you'll recall, fighting off a thousand of their snipes and a goodly number of those big, ugly clunkers alongside the *Constellation*."

Krishnard took another sip. "Point taken."

Eskridge signed out. Krishnard faced the command crew. "As much as I didn't want to do this, up the station's alert status. Make sure all extra eyes are keeping watch around Heliopolis, the solar farms down there, and the basin."

The basin, and *Messenger*. For the first time since his arrival to the city, Krishnard decided it was time to visit the place that would soon take Darren away from him, perhaps forever.

In a vessel considerably so much smaller than a lightship or tanker, the chop verged on violent. The spacesuit's bulk added to Krishnard's discomfort.

"You've never traveled from the city to the surface, Commander?" the pilot asked, his voice bookended by crackles over the suit's radio.

Krishnard assumed it was the look on his face that gave him away. "Not until now."

As if on cue, the shuttle jolted. The pilot—the name on his helmet read *Boseth*—made another course adjustment. "Don't worry, we aren't far from our destination."

"Who's worried?" Krishnard lied.

With warning levels across Nor-Hem space rising from cautionary yellow to the dangerous territory of red, from Helsinki to Heliopolis, from Moon City to Olympus Mons, Krishnard's pulse was already in a gallop. Dropping down into the shadow of Mercury's night made it race even faster. A behemoth lurked in the darkness, but its presence had turned the planet's shadowy face a ghostly blue-white.

"There she is, Commander. NLS *Messenger*."

Krishnard's next breath hitched in his throat. Seeing the intergalactic lightship on 3-D projections screens was one thing; up close was quite another.

The *Messenger* stretched out along the center of the crater, elegant and ominous at the same time. Her six V-light engines alone lit the night face of Mercury for a hundred kilometers in every direction. The two smaller sister vessels floated in protective formation around her, both looking considerably lesser in scope than Krishnard had imagined possible of a lightship. Compared to the vast body of *Messenger*, the light-shuttle seemed insignificant, no bigger than a cell.

"Holy gods," Krishnard whispered.

The shuttle made a flyby. "Thirty decks, six colossal V-light engines capable of sustained light speed, a fully-functioning biosphere and genetic bank capable of establishing a thriving ecosystem on Planet Gamma—should those dead city images from the probe result in a clean slate for the mission to work with. She carries ten Type III light-shuttles onboard housed in two separate landing bays, earth movers, and the makings for a construction project as ambitious as Heliopolis," Boseth said.

"Magnificent," Krishnard sighed.

And truly, she was. Suddenly, *Messenger* wasn't the enemy, the other lover, or a threat. He understood Darren's enthusiasm to go, even if he didn't agree with it.

"Take us in, Lieutenant."

The light-shuttle arced toward the monster's portside wing blade, under her armor, and into the vast landing bay, where a continuous stream of supplies were being offloaded. They touched down gracefully. Krishnard stepped out of the shuttle, then the spacesuit. *Messenger's* captain, dressed in the drab olive color of the mission's official uniform, met him just shy of the maglev.

"Commander Krishnard, I heard you were stopping in to say hello," said Captain Vance Gallender. "It's about time."

He knew Gallender from when he had captained NLS *Prominence* and had always liked the man. Now Krishnard resented him. Even as he shook Gallender's hand, he was jealous, wishing the brass had put him in the big chair on *Messenger* instead of the satellite wobbling above her.

"Thanks for making the time."

"Not at all," Gallender said. "We're excited to have you here, given the latest chatter. Galleons, out this far? It looks like that estimate of ten years to adapt Chinese V-light tech to those ugly clunkers was a bit over-inflated."

"It does, though their Imam swears it wasn't them."

"Surprising," Gallender said, his sarcasm clear.

Everything Gallender showed Krishnard was new, bright, top of the line and state of the art. The maglev systems moved faster and quieter and lacked the bitter edge of ozone. The colors wherever he turned were fresher, the ship's systems as yet only touched by the hands of the builders, not three duty shifts a day over a decade or more's worth of dates. In the propulsion sector, the monstrous pounding of the V-light giants required protective ear gear.

The Arboretum was as green as anything he'd seen on Moon City or their version on Heliopolis. Hell, only the Earth herself trumped *Messenger* in terms of sheer believability and sustainability. A false sun turned above the vegetation, the radiant bulb so bright as to be convincing at a quick glance that it was the genuine article, giving warmth and life to its third-closest planet.

They would have bypassed Central Medical had Krishnard not requested that the tour take a brief interlude. He wanted to speak with his soon-to-be-former CMO.

"Of course. Contact me on the radio when you're ready to resume your meet-and-greet with Messenger."

"Will do," Krishnard said.

He strolled into the open white expanse, a point of charcoal gray color among numerous bodies dressed in drab green. Only one other body distinguished itself from the rest in a pop of cobalt blue. Krishnard moved toward the familiar blue uniform, fighting the urge to smile. V-light had become Nor-Hem's greatest achievement, a feat celebrated in the names of its ships and this new ambitious endeavor to reach beyond Earth's solar system. But there was nothing or no one as glowing to him as the man in that blue medical uniform.

"Doctor Bendewald," he said.

Darren glanced up and, for an instant, Krishnard saw a similar sunrise reflected in the other man's expression.

"Commander," Darren said. "I wasn't aware you were here."

"It was spontaneous. I figured it was long past time for a visit."

Darren smiled. Though it had been more than five years since their time together onboard the NLS *Aurora* when everything had been so fresh, new, and exciting as the *Messenger*, Darren was as beautiful to behold now as that first moment when chemicals had sparked between them, and love was as sure as the certainty of sunrise over the Earth. Krishnard had suffered plenty of battle damage since *Aurora*; the look on Darren's face spoke of love's newness, too, regardless of the wounds.

"Show me your new stomping ground."

Darren nodded and his smile widened. "Sure, come on."

The two men, dressed differently from the others, moved away, charcoal and blue. And, for a short while, all was right in their corner of the universe.

The snipes raced in sharply, two hundred strong, and broke upon approach to Heliopolis. Half of the wing took aim at the city, while the remaining attack jets raced down and toward the night face of Mercury. Three of the second force strayed too close to the daylight boundary; without sunshields, they were instantly vaporized.

"Commander Krishnard, the station's come under attack," Boseth said.

"I see that, Lieutenant." Krishnard reached for the radio controls. Keidi's face appeared on the 3-D screen. "Heliopolis Command, status report."

"Sir, so far, we're tracking 197 individual snipe attack craft, no Galleons."

"You know those snipes didn't get all this way from Earth on their own. They're out there. Target and respond, Commander."

"Understood," Keidi said.

Voices ricocheted over the radio—Ronson on *Light Brigade* and the captain of *Effulgence* below, and from *Luminous* and *Daylight* above in the wobble surrounding Heliopolis. The first bright streamers of weapons fire from the satellite and lightships lashed out, resulting in explosions.

The *Luminous* opened fire. Salvos of blue-white energy surged, volatilizing numerous attackers. Lesser, dirty orange energy ribbons answered, the telltales of particle weaponry and missile contrails. The same sunshields able to navigate and channel the solar glare into V-light engines repelled most of the initial damage, but as the shuttle swerved to avoid the incoming enemy traffic, NLS *Daylight* took a direct hit that sent a mushroom cloud of dark smoke and shrapnel up along her command tower.

Krishnard swore and cursed them, Zaher and all of I-Sphere, who'd used the situation and the threat of an attack by the Chinese to launch their own gutless assault on Nor-Hem. The rage nearly overwhelmed him in its fierceness, but the emotion only occupied the top tier for another moment before an even greater one trumped it.

An instant before Boseth delivered the bad news, Krishnard saw the three snipes coming in fast, headed their way.

"Son of a bitch," Krishnard said. "Patch light-weapons to my console. You get us home to Heliopolis."

"Aye, Commander."

The panel activated. Krishnard stabbed the appropriate buttons and a 3-D holographic representation of the targeting system lifted into play.

"Coming into range in five...four...three..." Krishnard counted.

In the final two seconds, the snipes broke formation to flank them. Krishnard targeted the lead ship and punched his forefinger into the 3-D trigger. The light-shuttle's forward cannon pounded out a blue-white energy beam, leaving debris where an I-sphere snipe had been.

He got off another shot and took out the snipe at starboard. The surviving fighter at port changed course and tactics and rammed into them, sending the light-shuttle spiraling toward certain destruction.

Boseth was dead.

Another threat loomed directly ahead of the corkscrewing shuttle in addition to the others already chasing him down: beyond the expanding spider's web of the cracked forward space window, the darkness of Mercury's night had grown considerably less murky.

Dawn was breaking. On its present course, without sunshields, the shuttle was headed for vaporization. Cursing when he should have been praying, Krishnard checked the pressure seals on his spacesuit, closed his visor, and hit the emergency eject button.

He'd done freefall over the Northern California coast, shocked at how big the redwoods looked even from that high up in the troposphere, and spacefall over Crater Plato and the Mare Imbrium outside Moon City's breathtaking silver wheel. But nothing in Norberto Krishnard's past experience prepared him for floating in space at the center of the greatest battle ever witnessed this far out from Earth

Above him, *Daylight*, *Luminous*, and the city's defense systems were engaged in a fierce retaliation against three of the enemy's galumphing but well-armed Galleon-class capitol ships. Though it lay gutted open, one Galleon fired continuously, not yet aware that its demise was imminent. The light-tankers had pulled back; the wan blue dot in the distance was either *Acropolis* or *Chaparral*. The lightships continued to fire, while the Galleons were standing their ground in a way no I-Sphere assault craft had ever previously demonstrated.

Below, the Galleons' compliments of snipes were inflicting considerable damage on *Effulgence* and *Light Brigade*. Krishnard wondered if similar surprise attacks were taking place across the rest of the Nor-Hem territories on Earth, the moon, and Mars. An Inner Planet, all-out war.

The radio crackled, shocking him out of his thoughts.

"We're sending help, Commander," Ukiah said. "One of their snipes made it through the countermeasures and slammed into our light-shuttle hangar, but we've almost cleared the debris."

Krishnard floated. The light breaking through the night crept closer. "You'd better clear it fast, Ukiah, or you'll be taking your orders from Keidi in about…four minutes."

"Wouldn't want that, Sir," Ukiah said lightly.

The light.

Not sure why, Krishnard glanced into the rain of blood-red and purest-gold spilling across the wobbling planet's day-night dividing line. Just for a second, not more than two, a rush of icy-hotness surged through his blood.

Contained within the glare was something beautiful, something merciful, he was sure of it. Though madness and malevolence surrounded him in all other directions, Krishnard knew that everything was going to be all right because the light told him so, not in spoken words, but promised through a higher form of communication.

Krishnard stared into the light and for that second or two, the light gazed back at him. He didn't know if it was Brahman, the Buddha, or Christ. Maybe it was Allah. All of them. None of them. But it was there, it was real, telling him all would be well, there one instant, gone the next.

Krishnard floated, and the light swept closer. Now, the nearing glow only represented certain death.

"Heliopolis Command, what's that rescue shuttle's ETA?"

"Hold, Commander—we've got additional enemy contacts closing rapidly on our position."

The peace that Krishnard had so briefly attained evaporated. He could accept dying out here, his body reduced to ashes and scattered in the solar winds, his dust perhaps scooped up by one lightship's solar collectors to power its engines and shields. But what he couldn't and wouldn't agree to was Darren being harmed or the *Messenger* mission falling to these thieves and cutthroats.

They moved quickly out of the wobble, four more Galleons. Even given the distance, Krishnard saw that the lead ship's snubbed nose was decorated with crossed cutlasses, the swords identifying it as the I-Sphere's flagship.

Krishnard swore, screamed.

Two of the Galleons made a run toward Heliopolis, one at the *Messenger* and Caloris Basin. The flagship lumbered toward him.

"Come on," Krishnard shouted. "You want me that badly, come and get me!"

The light inched closer, and Krishnard welcomed its hunger—better to burn in an instant than suffer an eternity of torture at having failed Darren. But the I-Sphere flagship moved in close, cutting off the sun's glare before it could do the deed.

"Commander Krishnard," a familiar voice crackled over his radio. Zaher. "You asked for actions to back up words, and you now have them."

The Galleons opened fire.

On the other Galleons and snipes.

The two men stood beneath the trees. Heliopolis' glass fountain cast a geyser of pure water into the air, as if in celebration.

"Thank you, Zaher," Krishnard said. "*Imam.*"

Zaher nodded. His smile seemed far less contrived now, almost genuine. "I told you we were not behind the provocations or attacks on your forces, Commander. But I, myself, had to confirm this for the benefit of both our governments."

"The Chinese," Krishnard said.

Zaher waved a hand. "They claim it was a rogue faction of their military that hoped to stage a coupe by drawing Nor-Hem into an armed engagement. The Galleons and snipes that attacked Heliopolis were part of a secretly negotiated arms trade done during our recent diplomatic treaty with New Beijing. As you saw by their aggressiveness and maneuverability, the Chinese made several modifications to those ships."

Krishnard nodded. Damage to the station was extensive, but repair teams were already making excellent progress. Less pain had been inflicted on *Messenger* and for that Krishnard was grateful.

"You'll excuse me, Imam, but as you can imagine, there's much that requires my presence in Heliopolis Command."

"I understand."

Zaher extended his hand. This time, Krishnard shook it.

"Imam, we'll speak again soon. My office, if you'd like."

"Of course, but only after you get the *Messenger* on her way to Planet Gamma."

The behemoth rose up, free of the umbilicals feeding massive amounts of pure energy into her V-light engines. She made a graceful pass over the Caloris Basin and the surrounding hard-scrabble of Mercury's pitted surface. The two lightships flew escort and would follow her to the edge of the solar system before turning back.

She passed by Heliopolis and the wobble before turning her face toward Centauri's trinary system, specifically the fourth planet from the red dwarf sun, Gamma.

"You did it, Commander," Keidi said. "Not only did you stop the war, you got her on her way."

"We all did," Krishnard said, watching the *Messenger* go. Truly, it was the second most beautiful sight of his day.

Through the cheers and excited chatter, Ahearn said, "Commander Krishnard, you've got an incoming call from NLS *Messenger*. I can patch it through to your office."

Krishnard nodded and hurried up the stairs. He activated the 3-D screen and the beautiful vision that held top honor materialized, Darren Bendewald.

"Norberto," he said. Though smiling, Darren's eyes held a haunted look. "I…"

Krishnard shook his head. "Don't speak. Let me go first."

Darren's lower lip quivered and Krishnard wanted nothing more than to reach out and still it with a kiss.

"This morning, they began laying the keel of *Messenger* II, just outside Olympus Mons. I spoke with Admiral Rispard and he made it official."

The haunted look in Darren's gaze softened. "Captain?"

"You're looking at him. So stay safe and have your fun as the first human explorers on Planet Gamma, but expect me in about five years time. Think you can wait that long?"

Darren nodded. The darkness was gone completely from his eyes.

"I'll have a nice little villa on the shores of Gamma's southern sea built and waiting for you."

"For *us*. It sounds perfect," Krishnard said, his voice softening.

He reached toward the photonic image and cupped Darren's chin, at least in his imagination.

"I love you."

"Me, too," Darren said. "I'm counting the days, starting now."

No further words were exchanged across the widening distance, for they weren't necessary. The signal ended, and Krishnard returned to the chaotic bustle of Heliopolis Command.

"All right, people, the show's over," he said. "Let's get back to work—we've got a station to repair and run."

The new commander of Heliopolis set about fulfilling the demands of the duty shift, telling himself that he needed to stay busy, and that tomorrow would bring him one day closer to Planet Gamma and his reunion with Darren Bendewald.

Gregory L. Norris is a full-time professional writer with numerous publication credits to his resume, mostly in national magazines and fiction anthologies. A former writer at Sci Fi, the official magazine of the Sci Fi Channel, he once worked as a screenwriter on two episodes of Paramount's modern classic, Star Trek: Voyager.

RUSH
Andrew Wolter

A SWARM OF BUTTERFLIES INVADES HIS stomach as he grabs for the scalpel.

With the first incision, starting behind the left ear, a burst of adrenalin causes his heart to race with anticipation. He closes his eyes, takes a deep breath through his nostrils, and a smile etches his hatchet-sharp face as the tip of the scalpel penetrates the tender flesh. Just as he learned in pre-med, before he dropped out, the man maneuvers the scalpel from behind the left ear, over the crown of the head, and to the back of the right ear. The entire time, he ensures that the scalpel is deeply embedded into the soft flesh.

Setting the scalpel aside, the man applies even strength to peel the front flap of the scalp forward and over the face of his once androgynous victim. The combined sounds of slurping and velcro being separated accompany the man's excited laughter. The back flap of the scalp is easily pulled backwards over the nape of the neck.

The entire top hemisphere of the skull reveals a reddish-pink treasure. The man grabs for a bath towel and begins blotting the sticky remains of flesh.

A memory:

"What do you mean you dropped out of school?" Dad's reddened face expressed his fury.

"It's not my calling, Dad. It's always what you and mom wanted for me!"

"You could've had a good life. You had your mother and me to back you up through your first two years of medical school. Now you want to quit?

97

"I have no clue how you plan to support yourself, but you won't be moving back home. That's final!"

"Don't worry, Dad. I'll make a living. There's an opportunity on every street corner in this city."

It usually takes a day for the skull to dry.

In the past, the man has used various instruments to shave the bone of the skull into a fine dust. Once, he had even resorted to using a cheese grater. However, the particles of the skull resulted in large slivers. After endless experimentation with his first victim, leading to an unusable product, the man decided to use an 80/80 metal grit file. The abrasive was coarse enough to grind the skull. Although, it took nearly two hours to prepare one eight-ounce bag of powder.

He vigorously moves the file back and forth upon the rounded front of the skull, stopping every fifteen minutes to push the fine particles into a metal baking pan. Enthusiasm mounts as he discovers a constant rhythm of movement with the file. His heart speeds to a thrilled race and the tickling sensations of giddiness travel from his stomach to his tingling limbs. His breathing is erratic and rushed by the mixture of awesome sensations. After an hour and a half, the man feels a warm wetness between his legs and is both exerted and satisfied.

All he has left to do is dismember the corpse, bake the powder, and package it.

The dealer has met with the elusive man twice a month over the past year. Sometimes, he wonders if the guy is an undercover cop, what with his well-groomed outer appearance and the fact that he always shows up after one of the young men the dealer pimps out goes missing.

The man arrives at 9 o'clock. The dealer watches him with a cautious eye, studying every gesture to ensure that he is not making mental observations of the place. Each time, the dealer anticipates the man's numerous questions; however, they never arise.

Just like tonight.

The man sits across from the dealer. He retrieves an eight ball of powder from his right jacket pocket and sets it on the plywood of the makeshift table.

Keeping his eyes on the man, the dealer reaches forward and grabs the drugs. He untwists the tightly wound baggy and dips his long fingernail into the substance. Placing it to his right nostril, he quickly snorts the powder and winces.

"Damn, this shit burns!" However, the dealer knows the man's goods are worth it. He exhales, and his shoulders uncontrollably slump. "What a rush. You want a hit?"

"No, thanks," the man casually replies. "I've already had my rush."

The dealer slides two one-hundred dollar bills toward the man.

After grabbing the cash, the man nonchalantly exits.

In his hazy state of mind, the dealer hopes another one of his hustlers doesn't go missing tonight.

Andrew Wolter is the award-winning author of the books HAUNT ME AGAIN and MUCH OF MADNESS, MORE OF SIN. His short stories have appeared in several online and print anthologies. An active member of the Horror Writers Association, Andrew resides in Seattle, Washington. Visit Andrew on the web at www.AndrewWolter.com

CROSSBACK
Barry Lee Dejasu

RAYNA FOUND THE LOCKBOX THE WEEK after Lou moved in. It had come with him among the mercifully low number of boxes from his old apartment, and for several months, she didn't give it a second thought.

After nearly half a year of Rayna having to drive over an hour to see him in his cozy, if crowded, Vermont apartment building (and conversely, him taking the train to visit her in the second floor of a Rhode Island condo), it made less and less sense for them to continue traveling this much just to spend a couple of weekend days together. They were crazy about each other. Rayna had never loved someone so generous, kind, giving, and caring as Lou, and he had told her numerous times that she'd been as much of an exception in his own, ever-moving life. Moving in together had been one of the biggest decisions they'd made, but it excited Rayna to think that there would be other, even bigger ones to be made, soon enough.

When she found the lockbox, it was late in the summer, and the slowly cooling temperatures had begun to wilt the pride of wearing t-shirts and shorts. It had been shoved high up on a shelf, straddling the edge of the cheap wood. Rayna was sure it would fall on the next unfortunate person to bump against the shelf's front, placing the latest bag of clothes into the open cardboard box labeled "SUMMER CLOTHES – R." She straightened and stepped over to the shelf, looking up at the metal case peeking over its summit. It was about the size of a typewriter, which, in retrospect, was precisely what she'd always figured it was. But when she reached up to push it further back, she found it was far heavier than she'd expected, the flaking beige paint belying the strength of its metal housing. It seemed to stay put, and so she let go and turned away.

A tugging sensation on Rayna's wrist was the only thing that brought her attention right back to the lockbox in the split second before it followed her lowering hand. It sailed through the air, straight for her face; her lungs loosed a choked grunt at the approaching projectile, but her instincts were ready, and her other hand darted up and caught the heavy box in mid-fall.

She must've shouted, because she heard Lou's voice drift in from elsewhere. "Hun? You okay?"

Hefting the lockbox before her, glowering at it like it was a misbehaving pet, Rayna noticed now what had brought it down after her hand—her bracelet, a charm-studded double-hoop that Lou had given her for her birthday the previous month, was clinging to the front edge. She pulled her arm slowly away, noting how the bracelet clung until it could resist her muscles no longer, and snapped off of the worn metal surface. As an experiment, she moved her wrist closer to the lockbox again, and sure enough, her bracelet jumped forward and grabbed an invisible hold to the metal with a metallic snap. *Magnetic*, she thought as she flipped up the silver latch (itself devoid of an actual lock, she only later realized) and opened the box.

At first, she wasn't sure what she was looking at; the snarl of wires, dully shining metal discs and bands, and blocks of other, even more unrecognizable electronics inside the box could have been no different to her than the innards of her first car's dashboard, mid-dissection during its many tune-ups. As she raised the box and cocked her head, eyes roving over the tangle, she began to see where one circuit began and another ended; certain patterns formed. Whatever their individual purpose, Rayna was sure that every component was part of a larger design—a device.

Still only thinking mechanically, Rayna moved out from the foyer and into the den, where a coffee table's waist-high surface would suffice for putting the box down and lifting the curious electronic collection out from it. The wires were piled—shoved—upon each other, and upon the bulkier objects at the bottom; these she lifted out first, draping them up and over the edges of the box like tissue paper. She reached in, pulled the black cubes and blocks out, and feeling the box lift with its contents' magnetic properties, she held the box down and tugged the rest of the device free and held it aloft in the scrutiny of the afternoon's ambience.

The circuitry hung from Rayna's hand like the limp arms of a dead octopus, and she very gently poked and lifted at the dangling wires, noting how they were grouped into—indeed—eight arms radiating out from its center, each one ending in small metallic beads and round, flat pads of thick rubber. Unlit LEDs glistened like berries along the vines, and one of the bunched wires—the longest set of them—ended in a grey, flat box, little larger than a matchbook, one side of which was flat and shiny. She turned the device over in her hands, her fingers easily maneuvering each segment and section as she looked for some kind of logo or sign of manufacture; however, only the almost microscopic print on a few of the individual blocks were visible, and they gave no further clues.

Rayna lifted her gaze, and the rest of her head followed suit. Lou had disappeared into the spare-bedroom-turned-office-turned-studio only about ten minutes earlier, and Rayna knew it generally took him a good long while before he could settle down and focus on a sketch or illustration enough to need to be left alone. "Lou?" she called.

"Yeah?" he called back.

"What is this?"

A brief pause, then: "What is what?"

"This…" Rayna moved through the den and towards the studio's door. "This…wire thing?" She held the device out in the air before her as she stepped through the doorway, so it would be the first thing that Lou would see when he twisted around on his old, squeaky diner chair. "Uh," she heard him croak in the moment before she entered the studio and stopped to find him facing her.

Unbeknownst to Rayna, her face was mirroring the look on Lou's as she stared at him, and as he in turn stared at the device in her hand. Lou's beard only served to frame his lips as they puckered into a silent *O*, his eyes wide behind his thick-rimmed glasses.

After a few seconds that passed like minutes, Rayna said, "Lou?"

He seemed to start, and looked quickly up at her. "Care…" he muttered, and raised his hands before him, a charcoal pencil still clutched in his right. "Careful."

Rayna felt abruptly uneasy, and glancing down at the device, she suddenly had the urge to drop it—to toss it aside.

"L-Lou?" she said, and was surprised to hear her voice come out in a choked whisper.

"It's not a bomb," Lou said. "Don't worry." Some of the tension had leaked out of his features, but he still looked uneasy.

"That isn't helping," Rayna said, almost afraid to raise her voice.

"It's not a bomb," Lou said. "It isn't something meant to cause pain."

"Then what is it?"

"Just give it to me, carefully. It's…delicate."

Rayna brought it over, her hands almost shaking, and she watched as Lou easily took it from her. He looked at it, touching and moving its loose components with all the delicate familiarity and care that she otherwise would hope he'd someday show for their children.

"I'm sorry," Lou said. This was almost as strange and startling as the device he now held, and when he looked up, Rayna was shocked to see his eyes had a faint red tinge to them, like he was stoned—a proclivity he never indulged in—or about to cry.

"Why?" Rayna asked. "Lou…what is that thing?"

"I don't think I can explain it," Lou said, and the corner of his lips tugged, like a grin forming and dying all at once. "I think…you need to just find out for yourself."

"Lou," Rayna said, raising a hand and gesturing at invisible diagrams before her. "Remember how I said there are few things in this world that scare me? Well, one of those things is feeling I'm not getting the whole story from someone I trust."

"I promise you," Lou said, "I'll tell you everything."

"Lou, what—?"

"Just do me a favor. Put this on." He lifted the device and held it out before him.

"No!" Rayna didn't want to touch the mysterious thing.

"Sweetie," Lou said. "It's not going to hurt you."

"That's not at all comforting," Rayna said. "Why can't you just tell me what—?"

Lou seemed to think deeply for a moment; pursing his lips, he turned the device around in his hands, craned his neck down, and raised the masses of wires above his head. He unceremoniously draped it over his hair, then began to press the various beads and pads to parts of his scalp. Rayna immediately realized that its size and shape was intended for cranial application—and once again, she found herself focusing on the mere mechanics before her. Lou's eyes, unable to see the tasks he was conducting, darted back and forth, and once or twice met Rayna's, but the unspoken questions in her gaze went unanswered. His jaw twisted to the side as he worked at the wires, trying to put them in place.

"It had something like paste last time," he said, but didn't clarify. He fumbled with the device for one more moment, then grinned and lowered one of his hands, then the other. On his head, the device was like a bizarre new instrument for hair-styling, and for a moment, Rayna almost laughed, but his elusive attitude dominated her sense of humor.

He reached behind his head and brought his hand forward. In it, he held the tiny grey box on the longest set of wires. Although Rayna didn't see him do anything to it, its polished side unexpectedly lit up with electric blue light. As he lifted it before his face, his features became awash in the display's light, his eyes disappeared behind the warped reflections of twin, illuminated squares. Raising his other hand, he reached for the tiny unit when he gasped, his whole body shuddering. He dropped it and pitched forward in his chair.

Rayna shot forward. "Lou!" she shouted.

Lou threw up his hand, and Rayna clumsily halted within a couple of feet of him. After a moment, he lifted his head, took in a hissing breath, and slowly sat up, flinching. "When you were at your cousin's party, you saw Archie Brewster get that heart attack," he said in a rush. He reached up and tore the device from the top of his head. "You saw it through the back window."

Rayna's entire body shuddered. "What—?"

"You went to the bathroom, and because of how bad Jake…" he frowned, and looked down at the device. "Jake Di…Dina…"

"*Jake DeNapoli*," she heard herself whispering the name she'd not pronounced—not *thought* about—in years. She didn't like to think about that party, of the tragic outcome of that poor neighbor next door—the look on his face as he…

Lou was nodding, looking pale, and the blue light of the device's screen went dark where it swung at the end of its wires. He placed the device onto his leg as he spoke. "Jake DeNapoli stunk up the bathroom, so you had to open the window. You looked out the window and saw your cousin's neighbor, Archie Brewster, tumbling out of his house and seizing up and—"

"Stop it, stop it!" Rayna shouted. "What are you doing? And what the fuck is that thing? And how do you know about all that? I never told you that story!"

"You don't like talking about death," Lou said. "That's another thing that scares you."

"*How do you know all of this?*"

"You told me."

"I never—"

"Yes you did," Lou said. "I asked you, 'Tell me something that you've never told me before,' and you told me about a couple of stupid things— well, no, sorry, not stupid, so I asked for something more sig—"

"Lou, you're scaring the shit out of me right now."

"I'm sorry," Lou said, and took a deep breath. "What do you want to know?"

"I want to know what that thing is, and why you know so much about stuff I've never told you about."

Lou lowered his head, thought for a moment, then said, "I don't really want to talk to you in paradoxes or riddles, but it's kind of hard not to." Lou lifted the device. "You've seen what happened when I put this on. Somehow, I wound up knowing about something you never told me, right? So, why don't you put this on, ask me about something I never told you, and then activate it."

Rayna heard someone laugh, and realized it was herself. "Like hell I'll—"

"After everything that we've experienced together, and everything we've trusted each other with," Lou said, "I'm just asking you to trust me on this." He held up the device. "Put this on, and then ask me anything. Just make sure it's about something I've done before that I haven't told you about."

"Oh Lou, *please* tell me you're not about to reveal—"

"It can be about anything," he said. "Something totally innocuous. Just as long as it's something you never knew about me." He snapped his fingers and pointed, a smile challenging the tension on his face. "Ask me about the dead bird my friend Mike found."

"Lou…"

"*Please*, Rain," Lou said, and now she saw something in his face, something that might've been there the whole time: a pleading look of *yearning*, one she'd known all too well in the past.

That was what did it; she didn't know what the hell was going on or why she should participate in anything that he suggested—but she suddenly knew that, whatever his reasons—he genuinely wanted her to experience them for herself.

In a tiny voice, Rayna said, "You said that device won't hurt."

Lou nodded, and then stopped, thought for a moment. "It might tingle a bit, and it's a bit startling when…when it works, but it isn't painful. I promise you that."

Rayna closed her eyes, took a deep breath, and let it out in a tired sigh. "Oh, why the *hell* am I doing this?" She moved forward and reached for the device.

"Because you love me," Lou shook his head. "And I'm not emotionally blackmailing you, Rain. That's the truth. You love me, you trust me… and so I trust you to do this."

Without a word, Rayna took the device from him.

He began to tell a story of when he was twelve and attending summer school in Providence. As he did, he stood up, reaching to help her place the device on her head, but she stepped away; right now, she didn't want him to touch her. He respectfully acquiesced, but between parts of his story—in which his friend Mike had found a big, dead bird, probably a crow, behind the metal door at the base of one of the building's furnaces, and how they'd obnoxiously kicked it around and eventually clipped it by its wings to the empty flagpole and raised it to half-mast—he instructed her on positioning the device on her head and attaching the sensors to her skin. The sensors were warm, and were a little loose where they touched her. There was indeed a tingling sensation, but in her state of baffled wonder, Rayna figured that could've just been her nerves.

Lou finished telling his morbid story; on any other day, she would've shaken her head and said, "Boys are weird," but now she remained silent. He then told her to pick up the tiny grey box, which was some sort of controller, and then to wait.

"After," he said, "later, I mean, I want you to ask me all about it." He pointed at her head, at the device.

"Why can't you just tell me?" Rayna said.

In response, Lou told her to push the button beneath its display. Rayna took a deep breath, held it, and finding the flat, lozenge-shaped panel of rubber, she squeezed the grey box into her fingers as she pushed her thumb onto the button.

Rayna was temporarily blinded by the light that filled her eyes, surprisingly bright from such a tiny screen. She blinked, trying to concentrate on the digits that had appeared in the electronic shimmer, but the afterimage was so powerful that she found at first she couldn't even see. She blinked a few more times, waiting for her eyes to adjust—

Something's wrong; Lou's not in front of—

A shudder bolted through her body, and she gasped and stepped back, turning to leave the studio—

But she wasn't in the studio anymore.

She was back in the foyer, back in front of the bookshelf. Instinctively, she looked up; part of her wasn't all that surprised to find the lockbox was back on the top shelf, precariously balanced.

"What the *fuck?*" she heard herself whisper.

"Hun? You okay?" Lou called from the studio, his voice as comfortable and cool as when this crazy ordeal had first started.

Comprehension had begun to dawn on her, but she didn't—couldn't— give it any further thought, not yet. She grabbed the lockbox down from the shelf and all but ran into the studio.

"It's a…time machine?"

Lou, back atop his stool, jolted to his feet and spun to face her, wide-eyed.

"It's a time machine," she repeated, trying to wrap her mind around the combination of words, and their significance.

"How—?" Lou blurted, then blinked, trying a different tact. "What are you—?"

"You told me to put it on, and then you told me about being in your summer school, and how you and your friend Mike found that dead bird in the chimney, and—"

Lou's body rocked with a slight shiver. "I...did?"

"Yes." Rayna shook her head. "I guess you wanted me to tell you something that I couldn't have known unless you told me."

Lou's eyes darted off to the side, then back to Rayna's face. "What else did I tell you?"

"Not much, really," Rayna said. After a moment's recollection, she added, "You told me to ask you 'all about it.' I guess you meant this." She hefted the lockbox, then lowered it.

Lou sighed, lowered his head and nodded. "What do you want to know?"

"Well first of all," Rayna snickered as the next thought bubbled to the surface, at how absurd it was—how absurd *everything* was. "*Is* this a time machine, or am I possibly having a psychotic breakdown?"

"I don't date psychotic women," Lou said, "so...it's a time machine."

Rayna caught herself before she had a chance to let loose a laugh that would have made her pursue the question even further.

"Well? What can you tell me about it? Where does it come from?" She thought about it a moment, then asked, "*When* is it from?"

"Honestly?" Lou looked up at her, and the wideness—the depth—of his eyes was an open door to a world of sincerity as he said, "I'm not sure."

"And why do you even have it?"

Lou's mouth twitched with the possibility of a smile, but it was dead on arrival. "It's...kind of a long story."

"I have time," Rayna said, and almost regretted her choice of words. Lou, however, didn't seem to notice.

"So you used it," Lou said. It wasn't a question, but Rayna nodded. "I guess I wanted you to know what it does—that it really does work—before I explained anything." He gritted his teeth and hammered his fist through the air, but it had no surface upon which to impact, and he wobbled atop the stool. "Stupid, *stupid*."

"Excuse me?" Rayna asked, an edge creeping into her voice.

"Not you," he said. "Me. That I would just…send you back like…" His eyes widened. "When did I do this? I mean…when did you…?"

"About five minutes ago," Rayna said, then thinking back on what she'd just experienced, she closed her eyes. "I mean…I've only been *here*, now, for about five minutes, so maybe two minutes before *that*."

Lou's eyes widened slightly. "Did I tell you how to use it?"

"No, he—you—*God!*" Rayna was getting a headache from all this. She composed herself—something she did well, and that Lou often admitted was one of the things he liked most about her—and tried again. "*You*… used it first, I think. You were talking to me, you put it on, you sort of… spasmed," she pointed at his stool, "and then you revealed you knew about my cousin's party."

Lou cocked his head, genuine puzzlement in his face. "Your cousin's party?"

Thank God, Rayna thought. "Something that I must've told you before…I mean after…" Rayna closed her eyes and cursed under her breath.

"I think I understand," Lou said, looking away. "So I could show you how the tech works, I asked you to tell me a story I'd never heard, waited until it was over, then crossed back and recited it back to you."

"Creeped the shit out of me," Rayna admitted, and looked back at him.

"Sorry for that," Lou said.

Rayna would've told him it was okay, but it wasn't. None of this was.

"So when I had you use it," Lou continued, "did I set the controller, or did you?"

"You did. I just pushed the button."

"Probably set to five minutes…" Lou murmured, more to himself. "Okay." He looked up at Rayna, took a deep breath, and let it out slowly. They stood there facing one another, in pregnant silence, for a long, minute before Rayna finally spoke.

"You didn't answer me before."

"What did you ask me?" He chuckled weakly. "*When* did you ask me?"

"Just now," Rayna said. "Just a minute ago. *Why do you have this?*"

Lou took a deep breath, his lips tightening until his beard seemed to devour them, then spoke slowly. "Someday, all sorts of things will be possible. You think iPhones and 3D TVs are a big deal now?" Lou snickered. "Just wait."

Rayna felt a chill as he said this. "So…what, you somehow jumped into the future, found one, and jumped back with it?"

"No." Lou shook his head. "It doesn't work that way."

"Did a time-traveler jump back and give it to you?"

"No," Lou said. "This isn't *Doctor*—"

"*Then why the hell do you have a time machine, Lou?*" Rayna nearly shouted, then closed her eyes, feeling the stinging hint of tears behind them. She inhaled sharply, let the breath rejuvenate her senses, then opened her eyes, relieved that they weren't teary. "Why would you keep that from me?"

"Simply put...I didn't want to scare you off," Lou said. "It's crazy, this tech. Most people don't understand it. It only crosses back, and it's only for intrabiophysiological repopu..." He broke off, sensing— then seeing—Rayna's bafflement. "The tech only goes backwards. It can't—*I* can't—go to a future. Not with that."

"So...what?" Rayna said in a small voice. "How did you get it? How long have you had it? *When* did you get it?" Her eyes widened slowly as realization, such a repulsively oversized insect, crept onto the floor of her senses, and she asked in a very tiny voice, "How old are you? Really?"

Lou held his hands up. "Don't freak out."

"That's not helping, and it's not answering me," Rayna said. "How old?"

"I'm thirty-eight," Lou said. "Sorry I lied about the other seven years."

Tears rebelled against Rayna's eyes again, having grown in number. "You *lied?*"

"No, Rain!" Lou said. "I mean—yes, I'm not thirty-one, I'm thirty-eight, but all of what I've told you is true. My father worked in that theater, my sister's a lesbian, my favorite ice cream topping is Froot Loops, uh..." he shook his head, hitting a mental wall. "All of it. It's all true. Just..."

"Not the whole truth, obviously."

"No, not all of it. I didn't want to scare you off."

"You're certainly losing that battle." Rayna felt her right eye get moist, but didn't reach up to wipe it; didn't want her hurt to show.

"Look, Rain," Lou said. "I'll tell you everything. Isn't that all you've ever wanted from me? Total trust, total honesty?"

Rayna's lip curled slightly as she said, "All I *wanted*, yeah."

"Please—" Lou raised his hands, eyes widening; were they getting red behind his glasses? "Please. Wait."

"I'm still here, aren't I?" Rayna said weakly.

"Yes you are, and so am I."

"If you were holding this right now, though," Rayna said, lifting the lockbox before her, "*would* you be? Would you still be here if I'd told you I knew about it?"

"Of course I would!" Lou said a little loudly, and Rayna really wasn't sure if she believed him or not. A moment later, he said, "So…what else do you want to know?"

"I need to sit down," Rayna said.

"Of course," Lou said, getting up.

Several minutes later, the two of them were sitting across from each other in the den. Lou probably sensed—or at least had been able to respectfully imagine—that Rayna didn't want him near her, so he'd sat down on the worn, green-painted leather chair he'd picked up at a thrift store several months before. He'd asked Rayna if she wanted anything to drink, and although she could've used a heavy dose of vodka, she'd settled herself to ask for water instead, and now clutched the bottle tightly, wringing its plastic between her hands so it popped and cracked. The lockbox sat on the long, squat coffee table between them.

She couldn't remember when Lou had started talking, or if she'd even said anything to incite the conversation; she just became aware as certain dates began to settle in, years like 2018 and 2021, and something about a farm, and somebody named Paul.

Rayna interrupted Lou as he started to explain something about wrinkles. "So it only goes backwards?"

"Yes. If they eventually find a way to jump into futures, I haven't been around for that yet."

"So you jumped back seven years?"

"Ultimately…yeah."

"'Ultimately?'"

"I was born in 1982," Lou said, "and in 2021, I found the tech, and made a crossback, for a couple of months, then I made another one for a few years. Then…" He shrugged.

"How long?" Rayna asked, trying to wrap her mind around the scope of it all. "I mean…how many times?"

"Honestly?" Lou said, "I've started to lose count. Ten, twelve times maybe?"

Rayna shivered. "But…why?" She looked up at him. "Why would you do that?"

"Have you ever faced a situation, and wondered how things could've been different? You know, 'I woulda, coulda, should, didn't?' Or think to yourself, 'if I could do it all again, I would?' Well…" He trailed off, then shrugged. "I did."

Rayna shivered again.

"Anybody who's ever had even the slightest bit of an imagination has wondered about *possibilities*, about how their future could've gone if things had been even slightly different. I've been able to determine some things about myself—certain constants that simply…don't have to be. I've tried a lot of things out, and I know more and more of what works, and what I want out of life."

"What *do* you want?" Rayna asked.

"What I've come to decide is…I want to figure this out." He pointed at the lockbox. "I want to figure out how it works, what its design is like, memorize it, and…"

"You want to make another one."

"It only goes back seven years. I think it has to do with, you know, how cell regeneration works? I think it needs some kind of 'constant' in the user's body to jump back on, like some kind of anchor to recognize where it's sending you. But it doesn't make the crossback with you. It just sends your consciousness, your soul…something. I'm not sure of any of this, you realize. It didn't come with a manual."

Rayna squeezed the bottle again, crunching the plastic. "Why, though?"

"Why don't I have a—?"

"No, *why*, Lou? Why would you have something like this?"

"I want to be able to fix things, to just go back and…make sure things just go the way they *really* should be."

Rayna held her hand up, buying herself some time to think of the proper words for her thoughts. "How…how can you know that? What should be?"

"I've seen the big picture," Lou said, then narrowed his eyes. "Well—some of it. I can tell you a lot of things about what's to come. You'll love the next election."

"I don't care about any of that," Rayna said. "I want to know about where *you and I* fit into that big picture."

"Well, I can tell you this much—it's been really lonely for me, doing this."

"So why couldn't you just tell me? Why wait for me to find it?" She thought back on the look on his face when she had first arrived from the jump—the crossback, as he kept calling it; he looked so shocked, so embarrassed. "Why does it feel like I *caught* you doing something wrong?"

"'Hi, nice to meet you, Rain. You're very pretty. Let's go out sometime. By the way, I'm from a different future. Want to time-travel with me sometime?'" He laughed. "'Hey, where you going? Come back...'" He shook his head. "If I'd told you any of that, you'd probably have left to hide out with your mother and think about things, and I'd've probably had to crossback to some point before I met you, so I could know to not scare you off."

"Did you?"

Rayna immediately regretted asking it, but instead Lou said, "Life *can* be like *Groundhog Day*. You can go back and fix things."

All that had been so perfect for them, all the pleasures and fun and romance that they'd had...what did any of it mean, now — literally *now*?

"So...what, then?" Rayna asked. She reached out to the table and planted the water bottle next to the lockbox. "Did you? *Did* you 'go back and fix things?'" Lou started to answer, but she kept going. "What did you have to 'fix,' anyway? What could've been so imperfect in your life that you had to jump back in time ten or twelve times? Did you screw up, or something? Did I leave you? Did it any of it even involve me?"

"Rain—"

"*Did any of your 'possibilities' involve me?*"

"Yes," Lou said, then after a moment, he added, "Ultimately, they did."

Rayna set her jaw, her teeth a rumbling grind in her head. She'd heard enough. She grabbed the lockbox and pulled it onto her lap.

"Wh—what are you doing?" Lou asked.

"What I should've done a while ago," she said, flicking open the latch and tugging the lid open. Her bracelet clung to the side of the box where the magnetic part of the device was, and she tore her arm away as she reached inside and pulled the tangled affair out.

"Rain, don't! It's the only one that exists in this timeline!"

She stopped for a moment, looking down at the device as she ran her fingertips over the grey controller, then back up at Lou.

"Rayna, please," he said. "Don't do this. Don't destroy it."

"I won't," she said. She wasn't entirely sure of what she was doing as the screen lit up. She saw a series of numbers appear, and a grid of various symbols and in-screen controls below them. She pushed one a few times, saw one of the numbers increase by a couple, then looking up at Lou—now on his feet—she rose to her own feet and stepped cautiously backward.

"Rayna, don't," Lou said. "Please. I can make another one. We can go together. We can live together—forever. We can be immortal, if we want."

"That's not what *I* want," Rayna said. She held up the device. "You'll still have this, right?" She didn't wait for his answer. "So maybe, you can try to figure out how to go back to before you ever met me."

She planted it atop her head, but Lou didn't make a move to stop her. She pressed the various sensors and transmitters to different parts of her scalp, to the best of her memory.

"Goodbye," she said, and pushed the button before Lou could speak.

"Hun?" Lou called from his studio. "You okay?"

Rayna started to cry as she pulled the lockbox down from the shelf and opened it. "I'm fine!" she called back, hoping her voice didn't quaver too much. Lou said nothing.

She had to figure out how the device worked before she used it any further. It was a daunting task, and she knew it would be tricky. Then she slowly began to smile, and sniffed back her tears.

She had all the time in the world to figure it out.

Barry Lee Dejasu is a columnist for the movie blog Cinema Knife Fight, as well as an editor for Shock Totem Publications. He lives in Rhode Island with his lover, author Catherine Grant.

ONE SHOE
Laura J. Hickman

THE ONE SHOE, TOPPLED OVER ON its side, with no child to wear it. Tears trickled down her flushed cheeks from puffy eyes, the dying sirens echoing in the distance. She longed to touch the shoe, to hold the already fading memories of the last year and half with the one person who loved her.

Hate and guilt filled her heart. She should have been faster, paid better attention; his laughter would still fill her with warmth and happiness if only she was a better mother. The only sound screaming in her ears now was the revving of the engine and the crushing of bones.

The eyelets on the shoe stared her down, mocking her. The tongue lashed out and laughed. Her brain tried to rationalize what she heard and saw, but she knew she deserved it. She let him die. She didn't watch out for him. She let him down.

No more nights rocking him to sleep, reading to him, holding him. The shoe laughed again. That tongue was ruthless. Without a thought, she rushed to the shoe and began to tear at it, the small memento of her lost boy ridiculing her. She never deserved a child. She had problems taking care of herself, how did she ever believe she could be a good mother? The shoe, the final proof of her uselessness. As the seams loosened and split apart, so did she.

Living without her son was not an option; the guilt was too much. She calmed herself and headed to the house, clutching the past in her hand — so small, so innocent. At the cabinet, locked to keep him away, she found the dangerous bottles. She poured them into the food processor, dropping the torn shoe in with them. The mixture bubbled and fizzed.

Memories of past drinking and carrying on, more proof she was a bad mother. She clicked on the massive machine, allowing the whirling and churning to echo around her.

Once there was nothing but liquid flecked with a few remaining pieces of her son's sole, she poured the concoction into his favorite sippy cup. She raised the plastic container to her lips, whispered his name, and drank it down, allowing it to overtake her as she dropped to the floor.

Laura J. Hickman started writing as a child and had numerous short stories published by Necon ebooks, Six Sentences, and Angelic Knight Press. She would like to thank her friends and family for all their support in her writing.

DARK HIGHWAYS
Dan Foley

I WASN'T THRILLED ABOUT BEING BACK in Maine, and now, somewhere between Augusta and Bangor, the radio in the 2007 Impala SS rental car died.

"Damn."

It was two o'clock in the morning on a moonless January night. Interstate 95 stretched out in front of me like an endless black macadam snake and I hadn't seen more than three other cars since passing Waterville. Since my brother's accident I didn't like driving at night — my mind tended to wander. What was I going to do without the radio to distract me?

When I found my thoughts drifting into dangerous territory, I rolled down the window to shock myself back to reality. It was five below zero outside *without* the wind chill. The cold attacked me like a swarm of angry bees, stinging my skin and making my eyes water. I stood it for about a minute before my hand searched for the button to close the damn thing. I drifted to the right and hit the rumble strip. The car immediately filled with a deep, throbbing noise and the steering wheel jumped in my hand like it was possessed. That got my attention (it also just about scared the piss out of me). I was going to have to find a rest stop soon.

Twenty minutes later I was squirming in my seat and I knew I would have to stop. The problem was I hadn't even seen an exit, let alone a rest stop, for the last half hour. I threw caution to the wind and just pulled over on to the shoulder. Without even putting on my coat, I turned the lights off, stepped outside and walked to the back of the car where I unzipped, checked for oncoming headlights, and tried to relieve myself.

"Come on, come on," I told my reluctant dick as I stood there shivering. Finally, a steaming stream of piss emerged and splashed onto the gravel shoulder of the road. By the time I finished my teeth were chattering. It was so damn cold I didn't take enough time to shake off before tucking myself back in and wound up with a damp crotch to go along with a frozen dick.

Before I could get back into the car, something moved off the side of the road. I could hear it in the dark, and even though I couldn't see it, I had the distinct impression it was big. Moose or bear I guessed as I scrambled back into the Impala and slammed the door shut. As I was putting the shifter in drive, I thought I heard something tapping at passenger side window. I flipped the headlights on, hit the gas, and found myself shivering.

I'm not an imaginative person, but for some reason that old urban legend about kids parking and a man with a hook for a hand jumped into my mind. It just blew in and chilled me as effectively as the wind had earlier. *Stop*, I told myself, missing the radio more than ever. *It's the dark and the quiet… nothing more.*

When I was safely back to sixty-five I resisted the temptation to set the cruise control. That was all I'd need, one less thing to keep me occupied.

I sped through the night, realizing just how much I hated the silence, when the dash lights flickered once and went the way of the radio. I'd have really been pissed if I weren't so nervous. Without the dash lights the night seemed to close in around me. The cocoon of safety the car's interior had provided vanished like smoke on the wind. *What if the headlights go next?* I thought, and could feel my heart rate accelerating.

I didn't know where the thought came from, perhaps it was the weirdness of the situation, but it was a killer. For some reason I remembered that Steven King lived in Maine, in Bangor if I wasn't mistaken. Then, as if the mere thought of the man was an invitation to the unexpected, I could almost make out shadows just out of the reach of my headlights, pacing me down the highway. I flicked to the high-beams only to realize they were already on. Instead of increasing, the cone of light dragging the Impala through the night instantly shrank to half its size. My heart jumped into my throat as I realized the speed of light isn't nearly as fast of the speed of dark, especially if you're driving into it at…God, I couldn't even guess at how many miles per hour. If I hadn't just taken a leak, I would have pissed myself right then and there.

Fighting the panic that was blossoming in my chest I almost tore the turn-switch off the steering column trying to get the high beams back on. When the twin beams from the Impala's front end jumped out to their former length I was sure I caught a fleeting glimpse of black figures darting into the depths just beyond their reach. I instinctively let up on the gas. *On no!* I thought, as the Impala started to slow, and jammed the pedal back down toward the floor.

Lost in the night, chasing an untouchable splash of light that was forever out of my reach, I felt myself shrinking, becoming nothing more than a speck in the universe. It was a feeling I thought I had discarded with my youth, left behind with boogie men and monsters under the bed. Hands trembling, I turned on the overhead lights and the interior was flooded with light, but unlike the nightlight in my old bedroom it did nothing to dispel my fears. Instead, it made things worse. With the interior lit, the windows became mirrors, throwing my fear-etched face back at me. The night outside seemed to grow darker, pressing tighter on the windows of my prison. I turned them off and for a second another face, a very familiar face, peered at me from the darkness beyond the passenger side window. Had it been real, or just an image of myself, temporarily burned upon my retinas? The latter, I told myself. It had to be the later.

Trapped in the safe but unwelcome dark of the Impala's interior, I couldn't stop my mind from wandering off on a journey of its own. With nothing to concentrate on but the unchanging pavement in front of me it was free to travel where it might and I found myself racing through the past on another night, on this same stretch of road. The top was down, the night was hot, the speedometer was passing ninety and "Born to Be Wild" was blasting out the Vette's speakers. My little brother was on my left in his Porsche, matching me RPM for RPM. Ricky was two years younger than me. He always had to match me, or beat me. Like the old song, it was a game for him. "Look at me, big brother. I can do anything you can do better. I can do anything better than you."

He had always been like that, refusing training wheels on his first two-wheeler because I didn't have them anymore, going out for football in high school even when he was six inches shorter and fifty pounds lighter than me. It cost him a pair of scarred knees (the bike) and a concussion (football), but when he succeeded (and he always did), I was the first one he came bragging to.

I think he set his mind on the Porsche the day I bought the Vette. Everything he did from that day on was based on getting that car. The second job, the scrimping and saving, even breaking up with Sandy to save money, it was all based on getting that car. I knew it too, and I loved it. For at least a little while, I had something he couldn't match. But then he got his Porsche and everything changed. But this time I wasn't going to let him come out on top.

That's how we wound up speeding down I-95 at two o'clock in the morning. I couldn't hear it, but I knew the 911's interior was rocking – Springsteen's, "Born in the USA," or something from the Stones. I flipped him the bird, he laughed, flipped one back at me. Sara, his latest conquest, mooned me as our speedometers climbed past a hundred. He wouldn't run out of road for another five miles.

I was jerked back to reality when the steering wheel jumped in my hands and the roar from the rumble strip exploded in my head for the second time that night. I spun the wheel and barely missed the car that had suddenly appeared on my left. It blew by me and cut in front of me almost before I knew it was there.

At the speed it was moving it should have been out of my headlights in a flash, but it hung there, caught in my high-beams like a red-eyed moth unwilling to leave the light. Then it was gone, its taillights receding in the dark, but not before I realized it was a jet-black, 911 Porsche. "Fuck," I swore, and radio snapped back on, assassinating the silence. Unbelievably, "Born to be Wild" by Steppenwolf assailed me. I didn't even feel my foot pushing the Impala's pedal to the floor.

I was shocked when the dash lights came on and I saw that I was passing a hundred. Fear gripped me for an instant. I hadn't driven this fast since…well, since the accident. I wanted to let up on the gas but I couldn't. The Impala's 240 horsepower, supercharged, V-6 was talking to me, begging to be let off its leash… and there were those taillights in the distance. Still, I almost did it, almost eased back, but then the adrenalin kicked in and I was lost. Speed, the ultimate aphrodisiac, my private Jones had me by the nose.

At one-twenty the taillights in front of me fishtailed, disappeared, and came back again, blinking on and off like a pair of Christmas tree lights. It was the jolt I needed to let up on the gas. I had been here before. Then the Porsche was off the road and tumbling like a toy a child had tossed away in a fit of anger. When it stopped, a single high-beam pointed toward the sky like a beacon for disaster. I knew what I was going to see when I reached it and it wasn't going to be pretty. Bits and pieces of the Porsche and the driver were going to all over the highway.

I had the Impala down to forty when my headlights picked up the first bits of wreckage; shards of broken glass and loose pieces of trim. I was almost to the car itself when the single headlight winked out. It took me a few seconds to realize the wreckage on the road had disappeared along with it. Make that the wreckage and my radio. Except for my breathing and the wind noise from outside, the Impala was once again filled with silence.

Before I had time to wonder what was going on, Steppenwolf burst from the speakers and a pair of headlights materialized in the Impala's rearview mirror. Soon, too soon, it was pulling beside me. I refused to look over at it, but I didn't have to, I knew it was a black Porsche.

The damn thing hung there, at the edge of my vision, refusing to pull ahead or drop back. I snuck little sideways glances at it without moving my head. Each time I did, it seemed to be closer. Finally, I had to look. We were barreling down a dark highway with no more than six inches separating us. The Porsche's interior was as dark as my own and when I tried to see the driver's face a ghostly white fist appeared at the window, its middle finger extended to the sky. I floored the Impala but the Porsche leapt ahead of me like I was stuck to the pavement. Before it passed out of my headlights I saw its license plate – LIL-BRO. Then it was gone. A minute later its taillights were once again tumbling ass over teakettle through the dark.

This time I didn't slow down. I blew through the accident site like a cat with its tail on fire. I cringed when the Impala T-boned what was left of the Porsche. The temperature inside the Chevy dropped like a stone while the Porsche dissolved like a bad dream when you're jarred awake in the middle of the night. I breathed a sigh of relief until the now familiar headlights once again filled the rear view mirror.

"What do you want?" I yelled at the Porsche as it pulled even with me on the left. This time when the hand appeared in the window, it motioned me to slow down.

Fuck that! I thought, and depressed the gas pedal a little closer to the floor. The Impala crept forward but the Porsche kept pace. Then it was drifting right, slowly erasing the gap between us. I edged over until I hit the rumble strip. Without thinking, I jerked the wheel left, slamming the Impala into the side of the Porsche. Instead of the screech of metal I expected to hear, silence caressed me as the Porsche passed through the side of the Chevy. Then all hell broke loose.

Springsteen roared in my ears, Sara was squirming on my lap, grinding her bare ass into my groin, my heart started racing and my breath came in short, choppy bursts; a second later the Impala coughed twice and died. I fought for some kind of control as I rapidly lost speed. By the time I came to a stop, my mind was numb. My hands and arms ached from fighting a steering wheel that felt like it was suffering from rigor mortis.

The Impala had barely stopped rolling when my door was yanked open. "Thanks for stopping, Bro," Ricky said, as he stepped back to let me out. "Leave the keys in the ignition," he added when he saw me reaching for them.

"Yeah, we might need them," Sara said, as she climbed into the passenger seat. One look at her was enough to know I didn't want to see anymore. She still wore the effects of the accident. There was a huge gash on her head and her scalp hung down over her right eye, her left tit was exposed through the rip in her blouse, she wasn't wearing a bra. It was missing the nipple, torn away by pavement.

Ricky looked even worse. His right eye was nothing more than a gaping hole and his left arm was missing entirely. I knew there was a hole in the back of his head where he had struck a guardrail. I prayed he wouldn't turn around. There was no way I wanted to see that.

"What happened to you?" he asked, when I got out of the car.

"What do you mean?" I said, trying to keep a grip on my sanity.

"This," he said scornfully, smacking his remaining hand on the Impala's roof. "What are you doing driving a piece of shit like this?"

"It's a rental," I said.

"Really? Well, what's your ride these days?"

"Toyota Camry," I said after a moment's hesitation.

"A fuckin' rice burner? You're driving a fuckin' rice burner? At least tell me it's a six-banger."

I couldn't. It was a stripped down, white, four-door, four-cylinder model.

"Jesus Christ," he finally said. "I may be dead, but I'm still more alive than you are. What ever happened to "if the top's up it raining," to the "need for speed"?"

"I grew up?" I answered.

"Grew up my ass," he said. "Your soul died."

I started to say something but was interrupted by Sara. "Come on, Ricky. Let's get this show on the road."

He looked at me and shrugged, pity in his one good eye. "Damn, I even died better than you," he told me. Then he added, "Hey, Bro, gotta go. The road calls," and climbed into the Impala next to Sara.

"You know, this ain't half bad," he told me through the Impala's open window as he revved the engine.

"Hey, what about me?" I asked, before he dropped the Impala into drive.

"You? Get a fucking life," he said. Then he cranked up the radio (Springsteen's *Born in the USA*, of course), spun the Impala's tires, and put it back on the road. I tried not to watch as he drove away, but I couldn't tear my eyes off him. Before the darkness swallowed them, Sara mooned me out the back window.

I froze my ass off before a kid in a beat-up Ford Pickup gave me a lift. I reported the Impala stolen to the rental car company, the State Police, and my insurance company. Believe me, I wasn't stupid enough to tell them who stole it. "Oh yes sir, it was my dead brother and his girlfriend. Traded me for a wrecked Porsche." Yeah, right! I'd still be talking to the doctors.

I got a call a month later from the Maine State Police. They wanted to talk to me about the Impala. Seems it had been sighted several times, always at night, always on I-95, always at speeds in excess of a hundred miles an hour, and no one had been able to catch it. I told them I didn't know any more about it than I had already told them. I did wish them luck though.

Ricky was wrong, by the way. My soul didn't die. It was just sleeping. After his accident I gave up anything even the least bit adventurous in my life — the Vette, snowboarding, my job as an EMT, even dating. Shit, I took up golf and got a job selling insurance. I wasn't dead, but I might as well have been.

Well that changed. I traded the Camry in on a 2007 Ford Mustang GT 500 Convertible (red, of course) with a three hundred-horse power V-8, 5-speed manual transmission. When it gets here, I'm going to drop the top, pop some Steppenwolf into the CD player, crank that baby up, and hit the road. I'll find a hot chick who likes speed and get laid. I might stop when I reach California. Then again, who knows, Mexico sounds interesting.

Maybe somewhere along the way, on some dark highway, I'll see a 2005 Chevy Impala SS driven by a dead guy. If I do, I'll blow his fuckin doors off.

Dan Foley is the author of the novel "Death's Companion", and "The Whispers of Crows, a collection of short stories, both are available through Necon e-books, Amazon and B&N. He has also published in various anthologies and magazines in the U.S. Canada, England and Australia. Find him at www.deathscompanion.com..

A CHORUS OF PLASTIC SONGS
Scott T. Goudsward

THE SUN LOOKED LIKE A RAISED white welt in a bruised purple and gray sky. Dark clouds hovered low and threatened rain, and the air smelled of lightning. Elliot sat on the porch, looking at his handiwork. He'd decorated the overgrown shrubs and bushes lining the driveway, and now it was time to sit back and enjoy the view.

"What'd you do that for?" his father asked. Elliot jumped, not hearing him come outside. He'd thought he was still asleep on the couch. He heard the distinct *pop* and *hiss* of a beer can being opened.

"Seemed like the thing to do." Elliot shrugged and pushed brown curls from his eyes.

"Looks too much like damn Christmas. Take all that shit down." Tears threatened. Elliot fought them back. Last time he cried from his father's words, he'd dressed him up like a girl.

'Cause only girls and faggots cried and he wouldn't have his only child dressed like a faggot.

Elliot stood up and brushed off the backs of his shorts. Thin for his age, but Elliot's brown eyes seemed much older than seven.

"Take them all down, Daddy?"

"Every last one, boy." Elliot sighed and headed down the walk to the driveway.

"What if it rains?"

"Then you better work fast." Elliot turned to see him sit in the old rocking chair near the door. He set the beer can on the cooler, settling in to see the show, or sleep off the drink.

He approached the first bush. The "ornaments" looked back at him. Plastic eyes with lids on springs danced on the breeze. The doll heads had taken him a long time to collect. His father lurched up from the chair and pulled a bundle from his pocket; he threw a high lob at Elliot, whistling so Elliot would see it coming. Elliot caught it, before it bounced off his head; it was two trash bags tied together.

"One for the heads, one for the strings. I got a surprise for you, when you're done." Elliot worked the knot out of the bags and started the task. He pulled on the first piece of twine carefully wrapped around the doll head. It had a weak eye that didn't open properly and blond strands of hair were falling out. The head dropped into the trash bag; in the other bag he dropped the string.

He wondered if his father would punish him and make him tie the strings back together. When the bag of heads was near bursting, Elliot lugged it back up the gravel and dirt driveway. The first fat drop of cold rain fell. The trees, bushes and shrubs were bare. It'd taken him hours to decorate them. It took far less than that to destroy what he'd done. The rains masked his tears as he stood on the porch stairs.

His father snored from the rocking chair. There were seven empty cans around his feet. Elliot tied the bag shut best he could and dropped it on the porch. His father startled awake.

"Get out the rain, boy. You'll catch your death and I'll have to explain it." Elliot stepped up to the porch and used his shirt to wipe his face. "You're damn near soaked to the bone. Go on inside get changed." Elliot emerged from the small house minutes later. His father had two wrapped packages on his lap.

"I know we missed your birthday…" A wide smile spread across Elliot's face. "Don't get all emotional on me." He handed the packages to Elliot, not wrapped in colorful paper, but old brown paper bags. He tore at the wrappings and squealed at his presents. His father sat forward in the chair, excited at seeing his boy happy.

Elliot rushed over and hugged him. He stepped back and looked at the gifts.

"You like 'em?"

"Yeah, Daddy." In his small hands were a shiny new staple gun and box of staples.

"When it stops raining, I'll show you how to use them." Elliot smiled and nodded and thought of nothing else the rest of the day.

Elliot stared at his feet walking past the shed. He counted the steps to himself, moving his lips with each number, so his father wouldn't hear, even though his father was face down on the couch. In one hand he held the trusty staple gun, now three years old, a box of staples in his back pocket. In his other hand he carried a doll, in one piece, all limbs and head attached.

He walked past a tree, a birch, split in two from a lightning strike. Fresh growth showed through the burns. Elliot whistled softly, took the doll and stuffed it into the crook of the tree, stapling the hands to the bark, like it was hugging the burn.

Elliot spun in a slow circle headed for the ground. Jack Chaffer towered over him, fists clenched, eyes wide with rage and bloodlust. Elliot stirred, tried to force himself up, and collapsed into the dirt. Blood and spit clung in strings to his split lips and danced across ground when he coughed.

"Stay down, freak." Chaffer gloated. Elliot eased onto his back, making his gut the perfect target for Chaffer's boot. Elliot curled into a ball and whimpered. The other kids, gathered into a circle, and cheered for the next blow.

"Stop, please." Elliot whined. He feebly raised a hand and Jack swatted it away.

"What did you learn today?" Elliot coughed, tears rolled down his face. Chaffer raised his boot again, ready for the next stomp into the soft flesh of Elliot's gut, or groin. "Say it."

"Walk the other way, always." Elliot swallowed, tasted blood. Jack kicked dirt on him; his cronies did the same, until Elliot looked like he was lying in a bad shallow grave.

"Don't look at me again, either, ever." Chaffer pushed his way through the circle and moments later it dispersed.

Elliot lay in the dirt of the eighth grade playground and opened his eyes. He was alone, abandoned; even the teachers were inside. He eased up, using his arms for support, and looked around the school lawn. He stood, brushed a little of the dirt off him and headed up the street leaving a cloud of dust with each step.

"What happened to you, boy?" His father yelled.

"What do you think?" Elliot absently wiped at the dirt on this arms.

"I thought we worked on that?"

"It didn't work." Elliot spat.

"You do what I tell ya?"

"I went to kick him in the nuts, he slapped me so hard I bit my tongue."

His father walked over to him. He'd been in the rocking chair, drinking from a thirty-pack. From the cans on the floor, it might be empty. He stared at the muddy streaks down his cheeks.

"You cry in front of him?"

"I bled in front of him too." Elliot stepped around his father, heard the whispered comments, *asshole, pussy, wimp.* He let the screen door slam and went for a shower.

His father was out cold in the rocking chair, where he was, more often than not. Elliot gathered up the empties and stuffed them back in the box. He eased his father's feet up onto the cooler and walked down the steps. Over the years, that one garbage bag full of doll heads turned into dozens. The only true friend Elliot had was the staple gun. He retrieved it from the shed and a fresh box of staples. There was a bag of dolls on the floor. His father had been busy.

"You're next" he whispered and shook the staples at them. "Maybe I'll make a nice bouquet of you." Elliot lovingly ran his fingers over the cool metal of the staple gun. A smile played at his lips as he closed the door.

The Garden was out beyond the shed. Elliot had the path worn into the ground before his tenth birthday. The heads in front of the house had freaked out the social workers and police. His father made him take them all down, again, all the while mumbling in a drunken haze *"what doesn't strong you, makes you kill."*

Elliot gasped as he often did on seeing his creation. There was a ring of birches; the trees facing the trail had dozens of doll heads staring at the shed. As the ring continued, Elliot had placed the heads, so they were always looking straight ahead. To him it made the area safe, eyes on every angle. The heads in front were angry, with missing eyes and rips and holes in the plastic flesh.

Elliot kissed his fingers and pressed them to the first face he passed. The eyes were faded but still blinked in the breeze, strands of black thread clung to the head. The rest of the doll rested in the lightning scar "V" of the tree, the limbs trapped in the wood, from where the tree had grown around it, in a grotesque twisting of branches and plastic limbs.

Inside the circle of birches, Elliot had landscaped and manicured shrubs and bushes and from their branches hung heads on bits of twine. In the center of the bushes was a bench Elliot had stolen from the park and dragged home. He sat down and looked at his friends. He placed the staple gun down next to him, keeping his fingers on it.

From under the bench he pulled out a green trash bag, mostly empty. He dug around the inside and pulled out the next head. Bright eyes flashed in the afternoon sun. He jostled the head, watching the eyes open and close. There was a hole in the base of the red plastic lips, for "feeding."

He raised the head, pressed the neck hole to his lips, still cracked from the beating, and blew. A high-pitched whistle escaped the doll's lips. Elliot smiled as a trickle of blood leaked down his chin.

Elliot strolled back to the house, empty garbage bag dragging in the dirt behind him. He licked his cracked lips to keep them moist. In the shed, he dropped the bag on the floor and put the staple gun and box of staples on the shelf. Tomorrow, when he came home from school, he knew there'd be more. His father was a scavenger, a damn good one. Half the time between state checks, they lived off can deposits. His father had no qualms about walking down the road and burrowing through trashcans. He'd been picked up for digging through the dumpsters at the schools more than once.

He was in his chair, head back, ball cap pulled down over his face; loud bear-like snores escaped his mouth. Elliot used to play a game, pinch his lips shut and see how long it took for him to bolt awake. It never occurred to him that he could have suffocated him in his drunken sleep. The beatings had been legendary; even the bullies at school left him be 'til he healed up.

Now as he stood on the porch, absently picking a blister on his hand, Elliot wondered what'd be like to staple a real head to a tree. How many staples would it take? Human heads were much heavier and not so hollow. He'd seen on TV where people boil heads to clean them. But would the staples go through bone? And how would he get the eyes and brains out? The rest of the meat would just slough out, or so the TV man said.

"Beetles," he whispered. The blister broke in his hand. Elliot winced and ripped the skin off.

"Beatles?" his father slurred. "We don't want none of them Brits here. You go upstairs and play some Lynyrd Skynyrd." Elliot watched him, try to roll over in the chair. He shook his head. There'd be no way to get enough beetles to strip the head clean.

Elliot lay in bed, the moon streaming in through the lone window in the cramped room. He'd moved the bed to the window so he could look out when he couldn't sleep. And tonight his mind raced with thoughts of human heads, beetles and staples. He'd come to the conclusion that the staple gun just wouldn't work. There was a hardware store in town that rented nail guns. But the problem remained: where to get a head, how to boil it, leave it whole and deal with the stink, or try and get some beetles to strip it.

Elliot sat up. He looked towards the garden. The night was like lake ice; dark, clear and sparkling. Off in the distance, past the path, he saw the birches; they were mostly hidden by the shed and in shadows. Elliot could see some of the eyes, unblinking, watching him. It made him feel good knowing they were there and looking out for him when no one else would.

He glanced up at the Tropical Fish calendar tacked to the wall. Tomorrow was Saturday and the thought ran a cold shiver down his spine. Elliot wrapped himself in the blankets, despite the mid-spring heat and humidity. Tomorrow was cleaning day. While his father was out scrounging for cans and dolls and maybe some food, Elliot would be in the garden, cleaning out the heads. He was always terrified what would be inside the hollow plastic faces. Sometimes it was dirt, other times, the occasional leaf. It was when the spiders crawled in and clogged the inside with web and dead bugs that made his skin crawl.

He wondered if they felt stuffed up. Did being packed with dirt and bugs do anything to them? A doll was a friend to someone once. Then they got discarded, thrown away and forgotten about. Elliot was doing his best to help them remember; the heads needed peace. And though he couldn't sit and stroke each one lovingly, he wanted to, desperately. Were the heads packed with dark thoughts?

Elliot shut off his brain for a moment at the hint of a breeze. A warm wind blew off the back fields, through the trees he didn't walk through anymore, down past the pit, and the dump and the meadow. He heard a sound, small at first, barely audible. It was too long to be a bird chirping, too high-pitched. The noise was different than peeper frogs. It grew louder with the passing seconds. The frogs stopped, and what few birds were there rustled and flew off.

The sound grew louder as the wind picked up. It was too clear for a storm; didn't smell like rain either. Elliot leaned out of the window; he'd taken the screens out ages ago to see the garden. He saw the moonlight reflected off the eyes, blinking in the breeze. There was a tune to it, something soft and gentle. His heads were singing to him, whistling a song through their plastic lips.

Elliot didn't cry the night his daddy died. He'd barely even known he was gone. The doll heads had sung him to sleep, whistling their siren's song. In the morning, Elliot had gotten ready for the cleaning, armed with paper towels and glass cleaner.

He was still in the chair, or part of him was, he'd managed to roll over in his sleep, his neck bent and caught under one of the chair's wooden arms. The thoughts of real heads and nail guns came back to him and he hated himself for thinking about it.

"I better call someone," he muttered. Elliot dropped the paper towels and glass cleaner on the porch. He stopped again to look at the queer angle of his father's neck. He didn't hear a scream, or a call or a cough; there was no sound from the porch.

"Someone kill you, Daddy?" He waited for an answer, for how long he didn't know. "I'll take care of it all." Elliot went inside, picked up the phone, listened to the solid, reassuring tone and tried to figure out who to call.

With an armful of plastic grocery bags, Elliot stopped on the corner of the street. There was no traffic and no people. The town seemed deserted. He stared deer-like into the window of Gibson's Toy Emporium. Toy trains ran through a mountain-scape and across bridges crossing valleys. Interspersed through the display, were dolls, sporting equipment, toy trucks and empty electronics boxes.

Elliot's breath oozed from his mouth, as he saw the box. "Sarah Sings" a lifelike 36-inch doll with "real skin." She said fourteen different phrases, her eyes opened and closed and you could feed her from a bottle. Elliot reached for the door, before realizing he had taken that first step.

Elliot sat on the ground near his father's burial mound. He buried him deep, wrapped his father's corpse in a blue tarp, covered him up and then neatly stacked stones over the bump. The ground was damp and he felt the cold seeping through his pants. The Sarah doll stood within arm's reach still in the box. Elliot licked his lips. Scattered around him on the ground were the staple gun, a hacksaw, a gardening shovel and a rechargeable drill. He waited until the moon "looked right" to him and reached for the box.

The doll with blue eyes and blonde hair looked innocent to him. He stared at the red painted mouth and the small hole between the lips. Elliot tore into the box, tossing pieces of ripped cardboard and plastic over his shoulders. When Sarah was free, he held her up, looked into her eyes and pointed her at the moon. Elliot stood, oblivious to the damp spot on his pants.

"See them, Sarah?" Elliot held up the doll and spun in a small circle, showing her the other heads in the garden. He tucked her under his arm and held her close to his chest. "They're all your brothers and sisters." He stroked the thick blonde hair and lifted her close to his face. "Tonight, you're going to sing with them, all the others. Sing me a lullaby by the moonlight." Elliot walked around the mound, wishing he'd kept the old bench in the garden. "Family first," he muttered, just like daddy used to say.

Elliot looked at her outstretched arms, just ready for a big hug, and those eyes that caught his gaze and reflected his face. Her lips were kissable, maybe even lickable. He brought the doll a little higher. On her left arm was a small sticker that read, "press here." Elliot licked his lips, still thinking about her mouth, and pressed down on the spot.

"*Will you be my best friend?*" A high-pitched electronic voice rang out, spoiling the harmony of the garden.

"No." He pressed again.

"*Are you my new mommy?*"

"Daddy didn't raise no girls or queers."

"*I love you.*" A wide smile crossed his face and without a second thought, Elliot twisted the doll's head off the plastic body. It came off with a satisfying plastic *pop*. He didn't need the hacksaw like originally planned. He dropped the body in the dirt, stepping over it to get to the drill.

First he held the neck hole to his lips and blew. He listened to the other heads humming with the breeze around him. He blew again, picking up the drill, he widened the mouth hole, gently blew the plastic shavings away. This time the pitch sounded perfect, Elliot smiled and held the head to his chest.

"I hope you'll like it out here with all the others. They'll be nice to you, or they'll have to deal with me." Elliot looked over his shoulder at the other doll heads, as if they were plotting. As he stared down some of the other heads, something new caught his eye, maybe something a little sinister. Elliot scowled and reached for the staple gun. Looking for the best spot to overlook the mound, he ripped one head off a tree, dropping it and then carefully stapled Sarah in its place.

He looked down at the head lying on the stones covering his father. The head landed there. It looked at him, with dirty cheeks and one gimpy eye that stared off into space. The other one, locked right on, like it was looking through him. He went to kick it, but remembering where it was, Elliot gently lifted the head off of the mound and dropped it. When he thought none of the other heads were looking, he stomped on it. He picked up the ruined head and Sarah's doll body and stalked off into the woods.

The grass was damp and the path not so worn. The trees grew thicker and the heads he'd placed up on the trees to keep watch had mysteriously vanished. He always assumed it was his father ripping them down in a drunken stupor and throwing them deep into the dark woods. Elliot looked back towards the moon. A cool breeze rushed by, chilling him. From this far back, he could barely see the outline of the shed.

There was no more path, but Elliot knew the way—he'd been playing back there since before his mother died. He walked slowly, dragging his feet so as not to trip over anything. The doll's body seemed intolerably heavy. He screamed and threw it hard as he could, waiting to hear it collide with a tree and the arms and legs fly off in different directions.

"*I love you.*" Elliot shivered. The doll hadn't gone far at all, and it was still in one piece, sans head. He picked it up and continued. He broke through the tree line to a small clearing, the moon shone bright here. The night sky was cloudless, an infinite number of stars winked down at him. Elliot hummed something to take his mind off the next deed.

He hated this place, and Elliot knew that it hated him too. Before the town really built up decades ago, this clearing had been used as a dump. There were rusted out cars, old appliances, layers of broken bottles and rotted boards and furniture.

"This place has a soul," he said to the body. "I never found anyone buried out here." In front of the biggest pile of junk was a deep gulley. Elliot stepped closer to the edge. Down among the moss-covered rocks and fallen branches were hundreds, if not thousands, of discarded doll bodies. Plastic arms and legs bent out at impossible angles. Dirt covered fingers pointed at him accusingly. Liquid shadows fueled by moonlight caressed the jagged ground and ran like swarms of inky insects across the stones.

"I'm sorry," he whispered and tossed the body. It fell with a wet squeak of plastic against plastic. It tumbled neck over feet until it stopped in a pile. The cleanness of the new body shone like a beacon. Elliot inched back. A shadow moved in the gulley, and something shifted with a dry rustling. He looked down at the crushed head in his hand. Something moved inside; something dark and fluid. A spider scuttled and ran up his arm. Elliot screamed and threw the head, batting at the spider.

Elliot squatted on his haunches in the alley behind the toy store. His bike was up against the brick wall. He ate stale cookies from the bakery next door. The day-old goods were always cheaper, and just as good. His daddy had drilled that into his skull. Elliot thought about his father, dead now sixteen years.

Elliot had been caught by the state, sent away and forced to perform community service. Mark Lambert's body had been exhumed from the garden and laid to rest in the paupers field next to the local cemetery. The bullies in the minimum security prison had done far worse to Elliot than the kids on the playground had ever done. The local and state press had been all over the story of the body buried in the backyard. When the pictures hit of the plastic heads, Elliot had become somewhat of a local celebrity.

When his term was over, Elliot moved back into the old house and there wasn't a day when the driveway wasn't packed full of cars of curiosity-seekers wanting to see what he'd done. Some asked him questions, *how... why?* Others just walked past him, keeping a suspicious eye leveled, waiting for him to pounce. Elliot kept the answers simple and did his best not to talk to any of them.

The side door opened with a squeal of hinges. Elliot stood up and brushed the crumbs out of his shadow of a beard. Mr. Gibson poked his head out and nodded, seeing Elliot. He pushed on the door, as if it was fighting him, until it swung wide. Elliot wiped his hands on his pants, suddenly anxious at the new treasures being brought out.

Gibson dragged out the trash bags full of dolls, heads, arms, and bodies. The manufacturers had discontinued a line and didn't want them returned. Elliot always took the throw-aways; it was so much easier than digging through dumpsters. He helped Gibson with the bags, taking the weight away from the older man.

"Got a lot for you today, Elliot." There was a waver in the man's voice.

"Thank you, Mr. Gibson." Elliot pulled a small roll of bills from his pocket and handed it to him.

"You're not looking right, Elliot. Everything okay?" Elliot tested the weight of the bags, tried to balance on the bike with the bags thrown over his shoulder. He fell over in a pile of plastic corpses. "Leave the bike, Elliot. I'll bring it in the store. Knock when you come back."

"Thank you." Elliot stood, oblivious to the people stopped at the mouth of the alley, staring at him. Cell phone cameras snatched pictures. He gathered up the bags, threw them over his shoulders and started towards home, like a homeless Santa Claus.

Elliot stood at the base of the driveway and dropped the bags on the road. There were cars here, despite the chain he'd strung across it. The cars were on both sides of the street; there was never any quiet time, except at night when his treasures sang their plastic serenades to him.

Elliot unlocked the padlock, and the chain fell limp across the dirt and gravel. There was no use locking it back up, not with people at the garden. He dragged the bags behind him as he walked, kicking up storm clouds of dust.

He dropped the bags off at the porch, from the cooler; he took out a bottle of water and drank deep. He poured water on his hands and splashed it on his face. On the boards near the rocking chair was an old pickle jar with cash stuffed in it; the admission jar. Elliot never could figure out what to charge people, so he just left jar out and people stuffed in what they wanted. It helped with the bills and every now and again, he'd get an interview that would bring in fresh eyes to his garden.

"Thanks for coming, folks." He waved to a family walking down the driveway. They kept their kids tucked safely between them. They nodded and Elliot looked away. They quickened their pace, forcing smiles until they were out of eyeshot. Elliot heard their car starting. He waited until the last of the people left. When he was sure he was alone, Elliot set the chain across his driveway and went for his bike.

Elliot sat on the porch eating chicken from a bucket. All around him lay the carnage of the night's work. His feet were covered in plastic shavings from the drilling. The hatchet lay on its side, unused. The boards were strewn with plastic arms and legs, some twisted, others still attached to the bodies bent at impossible angles. He stopped for a moment, his hands wrapped around the throat of his next 'victim.' A car rolled by slowly on the street, and he heard it stop near his driveway. There was some muffled talking. Elliot reached for the hatchet. When the car sped up, Elliot resumed his death grip on the doll's throat.

He imagined the cheery face turning pink and gasping for air, the little plastic hands beating against his to get free, the glass eyes bulging. With a sick grin and a vicious twist Elliot popped the head off. He watched it bounce across the porch and land in the dirt. He dropped the body in a bag, wiped his hands on his shirt and reached for the next one.

Carefully, he examined the mouth. There was no hole for a bottle, so he drilled one, cautious not get any shavings on the fried chicken. He tilted the doll up and down and watched the eyes open and close. Those were his favorite. Though he used the ones with the painted eyes, the ones that blinked always seemed more alive to him. Elliot stood and unceremoniously stepped on the doll's torso. He watched the head go shooting off and roll across the driveway. A smile played at his lips and bits of fried chicken fell from his wispy beard.

When the last doll was dead and gone, Elliot got to the gruesome task of stuffing heads into one bag, limbs and bodies into the other two. He retrieved the two from the dirt and tied off the bag. Footsteps crunched on the driveway.

"We're closed."

"I told you never to talk to me, freak." Elliot's jaw dropped. The bag in his hands slipped free and rolled away from him.

"What do you want, Jack?"

"You talked to me, and you used my name." Jack Chaffer stood in the circle of light from the lamppost near the porch. Elliot reached down, picked up the bucket of fried chicken and set it down inside the house. Then he dropped an empty trash bag over the hatchet, hiding it.

"I'll call the police. You're trespassing."

"You going to cry again when I kick your ass this time?" Jack stepped closer. Elliot saw the stagger; he'd seen it a thousand times or more with his father.

"There's nothing you can do to me to make me cry."

"Looking at me, talking to me. Looks like you're all grown up now. Except men don't play with dolls, just girls and queers. And I know you're not a girl…" Elliot stepped back, sliding the chicken further into the house. That bucket would have to last him a few days and Jack Chaffer wasn't going to ruin his meals. He grabbed the phone from the wall and came back outside. Jack was standing at the edge of the porch.

"No matter how fast you call, I'm faster." Jack clenched his fists, the knuckles popping with each tightening of his fingers.

"What's the matter, Jack? You beat on your wife and kids too much this week, so now you have to bother me?" Chaffer's eyes bulged with rage. Spittle flew from his lips as his head shook.

"I'm going to fucking kill you." Elliot slammed the door as Jack charged him, stepping to the side. Chaffer ran headfirst into the side of the house. Something inside fell and broke. While Chaffer was dazed, Elliot swung and smashed the phone on the back of his head. He saw a bit of blood blossom. Chaffer staggered back, grabbing his head, saw the blood on his fingers and screamed. He was a wild animal and Elliot knew he had to keep his cool, and not show his fear. All he wanted to do was curl into a ball and take the beatings 'til he pissed himself and passed out. Then he'd be left alone again, for a good long time.

"*Every now and again, a man's gotta take a stand for himself.*" His father had said that one night pre-stupor and right now, the words felt right.

Chaffer launched himself at Elliot, caught him around the waist and drove him out to the driveway, knocked him sprawling in the dirt and gravel. Elliot flinched, getting back up, the meat of his hands scraped raw. Chaffer got down in a football stance, something he'd done through high school and college. He surged forward like the tide, and leapt at Elliot who barely got his hands up in time to deflect some of the hit. Elliot flew high over Chaffer's shoulder and landed hard on his back. A pained groan escaped him. Elliot lifted his head to see where he was and the staple gun gleamed in the porch light.

The first kick caught Elliot in the side, lifting him off the ground, like he was an empty sack. Chaffer grabbed his collar and belt, hoisted him over his head and tossed him, like one of his dolls. Elliot hit the ground and rolled with the throw, felt Chaffer's arm slip just a bit. Was he getting tired? Maybe the booze was too much. Elliot stood holding out his arms for balance and spit dirt at Chaffer.

"You don't know when to stay down." Chaffer charged him again, and this time Elliot was ready. He cocked his leg back and when Chaffer was close enough, punted his balls into the end zone. A pained gasp that drew out into a wheeze escaped Chaffer's lips as he collapsed in the driveway. Elliot stumbled as he stepped over him. Chaffer weakly made a grab for his leg. Elliot went to the porch, took a drink of water from the cooler and reached for his staple gun.

Elliot sat on the bench in the garden. He looked down at the spot where his father had been buried. Instead of the neat rounded mound of stones, there was now the grisly staple-ridden body of Jack Chaffer. Elliot had gotten several shots off to the face; the staples didn't get through his skull, but they were in there tight. He remembered the screams as each staple *thunked* into skin and bone. After his head, Elliot went to his arms and legs until Jack passed out. As an afterthought, Elliot had planted the hatchet deep in the side of his neck. Jack Chaffer would not bully anyone again.

Elliot ran his blood-coated fingers across his father's name carved into the seat of the bench. For a moment he imagined his father sitting next to him and smiling. Proud he had stood up to the bully, finally. But Elliot was alone in the garden. Even the thousands of sets of eyes staring at him brought no comfort. He felt exposed and alone. Now that people were coming to see his Garden and marvel at the "art" there was no place to hide the body. Even if he dug all night, there would still be evidence, and Jack was a big man, the scar in the Earth hiding him would be much bigger than his father's grave.

Elliot knelt on the ground pulled the hatchet free. It came out with a wet sucking sound that almost made him cough up his dinner. With several more fast, hard chops, he separated the head from the body.

"I still need beetles, no matter how much I boil your ugly head."

Elliot picked up Jack's head by the hair and tossed it to the side, out of the garden. With a grunt, he stood and emptied the trash bags in the center of the garden and rolled Jack's body in them, stapling the bags to the dead flesh so they wouldn't unravel. Grabbing the body by the feet, Elliot dragged it from the garden, down the wooded path; past the spot he stopped hanging heads and built a fence. He unlocked the gate and continued. He walked slow and sure by the moonlight, guiding his path. From behind he heard the songs and felt the cooling breeze that carried them. They were telling him he'd done the right thing.

Elliot stopped at the gully that held all the doll bodies. He looked down at them. There was no way he was ever going to get Jack's body to the old dump; he was too hurt from the fight and too tired. There was so much to do and clean up before morning brought the next batch of curiosity-seekers to his door.

Elliot eased himself into the mass grave of plastic bodies. He cried out, imagining the plastic arms reaching for him, trying to grab his neck and dig at his chest. Little plastic fingers and toes poked and scratched as he cleared out a hole in the dirt-caked and moss-covered little bodies. He grabbed hold of Chaffer's leg and pulled until the body rolled in on top of him. Elliot screamed, drowning out the plastic songs. He struggled out from under the dead weight and clawed his way free of the gully and the plastic bodies fighting his retreat.

Elliot got back on higher ground, and caught his breath. The moon reflected off the trash bag wrapped corpse. He quickly covered Chaffer's body with hundreds of dismembered dolls and ran for the gate.

Elliot rested on the bench for a moment to catch his breath. Out beyond the ring of birches, Jack's head stared lifelessly at him, mouth agape, jagged flaps of skin hanging, touching the grass. Elliot clutched his side, afraid to lift the shirt and expose the massive bruise that must be growing there. Gingerly, he pressed his fingers to his ribs and let out a hiss. Standing, he grabbed his staple gun and looked for a spot in the Garden. The only place not already crowded with plastic heads was the bench.

He stepped towards the birches. The outside and inside of the trees had heads overlapping, pressed so close there was no room to slide even a slip of paper between. Elliot looked up to the moon; normally the warm glow gave comfort, but now it filled him with staunch horror. Dropping the stapler, he grabbed Jack's head by the hair and took off down the path, abandoning the bag of heads and all the assorted parts on the ground.

Back in the safety of the house, Elliot put on a pot of water and slipped Jack's head in. Elliot watched it sink to the bottom of the pot, staring at the white eyes and pale lips. Elliot adjusted the heat and went upstairs to shower and wash the blood from his hands.

Elliot woke up from a dead sleep, framed in moonlight streaming through his window. He'd fallen asleep straight out of the shower, sitting for just a moment to dry off and change. The clothes he had on earlier would have to be burned. If Jack's car was still on the street it would have to be moved, not to mention removing the blood on the porch, driveway and garden. Then he smelled something cooking. A wave of nausea swept over him and he ran to the bathroom to vomit. Elliot rinsed his mouth and eased down the stairs into the kitchen. He shivered, remembering the plastic arms and hands all over him earlier. At the base of the stairs, he pressed his back to wall and slipped into the kitchen.

It was still dark out, the time on the clock radio flipped over to 3:09. Elliot inched over to the stove, the burner glowing orange with heat. He grabbed a fork from the drawer and poked it into the brackish water. There was a swirl of fat and oils in the dark water. Elliot drew his hand back, letting the fork fall into the pot. He turned off the heat and covered the pot, and ran gagging for the sink.

When he was empty, Elliot got dressed, got a bucket, scrub brush and soap and went to work on the porch. When the porch was to his liking, Elliot got a shovel and a bucket from the shed and gathered up as much of the stained gravel and dirt as he could. He left the buckets near the house and walked down the driveway.

At the base as expected a car, a dark green SUV with a baby seat in the back. Tentatively Elliot tested the door, expecting the alarm to blare out, but it was open. He checked around the seats and glove box, the registration was to Jack Chaffer and the keys were in the ashtray. Elliot started the car, and then unlocked the chain, keeping the lights off. He drove it halfway to the house, then set the chain back in place.

After loading the buckets and the pot in the SUV, Elliot drove it down the path, this time with the lights on, trying to avoid and holes or roots. He didn't want any more of the bloody water or head soup to slosh around the SUV. As he drove slowly past the ring of birches, he scraped off levels of heads and paint and bark. He cringed, imagining the tiny screams from each head. When past, he opened the car, there were long scratches down the side.

In the Garden, Elliot cleaned up again, gathering up dirt and washing down the bench. The sun was rising. If in fact Chaffer did have a family, they'd be looking for him soon. Elliot finished his trip, stopping to open the gate and drive far as he could into the back woods. He got to the gully. Driving carefully and slowly, he maneuvered around the mass grave of dolls. He stopped the car near the old dump. The husks of old cars stared back as if hungry for their new arrival, fresh "meat."

Elliot climbed out. He dumped the buckets and pot into the decades-old debris, then climbed up through the piles of rusted metal and rotted boards. He pushed and pulled as much detritus as he could to cover the SUV. Without looking back, Elliot ran for home.

Elliot sat in his father's old rocking chair to catch his breath. Panic surged through him like the tides. His heart was racing so fast he feared it would explode in his chest. He rocked slowly, hoping the motions would ease his tensions. The creaking porch boards made a racket that was barely tolerable. He stopped to hear a song on the breeze.

His friends were singing to him, helping him to calm down. Elliot closed his eyes and listened as the spring breeze caressed him. The notes and harmonies soothed. A smile crossed his face as the morning sun started to warm him. Elliot heard the voices on the wind, calling to and singing to him. He slid down in the chair a little as the dolls lulled him to a troubled sleep.

When the first carload of tourists that day found Elliot he laid twisted in the chair; his neck bent and broken under the arm, surrounded by the headless corpses of hundreds of dolls.

Scott T. Goudsward is a New England writer. A slave to the cubicle world during the day and slave to the words at night. He is one of the coordinators of the New England Horror Writers. New in the writing world, Scott has a non-fiction book co-written with his brother David, "Horror Guide to Massachusetts," an anthology co-edited with Rachel Kenley, "Once Upon an Apocalypse." His short fiction has most recently appeared in "Atomic Age Cthulhu," "Wicked Seasons," "Dark Rites of Cthulhu" and "Bugs!" Readers can learn more at www.goudsward.com/scott.

TSUNAMI

T.T. Zuma

A SENSE OF UNEASE WEIGHED ON Emily as she stared out over the ocean. The atmosphere on the beach had changed, turning oppressive. A slight breeze cooled her sun-broiled skin. For the life of her, she couldn't figure out why she felt so unnerved, and no matter how hard she tried, she couldn't shrug it off. Reaching up, she caressed the small gold cross hanging from her neck.

She glanced over at her husband Carl, building sandcastles with her son. While her thirteen-year-old, Stephen, enjoyed the sculpting and the playful banter with his father, her youngest, Samantha, sat a few feet away from them scooping up fistfuls of sand and letting it flow through her fingers. At seven, Samantha was a mischievous child, a free spirit who questioned everything, endlessly it seemed. Emily kept an eye on her, as there was no telling if Samantha would wander off and get too close to the shoreline.

The island they were vacationing on was not large or commercialized, which was what attracted them to it in the first place. It didn't offer many amenities other than a decent hotel and a first-class beach located in a small, private cove surrounded by palm trees. There wasn't a lot of tourists on the island, which left Emily and her family plenty of space to play and relax. The beach itself was spectacular, with the cleanest white sand she had ever seen buffering the hotel from the ocean. The saltwater was sparkling clear with only a touch of cobalt — appearing as fresh as any pond or lake back home in the mountains of New Hampshire. Best of all, the water was pleasantly warm and refreshing, a far cry from the freezing temperatures they had left behind.

Samantha stopped playing in the sand and rose to her feet. After a few moments of twirling and imitating the seagulls that flew overhead, she walked over to her father and brother. While they tried to involve her in the construction of their castle, Samantha wanted no part of it. Instead, she moved a few feet from them, stopped, and then looked out over the ocean.

Then, just as Emily had feared, Samantha began to saunter toward the shoreline. Emily was on her feet in seconds, chasing after her daughter. Samantha was quick though, and she was already into the water up to her knees before Emily could get to her.

Reaching her, Emily scooped Samantha up with one arm, preventing her daughter from wading any deeper. But Emily's forward momentum prevented her from coming to a complete stop and she lost her balance, causing both of them to tumble into the surf. Emily's head brushed the sand when they went under. There, a large shard of glass from a broken bottle jutted up from the ocean floor. She stood quickly, hefting Samantha and holding onto her tight. She silently thanked God that neither she nor Samantha had landed on the glass. Walking back to the beach, she swept the thin blond hair out of her daughter's eyes. Samantha seemed none-the-worse from the experience and Emily kissed her forehead. "What's the matter honey? You don't want to play with Stephen and your dad?"

"No, Mommy. I want to play with that woman." Samantha lifted her finger and pointed to the sea.

Emily lifted one eyebrow and cocked her head at Samantha. She followed Samantha's gaze.

"Honey, it's probably a boat or a dolphin…" she began, but Emily froze when her eyes caught sight of a figure in the distance. At first glance, it did appear to be a woman and, oddly, it looked as if she were standing on the surface of the water.

Indeed, it was a woman, nude, her hair dark, wet, and long enough to cling to her waist. Even from a distance, Emily could see that the woman's breasts hung heavily from her chest.

She had to be standing on something.

"Can I play with her Mommy?"

Emily was about to give Samantha a hastily thought out, "no", when her daughter's eyes suddenly went wide. Samantha once again pointed at the woman and then said, "Ohh-look!"

Beneath the woman, a wide column of water lifted her skyward.

Emily stared, her mouth agape. From where she stood, the column appeared to be round, at least twice the diameter of the woman and its surface as smooth as ice. The water at the base was undisturbed. There was no spray from the small waves as they collided with the column. It was as if the ocean were diverting around it. Emily wrapped both her arms around Samantha as the column rose, lifting the woman up further into the air. For a brief moment Emily had the impression that the woman was falling, but then she realized that the column had stopped rising. She looked down upon Emily and Samantha.

Emily turned toward her husband. He and Stephen were absorbed in their work, neither of them aware of what was occurring offshore. She swept her gaze beyond them and across the beach. The other tourists were continuing about their business of sunbathing and chasing their children, she couldn't count one person who was looking out over the water in shock or amazement. *Were they the only ones who could see the woman and that gigantic column of water?* An urge to shout overcame her, to get Carl to look toward the sea. She turned back to face the ocean. When she saw what was happening, she thought for certain that she was hallucinating.

In the brief time she had looked away, the column had widened. It was now a huge wall of water, as wide as the entire beach was long. At its ends, the wall veered in, bracketing the beach at ninety-degree angles. Behind Emily, all had gone quiet. The adults, the children, even the seabirds were silent and they all now stared in wonder at the ocean. Carl and Stephen stood looking out over the water, her son pointing at the wall with a look of amazement while her husband had turned toward her in fear. Their eyes met and a chill ran though her body. She wanted to reach out to Carl, to hold him for what she intuitively knew would be the last time, but a strong compulsion to face her fear overcame her. She turned from her husband toward the ocean. Focusing on the woman, Emily immediately regretted her decision.

Below the woman, large gouts of water, resembling solid tubes, exploded out from the length of the wall. The tubes, too many to count, were as wide as boulders and racing through the air, and they were headed toward the beach.

Emily turned away in a panic, cradling Samantha and throwing herself to the sand. Lifting her head, she managed a single sob as she watched her husband and son crushed beneath one of the tubes of water. They were gone in an instant, washed away in the unrelenting tide of water that followed.

The tubes reached them all — men, women, their children, hammered into the beach sand and then swept away. Emily braced herself, praying that her body would provide enough of a cushion to spare Samantha a crushing death.

The tube of water that came for them somehow missed its target, making contact with the beach a few feet before them. The sand beneath them shook, and then less than a second later the tide swept them forward.

Emily struggled to grip Samantha as they propelled through the water. She had a tight hold on both of her daughter's arms but she could feel Samantha slipping away. Something was tugging at her daughter, trying hard to loosen Samantha from her hold. With every tug Samantha slipped further down Emily's arm until, with a strong yank, Samantha was ripped from her grasp. Emily screamed, and seawater rushed in between her parted lips.

Reflexes kicked in, and Emily gagged from the water that she had swallowed. Stomach heaves assaulted her body, and she found herself spasming. She fought hard against it, trying to keep herself from expelling what little air remained in her lungs. She willed her legs to kick, to try to lift herself to the surface, but the current was too strong.

Nearly out of air, Emily stopped struggling to save as much oxygen as possible. After gagging a few more times the convulsions subsided, and she found herself drifting along with the current. An overwhelming feeling of calmness descended upon her, and the rapid sensation of being pushed forward in the water diminished to the point she thought she was barely moving. She tried to focus, desperate for one last look to find Samantha.

Emily wished that she had simply closed her eyes and let her mind drift away into the darkness.

Bodies, with their heads bowed and their arms hanging uselessly in front of them, rotated leisurely in the water around her. The dead were everywhere, in a macabre dance as they drifted and then bounced off each other in slow motion. Most were seriously injured, from missing limbs to severe lacerations. Blood, still oozing from their wounds, created small, puffy and red tinted clouds that slowly dissolved in the water. When the gentle current turned the bodies, exposing their faces to her, Emily cringed. Their facial features were beaten to pulp. Eyes were missing, noses flattened, and pieces of bone jutted through their flesh.

Before the water could claim her, she came to a sudden stop — a pressure against her back, something solid, unyielding, holding her in place. Moving her hand to her back, she realized it was the trunk of a palm tree.

Gathering reserves she hadn't realized she still possessed, she wrapped her hands around the trunk and began to pull herself up, forcing herself to climb.

When she broke the surface of the water, the air racing into her lungs hit her like a sledgehammer and her chest erupted in pain. A coughing fit followed but she held on to the trunk. When her body settled enough to where she had control over it, she put her forehead against the palm's rough bark and relaxed. After a few minutes of rest, she lifted her head and gazed past the palm tree.

A short distance away stood a series of buildings. She recognized them as part of the resort, but oddly, her view was skewed. For some reason, she was looking down on the buildings.

The resort had not suffered any damage from the tubes nor did it look as if the tidal waters had reached it. She noticed people — staff from the look of their uniforms — all gathered at the front of the hotel and pointing up in her direction. None of them made a move toward her or the beach.

Why is the resort so far down, and why are they all pointing at me?

After lowering her head slightly, Emily's eyes went wide. Only a few feet beyond her, the ocean ended abruptly, vanishing into thin air.

In a panic, she clung so tightly to the palm tree that the muscles in her arms began to lock up. When she was convinced her hold was secure enough to prevent her from drifting off to the edge, Emily turned her head around, to look back at where the beach had been. She saw nothing but a flat expanse of ocean. It was as if the wall of water had come ashore and then run up against an invisible barrier.

Emily maneuvered herself around the palm tree to get a better look. When she settled on the other side, her back now to the resort, she poked her head around the trunk of the tree. She gasped at the site.

Emily was on top of what looked like a gigantic fish tank.

Gazing out over the water, she noticed that many of the dead were floating on the surface. Thoughts of Carl, Stephen, and Samantha stabbed at her heart, and her tears mingled with the seawater.

A movement around one of the bodies closer to Emily caught her eye. It was a man, belly up with his arms stretched wide. His body bobbed a few times, and then it was gone, pulled down into the depths. She watched as one by one, the same thing happened to other bodies. Sobbing, she waited for whatever was in the water to reach her. She didn't have long to wait.

Small waves began to brush up along Emily's right side. They weren't powerful, but they were strong enough to catch her attention. She turned in their direction. Ten feet away the seawater was boiling. Dozens of large bubbles were pushing their way up through the water and then bursting when they made contact with the air. Something was coming from below. When it broke through, Emily could not pull her eyes away from it.

A woman was rising out of the water. Her features were bloated, her skin tinted blue. Small sections of her body were missing, including most of her fingers and toes. The woman continued to rise until the soles of her feet were even with the surface. She stared at Emily, her eyes milky and bulging from their sockets.

At the sight of the woman Emily wanted to let go of the tree trunk and swim away, but her hands refused to let go. Her heartbeat accelerated and she began to tremble violently. A scream fought its way up her throat, but before she could take a deep enough breath to expel it, her head grew heavy and her mind clouded over. Her heart rate slowed and her shaking subsided.

This muddled feeling lasted only a few more moments before it vanished as quickly as it had come. She began thinking clearly again and, oddly, she found herself less fearful of the woman. Emily faced her, staring deeply into the woman's opaque eyes.

"You survived."

The words were not spoken aloud but had appeared in Emily's head.

The woman approached Emily, gliding inches above the surface and stopping a few feet before her. An image of Jesus walking on the water flashed into Emily's mind.

"Ah, the man called Jesus", the woman noted. "I have seen the image of this man several times in your people's minds, but this is the first I have seen it associated with traveling over water. He is usually thought of in the moments associated with imminent death."

She's in my head. She can read my mind.

"Yes."

The woman's reply was clear, though it possessed a faint echo, originating in the back of Emily's head, and spoke in Emily's own voice.

Though Emily realized there was no shielding her thoughts from the woman, she felt more comfortable speaking aloud. "Why? Why did this happen?"

After a few moments of silence the woman spoke.

"You are frightened of my countenance. Before I answer your query, I want you to feel at ease. Briefly, close your eyes."

Emily did as she was told, and when she reopened them seconds later she reared back at the sight. Standing before her was the Virgin Mary.

This visage of the Holy Mother was a duplicate of a picture that hung in Emily's church. She was clothed in an ankle-length white flowing gown, with a matching veil that completely covered her hair. An expansive blue robe, long enough to touch the water, was draped over the woman's shoulders. A strip of blue fabric was cinched across her waist, with the knot tied in front, its two ends hanging free. Her face was beatific, and the bright glow emanating from behind her head left little doubt as to who the woman wanted Emily to identify her with.

The woman's appearance was sacrilegious, but Emily had to admit it was preferable to the rotting body that she knew actually stood before her. In the recesses of her mind, Emily heard the woman speak.

"I see this is more pleasing."

Emily nodded.

The woman echoed Emily's earlier question. "Why?" A pause, then, "we do it because, like you, we need to feed."

Emily's gut roiled. Visions of hideous creatures feasting on her family immediately came to her, and her face contorted in revulsion. Seconds later the image vanished, and Emily could recall them only vaguely as the woman continued on.

"No, that is not who we are. We do not feed on the flesh. We take our nourishment from your life's essence, what you call your soul. It sustains us, allowing us to survive for long periods in the deep. We thrive on your emotions, your moral deliberations, your guilt, and your joy. We relish your ambiguity, delight in your successes, and we question and analyze your failures. We are, in essence, the Christ figure that you have mythologized. We appraise your transgressions, evaluate your responses to them, and we acknowledge your remorse. We grant you absolution. Your souls are the repository of who you are, what you have been. We absorb your souls and you become one with us. It is the only way to insure your eternal, peaceful existence; otherwise, contrary to your beliefs, your souls perish along with your flesh."

Emily trembled, her head shaking violently in denial. The woman's words upended the very tenets of her religion, but as she took a look around and viewed the carnage surrounding her, doubt took root in her mind.

If there is a God, would he have allowed this to happen? And, these-these-creatures, surely they could not be God or God-like!

"No." The word was spoken firmly in Emily's head, followed by, "We are not your God."

"Then, who?" Emily asked.

"We are *The Recorders*. Our mission is to gather information. We will be called back one day and asked to share all we have learned, to share all that we have become. When that time occurs, the souls we have taken possession of will not only continue to feed others, but they themselves will be nourished in the sharing."

"The Recorders? Who are you recording for? How long have you been here?"

"We arrived in 365 A.D. — your calendar — in the region you call Alexandria. After we feed, it takes many years to digest and absorb your souls, so in most cases there are long interludes between harvests. As time progressed so did your science and social skills. We had to adapt or be discovered. Using an empty human vessel, we contact our feeding grounds in advance, make arrangements with them, and offer the majority of their population safety from a harvest as long as we fed on the few. We have found that the threat of annihilation, along with a demonstration of our abilities, always leads to negotiation in our favor."

Emily turned to face the resort below her.

The Virgin Mary nodded. "Yes, they were prepared for us."

Tsunamis. They come in the guise of a tsunami.

Once again The Virgin Mary nodded. "We do, but not all tsunamis are of our making. Most of them are natural occurrences, harvesting far more souls that we could possibly feed on. With your science so well advanced you now possess your own recording devices, so we feed in more secluded locations to avoid detection."

"Where do you come from?"

Emily saw what could pass for a smile as the woman replied, "That is not your concern at this moment."

Emily paused, and then asked, "What are you going to do with me?"

The Virgin Mary looked down on Emily, this time with a smile that Emily thought genuine.

"You are a survivor," she said. "And you can remain a survivor if you choose. Shortly, the water will recede and you will be able to continue with your life as it is. However, your husband and children are with us. They, too, will continue to live on. You have a choice to make, but you do not have much time to decide."

With those words, The Virgin Mary began to glide away from Emily. As the woman retreated, her body descended into the depths.

Emily did not react. She continued holding onto the palm tree and watched in silence until the top of the woman's veil disappeared and only calm water remained.

Emily was exhausted. She wanted to rest her forehead against the tree trunk and take some time to think about what had just happened, but as she moved forward she noticed that the water surrounding the trunk was receding. Emily loosened her hold and let the water guide her to the ground.

When Emily's feet touched the beach sand, she relaxed and leaned against the tree for support. She scanned the beach. The water continued to backtrack toward the sea.

"You will have a choice soon, and not a lot of time to make it."

The woman's words echoed through Emily's mind as she watched the ocean ebb. The water made steady progress, and in less than five minutes the beach would be restored to its former size. Emily turned, looking back toward the resort. The staff must have believed the threat over as they were making their way toward her. She saw a mixture of amazement and guilt on their faces, and she wondered how they could all live with themselves after the collective decision they had made. Now, she had a choice of her own to make.

She could pull herself away from the tree and approach the hotel staff, accept their pity, their offers of assistance, and then move on with her life. There would be a price to pay for this, and it would be steep. She would be forever trying to suppress the images of the death and destruction during her waking hours, and unable to banish the terror of it all in her nightmares. The images of Stephen and Carl crushed into the sand and the horror of Samantha taken away could never be shared with anyone back in New Hampshire. No one would believe her.

As she had done so often in her life when she was besieged with doubt, she grasped the cross hanging from her neck. Instead of gaining solace from the icon, Emily felt empty, lost. The gold cross had always been a tangible reminder of her faith, giving her strength or, at the very least, hope in times of trouble or confusion. Now it was just a piece of cheap jewelry weighing heavily against her chest. For a brief moment, anger flared. How could she have been so misled all these years? How could she have been so naïve and trusting?

Emily looked out over the beach. The water had receded quicker than she had thought it would, and the shoreline almost looked as it had before the tsunami.

Gazing up, Emily saw the woman, the true form of the woman, standing on top of the ocean a short distance away. The woman's stance appeared casual, neither beckoning nor reproachful. She was waiting.

A vision appeared in Emily's mind. Though the image fluttered as if it were drifting along casually on an ocean wave, she had no problem identifying it. The three of them, Carl, Stephen, and Samantha, were all standing together on a mountaintop staring off into a night sky glittering with starlight. They appeared to be at peace, and judging from the looks on their faces, in a state of spiritual awe.

Emily made her choice.

She tore the cross from her neck and threw it to the ground.

Gathering her strength, she sprinted to the shoreline. When the water was up to her knees, she dove in, swimming toward the woman. Kicking her legs hard and taking broad strokes to reach her, Emily pushed forward. The thought of reuniting with her family provided enough fuel to keep her tired body from burning out. Her life would not be worth living if she couldn't feel the warmth of her husband's love or experience the joy her children brought her. This was her chance to be reunited with them, and she would not be denied.

When Emily had covered half the distance to the woman, she felt a tug on her left leg. She ignored it at first, but when it happened again she couldn't dismiss it, whatever had been tugging at her pulled her completely underwater. After flailing for a moment, she rose back up and treaded water. An odd tingling in her left thigh had her hand reaching down to it. She felt nothing wrong so she continued along the length of her leg. When her fingers brushed her ankle she paused, a feeling of dread passing through her. The flesh at her ankle was torn, and it felt stringy. Below the ankle, her foot was gone. Stunned, she probed the area, and when her fingers touched exposed nerves, pain ricocheted throughout her body. The water around her was turning red. There was another tug, a more powerful one this time, and she was dragged deep into the water. She looked down, and saw that her leg, up to her knee, had been torn off her body. Her mouth opened in a scream and seawater rushed in. Her body bucked wildly as she gagged, and the torrents of blood pumping from the stump made the water too hazy to see through.

A voice, sounding like her own, entered Emily's mind. There was no mistaking its mocking tone.

"You are very gullible."

Confusion now kept company with Emily's pain. Why would this woman go through all this trouble to torment her? The woman had plenty of opportunity to kill her earlier, why had she been toyed with?

The answer to Emily's questions came swiftly.

"I enjoy playing with my food."

As she tried to make sense of the woman's words, new images flashed in Emily's head. They were of the last moments of her life, only in reverse order. She saw herself swimming toward the woman, seeking salvation and hoping to be reunited with her family. Then she was on the beach, watching the resort staff making their way toward her. Next, she was holding onto the palm tree and watching as the dead were dragged down into the water. She watched as Samantha was pulled from her hands. Following that, she saw her husband and son crushed by the giant tubes of water. The next image to fill her mind lingered longer than the others. It was of her floating motionless in the water, a large shard of glass protruding from her head as the water darkened, and Samantha nearby, crying.

When that last image flickered away, Emily realized who the woman really was.

Emily slowly brought her right arm to her chest, then, reaching out with her fingers, she placed them just below her neck. Her fingertips moved tentatively, searching for what she believed would be her true salvation.

Emily's fingers came up empty.

The next words she heard only served to increase her suffering.

"Unlike faith, old habits die hard, don't they Emily."

T.T. Zuma has had numerous horror and noir stories published in various print anthologies, magazines, and websites. Zuma also write reviews of dark fiction and horror novels for Horror World *and* Cemetery Dance *magazine. He lives in New Hampshire with his wife, Paula.*

A Tale of Chivalry

A TALE OF CHIVALRY
Ogmios

For my Grandfather Michael Hunter

Oh dear, oh cheer,
Look yonder lass.
I say, look there.

Oh dear, oh dear,
You say look where?

Look past that tree,
Not quite to the sea.
He comes forth,
Metal clad knight so fair.
So fair indeed,
As to send sparks through the air.

So say you,
I care not for his name.
Say you true,
What deed claimed his fame?

Ahhh, A deed you need,
A need indeed.

Why, he stands afar,
As brilliant as a star,
As stern as a ship,
And quick as a whip.

Many tales I could tell you.
And no less than the other,
They all would stand true,
Like words from your brother.

Tis not a needless conquest I'll share,
But one of concern for all to care.

Why, just over a year, or so, ago,
The land was endangered by the dragon named KaLo.

Now as you know young lass of the land,
Each Spring Equinox brought,
Years of generations of knowledge taught.
Sown into the ground,
Grown tall golden brown.
Stored for winter food,
And gold at Barter Town.

Each harvest brings darker days,
Shorter light and longer night;
And the fear of KaLo with his hideous ways,
Claiming taxes on lands that are his by right.

Now the people of the land,
Knew he had not right.
But they felt it wise,
To pay and not fight.
Just one attack and KaLo would bring,
A harvest of ash and winter suffering.

Now as you know,
Young lass of the land,
The cycles of growth,
Don't all go as planned.

Lack of gold required,
A new plan you see,
When the dragon came,
To collect his yearly fee.

KaLo was enraged,
And gave three days,
And the land's people knew,
They had only two ways.

They could leave the land,
Which they loved and worked;
Or take over the mountain,
Where the dragon lurked.

Now the name of the knight,
Which you care not to hear,
Is the name known to dragons,
Both far and near.

For it was he,
Who championed the cause,
Riding fierce and hard,
Accepting death before pause.

The moon drew high,
With the night's approach,
And with the cold wind,
The knight tightened his broach.

Into the mountain on foot,
Sword and torch in hand,
Gulping back fear,
Brought on by the lands.
Lands, which took hours,
Upon hours to ride,
With thoughts nothing more,
Than insults to his pride.
For if his people shall survive,
In these caverns his strength must thrive.

Hours of searching tested his will,
Till at long last his eyes did fill,
With the reckon-less sight,
The dragon's fierce glare,
Head cocked, prepared,
To spew flames of despair.

With valiance and skill,
The knight did defend,
Dancing with flames,
Choosing blows to send.
Still, strength and agility,
Did the warrior naught,
And in his anguish,
He found cover… and he *thought*.

Jumping true and stern,
Caught KaLo by surprise,
As the knight leapt,
Hurling his torch for the eyes.

The dragon dodged,
With movements so keen,
However distracted,
Leaving the knight unseen.

KaLo burned with rage,
Not finding his foe.
And careless impatience,
Led to the fatal blow.

The sound of coin came from the right,
But the left gave way to the charging knight.
Thrusting deep his mighty sword,
Claiming both KaLo's life and hoard.
Eyes of jewels,
And claws of gold,
Lay credence to,
Words so bold.
For he wears both on his vest.
And to the people went the rest.

And now you know,
He who draws neigh.
And the reason why,
His head rides so high.

For clear as day,
And loud as thunder,
Remember the knight,
Named Sir Michael Hunter!

Ogmios is an artist, writer and the publisher for Outside The Box Comics. He also works for authors and publishers providing book covers, graphics and illustrations. His primary focus is myth, fantasy, horror and sci-fi. For more from Ogmios and Outside the Box Comics please visit www.ArtByOgmios.com.

FUND-RAISER
Thom Erb

T.D.'s Cordial Lounge & Gentlemen's Club
South side of Pinnacle City.
7:39pm.

The dark, aging strip club smelled of dollar store cologne, stale beer, b.o. and urine. Red, white and blue lights chased the each other as less than "in-their prime" strippers tried unsuccessfully to shake their jiggling money-makers on the peeling, linoleum stage. The blown PA speakers blurred out "Pour Some Sugar One Me."

Besides the two less, than enthusiastic dancers, only five other people sat in the dive. One, a portly bartender picking his nose while cleaning beer mugs and a skanky cocktail waitress pulling her thong out of her ass with the couth of a fishmonger ripping a trout's guts out. The other three men sat at a corner booth on the far side of the room, milking their drinks and looking frustrated. All of them looked like they walked off the set of a Scorsese flick on a *Clerks* budget.

They all seem to be roughly the same size except for the goon on the end who looked like he was stunt double for the Incredible Hulk. Same flat hair cut and all. After much silence, the guy overly-slicked back hair in the middle spoke first.

"Can you believe this shit?" He shook his head, tapping the newspaper on the table.

"Wha? Whose bangin' whos, now, Ritchie?" The big man with the chin the size of a vice muttered. "Oh, let me guess. It's that hot, but crazy as a shithouse rat, Lohan broad, ain't it?" Mikey smiled.

After a double take, Ritchie said. "Nah, it ain't nothin' like that. It's those dame Duck Dynasty stronzos, Damn." Ritchie stubbed his thick finger at the paper and nods his head with a wide smile that could swallow the table. "Bout time they tells 'em tree huggin' liberals where the bear shits in the buckwheat."

The big man tilted his head to the side, like a dog, "Duck what?"

Richie lets out a frustrated breath and shoves the paper toward the hulk.

Mikey "The Chin" Criscione looks at it like he's never seen a paper filled with words before and shrugs his wide shoulders.

"I don't get it." His low voice nearly lost in the thumbing bass of Van Halen's "Beautiful Girls."

Ritchie shook the paper in the Mikey's face and shouted over the loud music. "Ah, C'mon, you dumb fuck, don't you read the papers?"

The bald guy had enough. His thin face was bright red with frustration and shot death glares at both of pals.

"Enough." Tony Foti yanked the paper from Ritchie's hands and shoved it back into his chest.

They all fell silent, hiding their faces.

"We've been sitting here for hours and you two have been circle jerking for the bitches and we still ain't got nothin' to show for it." Tony said, shaking his empty glass at the nearly sleeping bartender.

"Sorry, boss." Mikey and Ritchie uttered in unison.

The loud music pounded on as more losers and pervs filled the club. The waitress came over and replenished their drinks and sauntered off, with a red hot hand print on her ass.

"Hey, I like titties and booze as much as yous guys do, but let's get down to business. Let's hear what yous guys got for me. so as to be better earners for the family? There's no way in hell any of us is gonna be made if we don't give them something....bigger...better." Tony sipped his fresh drink and stared off at the Puerto-Rican chick with the huge nipples. "And, I don't know about you two boombats, but this guy's sure as hell isn't gonna be just a street prick all his life."

Tony shifted in his chair slammed the glass down.

"We ain't getting no where until we can bring the family some serious cake." He waved the waitress dressed in a hot pink bra and thong that barely covered her yummy parts back over.

"Wait...what? We getting cake? Some black forest cherry cake with cream frosting sounds delish." Mikey licked his chops.

Tony ignored the stupid question and yanked the bottle from the girl's hand, shot her a wink and slapped her on the ass, shooing her away.

"See. Big Dickey Marchione and his crew will be coming in here *heavy* tomorrow night and if we ain't got any cash or at least, a solid line on something, we'll be, yeah, you know." Tony poured himself a drink and set the bottle on the table.

"Wait, we ain't getting no cake?" Mikey pouted as he watched the waitress walk away.

"Ah, stugots, you mook. There ain't gonna be no CAKE. See." Ritchie bitch-slapped the big man on the back of the head. "Boss was talking about cash, moolah, greenbacks, got it?"

"Wha...why yous gots to be hitting' me for? Tony said we was getting' cake, right?" Mikey shrugged, looking at his boss.

"Oh, maron', knock it off, for christ's sake. You stupid shits ain't doing nothing, but giving me a damn headache." Tony sat back and rubbed his bald head.

They all sat in silence for the next few minutes. Tony, tried to chase the headache away and figure out what to do next, but nothing was getting through the numbing migraine creeping in. Ritchie began scouring the Pinnacle City Herald for anything that could help them out.

Mikey wiped drool from his chin while thinking about a delicious, black forest cherry cake the nice girl never brought back.

"You Shook Me All Night Long" blared through the PA system when suddenly Ritchie jumped, knocking the bottle over, spilling the whiskey all over Tony's pants.

In complete pissed-off chorus, Tony and Mikey shouted, " Whoa.... hey...?

Ritchie jammed his forefinger into the newspaper and bounced in his seat

"Here. Right here, boss. I think we got something here that will make the Family smile and welcome us with wide arms," He said.

Tony dabbed a napkin at his crotch and shook his head in disbelief. "If that's another one of your batzo, lottery winners eats at the 10th and Maberry Subway, I swears to god I'll clip your sorry ass right here."

"Nah, boss, I swear. We have us here, a winner." Ritchie shoved the paper over to his boss and puffed out his chest in triumph.

After wiping off his seat, Tony sat down and reluctantly grabbed the newspaper and pulled out a pair of reading glasses from his black jacket. He scoffed.

From the Lifestyle section.

He read aloud:

"Pinnacle City's Most Celebrated Millionaire Recluse Rebellious to the End!"

Tony read the rest of the article silent. His big lips moved with each word. His smile grew wider and wider with each paragraph he completed.

"Uh, huh... Am I right, or am I right? Uh huh!" Ritchie nodded his head like one of those stupid Mexican dogs in the back of a low-rider from the south-side.

"The old bastard hates banks and the government. You know damn well what the hell that means, don't ya?" Tony started to nod along with the other guy.

Ritchie shot down his whisky and added, "And...He don't trust nobody, 'cept his black nurse Joyce, *who gives a shit*," so...we can kick the goddamn door in, ransack the place, in and out, easy fuckin' easies" He finished with a laugh.

"Cake?" Mikey said in a dull tone of guessing.

Tony and Ritchie let out a huge, collective laugh.

"What, I say?" Mikey asked.

"Shoot 'em up fellas. We can make it to old man Fund's mansion in twenty minutes." Tony downed the shot and dabbed the corner of his mouth.

"C'mon, it'll be a piece of cake." He laughed.

Tony left a tenspot on the table, took the bottle with them as the three of them left the club.

"See, I told ya we be getting cake, Ritchie."

"Oh, maron'."

Within minutes, the three wannabe wise guys were on their way to Elmore Fund's house on the east side of Pinnacle City.

On the way to the old man's joint, Ritchie Googled the old man's name and read the details of recluse's live and his vast fortune. The dulcet tones of Tony Bennett gliding their ride along was starting to help Tony's headache to lessing. He was sure Tweedledum and Tweeddledipshit would ruing right quick.

"Holy christ. It seems this old coot dumped a crap ton of cash into a little company called IBM and then parlayed that into goddammit Microsoft." Ritchie held his cell phone's light over the paper as the car bumped and thumped through downtown.

"I like Apple." Mikey said, pouting in the backseat.

"No shit, *Emeril*. Everything's food, with this guy" Ritchie nudged Tony's arm.

The night flew by as Ritchie regaled the others with the rich and he did mean, rich, history of the dying man and their penile wallets grew with each fiscally exciting sentence.

Tony sat silent for most of the drive then finally said. "So, wait. The old bastard ain't got no security at all?"

The car turned right and headed into a dark part of the city even these hardened tough guys regarded as scary.

"Nothing. Not even a pit bull or some such shit." Ritchie frantically looked through the newspaper, not finding anything.

"Damn." Tony motioned toward the glove box. "Easy easies, then. Let's have a snort then."

"So, what yous mooks gonna do with your cut?" Ritchie opened the box and pulled out a bottle of whiskey, smiled, took a sip and handed it to the driver.

"Salute'" Tony nodded, sipped and handed it back.

"Me? Well, I've had my eye on on this shiny, brand spanking' new slick black Cadillac. It's sweet!"

All three of them let out an agreeable howl.

"What's about you Tone?" Ritchie said.

Tony drove through the rainy night and thought long about all the cash.

"Ah, yous knows me. My Momma needs a new hip and hey, what's a good son to do, eh?" Tony took the booze from Ritchie's hand and smiled. He hoped they hadn't caught on yet.

"You're a good son, boss." Mikey said while flipping through is cell phone.

Ritchie smacked Tony on the shoulder and nodded. "He's right Tone, and ya knows I don't never agree with his Captain dumb ass." He laughed.

Tony joined in, hoping it didn't sound too forced.

"What about yous, big guy?" Tony said.

"Disneyland." Mikey's baritone voice came out almost before Tony could finish the question.

Tony hesitated and then shot a look to Ritchie, who was shrugging his shoulders.

Harsh streetlights flitted through the windows as Tony liked the change of conversation. He asked. "That sounds like fun and all, but, yous don't got no kids."

"No kidding. And, ain't Florida closer?" Ritchie laughed.

"Oranges." Mikey said simply.

"Oranges. Wait...Wha..Why?" Ritchie turned to face the big man.

"I hate 'em." Mikey's tone and face were made of stone.

Tony decided it wasn't worth the bullshit-filled rabbit hole the conversation would take them down so he took another sip and handed the booze back to Ritchie who was still staring slack-jawed and Mikey in the backseat. He tried to fight the smile back and let the shadows of the night hide his ulterior motive for tonight's robbery.

A glowing, sliver of a moon guided the Cadillac down the street until it came to a stop a half a block from the Fund Estate.

"He better gots some pie."

"Shut the fuck up," Tony and Ritchie ordered.

Elmore Fund's Estate, Kitchen.

The entire room pulsed with heavy bass-line of Gloria Gaynor singing how'd she *survive*. The old man danced and grooved with the agility of a man, twenty years his junior. A black, silk kimono with a gold lamay dragon scrawled down the back, hung over his skinny frame, Upon his pale head, was a well-crafted toupee' that bounced with ever hip bump he performed against an imaginary partner. A red-dotted joint hung loosely from his wrinkled lips. Spinning deftly on his slippered heel, the old man pirouetted and gracefully unloaded a steaming hot cookie sheet of piggies-in-a-blanket from the oven.

Elmore could hear the other partiers in the living room hooting and hollering and the thought of the young girls and their tight, gravity-defying bodies made him adjust his medicinally-enhanced penis as he sipped from the crystal class full of Grand Marnier. He spun around in a circle with one, stick-like leg touching to the floor and held his hand high.

"You coming back, Lenny?" A sultry call came from the living room.

"Ohhh, yeah, we're getting really hungry," Another girl cooed.

Elmore Fund gave his rather thick member a quick tug, chugged the remainder of his drink and fetched a big baggy filled with cocaine from the under the sink. Makin' It began and he dumped a pile of the devil's dandruff onto half of a large silver platter. A little bit spilled onto the counter and he paused, shoved his long picky nail into the mess and promptly used his large nose to make it disappear in one hearty sniff.

"Daddy's coming, and he's bringing party favors." Elmore busted a move and filled the rest of the platter with the piggies-in-a-blanket and shuffled to the living room. The coke hit him like a hammer filled with electricity and he was standing in a bathtub. He didn't care. He was getting some tonight, one way or another. Even it if killed him.

The room erupted, as the oldest, unknown to the public, *made man* in the Marchione Family entered the room lit with a rainbow of flashing colors and enough drugs to choke a T-rex.

Outside the Elmore Fund Gate.

"Think old Bag-o-bones up there, has any idea we're coming?" Ritchie asked as he opened the trunk lid.

Tony gathered the shotguns and quietly closed the trunk.

"For your sake, I hope not." He handed them their weapons and chambered the shotgun.

Cold rain poured on them as they walked to the north side of the property. The Fund building took up one of city block. It was a butt ugly-ass piece of property, but a sizable ass it was and filled with cash. Tons of it.

The rain washed in, soaking their leather jackets and seeping down into their JC Penny suits.

"So, what's the plan? Ritchie asked, wiping rain from his face.

Tony had taken the last ten minutes to recon the rundown shit-hole. It was an old Victorian that once was the the centerpiece of the neighborhood Back before the blacks moved in and chased all the rich white folks up town.

It had three stories that looked like only the first floor was livable. The waving shingles gave away its rotting age. The white paint peeled in jagged strips away from the house like a boxy snake fighting to get away from its itchy old skin.

"I say we don't pussy-foot around. Let's just knock on the door." Tony racked the shotgun smiled wide and took a shot from his flask and handed it to Ritchie.

We got your six, boss. Easy peasy and I gets some pie," Mikey grinned.

Tony shook his head, and shoved Mikey forward and the man with the big chin opened the rusted metal front gate and stepped through.

The thumping sounds of "Jive Talkin'" reverberated through the overgrown courtyard.

"Ooh, the Bee Gees, nice." Mikey faked Travolta's walked as he big man swaggered as if carrying two paint cans.

No job was every easy with these two stooges. Mikey with his obsession with cake and Ritchie with talking about yanking his meat every ten minutes. Tony had enough. He'd been counting the seconds he could put a bullet in both of them. He'd hatched the plan to take out the old man, but he needed dumb muscle and a couple of patsies. These guys were perfect for the job.

Tony was damn tired of being a heel-sniffing bitch to the Family.

Knowing full well he should've been made at least two years ago, he'd had enough. He had a sit down with the right hand of the Tortarella Family from the Shorelands, and Tony made the deal. With the haul he'd get from this job, he'd be a made-man for sure. Just with a different family.

He pulled up the collar on his jacket and followed the big man- making sure to keep a safe distance. Ritchie followed close behind, Tony stopped and motioned for him to follow Mikey up the slick steps.

Tony gripped the shotgun and smiled at the thought of saving two slugs for this these two jamokes.

A light from a large bay window spilled multi-colored hues on the slack porch. Silhouettes of curvy girls dancing cast seductive shadows on the front lawn and sidewalk. Tony heard Ritchie's lecherous giggle.

They reached the weatherworn door and Mikey turned toward Tony.

The sounds of "Sister Christian" flitted out into the cold night.

Motioning for Mikey to try the door knob, Tony held the shotgun toward the door. He had to vigorously illustrate to the big man several times before he finally understood the command. That and a walk-up cuff from Ritchie.

The door opened with a shove and a yellow light blinded them as they entered.

It was a small foyer that greeted them with a garishly painted hooker red door at the other end.

Shaking the cold rain off, they enjoyed the warmth for it seemed the old man must have had the furnace cranked up to inferno. Some blues music filled the tiny space and the sounds of hooting and hollering mixed with it.

"I thought you said the old man was on his death bed?" Mikey said.

"Well, maybe he's livin' it up before he shits the bed. So what? Don't change nothing." Ritchie adjusted his hat and nudged his big nose toward the red door.

Tony shoved his way between them and grabbed the pitted door knob and held the shotgun up. "He's right. It don't matter. We're here for one reason and what's that?"

"Show me the moo la" Ritchie smiled and Mikey joined in the chorus.

"Hells, yes." Tony nodded and pounded on the door. Big flakes of paint fell from the door, landing softly on their shoes, like ashes from a burning fire.

Elmore living room.

The large room was filled with a multi-colored light show that would make attendees at a Pink Floyd concert jealous. The smell of German hash, booze and sweat filled the thick air. Six naked girls danced and paraded around the spacious room. The worn walls were covered with black and white photos of wise-guys from days gone-by. Elmore let out a big breath, sending a wall of smoke into the air. Between between his legs on her knees, was Kendra — a hot Jamaican girl he'd met downtown at Louie's Cordial Lounge a few months back. He loved black girls. They knew what his old white-ass liked. It didn't hurt that she didn't take any shit. And, of course, it also helped that he paid them well and always sent them home more than happy and well fed.

Realizing his glass of Svedka vodka was empty, he motioned to Raymond, his ex-MMA fighter, body guard, who was busy talking to the cute Puerto-Rican girl bouncing lively on his big lap.

"Ahuuummm. Raymond." Elmore shook the large empty glass, save the annoying ice cubes clanking around inside it.

"Oh, yeah, sure boss." Raymond shoved the small girl off him and zipped up and swiftly snatched the glass from Elmore's hand and disappeared into the darkness of the kitchen.

"As you were, my dear." Elmore smiled a wide very expensive, dentured-grin. He gently shoved the girl's head back down into *service mode*. He waved at the other girls dancing, smoking, drinking and groping each other. Sometimes it's damn good to be the uncle of the biggest mob boss on the east coast. Elmore thought.

Another reason he loved black girls. A deep breath caught in his chest, as he exploded in climax.

Then the room exploded in chaos.

"Alright you motherfuckers. Kiss the goddamn floor!" Tony shouted from behind Mikey and Ritchie as they bashed in the old door.

The room erupted with screams, gun fire and pounding sound of Lady Ga Ga's Bad Romance.

Tony tried to locate the old man but the room was so dense with smoke and the gay-ass lights, he could barely see Mikey's back.

He moved to the side, "Ritchie, take the living room."

Before he could tell Mikey what to do, the shotgun roared and panicked screams racked his ears. He shoved the big man aside, and saw a naked girl sprawled out on the floor to the right. He paused. She lay in a pool of brain goo and blood. His face was a mangled piece of meat and bone. Thanks to the giant moron's Mossberg.

"Fuck me, Mikey." He let out.

Tony tried to make sense of the chaotic scene. He held his gun up and took in the room.

The twitching bitch at his feet let out a gasp, then fell silent. A large foyer offered a staircase sprawling up the left wall, while a hallway in front of them was washed in darkness and smoke. To the right, a wide doorway to the right housed the party.

Tony smiled.

"Mikey, get the door." Tony ordered, stepped into the living room and nodded as he saw the old man in his fancy robes, frozen where he sat on the couch. Five stunned, naked broads stared at him like dumbfounded deer in headlights. He heard the door slam shut behind him and he motioned for Ritchie to wrangle the bitches.

"What the fuck is this?" Elmore stood up, his erect pecker bopping in the smoky air.

Tony grinned and walked into the living room- the shotgun aimed at the old man's member.

"Chill out, *Woody*. If you play it cool, nobody will get hurt." He thought about the dead whore lying in a pool of blood and corrected himself. "Nobody, else, that is."

The room stood still- save the wispy smoke from the humongous hookah squatting in the center of the room.

The tinny sound of "Funky Cold Medina's" cowbell was the only sound in the room.

"Do you, *faccia di culos*, even know who you're dealing with? The old man stood straight up and walked around the end of the couch. Never covering himself.

Ritchie said with a crooked grin, "Oh, we know damn well, old man." He leaned against the doorway, laying the shotgun over his shoulder.

"Hell yes. You're the walking douche-bag whose gonna be our winning lottery ticket, to the Family." Tony said inching forward.

"Where's the money, old man?" Ritchie asked.

The old man turned, his stiff prick following his head. "Go fuck yourself, and take those two mooks with you're sorry ass." His long arm pointed toward the door.

The girls squirmed and cried, but the old man hushed them with one swift motion.

He slowly walked straight toward Tony and his raised shotgun.

This shitbag has some balls, Tony thought, trying to ignore that fact that indeed, he could actually see his family jewels swinging like a rusty grandfather clock.

Tony and Ritchie in unison pointed their guns at the approaching old man.

"What, big, bad young bitches bust into my home and think they can just take my money and get away with it? What do you think I am?" He walked straight up to the end of Tony's gun barrel and smiled, His fake tanned faced broke into Cheshire-cat like grin.

"You. You do know who I am don't you, stranzo?" He looked Tony deep in the eyes, a wide grin slowly grew over the man's wrinkled face.

"Yo, this guy, is batzo, Tone." Richie laughed like a hyena.

The opening piano strains of Dr. John's "Right Place, Wrong time," filled the room and everyone stood still. Tony smiled back at the man and shoved the barrel into his face.

Mikey spoke with an unusual tone, "Hey, boss,"

Tony ignored him.

"We don't give three-shits who you are. All we want is all the money you have in this house. So, make it easy on you and your bitches and just tell us where it is." Tony said.

"Oh, so you dumbfucks came here for the *dying old bastard's, vast fortune*, am I right?" The old man pushed back at Tony, smiling all the way. "Yous, thought it'd be easy as pie, ain't that right?"

Sounds of crying women mixed with Dr. John to fill the room with a sinister, dark and melancholy soundtrack to the dramatic scene.

"Tone, fuck this shit. Let's get the cash and get the hell outta here." Ritchie said.

"Raymond!" the old man shouted.

A flurry of gunshots rang out and Tony heard someone squeal in pain behind him. A loud thud shook the floor.

"Mikey." Tony shouted and rushed the old man, pushing him back onto the sofa- ignoring the cries of the strippers and shoved the barrel of the shotgun into the old man's chest.

"Go ahead, you big pussy. Shoot me. If you do, you best make damn sure you put one in my brain pan, 'cus if you don't, Boy, I'll gut you and your girlfriends , here." The old man smiled, splaying his arms while prone on the couch.

"And, you'll die a broke bitch at that." He finished with a mouthful of Mossberg.

The old man's fearlessness unnerved the Tony. Usually they were pissing and shitting themselves and begging for salvation at this point. Not this ancient coot. He was as cool cucumber shoved up Frosty the Snowman's ass.

Shit.

"Boss," Ritchie shouted louder.

"Go ahead, tough guy. Show me yours, I've already showed you mine. I'm thinking you're a wee-bit shy," The old man laughed.

Tony's sweaty finger tightened on the trigger. Gritting his teeth, he said, "Don't make me shoot yous, you old prick!"

A shotgun blast peppered the wall behind Tony, causing him to drop to a squat, never dropping the gun from the old man.

"Goddamn it, boss, I'm hit." He heard Mikey call from the foyer. The sounds of Ritchie racking his gun could be heard on the other side of the sofa. The whores were huddled in a corner crying behind him.

The old man laughed. "Nice shooting', Raymond. Took yous, long enough." He shot Tony a mocking wink. "Now, get in here and wipe these shitbirds off my shoe."

Tony could here Mikey grunting and fumbling around and the deep sound of someone laughing.

Then there was a rapid succession of shotgun blasts.

A loud groan... followed by the sound of wood and glass smashing came from the foyer.

A few seconds of silence passed then a big thud caused everyone to jump.

"Stugots, bitch!" Tony heard Mikey grunt.

The girls screamed.

Tony stood up, knowing damn well what had just happened. He wiped the sweat from his face and looked down and the old man stared back up at him. He still held that old-school tough guy mug, but it slacked a little after the gunshots.

"What were yous saying, old timer?" Tony said.

Ritchie stood up from behind the couch, shaking his head. "Well, you gonna take a nap down there or you gonna get off your ass?" He turned and smirked at Tony.

"Bite me." Was all Mikey muttered.

"Quit dickin' the dog, Ritchie and start tearing this room apart. I'll bet you, dollars to donuts, all the money can't be too far from this fossil's, saggy ass.

The old man's head spun around and shot Tony an odd look, then spun the other way as he watched Ritchie start yanking books down from bookshelves, ripping pictures off of the walls.

Mikey walked into the room and started on the opposite side of the room, near the strippers and tore into what looked like a very expensive antique desk.

Tony watched the old man grow more and more nervous as Ritchie continued his violent search.

He felt his stomach grow warm as he knew the boys were getting close to the brass ring. Finally. He would have the cash to get in the good graces of the Family. He squeezed the shotgun tighter. It'd been a long fifteen years. He'd paid his dues tens of times over and doing all the dirty work for the Marchione Family got pretty damn dirty. He didn't mind wet-work, but some of the shit was way beyond anything anyone should have to do. He shook his head, trying to clear the blood-soaked nightmares from his gutter-filled mind.

"Hey, Boss," Ritchie said.

The old man sat up, a stern look of deviance on his chiseled face.

"Hows about you freakin' hammerheads just quit while you're ahead. If you take your sorry asses out of here now, I'll forgive yous for killing my boy." He raised an eyebrow at Tony, then glanced back and forth the other guys searching.

"You should take a look at this," Ritchie said.

"But, if yous keep ripping my house all to hell, I cannot promise I won't stomp a mud hole in yo.."it was then he jumped up at Tony.

In a flash, the shotgun roared to life. A deafening blast filled the room. Followed by a howl of pain, as the old man was blown back onto the sofa.

The room froze as still as photograph—a smoky, blood filled image of death.

The old man lay dead. A red, gaping hole in his chest ushered out a gush of blood and soaked into his pajamas and the couch beneath.

Tony's arms ached. He gripped the shotgun so tight his hands pulsed with pain.

"Ah shit. This ain't good, boss. No good at all." Ritchie's voice sounded like a long distance call from a landline during a lightning storm- Filled with static and a cold echo.

Ritchie had to repeat himself a few times before Tony shook out of it. He didn't mean to kill the old man, just scare him enough to make him drop a deuce in his drawers, sure, but killing him was never in the plan. It didn't matter now. Shit happens and to him, it happened often, and in copious amounts.

"Boss!"

Tony felt his arm's drop—dead weight. The gun still tight in his hand.

"Well this sucks." Tony finally said. He let out a big breath.

"Boss, you need to see this shit." Ritchie quick stepped toward him.

"What's got your panties all in a bunch?" Tony felt the shock lifting. He took the picture frame from Ritchie's shaking hand and gave it a look.

Then Tony thought his heart would burst out of his chest and splattered against the wall.

"I freakin' told yous, boss."

"What is it?" Mikey asked.

Seconds, moments passed. Tony fought to breath. This couldn't be happening. No way in hell, any god could be this fucking cruel. No matter which way he tried to rationalize this situation. The end result came to the same cold, brutal, deadly truth.

He was dead. *They* would all be walking dead men, for certain now.

"C'mon, boss. What the hell's going on?" Mikey shouted.

Tony held his hand up to the big man and continued reading, analyzing the photograph in his shaking hand.

'Told, yous." Ritchie repeated.

"If you say one more goddamn word, I will shoot you myself," Tony said, never looking up from the black and white photograph.

Tony's skin grew cold- clammy.

"YOU said you did your homework on this old fuck, right?" Tony asked. He could feel Ritchie step back.

"You said, he was just an old rich, weird guy, nobody even gave two-shits about. Ain't that right? Tony stated coldly.

Ritchie stood frozen.

"In and out, easy-peachy, you said." Tony continued.

The strippers began to scream again.

Tony shot Mikey a look. The big man moved swiftly to the gaggle of girls.

He looked deeper in disbelief at the picture in his trembling hand. In the rich, cherry-finished frame, was a photograph. An image caught in time. Tony recognized two men straight away. The first, was the old man who now, lay dead on the sofa. It was the second man that made Tony's scrotum shrink and try to crawl back up inside his body cavity.

Seeing the second man in the picture turned Tony's blood to ice. Knowing that after tonight, there would be no being *made*. The only thing that would happen tonight, would be the Marchione family would discover this clusterfuck and then, their full brutal wrath would come down on Tony's head. And in a few days, some unlucky fishermen off the coast of Pinnacle City will find his headless, bloated body bobbing in the water.

That was the best case scenario.

The second man in the picture was Orazio Marchione—The Godfather of the Marchione Family.

A large group of wise-guys gathered what looked like a party of some sort. Maybe taken back in the early-seventies. Tony recognized several of them. They all looked happy. Their chemically fixed smiles stared back at Tony. But, it wasn't the image itself that made him feel like a railroad spike had been driven through his racing heart. No... it was the writing on the picture that seized him.

To Elmore, my favorite nephew, You're a good kid. You got a smart mouth, I like that. Keep your grades up and I'll talk your mother into letting you come to our cottage in Shoalewater Cove this summer!
Love,
Uncle Orz.

Tony dropped the picture. Glass shattered into a dozen shards and danced onto the carpet.

Mikey and Ritchie stepped back.

The strippers continued to cry.

"Shut those bitches up, damn it!" Tony shouted.

Within seconds, Mikey fired a volley of shotgun rounds into the panicked girls.

The screams soon stopped.

"What the fuck are you doing?" Ritchie shouted.

"Wha? Boss told me to shut the bitches up. So, I did? What for you want from me, geesh?" Mikey shrugged, shaking his large head.

"Like we ain't got enough crap to deal with, now yous gots to go and kill those broads. Dammit!" Ritchie let out.

"It don't matter. Not anymore." Tony's stunned gaze slowly osculated between the picture on the floor and the dead guy on the blood-soaked sofa.

"It's nothing, Boss. We've dumped bodies before. What's the big whup?" Mikey said, starting to stack the girls, still twitching bodies.

Ritchie stepped forward. Tony could see him looking at the blood splattered picture on the carpet.

"Uh, huh. Something tells me, we're in a world of shit, huh, boss?" Ritchie's words came out cautiously, As if he said them slow enough, the truth would be lost between the beats of the words.

Tony looked up at Ritchie, "Yeah. We're fucked."

"What's goin' on?" Mikey huffed as he dropped the last stripper on the pile.

"This dead piece of shit here. The one Ritchie said was just some rich asshole. And easy mark. Well, turns out. And pretty goddamn funny too," Tony dropped to one knee and roughly rubbed his chin.

"...is that, uh, yeah. He's the Boss's Goddamned uncle!" Tony's head sunk into his chest.

"Shit." Ritchie and Mikey whimpered.

The opening piano trills of Dana Summer's "Last Dance" flitted out of the speakers—mocking them. Tony jumped up and fired a round from the shotgun, silencing the song and exploding the stereo into a rain of plastic and vinyl.

Many thick, panicked moments passed until the dread silence was shattered when Ritchie started laughing like a hyena.

"What the hell is so funny?" Tony demanded.

Ritchie was rubbing his hands together and stepped close to Tony.

"This may be a long shot, but I think I just might be able to save our asses."

Mikey came running over. Tony stayed crouched, his face buried in his hand.

"How?" Mikey asked.

"Yous guys remember that old man down in Dutch Town? He's got that shop.

"Oh, that voodoo mook with all those dead chickens hanging from his front window? That place creeps me the hell out." Mikey squirmed. "And smells like roadkill."

"Yeah, that's the guy. They say he's old school Cajun wizard or some shit. I know it's a freakin' long shot, but we're running out of options." Ritchie reached down and grabbed Tony's shoulder.

Many long seconds passed.

"Boss."

"One second. Let me get this straight. Are we talking raising the dead here?" Tony finally spoke.

Ritchie squatted down next to Tony. "Maybe not like those stupid Resident Evil flicks and shit, but I bet yous, he can do something. I know it sound's crazier that a shithouse rat, boss, but I've heard this guy is good. Maybe he can work his redneck mojo and fix this old bastard up."

Tony thought for a minute. "Hate to take a dump in your punchbowl, but *Weekend at Bernie's* here knows we killed his ass!"

"Nuh, uh. Actually, *you* shot 'em, boss." Mikey smiled, nodding his head.

Tony gaze burned into Mikey and could have melted a tank. He turned toward the old man. His wide, unblinking eyes bore into him. As if in death, he still knew that he'd have the last laugh. The smell of cordite, copper and reefer filled the air.

"I know it sounds damn crazy, boss. But maybe the guy can work some kind miracle memory mojo. He won't have any idea we were here at all. Then we'd be off the hook, right?" Ritchie said, taking out his wallet. "I have his number..." He pulled out a piece of paper.

Tony saw no other way out. Desperation was filling him. "Ah shit. Go on. Call this witch doctor, of yours. Hell, worst case, we'll have one more body to add to the pile before we burn this place to the ground and head for Mexico."

Ritchie made the call. The storm raged outside and pounding rain and lightening filled their ears.

"Yeah, hello. Is this Mr. Bertrand Bartheleme?" Ritchie spoke into the phone. Long moments passed. "Great, Me and my associates are in need of your services."

The call took forever and finally, after twenty minutes, Ritchie hung up and smiled.

Time seem to crawl in reverse as the three gangsters kept the dead company.

The door opened and in walked in a short, fat guy. A twisted cross between Janis Joplin, Dr. John and dressed like he just walked off the stage after performing with the Parliament Funkadelic. He sauntered to the center of the foyer, without uttering a word. His limp wrists flailing like they were on swivels. Stork-like legs sat precariously on top of a bowling ball-shaped body. Tossing his rain-soaked wool coat over the newel-post, the weird guy wearing multi-colored boas, looked Tony and the other up and down, with pursed lips.

Ritchie stepped forward, hand extended. "Mr. Bartheleme, so glad you could make it. Sorry about the time."

Ignoring the hand, he peered into the living room, while he extended his own, pudgy hand, palm up.

"Who the hell is this guy?" Tony asked.

"How much is it going to cos— " Ritchie asked.

Tony held up his hands. "Wait. Back the bus up. How the hell can you know what to charge, when don't even know what the hell is what's going on?" His voice raising with each word.

"It's simple, tough guy. Just chill." The man said with a lilt. "Tall dark and creepy here, said you have one dead guy." He stepped forward and placed a hand on Tony's chest. "Flat rate charge of five-hundred. Plus expenses." He smiled, revealing a bright, shining gold tooth.

Tony recoiled.

Ritchie started walking into the living room. "Follow me, he's...um, in here.

"Wait... Plus expenses?" Tony said.

"Oh, don't worry your pretty little head, *Chachi*. Sometimes they let loose their bodily fluids, " He followed Ritchie. "And, dry cleaning gets expensive." He smiled back at Tony. He walked around the sofa and stopped quick, clapped his hands and smiled.

"Nice shot." He said and set his bag down and held his hand out— waiting for payment.

"No bread, stays dead, darlin'?" The glint from his tooth nearly blinded Tony.

Tony stormed across the room and jammed the cash into the man's sweaty hand.

"Can you bring him back?" Tony's question sounded more like a demand.

"Easy-peasy puddin'-pop."

"And, the whole amnesia thing?" Ritchie asked.

"Oh, yes. That. Not a problem, at all my dear. It'll just be an additional five hundred." He smiled at Tony and held his hand out again.

Tony felt his fist ball and if it weren't for the whole being hunted down and tortured by the largest mob family in city thing, his shotgun would be ribs-deep in this fops ass.

He took the remainder of the cash from his wallet and gave it to the man.

"Only have three hundred. It'll have to do."

The man sneered and after a second, shrugged and shoved it into this bag.

"Okay, Time to make with the mojo. First, everybody out." He waved them out of the room and grinned as he closed the pocket doors.

"It's an old family secret. I could tell you, but I'd have to kill you. No peeking, fellas." He said. The doors slammed shut.

"What the hell was that?" Tony stood in the foyer in utter disbelief.

"One freakin weird guy," Ritchie said, trying to peek through the slit in the door.

"Yous think? He's goddamn batzo." Tony said. "You better hope he pulls this off."

"I like 'em. He smelled like cake." Mikey said.

Tony and Ritchie turned toward the big man.

"Really?" They said.

Mikey shrugged. "Well, he does."

Tony ignored him and looked around. "Okay, while Bizarro The Clown works his *mojo*, let's tear this place apart and find that goddamn money. We're gonna at least get what we came here for."

They spent the better part of an hour systematically going through the upstairs, ripping it to pieces and finally, downstairs, in the kitchen, they hit the jackpot.

They all stood in the what could have easily been in a four-star hotel, kitchen. All staring at the same exact spot. The cupboards lay splayed open. Every box torn open. The floor was covered in everything from sugar, raw spaghetti, and finally... cake mix and a fifty-pound bag of flour.

Mixed between several duncan Hines, Black forest cherry cake mix boxes and the sack of flour, was the biggest load of money any of them had ever seen.

They all started laughing, slapping high-fives.

That was until a dank, foul odor began to fill the room. It smelled of sewage and rotting meat. Tony paused, while the other two continued celebrating.

Then the pounding and screaming began.

"What the hell?" Tony shouted and snatched the shotgun off the counter. He motioned to the others. "Bag all the cash up, we're getting the hell outta here."

"Got it, boss." They rushed to find something to toss the money in.

Tony crept toward the foyer, gun raised, while the pounding and screams continued to echo though the tall room.

The foul stench grew worse the closer Tony walked into the smoke-filled entry way. The doors to the living were still closed, but puffs of mustard-colored smoke tendrils slipped out from beneath the door. Tony pulled his undershirt up over his nose and made it to the door. The wood pulsed with pounding and the screams grew louder.

"You okay?" He heard himself shout.

Only unintelligible mumbles came from the other side of the door. Tony slid the doors open and a wave of thick, smoke pushed him back. It smelled of death, and pork chops. Fucking weird Tony thought as he caught his balance and breath.

The man tumbled and fell onto the floor—gasping for air.

Tony knelt down, trying to help him up. He got the fat man to his feet.

"What the hell happened?" He shouted.

The man shook uncontrollably and let out short blurts of words.

" Bad...dead. Alive...door...close."

It wasn't until the loud echo of moaning echoed into the room that Tony's rattled mind put it all together. He turned to see several shambling forms making their way to the foyer.

Tony dropped the shotgun and ran to the doors and slammed them shut. His mind raced at what the hell was going on. Either way, this wasn't a good thing.

The things on the others side of the door pounded and moaned but didn't show any signs of bashing through.

"What the fuck?" Was all Tony could belt out.

The man stood up and shaky legs, fighting to catch his breath. He smiled at Tony and the closed door.

After a few second, he said, "Shit, happens, Guido." the man smiled picked up has bag and walked to the door, opened it and turned around. "The old man is alive...well, sort of.but trust me.

Your secret is safe with him. Toodles." He sauntered out and slammed the door behind him.

Tony stood alone in the smoky foyer. Pounding zombies on the other side of the door and the dumb and dumber twins arguing which bag is better to use, the Costco or Sam's Club. He leaned against the door, his body bouncing with each strike the zombies pounded, and he didn't care. Slowly but surely a brilliant idea began to blossom in his flummoxed mind.

As the turd-bowl twins argued, Tony walked to the phone hanging on the wall and dialed a number he's only called once before. After three rings, someone picked up.

"Speak," The monotone voice spoke.

"Tony Foti calling," Tony said, trying to calm his breathing.A few moments passed.

"Who?"

"I'm part of Michelli's crew. I am calling with bad news about Uncle Orz. I thought the boss should know." Tony cast the dice.

Many long moments passed and the line clicked.

"Speak," Tony recognized the voice. It was that of the big man. The true boss. He fought to hold back a laugh. He had to play this just right. He drew in a deep breath and let out, slowly.

"Boss, it's Tony, I have some bad news. I came to do some favors for your Uncle and he's not doing too good." Tony said slowly.

"Is he okay?" The Boss panicked.

"You should get here as soon as possible, Boss." Tony heard himself spout the words.

Time froze.

Tony began to shit gold bricks.

"I'll be right there."

The line went dead. Tony smiled.

"Boys, put the bags in the car and get ready. We are about to move up." Tony smiled and held the doors closed as the zombie banged and moaned behind him.

The time had come for three low-rent wanna-be wise guys to take the leap to head boss. Tony checked the shells in the shotgun and walked to the door and opened it up.

Cold rain hit his face. He smiled and waited.

His time had finally come. Nephew would meet uncle and then.... Tony would be the Boss.

Moans of the dead and bowl-shaking thunder rocked the old Fund house.

Tony watched and waited.

Flesh would be eaten and destinies would be fulfilled.

Thom Erb is a genre fiction writer exploring all shades of darkness, light and the varying definitions of heroism and the reluctant hero. Refusing to pigeonhole his writing, Thom crafts tales blurring the lines of horror, fantasy, thriller and beyond. Find more at: www.thomerb.com.

THE LOOMING TREES
Penny Fey

KAT SAT IN THE PASSENGER SEAT of her ex-boyfriend's beat-up pickup truck, watching the night pass by. Eddie drove, and they spoke little. "Comfortably Numb" played softly on the outdated stereo, and the static was nostalgic and soothing in combination with the warm July air.

"Eddie, this isn't going to work, how am I going to get my car home tomorrow?"

He looked at her and groaned, "You want me to turn around now?" The frustration was clear in the way his jaw was set and in the edge to his voice.

Kat looked back at the familiar road ahead to gather her thoughts. Erickson Road was the road she grew up on. The truck rumbled around the corner near the frog pond and headed slowly in the direction of her parent's house. She felt uneasy, but she didn't know why. She looked at Eddie, opened her mouth to speak, to tell him to turn around, and she bit off her request. Eddie was squinting, leaning closer to the steering wheel.

"What the hell..." he muttered as he slowed the '85 Ranger.

Kat looked at his narrowed eyes and followed his line of sight to the left side of the road. Startled by the pair of eyes that were looking back at her, Kat caught her breath and her stomach flip-flopped with anxiety. On a large tabled surface of an old tree long since felled, was a spindly-legged deer. It stood alert, watching the truck and it's passengers. Then it bolted into the sand covered street and froze in front of the truck. Eddie hit the brakes and brought the vehicle to a complete stop.

The skittish creature was pale and ghostlike in the headlights before becoming spooked and gracefully bounding back into the darkness. Kat and Eddie exchanged a mild look of shock. The deer had startled them both, coming out of the darkness like a phantom, and disappearing just as quickly. Eddie drew his eyes back to the road, and kept both hands on the steering wheel ready for another deer to leap from the shadows. He released the brake, hit the gas, and the reliable old truck revved loudly jumping from first to second gear.

This road, like most in Apple Hill, had no streetlights. On the left there were dense acres of forest, that when navigated correctly, lead to Blood Hill. Blood Hill was affectionately named to pay homage to the Indian burial grounds that were a local mystery and said to have been located somewhere on the eastern slopes. To the right was an old apple orchard that was home to countless ancient, crooked trees that resembled old witches. It was late and though there was a full moon, it did not shine here. The apples were black, decorating the old misshapen trees that loomed in the distance. Even the halogen headlights had a difficult time penetrating the darkness.

Eddie and Kat scanned both sides of the road, watching for another pair of eyes to catch the gleam of halogen. Eddie slammed on the brakes hard. The headlights lit up a man in the in the middle of the road, standing in the darkness. He didn't flinch. He stood there unwavering, as still as could be. Kat's belly filled with horrified nausea. Eddie inhaled sharply. The man had long thin arms that hung by his sides. His legs were spread to the distance of his shoulders. He stared, his face concealed by a dark hood, at the young couple. The darkness that surrounded him had density, it was viscous and seemed to emanate from the stranger like blackened, inky tentacles.

A sickening, fleshy thud rocked the pick-up. Through the windshield, on the driver's side, a fleshy face appeared, bloated and discolored. It slid down the window, squeaking as it did, contorting the fat and swollen cheek into a lip-lifting snarl. The downward slide stretched the lifeless torso and revealed the stranger's neck, and the deadly, perfectly tied noose that was wrapped around it. He was on the hood, piled there like a rag doll, his limbs resting at unnatural angles. Eddie tried to back up, spraying loose pebbles from the tires before catching cracked pavement with rubber. The sudden reversal of direction relieved the body of its resting place and it swung in the still July air, toes dragging, drawing abstract lines in the sandy road. Kat fumbled with her cell and returned her attention to the man standing unnervingly still in the middle of the road. The stranger in the dark seemed closer, though she never saw him move. His eyes burned her very soul. He meant to kill them in the night, and consume them with his darkness, and no one would ever know.

"Eddie, go!" Hysteria pitched her voice an octave higher.

"I'm trying! I'm trying!"

Backing up, blindly and panicked, Eddie couldn't tear his eyes from the dark unmoving silhouette. The man in black, raised his slender arms suddenly, and his hood slid off revealing a face that was nothing but shadow and void where his eyes peered out. Kat's head was jarred violently backwards against the headrest. The truck came to a sudden stop, and behind them lay a bloodied deer, rattling its last breaths through punctured lungs and shattered ribs. Their heads rebounded back, and their eyes focused on the stranger, Eddie reached for Kat's hand.

Thump... thump...thump... thump thump thump.

Bodies began falling from the long limbed trees that canopied the road, ropes stopping them short. Men, women and children, floated inches from the ground, toes extended like ballerinas. A forest of corpses, suspended like puppets, swung in the soft breeze, blue and gray and lifeless — a ballet of death to a symphony created by the darkest of conductors.

Kat and Eddie stared, wide-eyed and horrorstruck, as their headlights flashed off and then on again like a strobe in a haunted house. Dead faces and stretched necks, dangling feet and clothes that spanned two centuries of fashion danced before their eyes. Just ahead, the man in black stood unnaturally still between a hanged man in suspenders, and young boy in footed pajamas.

Shadows wove between bodies, arms and legs, in ribbons of silkiness. Eddie and Kat rolled up the windows in a futile attempt at protection. The blackness knows no boundaries and flowed freely through the glass, and like the tongue of an evil lover, slid across their cheeks, and around their necks. The touch of darkness was cool and dry, reptile like and hissing. The conductor motioned quickly with his hands, pulling the shadow rope toward him. Kat and Eddie felt the constriction as the blackness tighten around their necks. Their eyes bulged as they were ripped mercilessly toward the conductor. The vehicle glass shattered under the impact of their bodies and the shadow ribbon swiftly snaked upward into the trees, suspending the two in the air.

The conductor made one final movement and the ribbon turned to rope. Kat and Eddie exhaled their final breaths, and melted into the darkness as the sun began to rise. The trees retreated back into the shadows of the forest. The conductor put his hands in his pockets and walked on down the road looking like he were out for his early morning stroll.

Later that morning…

An officer knelt and looked closely at the animal, noting the pieces of plastic protruding from the body. Picking one out, he recognized it was from the rear end of a pick up, a cover from the taillights… Someone *backed* over a deer?

Penny Fey (R.I.P. Michelle Beth (Hansen) Martens), writer, editor and artist: Penny was the primary writer and editor for "Summerlands Fanzine" by Outside The Box Comics. The Looming Trees is from her soon-to-be released collection of horror shorts "Apple Hill."

skin&hair teeth&bones
Kristi Petersen Schoonover

IT SHOWS UP AT THEIR DOOR, the package from his dead aunt's estate executrix. Jenn knows her husband Rob has been hoping for a substantial inheritance, but when she sees the beat-up Priority Box, its blue and red stripes runny from the rain, she is aware that this is all he is going to get.

Rob is next in line to possess the family's *Desuldura*, an ancient thing brought from the Old Country. It tells its user whether or not the current situation he is in is the result of a mistake in his past, whether or not he is on the right life path. After all, the future is too unpredictable—what one sees in the Tarot Cards or the Roving Eye or the Ouija Board can morph the second the querent makes a different decision based on his new, mystic information. But any mistake in the past can be corrected simply by changing the path of the future: marry the wrong man? Divorce him. Have a child you didn't want? Put it up for adoption. Take the wrong job? Look for a new one.

She brings the box into the house and sets it on the kitchen table.

Rob slides the coffee pot back into its holder and stands, holding his cup without taking a sip. "That's it, isn't it?"

Jenn looks up at him. His eyes have always captivated her, in a way that makes her want to go to bed with him, in a way that makes her want to envelope him. But as of late, there hasn't been much of that, and she has sensed him pulling away from her; sleeping with his back to her in the bed, failing to kiss her before he leaves for work. She has begun to wonder, in fact, if she has made a mistake, if she is on the wrong life path. "I think so."

He sets his cup down on the counter and approaches. For a moment, the two of them just stand, looking at it. Then Rob says, "We shouldn't open it. I don't want to."

Jenn knows the consequences for refusal and it is something not to be taken lightly. To dispose of it is to bring blight and even death to the household. "It's not a matter of want."

"I'm not saying get rid of it. I'm saying leave it, as is, in the back of a closet someplace. There's nothing anywhere that says you have to *use* it."

But Jenn *wants* to use it. She has one question in particular. She moves to the refrigerator and pulls a pair of meat cutting scissors out of a magnetic sleeve; when the shifts, she can see a ring of dirt around its former position.

"Don't," Rob says. "We can pretend it doesn't exist."

Jenn cuts the tape with care, as though there is paper beneath it she is afraid to damage. She peels back the flaps and peers inside.

Nestled in a bed of white tissue paper, a small, clear jar. Inside it, dried flakes of human skin, four teeth, bone splinters, a thick lock of black hair.

This, Jenn knows, is the stuff of dreams. Open the jar, dump the contents on the table, ask a question, get an answer.

"Ugh," Rob says.

She looks at him. "I want to ask it something."

"What?" Rob says. "What would you *possibly* want to know?"

She unscrews the jar. It smells like cumin and mold. She spreads the items on the table, closes her eyes, concentrates. In her mind, she asks, *Is this marriage where I am supposed to be?*

Then she looks down at the pieces. She waits for them to move, to spell out yes or no as she's seen them do before, once, at his aunt's house, shortly after they were married.

But the pieces do nothing.

Rob looks visibly relieved. He, in fact, laughs. "And to think I was worried."

Jenn listens to the rain pound harder.

In the quiet, after they've gone up to bed, there is the sound of scratching. It is faint in the living room. It is louder in the dining room. It is silence-shattering in the kitchen as skin&hair, teeth&bones slide around each other and finally give their answer.

Kristi Petersen Schoonover's novel, Bad Apple, is a Pushcart Prize nominee; her short fiction has appeared in several publications. She's received three Norman Mailer Writers Colony Residencies and is an editor for Read Short Fiction.

how you killed me
doungjai gam

it starts innocently enough—
a tendon that calcifies,
then nausea hits:
a black roiling smog
rendering my insides numb

with every rejection,
ossification spreads
through muscles and organs,
saturating the dermis

as I slowly asphyxiate
I reach into myself
to give you my final offering
you drop it,
stomp on it—
a pulpy mess
with bloody bits stuck to your boot

my stone flesh crumbles
as tears flow like rain
limbs shatter
as they hit the floor

and you:
the sole witness to my destruction,
can't even be bothered to pick up
the broken pieces of me
before you walk away
to start anew.

Doungjai gam , a native of Thailand, now resides in Connecticut with her family. She is a seven-time Necon E-Books Flash Fiction winner and has been published in LampLight Magazine. Find her on Facebook at www.facebook.com/ djai76.

INVIDIA
Marianne Halbert

INVIDIA ARRIVED WITH THE DAWN. SHE sat on the woven horse-hair divan in the front hall. When she heard the clopping of heels approaching, she stood and straightened her dress. She lowered her eyes, and when the woman stood before her, she curtsied. The mounting silence that grew overwhelmed her, and she spoke.

"Dunya Irinka," she said. "My father sent me, per your request."

"Invidia Zelenyee," the woman said, "Only seven years old. I hear you are a most responsible child. You better be, if I am to trust you with my Katja."

Invidia raised her eyes to meet those of Dunya Irinka. The woman towered over her. She wore an intricately woven scarf over her shoulders. A golden locket hung from her neck. Invidia had heard of this family, but never seen one in person. So it was true. The woman's head was as bald as an eggshell.

They walked upstairs to a room on the north side of the house. Dunya Irinka approached a crib, decorated with gold trimmed lace. She reached in and plucked the child and raised it to her breast. The babe was wrapped in a bone colored blanket, and wore a downy forest green cap.

"Katja has worn this cap since the day she was born. Remove it only to wash her hair, and replace it as soon as the hair is dry. You may blot it with a towel, but never rub. You will use a fan to dry it. Her hair is never to be touched by sunlight, lest it blanch. She is never to be near men, for they all smoke, and the residue will cloak the shimmer of her hair and rob it of its luster. The colonists overseas in Virginia will only pay top dollar for virgin hair. And no one provides finer red hair than the women in my family."

At that, Dunya Irinka brushed her hand over her smooth scalp, and closed her eyes, wistful. Then she opened them again and continued.

"She is never to look in a mirror. You will have four hours to yourself, every second Sunday. You will be taught to speak English. When Katja is sixteen, you will accompany her to America, where you will cut off her hair and prepare it for the wig maker. You will then apply the tonic to her scalp that will cause the roots to fall out, and never grow back. She will wear her baldness as a crown of honor upon her return and she will then begin to sire the next generation."

When Invidia made no protest to these terms, Dunya Irinka handed the baby over to her and left the room. Invidia held the girl in her arms. Ice blue eyes looked up into hers, and tiny fingers brushed her cheek. A stray strand of dark hair fell, and the baby grasped it, pulling.

"No, little Katja. You do not want my mouse colored hair."

She laid her down for a nap, and watched her for hours. Then Invidia moved to the rocking chair. Lunch was brought to her. Dunya Irinka came to feed the child, then put her back down for a nap. Invidia resumed rocking and began to doze. Then she heard a small sound and peeked into the crib. She drew in a breath. The cap had come slightly askew as the babe shifted. A tender curl peeked out from the cloth. Invidia reached toward it, halting her hand inches away. *But I am to wash the hair. I am allowed to touch it. The only one allowed. Dunya Irinka would want me to replace the cap*, she rationalized. Her fingertips moved forward, and she touched the fiery lock. It was soft as silk, and even in the afternoon shadow of the room, it seemed to create a light of its own. She pulled the cap down and Katja looked like an ordinary baby again.

The first time that Invidia washed the hair, Dunya Irinka watched, like a bird of prey eying a field mouse. She used her left hand to support Katja's neck, and her right to massage the soap into the soft red curls, and then to pour water from a pitcher, careful that the stream went back over the scalp. As she took a towel, she was desperately careful to do a gentle pat, then move the towel, do another gentle pat. Her eyes burned, wanting to look into Dunya Irinka's eyes to see whether or not she approved. But she forced herself to stay focused on Katja. On that red hair. She set the towel down and picked up a fan, holding it by the handle. She moved it up and down, creating a slight breeze. As the hair grew more dry, the curls bounced up and down.

For the first couple of years, it was nearly impossible to go outside with Katja unless she was strapped to a carriage. She was too young to understand the need to remain in the shade. Per Dunya Irinka's instructions, Invidia bound Katja's wrists to her side any time she tried to remove the cap. She eventually learned not to touch it.

At dinner, Dunya Irinka always gave the hunks of meat with the most fat to Katja and her older sisters who also wore caps. She said it would add shine to their hair. Sabina, the eldest, was bald, having already traveled to America. When Invidia reached for the butter, Dunya Irinka slapped her hand away. It makes the hair shine. It was for the virgin-haired only.

When Katja turned eight, Invidia convinced Dunya Irinka to let her take her to the park. "She'll be under cap and parasol the entire time."

"Please, Mamochka," Katja pleaded. She ran to her mother, and wrapped her arms around the woman's ample waist. The girl raised her pale blue eyes to her mother's face. "Invidia has told me so much about the swans on the lake. And it looks to be overcast all day. The sun couldn't find me, even if it tried."

"No little, one," her mother agreed, "you've hidden all the sunlight in your locks."

As they walked along the path to the park, Invidia was careful to keep the parasol over Katja's head. True, the sky was overcast with a tangle of gray clouds, but she was taking no chances. At one point, Katja raised her hand to her dark green cap and Invidia's heart leapt into her throat, but the girl was only pulling it down, not taking it off. She relaxed.

They found a bench sitting on a wide dock that jutted over the water. Invidia spread out a red cloth and laid out their lunch. Katja was leaning over the railing, her pale green dress blowing in the breeze as she watched large white swans paddling below, gray-tufted goslings racing to keep up. Katja was smiling, her dimples as deep as Invidia had ever seen. Invidia wondered if she'd caught her own reflection in the dull water below. The child's ice blue eyes sparkled, her gaze darting from the swans to the children chasing each other on the nearby hill. The urchins tossed a small basket back and forth, but one boy missed it and it rolled. A younger boy of about twelve, wearing a black wool hat cockeyed on his head, ran after it. The others called after him, *Pavel, hurry up!* Katja tore a hunk of bread from the loaf, and slathered it with butter. She held it out toward Invidia.

"No," she breathed. "I," she said, and looked around as though Dunya Irinka would be standing there watching, "I can't."

Katja used her other hand to brush her knuckles along Invidia's cheek. "This is the best day. What is a little butter compared to the swans, and the boys, and the sparkles on the water."

She accepted the bread and almost had it raised to her lips, the scent of it sweet in her nose. "Yes, the—" Sparkles? Her head whipped toward the water, a slight breeze creating gentle ripples. And peppering the ripples, there they were. *Sparkles*. She looked up to the sky and saw the rays of sun breaking free of the clouds.

She dropped the bread to the ground, vaguely aware that she crushed it underfoot as she stood and gripped the girl by the wrist, eliciting a shriek. Pavel, the boy with the hat, stopped playing, and ran toward them.

"Invidia, you are hurting me!" Katja screamed.

"Run." Her eyes darted around and saw a large tree, a large pool of shade. "There," she said, more to herself than to her ward. The boy blocked them, and put a protecting arm around Katja. "Fool," Invidia growled, "she cannot be in the sunlight." Still he was uncomprehending. "Ugh! She's a Belikov!"

The boy paused, then looked at Katja, the dark cap pulled down to her bright red brows. Just then an older boy ran past, and snatched the cap away, snickering. Pavel removed his shirt and draped it over her head. He swept her into his arms and raced for the shade, Invidia fast on his heels. He set Katja down. She hid her face in her hands, sobbing, but Pavel drew her hands away. He used his thumb to wipe away her tears.

"There, there, Little Belikov." He turned to Invidia. "Wait here."

She watched him go to the group of boys who were now using the cap for a game of toss. When he reached for it, the game turned to keep away. Within moments he had punched one boy, and tackled another. Then he came back to the tree.

He brushed the dirt from the cap and began to place it back on Katja's head. Invidia shoved him away. "I'll do it. I'm the only one allowed to touch her hair," she said. Then under her breath, she repeated, "the *only* one."

Invidia went to the dock to pack up their belongings and retrieve the parasol. As she approached the tree, she could hear Katja speaking.

"Maybe you could come by my house."

"You aren't allowed to be near men," Invidia spat. Then she directed her attention to the boy, Pavel. "You all smoke. The smoke invades your pores and clothes, and infects her."

He grinned and reached for Katja's hand. "Then I shall never smoke," he said.

Invidia raised her finger to her lips as they approached the door to

Katja's house. She held her ear to the door, and heard no sound. She opened the door and they tiptoed inside.

She was about to wash Katja's hair when she heard the familiar footfalls of Dunya Irinka.

"And how were the swans?"

Katja, stupid girl, was too shaken to speak for a moment. She stammered, looking at Invidia for guidance. "Oh, Mamochka, they were amazing."

The woman held her daughter's face in her hands, turning it. She lifted the cap to her nose and breathed in deeply. "Wait here, my Katja."

She took Invidia outside. She tore a small green switch from a nearby tree.

"Lower your shirt."

"But Dunya—"

Without warning, she cracked the whip across Invidia's face. The girl took a step back, stunned. The woman raised her arm again, and Invidia removed her shirt. She turned so that her back was facing her master, and dropped to her knees. Over and over the whip fell across her back. Trembling, she climbed the stairs, sensing the welts already raised before she made it to the top. Katja was waiting, her skin a perfect porcelain. She let Invidia rinse her hair, her fingertips more gentle than they'd ever been before. She rinsed it more times than usual. Little did the girl know, each movement was a torment to Invidia. Each shift sent a spike of pain racing across her back. As Invidia used the fan, Katja's eyes began to glaze over, and she dozed. Invidia studied every last strand of that red hair, *Belikov* hair. *What had I done to deserve such punishment? And what had this child done to deserve such reward?*

They did not return to the park. But a year later, Dunya Irinka traveled to America with one of Katja's older sisters. It was time for her grooming. Her hair washer had died, and Katja's mama trusted no one else with the task. Both Invidia and Katja followed the rules but they did go outside. They walked to the village. They sat in the shade of a building. There were no branches that could sway. No sunlight could reach them. They played a game. Katja would take off her shoes, and stick her toes into the grass where the sun was, describing the warmth. She moved so that it was up to her knees, and then her waist. Invidia made her stop there, not wanting to take a chance.

The boy, Pavel saw them one day as he was pushing a milk cart. He began to come by more often. He and Invidia would play in the sun at Katja's insistence while she watched from the dark. She wanted to experience the fun through them. They cartwheeled, and somersaulted, and laughed. And Invidia took advantage of the moments she could touch Pavel, relishing the hurt in Katja's eyes.

A few years later, she discovered them in the pantry, the door cracked open. She watched him kiss Katja. His hands caressed her neck, her cheeks, her temples, but never reached for the cap. Invidia knew how badly he wanted to see that hair again. How he ached for it. His kisses moved down her neck, loosening the front of her shirt. He dropped to his knees, his lips brushing her belly and a moan escaped Katja's lips. Invidia interrupted them and sent him home.

"You are fifteen. In a few months, we travel to Virginia. You will abandon your hair there and when you return you will couple with Yakov Zavragin."

"Don't." Katja's eyes brimmed with tears. "I envy you."

Invidia stopped. Invidia who resented the butter and fat given to this girl. Invidia who was jealous of the way that Pavel kissed Katja, the way he looked at her. Invidia, who from the moment she'd seen her, envied Katja and her fire red hair and all the life spoils it entitled her to.

"You, envy me?"

"Of course," Katja cried. "You are free. You are free to walk in the sunlight, to surround yourself with men and their dirty smoke. To let anyone run their fingers through your hair. To choose who you will couple with. And all the while," she said, yanking the cap from her head and tossing it to the ground, "I am tethered to this hair!" At this she gripped her waist as though she'd been punched, her long wavy hair glowing as it draped over her shoulders. "Yakov Zavragin." She spat it as though the name soured in her mouth.

Invidia scrambled for the cap, already fearing the switch across her back if they were discovered. She began to gather Katja's hair to replace the cap. Katja's voice was suddenly excited. "Maybe there is a way. I could cut my hair off. Cut it all off. Shamed, Mama will never let me carry on the line. She would see it as tainted. I would never have to be with Yakov, and I would be free to be with Pavel."

"No," Invidia said. The thought of Katja with Pavel pained her more than the thought of the whip.

They convinced Dunya Irinka to let Pavel accompany them to America for protection. When they arrived in Virginia, they took a suite in a row of rooms near a tavern.

The housemaid showed them to the shower. It was only a few feet beyond the back door. Made of brick, it was octagonal in shape. "Just pull on the cord, the water will shower over you."

Of course, Invidia couldn't use it. But Katja did.

"Could you wait for me, with my towel?"

Of course.

The night was warm. A horse and carriage clopped past, and moved down the lane. From a half mile away she could hear the hearty laughter and song of the men in the taverns. A low drum beat was followed by a fiddle and a fife. Then the drunken laughter of the colonists. The water showered over Katja, only her slender shoulders visible above the brickwork.

They went back inside, and had passed by a mirror in the hall. Invidia combed Katja's long hair.

"Just this once, may I see it?" Katja asked.

"No. After."

Invidia tugged the comb through a knot, relishing the wince of pain Katja exhibited.

There was a knock at the door, and Invidia put the comb down. She went to the hall, and a messenger stood before her. He had a letter. He said it was for the Belikov. He delivered the sender's instructions. Invidia accepted it, and after he'd walked away, she ripped through the wax stamp.

"Katja, kitten. Run away with me."

Invidia put the note in her pocket, and entered the chamber where Katja awaited her. She picked up the fan.

"Katja," she said, thoughtful. "You know upon our return, you can never see Pavel again. If you could deny your mother, and be with Pavel, would you still choose that life?"

The girl turned to her, the breeze from the fanning causing her eyes to blink. "Dearest, you are as a second Mamochka to me. You advised me against it."

Invidia paused, and pulled the note from her pocket. "He wants to be with you. I thought he only wanted you because you are a Belikov, but if he wants to run away, the riches must mean nothing to him."

Katja's eyes grew wide as she read the brief note.

"He awaits your answer. The messenger will return within the hour. All he needs is a yes. Or a no. To honor your mother, you must leave your heart. But then you have my blessing to follow your heart."

Katja didn't hesitate. She ran toward the desk, and the inkwell. She took the quick and scrawled a "Yes!" across the bottom of the note, in her swirling, fine handwriting.

Invidia nodded her approval. "Then it is done." She gripped the scissors. "You must hold very still. You must not release a breath." She stroked the hair, pulling it back. "You mustn't shudder."

She plunged the blade into Katja's young chest. Her ivory hands reached for it, but Invidia had already plucked it away, and the blood flowed freely. Katja tried to speak, but only a husky whisper escaped her lips.

"And then, we pull it back, like this." Invidia gathered the red bundle in one palm, and yanked it back. "And then, as though it had never been there, it is gone." She snipped with the scissors, and it was separated. Young Katja was tethered to her hair no more. Invidia tilted her head, noticing a swath of wet crimson shading the edges of the hair. Blood from the blade.

As Katja struggled toward her, Invidia moved to the side table, to the pitcher and urn of water. She gently washed and massaged the hair. While Katja drew in inconsistent and ragged breaths, Invidia fanned the gathered hair. "Almost there." A few more strokes and the strands were dry.

There was a knock at the door again, and Invidia stepped over Katja in her repose to retrieve the note. She went to the hall and handed it to the messenger. Without a word, she retreated to their chamber.

She picked up the bundle of hair and bound the ends, and used a tie to drape it over her forehead. She left one candle glowing and waited for the rap on her door.

"Katja," Pavel's harsh whisper came. She envisioned the image through his eyes.

He pushed the door open, and saw her there, her back to him. A slender figure. She held one hand out to the side, and he halted at her gesture. She reached up to the cap, hesitating, then slid it loose. A river of red flowed down her back, luminescent. She untied the robe, and let it drop from her shoulders, revealing thighs, calves, and bare ankles below.

Pavel took a tentative step forward. He reached for her, and she sensed his hands begin to brush her hair aside as he lowered his lips to the back of her neck. Not wanting him to see the scars across her back, she blew out the candle, and turned to him in the dark.

They made love through the night. In the morning, she watched the sunrise through the window as his arm draped over her chest. When he stirred, she turned to him. She pleaded for his eyes to welcome her, but when they fluttered open, they were confused. He shoved back from her, ashamed.

"Where is... *Katja!*" he screamed. He leapt from the bed, and knelt beside his Katja, a low moaning coming from him and he cradled her in his arms. Invidia struck the scissors into his side, below the ribs. He didn't fight. He just held his beloved, her ice blue eyes frozen, and his fading.

Invidia used the scissors to cut her hair. Then she applied the tonic and waited until mid-morning. She passed the time by writing a letter to Dunya Irinka, explaining how the young lovers had betrayed them both and eloped. How Invidia, having failed in her duty, was too ashamed to return to their homeland. She enclosed the note, written in the couples' own hands, as proof. Then she went to the octagonal shower, and let the last of her roots wash away. She draped Katja's gilded scarf over her shoulders, and clasped the Belikov locket around her neck. She tenderly laid the braid of hair in the silk-lined box and went to the wig maker's shop.

She approached, scaring away a few hens in her path. She walked in. At first no one noticed her. Then a woman casually looked at her, but then her gaze drifted to Invidia's head. How smooth. How bald. The woman whispered something to her husband. He turned, and they both took a step back. A young boy that appeared to be on an errand for his master ran out of the store, a box clutched under one arm. He fell into the street and scampered away. The wig maker turned, and upon seeing Invidia, he approached, and bowed.

"Miz Belikov. I have been looking forward to your arrival since your mother wrote me."

Another man turned, watching the exchange with interest.

Invidia said nothing.

"May I?" the wig maker asked.

She kept her eyes leveled on him. After a moment, she unlatched the box, and raised the lid, releasing a golden glow from the box. The man exhaled an expectant sigh.

"She told me," he said, "of all your generation, yours was the most exquisite." His eyes roamed up and down the strands. "She did not exaggerate." Invidia was fairly certain the man was close to drooling.

The other man stepped closer, and lifted the braid from the box. The owner seemed about to halt him, but something about the gentleman's status made the owner bite his tongue.

"This," he said with a thick British accent, then met Invidia's eyes, "came from you?"

Stoic, she did not reply.

"I may feel compelled to purchase it just to see it back on your crown." She breathed. He went on. "May I be so bold as to ask you to accompany me to the Governor's Palace this evening for the ball? I leave in a few days, and would gladly show you all of Europe."

"Let us see how the ball goes," she said. "Then we can talk about all of Europe."

He held out his arm, and Invidia accepted it. As they walked down the steps of the shop, she wondered whether she'd be on the ship when it left port, or if she'd be bound in chains and facing judgment by then. She paused before climbing into the prince's carriage, and watched the wigmaker place the hair in the window of his shop. Even as the carriage carted Invidia away, she could still see its glow.

Marianne Halbert's stories have been published by Coach's Midnight Diner, Midnight Screaming, Pill Hill Press, Necrotic Tissue Magazine, Blue River Press, ThugLit, Wicked East Press, Evil Jester Press, Static Movement, The Four Horsemen, Grinning Skull Press, Mystery & Horror LLC, Great Old Ones Publishing, Mocha Memoirs Press and more, as well as forthcoming stories with Screaming Spires Press and Evil Jester Comics.

DEAD THUNDER
D.B Poirier

THE SATURATED LAND TREMBLED AS TORRENTS of water rushed back to the ocean. Aquatic life splashed and struggled against the pull of the waves. Air cracked and space sundered as the kaleidoscopic bridge, Bifröst, entered the world, its ribbons of red, blue, green, and yellow vibrant across the sky but refracted—maligned—when they touched the newly-risen land.

"By the Nine Worlds, Heimdallr, where have you brought us?" asked the red-haired god.

Heimdallr stepped forward, his great horn looming large around his neck. "This is where he is; your prey, the Trickster."

Not all that rose from the depths had returned. Eels, whales, dolphins, and thousands of fish thrashed across the cursed land that was, moments before, submerged deep beneath the waves. Death would claim them soon. Gray silt oozed off, revealing jagged peaks of black rock. Multitudes of sunken ships littered the exhumed gravesite.

In the distance, a great stone city climbed hundreds of feet into the air. The structures were awkward in shape and defied rational thought; each tower a unique expression of madness and impossibility standing in mockery of a sane world.

The red-haired god scratched his beard with his free hand and clutched his mighty hammer in the other. "Are you sure? This is more a vision of Helhiem, if you ask me."

"This is Midgard, of that I am certain, Thor Odinson. We are over Midgard's greatest ocean far to the Southwest of the Geetlands and beyond two continents. He is here. I can sense as much." Heimdallr pointed to the twisted city and a look of panic suddenly crossed the face of the golden-toothed guardian of Bifröst. He gripped his mighty horn, bore it to his lips, and then hesitated.

Terror filled the Thunder God. "Why do you grip the Gjallarhorn so? Is it Ragnarök?"

Heimdallr released his horn and exhaled. "No, it is not Ragnarök but there is a presence here that feels like the end of the worlds. This place is old—older even than the gods. We should leave while we still can."

"You jest; few things in the nine worlds are older than my father."

"This is one of those things. This accursed place is ancient even by the All-Father's reckoning." Heimdallr placed a hand on Thor's shoulder. "Let us leave this forsaken rock. You can find the Trickster another time."

Thor shook his head. His red mane spilling over his chainmail shirt. "No, I must stay. It is my responsibility to assure the law is followed and punishment given to Loki."

Heimdallr's golden teeth retreated behind his grimace. "I fear I will not see you again, Thor Odinson. Please, do not linger long in this place."

Thor clasped the big hand of Heimdallr. "Fear not. I intend to return to my beautiful Sif and rouse her several nights thereafter."

Heimdallr's golden smile returned and he walked away with a chuckle. As Bifröst retreated from the world, Thor was filled with foreboding. He cursed himself for letting Heimdallr's words affect him and proceeded to the twisted city.

The terrain was rocky and slick. Even the surefooted thunder god found it a frustrating prospect to travel by land. Mighty hammer in hand, he leaped into the air and took flight. This form of conveyance was not often used by Thor. His enemies were almost always land-bound and the use of his hammer required close proximity to smite his foes. Above the ground, there was no leverage and he would easily be swatted away by giants and other colossal adversaries. However, from time to time when no one was watching he liked to exercise his full power as a sky god and fly.

When he reached the city, Thor discovered some of the buildings were as tall as the world tree, Yggdrasil. As he flew between them, their strangeness affected his mind. Distance and direction were distorted and he was forced to land lest he crash.

The space amid the structures shifted between light and shadow, without regard for the position of the sun. When Thor drew closer, he discovered the color of the stone buildings was not gray as perceived from a distance, but of a blackness that seemed to devour light itself.

Esoteric glyphs covered their exterior, but before he could examine them something else caught his attention: a trail of lingering shadows moving across the great avenues of the stone metropolis.

Where there were shadows, so too were the things that cast them. Or so Thor was inclined to think, though he couldn't be sure. *This place plays tricks on the eyes.* When he moved to investigate he did so with care.

Inhuman things slithered in procession, taller and bulkier than any man of Midgard. Skin of vomitous, glistening green and ivory streaked their naked bodies; their numerous extremities terminated in webbed claws. Unfamiliar denizens of the deep, Thor started to wonder if it were unwise not to heed Heimdallr's warning. Leaving this place was now a priority.

The scrape of claw on stone sounded behind Thor. When he turned, five of the aquatic creatures charged him, odd gashes in their necks pulsing. The sight reminded him of fish netted and pulled from their element. They were unexpectedly quick—all lunged for his throat.

Thor swung the mighty hammer, Mjölnir, a weapon forged for a god; forged for him. Two fell dead, their bodies crushed to pulpy stains upon the ground. Undaunted, the three that remained struck, their long claws sliding off his chain shirt. One abomination raked Thor's flesh at the base of his neck but his god's skin was unharmed.

What other evils lie in wait within this horrid city?

"Thunderer," called a voice from the shadows, "still meddling in things that are beyond you?"

Ignoring the three slimy foes that remained, Thor spun and hurled Mjölnir at the disembodied voice. The great weapon passed through shadow and slammed into the rock of a twisted tower. The stone, undamaged, resounded like a bell and Mjölnir fell to the street lifeless.

Loki stepped out of the darkness, a burst of flames erupting from his hands. Thor leaped away from the attack. The three remaining creatures were not so lucky and fell to the black street, immolated.

"To me, Mjölnir," called Thor. The weapon rose up and returned to his hand.

"Stay your fury, Thunderer, and grant me parlay that you may hear my words," Loki said.

Mjölnir slowly lowered to Thor's side. "What game is this, Trickster? What are those things?"

"They are the Deep Ones. At least according to scribbling of Odin."

Thor's expression grimmed. He raised Mjölnir high. "Do not speak foul of my father. Of what do you mean?"

"Slow-witted as ever, Thunder God." Loki spat. "This place, do you not know what it is?"

"I care not for this dark island. I came to put you back in chains."

Loki stepped fully into the light. Save for his breeches, his dress was feminine, in bold reds and yellows. His head bore a helm from which long horns stabbed up into the air.

"Look at this place," Loki waved his hand for emphasis and indicated the towering structures reaching high into the sky. "Surely you understand its significance. Or are you truly that stupid?"

Thor's green gaze followed Loki's hand. "This place is ancient. Heimdallr told me as much. More than that, I can feel its evil. We should not tarry here."

Loki walked over to one of the buildings and touched it. He pressed his face against the stone and with a delicate hand caressed the ruined surface as he might a lover. "These spires are of perfect and impossible geometric construction. They bend the fabric of the universe and alter the nature of reality. If you listen, you can hear whispers that reveal the secrets of creation."

A quiet calm came over the two gods and they heard the murmurs of countless alien voices. Sinister mysteries attempted to reveal themselves in a scope so vast that not even the mind of a god could perceive them in totality.

Mjölnir slipped from Thor's hand and he released a terrible scream of anguish that would have dropped a host of giants to their knees. "Stop… Loki… *Stop!*"

He placed huge hands on his head in a futile attempt to relieve the onslaught of pain brought on by revelation, clarity, and utter despair. Vomit powered past the Thunderer's lips and splashed the profane street.

With effort only Thor could muster, he reached for Loki and tore him from the wall. Sound evaporated, and they fell into a void of silence. Neither god felt themselves hit the ground.

After a time, Thor's mind stilled and the clambering of thoughts ended. He sat up and called to Mjölnir. The weapon answered but staggered toward him like a wounded animal, bouncing at times as it trailed along the ground. Despite its sluggish response, Thor felt better when the hammer landed in his grasp.

He turned and found the Trickster weeping, hands pressed against his face. Thor would have rebuked him, except that he understood Loki's malaise; a sorry realization for the god of thunder and battle.

"Loki," Thor said with uncharacteristic softness, "we must leave this place and warn the others."

The Trickster lifted his head and gazed upon Thor, his face wet with tears. "And tell them what? That we are insects compared to the Great Old Ones who dwell beyond the void? We cannot let another god touch these walls; they would die. Had you not pulled me from it my mind would have melted into oblivion."

With effort Thor stood and walked to Loki's side. He extended his hand. Loki took it and was lifted to his feet. "We must at least tell my father, Odin. He must know of this."

"Still the witless one, you are. Even after what we just witnessed, with the awareness and knowledge of the universe pouring through you, you still don't get it. Odin…he already knows!"

Thor lowered his head and grimaced at the realization that his father had lied to him. The All Father was not father of all; he was an insect just like the rest of the gods. Despair and hopelessness filled him once again.

Loki shook Thor. "The gods are old. Some like Odin are ancient. But that which sleeps in this city is *Eternal*." Loki began to weep once more, tears trailing from his cheeks. "And I have awakened him."

The red-haired god drew an arm across his mouth, wiping the dampness away from his beard. "Heimdallr," Thor called. "It is time for us to leave. Send the Bifröst that we may cross."

"There is no escaping this place," laughed Loki. "We can only try to delay the inevitable." Loki's voice grew louder, to an insane bellow.

Anger took Thor. He would hear no more of Loki's words. He had seen the same visions when Loki touched the wall but hadn't retained much of the picture. He was a simple god who viewed the world in simple ways. Loki, however, was the epitome of intellect, matched by few and surpassed only by Odin himself. Loki's mind had grasped infinity and eternity and all that transpired on that vast scale, if only for a moment, and now he was in the grip of madness as a result.

Thor slapped Loki hard, driving the Trickster to the ground. "Loki, come to your senses. Pull yourself from this lunacy or I'll call my wife Sif and have her beat it from your scrawny hide."

Anger flashed in Loki's eyes. "You will keep that harlot away from me, Thunderer, or next time I will take more than her hair!"

"Then stand and act a man that we may attack this problem you have created." Thor reached out and pulled the Trickster from the street for a second time.

A distant sadness filled Thor's heart. He missed his wife. Odin's command to retrieve the Trickster had interrupted his time with Sif. He could still feel her as they both lay nude atop a great bear rug, warmed by the roaring fire in their chamber's hearth. One of his great hands cupped her naked breast while he gently nuzzled her neck. Sif's magical raven hair, a gift from the Dwarves to repair the depredations of Loki, caressed his face as he whispered promises of pleasure into her ear. It had ended abruptly with news of Loki's escape. Anger gripped him and he smacked Loki again, hard across the cheek.

"What was that for?" roared Loki?

"That was for taking me from my Sif. Now how do we end this darkness you have unleashed?"

Before Loki could answer, four enormous creatures lumbered from the shadows, each three times the size of Thor, their gelatinous forms the sickly green of infected wounds. Three-digit hands sprouted dull yellow claws the length of swords. Most disturbing were their heads, which were dominated by a mass of writhing tentacles, parting on occasion to reveal dark dull orbs. The stench of dead fish grew suffocating around them.

"By all the gods, I have never seen such Jötunn," cursed Thor.

Real fear took Loki. "Those are not giants; they're Star Spawn."

"Spawn of what, a great squid? They smell worse than the insides of an eviscerated frost giant."

"Enough talk, Thunderer. These creatures will kill us if we let them." Loki took a deep breath, spread his arms wide, and conjured forth a gout of fire, setting one of the Star Spawn aflame.

Thor followed Loki's lead and let loose Mjölnir, sundering the head of the closest horror. Bone split under the blow, spraying black ichor on the wall behind it. The two remaining Spawn, undaunted by the fate of their comrades, attacked with ferocity. They first fell upon Thor with raking claws. The god ducked the first attack but not the second; it struck him in the chest, tearing away links of mailed shirt and god's flesh.

Despite the pain, Thor grasped the thing's arm and wrenched the limb from its socket. A jet of black fluid shot over him. As he cast the useless appendage aside, he raised a hand, and Mjölnir returned to his grasp.

The Spawn bellowed in rage; its tentacled face parting to reveal a toothy maw. Thor watched as its skin bubbled, a new arm sprouted, and its wound closed. Mjölnir launched again, crushing the head of the enraged Spawn. The thing did not rise anew.

Loki used his magic and created an invisible barrier between himself and his foe. The Spawn attacking him hammered at the barrier with clawed fists, each blow driving Loki farther back. With effort, the Trickster god enveloped the Spawn in a sphere of force, and then drew it in upon itself. The Spawn's tentacles flowed over the interior surface of the transparent globe and it screeched in pain as it prison slowly shrank, crushing its form. When the Spawn had been reduced to the size of a pearl, Loki set it aflame with his magic and cast it into the twisted sky where it exploded, lighting the sky in a ball of smoke and flame.

"We must find sanctuary and collect ourselves," Loki's rasped between deep breaths.

Thor examined his wound and torn chainmail. "What creature of Midgard is capable of injuring a god thus?"

"I'll answer your questions later. More of the abominations approach."

Dozens of the creatures appeared from inside the towering edifices.

"The nine worlds be sundered, how many of these things are there?" asked Thor.

"Too many to fight. We must run, Thunderer. There is a warded chamber among the buildings where I've been hiding; these things can't seem to enter."

Thor needed no encouragement and followed Loki. Hundreds of the Star Spawn pursued them on foot and in the air. Their journey was difficult; the spawn cut them off at almost every turn. After a short while it became apparent that their path was not one of their choosing. They were being herded.

"Loki," Thor yelled as he stopped running, "we need another plan."

"It would appear you are right. Every time we get close to the chamber they cut us off."

"We need to choose our path and break through their line."

Loki shook his head. "Are you mad? The Spawn will swarm us and we'll be killed!"

Thor smiled. "This may be true but at least we'll go down fighting. There is a chance we could break through their line, preferably its weakest part."

"How are we supposed to do that?"

"Well Trickster, it seems to me they are following us. We have control of their movements."

"I see," Loki regarded Thor with a sneer. "Simple god, indeed."

The two Æsir took flight again. This time Loki led them away from their desired destination, snaking through the twisted city. They ran in wide circles. When he was sure the Spawn were spread as thin as possible Loki rotated their direction a final time and headed for the chamber.

"Be ready, Thunderer. They will catch us in the courtyard ahead."

Thor did not hear him. The Thunder God was stirring his blood to frenzy. Loki had seen it before and it was a terrible sight to behold. In the berserk state, Thor was an animal. Whole armies had fallen to his wrath. Loki prayed it would be the same with the Star Spawn.

Six of the giants landed hard in front of them. Many more closed in on foot from every direction. They had only moments to break through or be overwhelmed.

Thor charged the six with bloody intent. He rolled between their thick legs, making it difficult for them to attack without striking a comrade. His speed and ferocity was too much for the monsters to match. Mjölnir struck knees and clawed feet, toppling the Spawn into one another.

Thor had cleared a path of bloody destruction for them to pass through. In moments, the Spawn lie wounded and confused, and the two Æsir continued on their way.

As he passed, Loki watched the Spawn's severed appendages suck into their bodies and new ones sprout. Long blade-like claws reached out and skewered Loki, and god's blood spattered the ground. The plan had been a good one; however Loki was too slow.

Mjölnir crushed the skull of the Spawn that had impaled the Trickster. Thor charged into the five remaining horrors, once again going for their legs. The Spawn desperately clawed at the Thunder God. Their attacks aided Thor as he worked his way between them; several Spawn grievously wounded their fellows trying to slay him. It wasn't long before Mjölnir had crushed all their skulls.

Loki tried to stand. Blood poured from his wounds. "You are a fool, Thunderer. I would not have come back for you, and now we will both die."

"I have no intention of dying. Be ready!"

"Ready for what?" demanded Loki.

"When I give the word, fly straight up as fast as you can. What I am about to do will kill you in your current state if you don't reach a safe distance."

The Spawn closed in, their faces twitching like masses of eels. The courtyard filled with the clacking of clawed feet. When they were but a step away, Thor gave the word. Loki didn't hesitate to achieve a safe altitude and it saved his life.

Thor reversed his grip on Mjölnir so that the hammer's head touched the bottom of his fist and then slammed it into the ground with all his godly might. The island trembled under the titanic blow and the stone of the courtyard peeled back like paper as Star Spawn and other ejecta were blasted into the sky.

There was a brief moment of silence as the area was cast in darkness by a cloud of pulverized rock. Then came the sickening impacts of Spawn as their remains rained down from the sky. It reminded Thor of an exploding cow he had once witnessed. A sickening wet noise echoed throughout the city.

When Thor walked into the chamber, Loki was already there. The Trickster god was in bad shape, blood still oozing from his wounds. Thor moved to help, tearing Loki's tunic off and ripping it into strips to bind his wound. Loki fell into unconsciousness.

Thor surveyed the chamber and was surprised to see that it was much larger on the inside. The interior was disjointed just like the city. Loadbearing supports were constructed in impossible positions. What caught his eye most was the odd sigil above the door through which he had entered: a distorted five-pointed star, an eye at its center, the monstrous pupil ablaze.

"It's called an Elder Sign," moaned Loki.

"Who put it there?" asked Thor.

"Very brave men of Midgard."

"This island has risen before in the time of Man? How could we not know of this?"

Loki struggled to sit up. "When the stars are right, R'lyeh rises for a brief time before sinking once again."

Loki doubled over in pain and began to cough. Dark syrup poured from his mouth. Falling on all fours, he began to tremble uncontrollably. The murky blood began to stream and pool on the black stone beneath him. Like a thing alive, the sanguine fluid flowed into a clotted mass.

The Trickster god transformed. His androgynous appearance became more masculine, his features more chiseled. Muscles grew larger and facial hair sprouted to the length of many weeks growth. When the blood stopped oozing from his mouth so too did his change in his appearance, and Loki fell onto his side, exhausted.

The clotted mass started to pulse, even as its form became distinct, that of a black heart.

Loki whispered, "You must eat it, Thunderer. I am too weak."

"Loki, what's happening to you?"

"It is the heart; I can no longer hold it. You must eat it before it is too late."

"How can you ask such a thing of me? I can sense its evil."

"Only a powerful god can contain it. Eat the Heart before she can manifest."

Thor considered Loki's words. "I won't eat it, but I have another idea."

He pointed Mjölnir at the beating heart. The power of the hammer manifested in the form of lightning and struck the black heart. The malevolent heart burst into flame but did not disintegrate. Thor willed more power into Mjölnir and the lightning turned blinding. The girth of its flow became as thick as Thor's arm. There was a sudden pop and a fine ash filled the chamber as the organ exploded.

"What is the meaning of this? What is going on?" Thor demanded. "More of your games no doubt."

Loki's breaths were shallow and ragged, though he remained conscious. Each time he tried to speak, he was struck by a fit of coughing. Finally he gave up on words and pointed past Thor. The Thunder god turned and to his surprise found something unexpected there.

It was a torrent of ash from the now destroyed heart. The swirling form was vaguely humanoid and grew more tangible by the moment. Before him coalesced a naked woman. She was beautiful by the standards of man or god. Long raven hair fell over her thin curvaceous frame. A tight cynical smile was all that detracted from her appearance. It was a grin that Thor would never forget.

"Kill her—now!" coughed Loki.

"How is it that the Witch Gullveig still lives? I saw her burned to ashes in Valhalla millennia past. Is this one of your tricks?" Thor's voice carried a deadly edge.

"I cannot be killed, Thunderer, merely contained for a time," said Gullveig. "Loki intended to use my power to awaken the Midgard serpent and unleash Ragnarök."

"Don't listen to her poison; hers is the power to manipulate the minds of gods," warned Loki, but it was too late.

Thor raised Mjölnir to strike Loki but the Trickster used his magic to carry himself across the chamber, narrowly avoiding the great hammer.

Gullveig gave Loki a wicked smile. "He is such a simple-minded god, so easy to control. Did you really think if he devoured my heart he could suppress my influence? Under my will Thor would have wrought devastation across Midgard."

Loki had no time to retort. Thor's furious blows were upon him and it was all he could do not to fall beneath them.

Thor swung again, "I should have smashed you long ago, Loki."

Loki dodged the attack. "Even your father could not kill me."

"You think yourself my father's equal?"

"Yes, it is why we became blood brothers," taunted Loki.

Thor flew into a rage at Loki's words; his blows wild and erratic. It was a necessary tactic; Loki needed time to recover his strength.

Now that Gullveig had emerged from his body, his full power was returning. Every moment that passed, Loki grew stronger as his body recovered from its wounds. More important was the recovery of his mind. Since the expulsion of the witch, his mind was his own. A voice of constant chaos no longer dictated his actions.

"You can't keep it up forever, Trickster. Thor will crush you and satisfaction will be mine."

"We shall see about that, Witch."

Loki dodged blow after blow. He did not dare counter-attack for fear Thor would strike him down. Instead, he led the Thunder God around the chamber, frantically avoiding his attacks.

"See what happens when you fight a real opponent Thor - you can't even touch me."

Thor flung Mjölnir at Loki and it struck his shoulder a glancing blow. Pain erupted throughout his body as the bones disintegrated. The hammer, continuing on its path, struck the Witch in the head, smashing it like an egg. The yoke of Gullveig's brain splashed the floor.

Loki's body slumped as a result of his injuries but he pushed on and staggered to Gullveig's decapitated body. Even without a head she was able to stand, blood frothing from her neck. Slowly the head reformed.

Flame erupted from Loki's good hand, and motes of fire trailed through the air as he plunged it into Gullveig's left breast. God's blood sizzled as it met fire. The fingers of the Trickster tunneled deep into the witch's chest cavity until he clutched her black heart.

"Thunderer, fight her influence!"

Thor's voice was distant. "I am hers no more. The spell is ended."

Gullveig's head reshaped fully. Her smile mocked Loki. "Such a thing we have done, you and I."

Loki's fiery hand flared and the witch glowed with an inner light. Ribs and lungs cast dark shadows through translucent skin. Smoke and tongues of flame flared from her mouth and licked the air. All the while she laughed.

"What are you talking about," asked Loki.

"You have touched the black walls of R'lyeh. You already know."

Loki's hand trembled even as he clutched her black heart. He let out an unhallowed scream of understanding. Gullveig turned to ash as bright flames engulfed her. A pulsing black heart, silhouetted in continuous fire, was all that remained. Loki dared not release it from his grasp.

"What did she mean?" asked Thor.

Loki's head sank almost as low as his fractured shoulder. "She was talking about the world serpent."

Thor shook his head, red locks slapping his chain mail. "The world serpent is myth, the creation of man."

"There is always a grain of truth in every myth. The world serpent is a metaphor for the release of a being as old as time; a thing serpentine in appearance, its darkness surrounding the world. He is awakening."

"So you have unleashed Ragnarök as foretold?"

"Yes, but not as prophesized; it's early."

"Don't play me for the fool. You speak as though you know the date of Ragnarök. Besides I haven't yet heard the Gjallarhorn."

"I know its true date. It was Odin who told me."

"My father's complicity in all this seems to grow each time you speak." Thor's voice once again filled with suspicion.

"It is not yet time to despair. That this is not the true time of Ragnarök means we can still alter the outcome of Gullveig's plans."

"Why should I trust you? Every time your tongue wiggles your story changes."

"Damn you to Helhiem. Open your eyes: it's me. The Loki you knew all those years past. Have you forgotten our adventures and the many times I saved you and the other gods from destruction?"

"How can I trust you? You just admitted your involvement in the release of the world serpent! I should just smash you now."

Loki in his frustration relented. "Okay then, smash me. I accept your judgment." Loki knelt and placed one hand on the ground and drew the flaming heart to his chest, unwilling to release it.

Thor looked down on his old friend turned enemy. "Get up Loki, I have not the authority to kill you in anything but combat. Father would be grievously disappointed."

"Then you trust me?"

Thor sneered. "Not even a little. However, if you are the old Loki I once knew then you must have a crazy plan to fix yet another of your mistakes. First, I want to know what it was exactly that you did to cause this."

"We don't have a lot of time."

"Then speak quickly. I want to understand how this happened. I need to know if I'm going to trust you."

Loki shrugged his injured shoulder, which was almost fully healed. "Your father and I are older than you can imagine."

"I am a god. I can imagine a lot."

"We don't have time to bicker, just shut up and listen. When the universe was young there existed many beings. By our reckoning they were incredibly evil and powerful. They have agendas beyond our understanding, and most of their actions appear madness to us. Maybe they are.

"There was a time when it came to pass that these beings went to sleep. Your father, Odin, and I did not understand why this happened, but we did not question our good fortune. We took our Kin and fled to the far corners of the universe with the hope that they would never find us.

"We discovered the nine worlds, our new home and created our own history. After millions of years, life spawned of its own accord and we ruled over it as its rightful gods. The Jötunn, elves, dwarfs, the Men of Midgard and more were all eventually born to this epoch. So too were many of the gods, like you.

"During this period Odin and I feared the eventual return of the Great Old Ones. We set out to learn if or when they would return. This is how your father lost his eye—but that is another story. Your father, through great trial, was able to discover the date of their return. It would be foreshadowed by an alignment of stars and the awakening of their herald on Midgard."

"I don't understand, are the stars not in alignment?"

"All but one, I moved the final star into position myself."

Thor's face showed disbelief. "You have such power?"

"As I said, I am a very old being."

"Why would you do such a thing?"

"It wasn't by choice: I was under the influence of Gullveig. Trust me when I say I regret it deeply, but it was my fate."

Thor began to understand. "That's why my father didn't put you to death for the murder of my brother, Balder."

"Yes, Odin understood that Gullveig had to be contained. Killing me would have released her."

"What is her role in this, why contain her at all?" asked Thor.

"You mean besides the fact she tried to kill all the gods? We did try to make peace with her. We asked her to enjoy this space of time between the rule of the Great Old Ones but she refused us. It was her desire to awaken them. We killed her twice, and both times she returned. The third time, I devoured her heart to contain her but she corrupted me."

Thor pondered Loki's words. "How do we stop their return? Is it even possible?

Loki let out a nervous laugh. "We can't stop them, Thunderer, only delay their return."

Thor lifted Mjölnir. "If I believe you and you're not lying, what are we to do?"

"We must split up. I have to move the star back to its rightful place and you must confront Cthulhu before he can awaken the other Great Old Ones."

The ground trembled at the mention of the Great Old Ones. The two gods looked at each other curiously.

"Didn't you say this being was beyond us; that we were insects compared to him?"

"Yes, but Cthulhu is the least of them—and he will be vulnerable when he first awakens. All you have to do is hold him off while I reorient the star. Once that happens, he will be forced to return to his slumber."

"Sounds like you're just trying to get me killed."

"You're right; you won't live without a little help." Loki placed a hand on Thor's shoulder. Energy, the stuff of gods, poured into Thor and he was overwhelmed.

Surprised by the incredible power of Loki, he pulled away. "How were you able to hide this power?"

"I never flaunted it in the old days, and after I absorbed Gullveig, the majority of my power was used to contain her."

The two gods exited the chamber together. When they stepped outside they met no resistance. Thor's crater was the only evidence of the conflict which took place in the courtyard. All the bodies were gone. Even the blood of the Star Spawn had been removed or consumed by the city.

"It is here that we part ways, Thunderer. Go to the heart of the city. There you will find the resting place of Cthulhu. You need not win; only hold him there as long as you can."

Thor clasped Loki's empty hand. "I never enter combat without the expectation of winning. I will defeat this thing."

Loki navigated the strange city with skill, the flaming heart of Gullveig casting shadows within shadows. The streets were empty; the denizens of this evil place were gone. No doubt they gathered in some dark place in readiness to welcome their malign god to this new day. He traveled beyond the city's edge and took to the air.

From a great height over the surface of the ocean he called out, "Heimdallr, send the Bifröst."

In response there was a sound unlike any Loki had ever heard. Its noise echoed across the nine worlds and its vibrations sent wrinkles through the universe. The Gjallarhorn had been sounded. Ragnarök had arrived.

The kaleidoscopic bridge sundered space and spilled through the night air. Heimdallr stepped through the dimensional breach, his sword in hand.

"What have you done, Loki!" yelled Heimdallr through golden teeth.

"Where is Thor Odinson?"

Lokie pointed toward the black city. "Thor lives. See for yourself."

With senses no other god possessed, Heimdallr peered into the twisted city of R'lyeh. There he perceived Thor and heard his words. The Thunder God chanted softly, Heimdallr trust Loki, over and over.

Loki presented the flaming heart of Gullveig, "Do you remember who this belongs to?"

Thor made his way to the center of the city. The middle of the dark metropolis was filled with its slimy inhabitants. They surrounded a titanic edifice of stone, a ziggurat, the tomb so enormous it could cover a mountain, the construction such that its Euclidean geometry added to the twisted city's profaneness.

The mass of creatures below slithered and undulated while chanting, "*Kathoooloo, Kathoooloo.*"

The drone repeated, as massive granite doors slid open in response. Stone scraped stone. Tremors rocked the city. Beyond the great halves was darkness, a starless night of evil, and Thor sensed oblivion within its veil.

Again the city trembled, as a thing of truly titanic proportions stepped forth from the blackness. Thor's consciousness elongated as it became disproportionate to its understanding of itself. His mind snapped in search of understanding that could not be had, not even for a god. As trying as it was, the touch of the black towers of R'lyeh paled by comparison to this experience. Madness took him.

Great Cthulhu stepped from his resting place, looked to the stars, and contemplated his premature awakening.

Bifröst traversed the vastness of space and carried its travelers to an unnamed star in the heavens. The fiery orb was blinding, such was their proximity.

"I knew the Bifröst could span more than the nine worlds," said Loki.

Heimdallr placed a hand on the hilt of his sword. "The Bifröst travels the whole of the universe, but that is not why we are here. Do what must be done, Trickster."

Gullveig's flaming heart still in hand, Loki leaped off the Bifröst and fell into the star. Intense heat consumed both him and the pulsing organ almost at once. However, Loki was himself of fire and so was not destroyed. He joined the complex reactions and conversion of elements and became the stuff of suns, liquid light.

Through fiery torrents and blazing rivers Loki traveled to the core of the star and felt its weight upon him. He expanded his godliness throughout every portion of the bright orb until it was his new form, his new body.

As he started the long process of moving the star, he couldn't help but laugh to himself. He had fooled everyone: the Jötunn, the Æsir, and the Great Old Ones. He had tricked omnipotence and gotten away with it and was about to do it again. Of all of them, only Odin knew the truth.

Odin was not the father of all, but he was the father of all that mattered, and Loki thought himself its uncle. The young gods had existed for tens of thousands of years, while Loki, Odin and Gullveig had existed for millions. The Great Old Ones were much older, their existence spanning lengths of time so vast they could only be measured in forgotten eons and dark epochs.

The power of the star was almost limitless; Loki understood how the alignment of stars could influence the great old ones. Still its power was not a simple thing to harness even for an old fire god like himself; it would take time. Thor would have to hold off Great Cthulhu until he had gathered enough energy to move the star.

Cthulhu stood above the buildings of R'lyeh, and his gigantic, bulbous form rippled as he stepped forward. Feelers as thick as ancient oak trees and as long as the Yggdrasil hung from his face, probing the air in front of him. Translucent eyes filled with black oil ignored Thor.

Thor's extremities trembled unconsciously. Somewhere deep inside, his consciousness unraveled and became separated from the rest of his being. Why Great Cthulhu was so large or powerful never occurred to Thor but it did enrage him. As the rage built, his consciousness somehow reorganized, and memory of his task came back to him.

With all his might, Thor flung Mjölnir. It struck Cthulhu's chest dead center and passed through his body. Thor heard a sucking sound as dark blood sprayed from Cthulhu's back where his hammer emerged. The wound closed immediately and the great old one moved on without taking notice of the Thunderer.

Thor let out a howl. "Damn you Loki! How do you stop something like that? I need to be much bigger, if I'm going to hurt this thing. "

Thor realized the answer. Using Loki's power he willed his form to change and grew to colossal proportions. He pushed for more size and when he thought he might burst he pushed for more, until he was half the size of Cthulhu. It would have to be enough.

Thor charged at Cthulhu's back and swung Mjölnir at his leg. A wet crack told Thor the leg was smashed and Cthulhu fell to the ground, its fall so great it created tremors that almost shook Thor from his feet. With the Great Old One vulnerable, Thor reversed his swing and smashed its ovoid head. Tentacles twitched spasmodically as colossal gouts of sticky black blood spurted from its crushed skull.

Like the Star Spawn, Cthulhu's leg sucked into his body, and a new one sprouted in its place. The head, too, was pulled in and a new one emerged. The great old one waved his clawed hand and an unseen force threw Thor into a twisted tower. The black building toppled under the impact.

Thor was shaken by the unexpected attack. He shrugged off the pain and climbed to his feet, ready to renew his assault. Cthulhu also stood, his attention now fixed on the God of Thunder.

"You noticed me that time, didn't you Old One."

Cthulhu's tentacles twitched in annoyance as he considered his opponent. The two converged and traded blows. Each time Mjölnir struck its target it did less damage. Thor, however, was not so lucky. Each blow Cthulhu landed cut deep into flesh, shredding his chainmail.

Thor had been in tough situations before, had nearly died more than once, but never had he found himself in such a hopeless one-sided battle. Now he understood Loki; the gods really were insects compared to such powerful alien intellects. If he was to die, it would be in glorious battle with the most powerful entity he had ever known. That at least gave him a measure of satisfaction.

Their battle raged and the island trembled. Such was the power of their steps that ocean water washed in from the coast. At times, enormous tidal waves spilled over parts of the city, washing its denizens out to sea. Still Thor fought on. The blows took their toll. Thor slowed.

Cthulhu raked at the young god. Whole sections of Thor's face were torn away, exposing white skull and cheek bone. The Thunderer's eye hung precariously from its socket, attached by the thinnest of strands. Rivulets of blood poured from the ghastly wounds.

Thor reached up and felt his damaged face. He realized the wound would have been fatal to any mortal of Midgard and many gods alike. *It's a good thing I'm not just any god.* As the Thunder God stood, he tore free his useless eye and threw it at Cthulhu in defiance.

Cthulhu caught the bloody orb between clawed fingers, flaccid nerve bundles draped lifeless over his digits. The tentacles of Cthulhu's face parted to reveal a toothy cavity and he devoured Thor's eye.

Rage filled the God of Thunder and he charged headlong into death. Thor swung Mjölnir with everything he had left. Cthulhu caught the head of the hammer in his left hand and took Thor by the neck with his right. Struggle as he might, Thor could not move and watched in horror as the tentacles parted again and a toothy maw descended upon his head. The tooth-filled aperture affixed to his scalp and bit into skull bone. Tentacles flowed over him and tunneled into flesh, penetrating skin, muscle, and sinew.

Thor roared in pain as Cthulhu ate him alive. He heard Mjölnir crack and pop under Cthulhu's grip; his beloved hammer was crushed to rock and dust. With a final effort Thor kicked the monster and pulled free. Hair and scalp were torn from his head; it was the price of his escape.

Again Thor took inventory of his injuries. His body had been perforated in dozens of places by tentacles. All that remained of his scalp could be seen protruding between the mass of undulating tentacles of Cthulhu's face. His head was now the white of exposed bone. Finally his weapon, the very symbol of his godhood, had been reduced to a nub.

He would die. Thor understood this now. Loki had been right, there was no defeating a power of this magnitude; one could only hope to delay him. Thor had delayed him and hoped it was enough.

A wet slurping sound drew Thor's good eye to Mighty Cthulhu and he watched as his red locks were devoured just like his eye before it. When he was done, Cthulhu raised one of his massive clawed hands and the power of the Great Old One tore a rift in the fabric of the Universe. Living blackness devoured reality, and anything it touched was pulled in and torn from existence. A black tendril of organic lightning struck out at Thor's left arm. It was ripped from his body and sucked into the dimensional aperture, gone forever.

Thor collapsed; his divine being could stand no more. Even infused with the power of Loki, he could not go on. Lying on the ground, he drew comfort from the remains of Mjölnir still in his hand. Despite all that had happened, he had been able to hold on to his beloved hammer. He thought it fitting that they die together. Thor had fought well, had done what he set out do. No one could ask more of him. He closed his one good eye and let oblivion take him.

Get up, Thunderer! You are not done yet, came a voice in Thor's mind.

Thor called back to the voice, *Loki? Is that you?*

You yet live, Thunderer. You, the strongest of the gods, the most resilient and pigheaded of the gods, cannot die. Not yet.

Trickster, I am finished. As foretold the World Serpent has vanquished me.

I need more time. You must fight. Now get up!

My eye and one of my arms is gone. Mjölnir has been destroyed. I have nothing left to fight with.

The power of this star is now mine. I will assist you.

Thor felt a flood of energy fill him. His wounds started to close and his desire for battle returned. He opened his good eye and with his one arm pushed himself to his feet. Cthulhu's face fluttered, twitched at the sight.

Loki's power, the energy of a star continued to fill him and Thor felt life return to Mjölnir.

Use it, Thor Odinson, we will do it together.

Thor rose into the sky and called to the lightning. Bolt after bolt struck Mjölnir. In response, Cthulhu spouted massive wings. Great veined sheets of leathery flesh stretched between bone carried him aloft in pursuit of the thunder god.

In just moments, the lightning turned into continuous streams of azure energy that arched to the weapon of Thor. Hundreds of bolts pouring power into Mjölnir. The sky was a web of pulsing power.

Now Thor, hit him NOW!

Thor pointed Mjölnir at his target. All that remained of the most powerful weapon in the nine worlds was a stone nub; but its damaged form did not inhibit its power. Blue lightning infused with the power of a star struck Cthulhu.

For endless moments Thor channeled all the power he could muster into Cthulhu and the flesh beneath the monster's skin began to liquefy and boil. His body expanded twofold, and a sound like thunder erupted forth. The bloated form exploded and scalding fluid, the boiling liquid flesh of Cthulhu, rained down upon R'lyeh.

Thor fell to earth unconscious, once again in death's grip. Loki's ethereal hand reached out and slowed Thor's decent and gently laid him on the streets of R'lyeh.

I will heal you, Thunderer. Then I must focus all my efforts on moving this star. When I am finished, I will return for you.

Loki drifted in the deep void, alone. He had shifted the position of a star for the second time in as many days and he was exhausted. In his left hand he could feel the pulsing of Gullveig's heart. He was afraid that might happen, that she might survive the heat of the star. She had made it out of the star the first time, so he knew it was a possibility.

Despite calling for the Bifröst, Heimdallr had not come for him. Loki was not surprised; he and Heimdallr were mortal enemies. In time Loki would find his way back to the nine worlds but that would take too long. It was time Thor didn't have. Now that the stars were back in place, R'lyeh would sink once again and Thor would be lost.

He called out one last time, "Heimdallr, bring the Bifröst. We must retrieve Thor Odinson."

Bifröst appeared under Loki, supporting his form. Loki stood and before him was Heimdallr. His form was bloody, his face the picture of madness.

"Asgard has fallen. Odin and many of the gods are dead."

Loki climbed to his feet, Gullveig's flaming heart in hand. "I'm sorry. I will miss them as much as you."

"You did this, caused this to happen! Was it worth it, Trickster?"

"This event was set into motion long before you were born, Heimdallr. We won, that's all that matters. We stopped Ragnarök and Thor yet lives."

"Don't you mean delayed Ragnarök? Why don't we just move the stars so the Great Old Ones never wake up?"

Loki shook his head. "We can't just play with the stars; the consequences are incalculable. They control the fate of all beings and moving them would likely wake the Great Old Ones. This is how it must be."

Heimdallr clenched his golden teeth. "Then we just wait for the inevitable? We all have to die at the hands of these Elder Beings?"

"We exist in a space of time between two epochs of universal Armageddon. One that came before us and one that will come after. We just pushed the one that comes after us off a few hundred million years. It's all we get so make the best of it." Loki's tone was harsh and cut into Heimdallr.

Heimdallr drew his sword. It was crusted with the blood of recent battles. "Why should I believe you? How do I know you didn't plan all this!"

"Odin planned it, fool. I don't have time to explain it all to you. We must save Thor before we run out of time."

Heimdallr rushed forward and plunged his sword into Loki's chest, knocking him prone and pinning him to the Bifröst. "The way I see it, if you're telling me the truth, there's no longer a use for you, and if you're lying to me then you deserve this death. Either way you should die for all the pain you have caused."

Loki felt his life force waning. He was going to die and there was no stopping it. All the fighting and effort of moving a star twice in two days had left him weak and vulnerable. "I forgive you, Heimdallr. My death at your hands was foretold by Odin a long time ago. You are playing your role just as I did. There is no shame in that."

Bending down toward Loki's face Heimdallr grimaced in denial. "If you knew this would happen, why did you call for me, why not run?"

"Because I had to try and save Thor. Odin foretold that he could be saved. For my blood brother's sake I had to try."

Heimdallr stood and started walking down the Bifröst. "I will save him. There is still time."

"No, Heimdallr, you have another charge." Loki tossed Gullveig's heart to him. "Eat it. If you don't, Gullveig will return and unravel everything we have accomplished this day."

R'lyeh shuddered as it slowly sank. The sounds of distant waves grew ever closer to Thor's unconscious form but he did not wake. In the sky above him a form coalesced. Features, arms, legs and head quickly became obvious. When the being was fully amalgamated and tangible, the sight of it would have driven even a god to madness.

It tilted its head and regarded Thor, tentacles fluttering. Great Cthulhu had returned. He looked to the sky and saw that the stars were in their rightful place. It was time for him to slumber once again. He bent over, lifted Thor, and clutched the fallen god to his chest. Cthulhu walked back to his resting place, the Thunderer's limp body like a doll held against its owner's breast.

The two entered the temple of Great Cthulhu, where they would slumber for an age. Cthulhu's purposes for Thor were unfathomable. Thor, if he emerged at all, would not do so with his mind intact.

The enormous doors slowly closed and the island trembled. They slammed shut with the sound of dead thunder and R'lyeh vanished beneath the waves.

The mind of D.B. Poirier is skewed, slightly, from the foundation of reality. He spends most of his time daydreaming about worlds and place most people are unaware of. A problem he intends to rectify through his writing. www.dbpoirier.com.

ENCROACHMENT
Craig D.B. Patton

KEVIN'S SON RAN INTO THE GARAGE.

"Dad, one of the chickens is dead! Come quick!" He looked sick with the news.

"Ok, Patrick. Show me."

He followed the boy around the house, past the rabbit hutch, past the gardens, and out to the small pond tucked in the furthest corner of the property. A white, six-gallon bucket and a butterfly net lay abandoned on the grass by the shore.

"I was trying to catch that big frog and I saw it swim over to the other side and I went around and that's when I found-"

"I see it Patrick. It's ok."

The chicken had been reduced to a jumbled heap of bloody bones with bits of meat and a few white feathers stuck to them. The legs extended at impossible angles from opposite sides, like two forks jammed handle first into the remains.

They stood over it.

"Dad...what did this?"

Kevin shook his head. "Don't know. Maybe a fox."

There were hundreds of acres of open land behind their property. The chance to live in closer proximity to nature was one of the main reasons they had moved to this rural suburb. But they were still learning about their non-human neighbors.

The boy edged closer to him. He was seven. Still young enough to want the comfort, but old enough to start feeling the pressure not to show it.

"It's ok, buddy," Kevin said, patting him on the back. "Just a fox. But we need to tell Mom. You go do that while I clean this up, ok?"

"Ok." The boy hurried away.

Kevin went and got a spade. He scooped up the remains of the chicken and carried it through a break in the green curtain of tangled undergrowth and young trees. When he thought he had gone far enough, he dumped the corpse.

The fox, or whatever, could have it.

Kristine met him on the back door landing. She was not happy.

"What are we supposed to do?"

He shrugged. "Keep them closer to the house, I guess. I mean, it was right by the woods. Easy pickins."

"But I'd rather they were over there. Less chicken poop to step in."

"We could get a dog."

"I think we've got all the animals we can handle right now."

"Hey, you kept saying how much you wanted to get back to nature."

She glared at him. "I just want nature to stay away from our chickens, that's all."

"Well, then we need to keep them closer to the house for awhile. Wait until the fox moves on."

"Think so?"

"I don't know, honey. It's worth trying."

But, two days later, Kristine found another dead chicken while watering the gardens before dinner.

"Ok," she said, erupting into the kitchen, where Kevin was washing kale. "There's a chicken head by the tomatoes."

He shut the water off. "What?"

"A chicken head."

"Just the head?"

She looked agitated. "Yes. Will you please come and get rid of it."

Kevin nodded. Kristine had few weaknesses, but dealing with icky stuff (Patrick's term) was always his job.

He went out. A few feet from the tomato vines he found the head. Kevin frowned. One side of the skull was laid bare, the eye missing. The neck ended in a jagged tear almost before it began. Thready bits of meat hung from it.

He felt a little sick, looking at it.

Kevin went and got the spade again. He carried the head out to the pond and catapulted it into the woods, listening to it crack off of leaves and branches before thumping to the ground.

"Let's keep them in the shed unless we're outside with them," he said to Kristine after he returned.

"But it's going to stink in there if we do that."

"You want to keep finding dead chickens?"

She frowned but shook her head.

The neighbors were sympathetic at the bus stop the next morning.

"That's frustrating," one said.

"Sure is."

"What are you going to do?" another asked.

"Don't know."

It was more than they usually said to him. Every other family in the development had been living there for decades. Most of the other parents at the bus stop had grown up going to school with each other. They were a close knit group and Kevin wondered whether his family would ever be accepted into the herd.

"It's like we've moved in on their territory," he had once said to Kristine.

She had nodded, scowling. "Maybe it just takes time."

"We've been here for over a year."

"Yeah, well, they've been here for thirty."

At least Patrick was happy. He had made new friends. He loved riding his bicycle without having to worry about trucks or stoplights. Loved climbing trees and finding all the constellations they couldn't even see in the city. Loved caring for the animals, especially Posey, his Himalayan rabbit.

Which was why imagining Patrick's reaction was the worst part of finding the hutch torn open early the next morning.

Kevin looked inside, examined the bent wires and snapped wooden braces. Posey was nowhere in sight. But the smeared blood and bits of white and black fur everywhere left no doubt about what had happened.

"Shit."

Something moved in the corner of his vision. He looked up.

A golden retriever stood on the lawn near the pond. He recognized the dog. It did not belong to any of his immediate neighbors. He did not know who it belonged to. But he had often seen it running through adjacent yards, dancing around the children, chasing or being chased by the dogs that lived there, or just...wandering. It was too thin and wore a fairly stupid expression on its' face that made him wonder if it was mistreated.

But, in that moment, Kevin did not care. Here was the culprit.

He started toward it. "Get out of here!" he hollered, waving his arms.

"Go!"

The dog curled its' tail between its' legs, scampered a few feet away from him and stopped. It looked at him.

"Go on! Go home!" Kevin shouted. He ran a couple of steps toward it.

The dog fled, its' body a tight, submissive curl as it scampered toward the road.

Kevin watched it flee until it was out of sight. He turned and walked toward the pond, to where the dog had been.

Sure enough, what was left of Posey lay in the blood stained grass. Nothing much. A few ribs. One foot.

Muttering, Kevin retrieved the spade and carried Posey's pathetic remains out to the woods. Thanks to the damn dog, it was becoming an impromptu animal graveyard.

After he had done his best to console Patrick, Kevin called the animal control center to file a complaint. They knew the dog. It had a history of complaints. He asked for the address of the owner but they refused to give it to him, assuring him that they would follow up on the matter.

That wasn't good enough.

It was a Saturday. So, after Kevin hosed off the hutch and the lawn, he asked around and found out who owned the dog. Its' name was Skip. The family's name was Carlson. They lived a few streets away, on the opposite side of the neighborhood.

He drove over to have a word with them. He had expected the owner to be some cigar-chomping, wife-beater-wearing ape the size of a refrigerator with stubble atop his head and tattoos in at least three places. Instead, Norm Carlson was a slip of a man with glasses perched precariously on the bridge of his nose.

"Yes?" he said, pushing the glasses further up.

Kevin introduced myself. "Is Skip your dog?"

"Yes." Norm looked anxious.

Kevin told him about the chickens. And Posey. And that Norm should keep his damn dog in his own damn yard. And how, if he had any decency, he should pay for the losses.

Norm blinked at him and pushed the glasses up again. "I'm very sorry about your animals, especially your son's rabbit. Skip does get away a lot. We got him at a shelter. His old owner used to beat him and I think maybe he got pretty good at escaping."

"Look. I don't really care. I've got a son crying at home because his rabbit was killed."

"But how do you know Skip did it?"

Kevin's voice grew shrill. "Because he was standing right over the damn body, that's how. You need to do a better job of controlling him or something'll have to be done."

Norm pushed the ridiculous glasses back up his nose one more time. His expression became frosty. "I'm sure it won't come to that."

"I hope so. Have a nice day." He turned and left.

Kevin went home and mowed the lawn, hoping he removed anything that was not grass along with the clippings. He watched for Skip until it grew too dark to see. The dog did not appear.

Until the next morning.

Kevin woke groggy after a restless night. The light was dim, the house silent. As he shuffled across the floorboards toward the bathroom, he realized that it was actually too quiet. Usually, he heard birds chirping in the branches of the red oak outside the bedroom window. But there was no chirping. There were no sounds at all. It was as though the world was holding its' breath.

He suddenly felt fully awake and alert. He peered out the bedroom windows, which gave him a view of one side yard and the entire expanse of the front yard.

Nothing.

Kristine rolled over in bed, making the mattress creak. Kevin glanced back, startled by the unexpected sound.

"Wha'izzit?" she asked, still half-asleep.

"I'm not sure."

She sat up, disheveled hair spilling around the worried expression on her face. "What do you mean?"

Kevin shook his head. "I don't know. But something's not right."

He went into Patrick's bedroom, being careful not to wake him, and pushed aside the window curtain to look out at the other side yard. Again, nothing.

That left only the backyard. There were no windows on the second story of their saltbox house that looked out that way. Kevin started down the stairs.

"Where are you going?" Kristine asked in a hushed voice as he reached the bottom.

He looked back at her, standing in her robe at the top of the stairs. There was no name he could give to his fear, no easily conveyed, rational explanation for the knot twisting in his gut. "Just checking."

Pushing aside the living room curtain, he looked out at the backyard and exhaled sharply in anger.

There was another body lying on the lawn near the gardens. Even in the gray, pre-dawn light, he could tell it was larger than the other corpses.

Kevin pulled on his overcoat, slipped on his boots, and stepped out onto the landing.

Everything was still. He stood there for almost a full minute, listening while he watched for any movement, for any sign of that damned Skip.

A jay shattered the silence with its' shrill cry. It sailed into view, bobbed across the yard, and disappeared into the forest. A crow cawed, as if in answer. More chirps and cries joined in.

The strange silence had ended.

Feeling reassured, he walked down the steps and started across the yard. Half way to the body, he realized what it was. His mouth dropped open in a silent expression of surprise and revulsion.

It was Skip. Or, at least, what was left of him.

The dog lay in a contorted heap. His head was tipped backward, eyes open and bulging. His throat was a bloody hole. Deep gouges marked his chest and gut, crimson-stained bones and organs visible within. His right, front leg ended half-way down in a gore-caked shard of bone.

Kevin threw up on the lawn.

What had done this? What *would* do this? And, he wondered, as the dread twisted back to life and burrowed deeper within him, was it still here?

Kevin wiped his mouth with his sleeve and warily stood up. For the first time, and too late for Skip, it occurred to him that something other than a dog might be responsible for everything. The forested ridge behind their property was home to all sorts of animals: coyotes, bobcats.... He glanced down at the deep slashes on Skip, at the gaping throat. Something big.

A black bear.

He knew what to do. "Hello, out there," he called. The sound rang through the morning quiet.

Black bears, he and Kristine had explained to Patrick dozens of times, only attack if they feel surprised or threatened. Or, if you get between a mother and her cubs. Otherwise, they startle easily and want to avoid people. You let it know you are there, and then you walk to the closest building and get indoors.

Kevin walked toward the house, watching for the bear. He saw none, which meant nothing, he reminded himself as he climbed the steps. It might have already left after depositing the latest gift on his lawn.

The thought reverberated with frightening implications. He hurried inside and shut the door.

Whatever was doing this was displaying intent. It kept coming back to his yard. His family.

He told Kristine to keep Patrick inside and called the police.

Things became more complicated when the police informed Norm Carlson about his dog's death. Norm described his conversation with Kevin the day before and, for an uncomfortable hour, the investigation centered on Kevin. But, then the animal control officer arrived to examine the body and told the police what Kevin already knew. Skip had been mauled to death by a large animal.

The neighbors were alerted. Information was distributed reminding everyone (again) how to discourage a nuisance bear: mount your bird feeders high, keep garbage cans locked up or inside a shed or garage, etc.

But Kevin no longer believed it was a bear.

"So, if it's not a bear, what do you think is doing this?" Kristine asked that night after they had tucked Patrick in bed with several rounds of reassurances and extra stuffed animals to snuggle.

Kevin shook his head. "I don't know. It's just a hunch."

"Maybe a cougar?"

He had considered it. Cats did leave dead animals lying around. And there were rumors that cougars lurked in the woods. But they were just rumors. Kevin had researched it online enough to convince himself of that already. "No. There's no proof that cougars live anywhere near here."

They looked out into the shadow-draped backyard, at the silhouetted trees lining the ridge beyond like black teeth against the starry sky.

"I don't like this," Kristine said.

"I don't like it either."

"Why's it keep coming here?"

He shrugged. "Maybe it goes other places, too. But we're the last house on this street."

She smirked. "Easy pickins."

"Something like that, yeah."

"Well, I guess we just wait until someone actually sees it."

He finished the last of his beer and set the glass down. "And then what?"

Her brow furrowed. "Call the animal control center. They'll come take it away. Then it's over."

"Great plan," Kevin said, scowling. "Except that it keeps coming in the middle of the night."

A trace of frightened irritation flickered across her expression. "Well, someone's got to see it sooner or later. We just have to wait."

Kevin hated waiting. But Kristine was right: someone had to spot it and call it in.

After they had gone to bed and Kristine was asleep, Kevin slipped out. He picked up the sweatshirt and track pants he had left folded atop the bureau and crept downstairs.

He had not told Kristine what he planned for one simple reason. She would tell him he was crazy and insist he stay in bed. And then they would wake up and find something else on their lawn. As he brewed some coffee and steeled himself for his lonely vigil, he imagined what that something could be.

Maybe a coyote. Maybe a bear, just to up the ante. Or one of the neighbors, starting their day with a fatal, pre-dawn jog. Or a tender, young high schooler on their way to the bus stop. Or...

He considered patrolling the first floor, checking out each window. But their nightly visitor always left its' calling card in the backyard. It probably came out of the forest back there. So he parted a slit in the living room curtain and sat facing it in the antique rocking chair like a hunter in a blind.

The night was clear. A waning, three-quarter moon bathed everything in pale, dim light. Crickets chirped. Their poor, confused rooster crowed inside the shed to announce it was dawn somewhere in the world. His coffee grew cold.

He refilled his mug and tried to read a novel using the travel lamp he had bought Kristine for Christmas. After he had read the same paragraph three times and still did not know what it said, he gave up and pulled out a massive coffee table book instead. It contained aerial photos taken all over the Earth. Each spread consisted of a single, enormous picture. Expanses of rice fields in Vietnam. Teeming shanties outside Rio. A packed stadium at a football match in London.

The book was an attempt at a portrait of the planet and its' inhabitants at the end of the twentieth century. An impossible project, of course, but it was impressive in scope and beautiful to look at. He remembered visiting the gallery where they had first viewed the photos and bought the book.

Kevin turned a page and stopped. It was a photo taken in the Serengeti. A lion was in midair, hanging off of the back of a gazelle that was separated from the herd. The lion's muscles were rippled bulges. Its' front claws were buried in the flanks of the gazelle, which had buckled under the impact. The lion's jaws were wide, baring the massive spikes of teeth for the killing stroke.

He wondered what Skip had seen the moment before his death.

Perhaps he had seen nothing at all, had no warning before the violent end. Kevin looked at the expression of stark terror on the gazelle's face. The glassy eye rolled back, the strain along the jaw line. He hoped Skip had died quickly and with little pain.

He flipped through the pages for some time, occasionally glancing up at the window. When he finished the book, he went to replace it in the bookcase. He had just slid it back when he heard a soft thump outside.

His senses sharpened. He saw his wife and son smiling from a portrait hung deep in the shadows across the room. He heard the primal drumming of his heart, the whoosh and hiss of his breathing. Then he noticed that the crickets had stopped chirping. The rooster was silent.

From where he stood, he could not see out through the gap in the curtain. He started toward it and then froze as the floorboards groaned and popped beneath him. In the absolute quiet that had fallen over the world, it was impossibly loud.

He winced at the sound. But he had to move, had to look, before it was gone.

Kevin slid his slippers across the hardwood, trading the creak for a softer, scratchy shuffle, until he stood a foot from the gap in the curtain.

Leaning closer, he peered out into the moonbeam painted yard.

He saw nothing. The night lay empty and silent, waiting.

A snuffling sound broke the quiet. Kevin jerked away from the window with a startled, strangled cry. It had come from the back door, not ten feet from where he stood.

He stared at the door.

The snuffling started again. A loud, snorting series of inhales.

"God," Kevin murmured. The word trembled as it left his lips. He stepped back toward the window. His hand shook as he reached out to grasp the edge of the curtain closer to the door and eased it back. An inch. Several inches.

He saw the shadowy outline of a massive form. It stood with its front legs on the landing and its hindquarters on the lawn, a full six-feet away. The hide was a coarse jumble. Thick tangles and twists that might be fur but seemed too irregular in pattern, too substantial in appearance. It reminded him of the snarled undergrowth of the forest. The choked stands of vines and shrubs and weeds. Camouflage, he realized.

He gaped at it, trying and failing to understand what he was looking at.

The snuffling stopped.

Outside, the thing moved. It stepped back. A great, wedge-shaped head lifted and turned to face him. The eyes, like pale-yellow globes, narrowed into slits, looking at him from amid the bramble patch of its' face. A widening sickle of jagged teeth shone dully below them. On the lawn, a serpent of a tail twitched. And Kevin knew.

It saw him.

He had only the single moment that it took for the thing to gather itself. He spun away from the window.

"Kristine!" Kevin screamed. Screamed at the top of his lungs as the glass shattered and the thing came through, all claws and teeth and hot breath. Screamed with the terror of the prey as the lion digs in.

Craig D.B. Patton writes in a 200-year old manse in Connecticut. His tales are in Anthology: Year Two - Inner Demons Out, Supernatural Tales, Illumen, and other markets. Learn more at flawedcreations.wordpress.com. Follow him on Twitter at @ craigdbpatton.

DOLLY, DO I HAVE A SOUL?

Philip C. Perron

OH GOD, I THOUGHT IRONICALLY, SINCE the folks that I was groaning about were the ones that would say otherwise about me — about my kind. Which leads to me. I had all the physical and behavioral health measures that a fourth generation descendent of a genetically modified person would have. And therefore I also had the negative connotation that came with it following me like a dog that was in heat.

Do you want to speak of appearance? Honestly, I held my own against any naturally birthed supermodel that walked the runways of old world Paris or the more prominent fashion shows now in Beijing and Shanghai. I turned heads wherever I went whether it was because of my figure, my high cheek bones, my jet black waist length hair, or my oval shaped brown eyes. I wasn't famous, mostly due to a self imposed separation from any notoriety, yet those many Friday or Saturday nights at the waterfront martini bars in Boston, I would attract the businessmen, the wealthy, and even the attention of Channel 8's head newscaster before he got the hint that I had no interest. After a few inane attempts, he went off to the next Ivy League alum that happened to be wearing a skirt too short and drinking a drink too big.

And speaking of Ivy League institutions, that brings me to intelligence. Some would say having a photographic memory is more God's punishment than His blessing. An old professor of mine from Brown University even told me once that such a thing wasn't the definition of brilliance at all but just a peculiar exceptional attribute that allowed otherwise normal folk to ascend to the apex of their respective fields. Yet no matter, I carried with me like the virtual tablet that I brought to work everyday, an IQ that read 164 which even then took into account the implicit mathematical downward adjustment that was applied to my score due to inheriting the gene manipulation my ancestors had received one hundred years prior.

But that wasn't what made me feel the outcast that I apparently was to many. It was much more than that. It was that very first hereditary manipulation impasse that was fought over many a night in the political halls and backroom offices of places like Washington, D.C. And all of it, all that wasted energy and empty cans of Red Bull that piled out in the marbled halls in front of oak doors, was ultimately a hoax. It was all inevitable. Scientific think tanks in faraway lands like Switzerland and China were protected by their own foreign administrations. No American jurisdiction could stop them.

Instead the births of Greta Hugentobler and Mei-li Wang changed the world one hundred and five years ago. I liked to refer to them as simply... well... *people*. But what started with Dolly, a cloned sheep in Scotland named after a famous Tennessee singer also known for her very ample breasts, resulted in the first two cloned human beings. No matter what the Chinese said, it was generally regarded that Greta, the Swiss-German, was "born" days earlier.

What ultimately was an extraordinary achievement in science would also be the commencement of the clash between comprehension and information with those so very different concepts of scientific ethics and theocratic principles. Some of the very same adversaries on such topics as immigration, space exploration, environmentalism, and various military interventions, were now incongruously eating at the same table so to speak.

Progressive intellectuals suddenly were standing non-figuratively with religious fundamentalists of all faiths in marches down Pennsylvania Avenue and United Nations Plaza protesting science in general, but also international irresponsibility to be more specific. Suddenly geopolitical foes like Iran were actually voting along with conservative American *neocon* administrations. The more fervent of the religious thought it was the end of days. Even Mei-li Wang was murdered at the age of twenty-three on the streets of Hong Kong by some crazed *Bible thumper* as being a spawn of Satan and an example of man's heathen ways. And so that was how the world ultimately transformed to what it is today.

When the clone came into being and was designated a common medical practice in nations other than my own, life as humanity had known it since the days of Adam and Eve was never to be the same. Cloning within a year's time rocked the world. A Swiss-German geneticist and a Chinese businessman begrudgingly shared a Nobel prize in medicine together to the outrage of many. For fifty years the practice went hand in hand with other genetic science such as chromosome manipulation and attempts at altering aging.

And then a young Egyptian newswoman named Sofia Chalthoum went off to find the disputed first clone. Greta Hugentobler, who married a Lithuanian businessman and became Greta Landsbergis, disappeared after a very bitter and pubic divorce from the self promoter and eccentric that her husband had been. And as time passed, she slowly became no more unique than any other cloned person other than being the first. Her very unwanted fame dimmed until her name became nothing more than an annotation in a textbook.

Sofia, though, was one of the best in her field. Her journey brought her to Lithuania, then to St. Kitts, and finally to Boise, Idaho, where an inauspicious grave marked the final resting place of one Greta Landsbergis, a naturalized citizen who's American dream had turned into alcoholism and mental health issues. Depression had overtaken the woman and everything from harassment equally from nihilists and the falsely pious drove her to drink. She was found at the age of fifty-three by the side of some railroad tracks with a tequila bottle in hand and an intravenous needle in pocket. Frozen from exposure. Gone to meet her God. And yet since her heart had stop beating, the death certificate instead read heart failure. Oddly very apropos.

So someone who probably should have been a rallying point of bravery and determination for someone like me, a clone, instead became the beacon of the now not outlandish union of progressives, conservatives, theocrats, and anarchists who rose Greta Landsbergis to figurehead of the *anti-cloning movement*. Therefore Sofia's drive to write the next nonfiction bestseller or create the next significant documentary instead drove a stake into genetics and their researchers who played God. Cloning essentially became that crazy uncle everyone was embarrassed about. What was once a fundamentally conventional practice became back alley science overnight.

But that didn't stop some. The eccentric rich and the progressively scientific hand in hand with the seedy remnants of the Jewish, Irish, and Italian-American crime rings continued illegally cloning without the government's blessing. So while people continued to procreate ending with male orgasm, elsewhere a clone would be "birthed" in a petri dish in some warehouse on the docks of Narragansett Bay or an old farm building rendered into a laboratory not too far from downtown Des Moines. It was thought that one in every 10,000 Americans born was actually a clone. In countries where the process had at least once been the commonplace, it was said that one in every 500 was more apt.

I happened to be lumped in with the folks that were quantified as one in every 10,000 Americans. That itself made me someone that the now peculiar group of associates who called themselves the progressive moralists, the religious righteous, the avant-garde virtuous, and the traditional *valuates* wanted to ferret out.

The fury over genetic manipulation in hopes of specific qualities like blonde hair or tanned skin was in some quarters frowned upon, but the clone ... oh the clone was something else all together. To begin with, the liberal and conservative thought the process was itself a moral outrage of science gone amuck. And with such a belief system also comes the intransigent characteristic of being a reactionary. As a result, that meant a person that happened to be a clone, who through no act of their own no matter how they felt, was themselves a moral outrage.

Though violence in all forms is unacceptable, depending on the judiciary and the part of the country that a crime against a clone occurred, justice was not impartial. Just last week someone that was outed as a clone was murdered in New York City, that anomalous mixed beacon of wealth and progressiveness, where the crime seemed to become a cold case in only three days. So that was the world I lived in today. Hiding as a clone, not from the government but from fanatics.

My originator, the person that I was cloned from, was no longer with us, having passed away years ago. I had been birthed as a "daughter" to her — a "delayed clone." One would probably be best to have called my mother a wealthy un-conventionalist. So with her no longer being with us, God bless her soul, there was no other "me" in a sense that was roaming the world.

So not being born the traditional route and having benefitted from an ancestor's genetic manipulation, I had always felt as if I was scrutinized. I was too perfect, too brilliant, too beautiful. And when someone appeared as if they had engineered DNA, it was the opinion they were more apt to have been a clone or a descendent of a clone. And that wasn't all that far from the truth as I knew personally.

So today was supposed to be just another ordinary Sunday, a day of rest for me and whoever else felt so inclined. My goal was an afternoon in the center of town to enjoy whatever delights would come my way. Thus when I pulled up in my car, I was surely disappointed.

Oh God, I thought as I got out of my vehicle. Over by the far side of the town green were a group of the anti-geneticist, one waving a placard, another passing out pamphlets. It was a mixed bunch. Nothing that I hadn't seen prior. Though a few were dressed in the common garb of the beatnik, the others were in customary summer wear. I strolled slowly around the edge of the green by the road before seating myself inauspiciously on one of the empty park benches that shown the sun invitingly.

As I began reading the half finished novel on my virtual tablet, a young group of teenage coed joggers were out enjoying the late morning, not much unlike myself. When the trailing girl tripped and fell hard, I should have felt a distressing omen over the proceedings. Her companions stopped to help her up. One boy brushed her off a little bit too familiar. I smirked knowing that the two would be somewhere somehow sneaking off a quick romantic interlude at one of their parents' homes later in the day.

As if on queue, two of the activists hurried over jostling their leaflets even as the girl was trying to regain her equanimity. I rolled my eyes gallingly and quickly gave my tablet's screen a tap as if the next virtual page would take me away from my displeasure. But in a moment, the auburn haired activist's eyes met mine before I could fix my eyes upon my tablet. And soon enough, I could hear him discussing something with his cohort that I could only wish was nothing to do with me.

Oh God, I thought once more as their attention ceased with the young joggers and were now focused upon me. All I could hope for was that they were no different than the handful of men who daily offered me a cup of coffee or queried me for my phone number. But knowing who they were — that they were anti-geneticist, or more apt, that they were anti-cloning — my appearance was no doubt a beacon for genetic manipulation. And that trail, alas, led to the matter of their discontent.

As I read about the romantic rendezvous of the two lead characters in the novel I was enjoying, a shadow of two figures crawled across my legs, over my skirt, and enclosed around me like a cave. When I looked up, their first appearance was simply that of dark silhouettes haloed by an injection of sun flares blinding my vision. But when one thrust a pamphlet in my line of site that read *Cloning: Humanity's Catastrophe*, oh, I knew I wasn't in for polite flirting and a quick brush off.

"Hi," a gravelly voice spoke. "We are giving out some literature about the risks of cloning and how it has endangered humanity's very existence." My eyes adjusted against the sting of the early sun. Soon I was able to focus, noticing that the auburn haired man was actually with a woman who styled her hair in a curiously fashioned reverse bob. I gave each a short smile and took the little booklet that the woman held attentively in front of me.

"There's a vote coming up next week," she said. "And we need your support with a vote of Yes on question seven. Can we count on you?"

Though worldly as I was, I couldn't even gather what election she was referring to since I was neither a devoted electorate or a political junkie, especially for the local ballot. My expression must have been telegraphed since she leaned down on one knee to be level with my posture.

Looking in my eye, she showed a strangely glazed expression upon her face. "Question seven is simply obliging people who happen to be clones to register with their respective town halls, specifically here in New Hampshire."

"Why?"

"For protection."

"But protection for… or *of* who?" I asked. I could feel my right eyebrow rise unconsciously. It was a quirk of mine that happened whenever I became agitated.

The strange, young woman rolled her eyes at my disdain. "It's about protecting our community." Her expression suddenly changed. "Do you even live here?"

"I do," I said. "And in all honesty I don't see."

"And by protecting the community we mean protecting the community from science's danger."

I swallowed hard and clenched my virtual tablet a bit too rigidly. My knuckles turned red which made them hurt. The sensation, though, gave me the enduring feeling of the fight. I loved playing the role of the politically undemanding; the one who promoted peace, love, and the global community way. I guess you could say it was more my nature having been told by the world that I was different in so many ways. For those of you who can't appreciate this train of thought, I suppose it was similar to being picked on in grammar school for being overweight or how the theocrat felt today in a world that was now very highly scientific.

"Are you implying that some people are dangerous?"

"Not some people," the young woman said. "But clones. Falsely made individuals that were created from the double-helix rather than from natural birthing." Such an inane term, *double-helix*, rather than chromosome or DNA.

"I'm sorry, but aren't all people created from chromosomes or DNA no matter how they came into existence?"

Her eyes closed tightly, making me curious whether she was trying to recall some political jargon that she had learned or if she was simply frustrated with my unconcern. "Clones are dangerous."

I knew she meant her belief was that the act of genetic science was dangerous, but I decided to follow obliviously with the thought of the clone, as a tangible constituent. Even if her convictions were more counter to the precise science, at this very moment the candid topic was more focused. This vote she was referring to was specific to a clone and the act of having a person of that persuasion be registered with the government not much unlike a sex offender was.

"Are you categorizing a whole group of people as one?" I asked, and then added, "Categorizing such people without instigation simply for the fact they are cloned?"

She opened her eyes and her bottom lip quivered for but a moment. "Clones are just preliminary to our agenda. It's a start. We have to put a face upon the whole danger of these Frankenstein's and their immoral and unethical methods."

And so there it was out in the open. This was where this odd melting pot of political and theocratic beliefs gelled no better than a recipe of bacon and ice cream. She was one of the progressives, the ones who believed that people should be born as they were and that any scientific manipulation was unethical. And yet these high minded idealists never thought that the cat was already out of the bag so to speak as they lived on the wrong side of history. And worse they were unsure what to do with those folks that were already manipulated, that were clones. We were here and we were here to stay — not by choice but simply because we were, that we existed. It wasn't as if their agenda would make us go away. And we, well, we had no agenda at all but to live a peaceful existence without maltreatment; to marry and have children, to work, to raise a family. Nothing any more nefarious than sneaking a joint after work or having a different lover the following Saturday night.

At this point I wondered if my conversation with them, my examination of their argument, was itself something that couldn't be put back into the bag. Suddenly my thoughts focused on that poor soul that was murdered in New York City days ago for nothing more than being outed for something he had no choice in. Being a clone and being alive. I sensed perspiration begin to form upon my forehead as imminent harm crossed through my thoughts. I felt the film of sweat that began to fuse into droplets upon my brow was suddenly giving away who I really was.

"Are you...," the woman began before letting the question fade.

"Thank you," I said while scanning through the pamphlet. "I'll most certainly consider your points and vote accordingly."

She got up from her crouch and looked down upon me. The two of them stood above me reminding me of how one of our country's far too many judges sat in a courtroom both with a superiority complex as well as their contempt at what they considered the latest degenerate in their midst. My first initiative was simply to tell them to burn in hell, but having seen in person the sudden violence of fanatics on the streets of our country's great metropolises I resolved not to provoke. Instead my most heartwarming smile fell into place upon my face.

"Do you know that the soul is lost?" the auburn haired fellow uttered out from what must have been some curious stream of conscious drivel that had passed through his mind.

"Come again?"

"The soul," he said. "People walk among us this very day without a soul."

Though I wasn't hungry, I suddenly felt as if any appetite I had was down for the count. "Do you mean they're damned?" I asked with a bit of confusion. Again it was foolish of me to continue to converse with them, but I sensed I was like a fox surrounded by the hounds. This was my only way to get them to scent out someone else. With the bizarre turn of the exchange, my defenses veered from defending against the progressive to that of the religious zealot.

"That goes without saying," he said. "Yes, the walking damned. That's just on principle. But what I mean is the incorporeal... the incarnate part of the person... there is none for the clone. Only God may create a soul. Not a scientist."

Faith. A trust without proof. And no matter what I was, I was myself a woman of faith. A true believer of God and one of the vanishing spiritual. I attended Roman Catholic masses weekly and even said grace before evening dinner. You may ask why? But it perhaps makes better sense when put into the perspective of my mindset. Just as everyone I too have a question of the meaning of life and what it all means. Why am I hear? What is the meaning of it all? What is the point? Seeing loved ones die, hearing of terrible tragedies in Burundi, or seeing the latest headline that another nation disappeared off the map as Russia makes another land grab.

The only question to ask is simply Why? Starvation, poverty, disease, mental illness, pain. And yet there I was weekly unfailingly at religious service gaining comfort in that search for cerebral wellbeing. Just maybe finding significance in my little carved out part of this world. That maybe I too was a child of God.

"Clones are soulless," the auburn haired young man said. "They are therefore aberrations of science and something to not be trusted. Don't you see? If one looks upon all of us as the children of God, the transcendent component of us is our soul. And the body is just a shell. The soul is passed along to our children leaving clones as nothing more than empty shells. Who knows what holds influence upon them?"

I looked over at the woman, expecting some sort of empathy. But there was none there. She had her own agenda and no matter how progressive thinking her anti-cloning thoughts were, her agenda was more in line with that old citation the *enemy of my enemy* is my friend. So I was alone to endure the presumption of both in their bizarrely united front against... me.

And so that's when I decided to step out of the closet, so to speak. I had told random folks at points what I happened to be. Now with my instincts intransigent and my rational indifferent, I spoke out with hardly any conviction. But by doing so I was drawing that figurative line in the sand that they wanted. "I am a clone," my voice said in an oddly conversational quality.

The auburn haired man recoiled from me as if I were a viper that were to pounce upon him. The woman, however, shown an expression of understanding; as if she had conjectured it all along. Once more I hoped for empathy from her, but instead I received a second expression. This time it appeared across her face in the likes as if she had been tricked into biting into a sour lemon. I was to get no compassion from there.

I pulled my virtual tablet up against my breast and waited for their first articulation of what I was. Being the town that I lived in, with its population of 11,000, that itself would essentially make me the only clone proportionately as a resident.

And what I had hoped would not happen did. "Heathen!" the man screamed as the woman turned to the remainder of their cohorts still on the other side of the town green holding up their placards and chanting whatever intone they came prepared to utter. "Over here," she shouted. "We have one."

Their yowling most assuredly drew the attention of the other seven activists that I counted, but fortunately or not, it also drew the glances of the young coed joggers to my little section of the commons. When the now large group of nine activists had formed close to where I sat quietly (and in fear, I must add), the short haired girl took one of the placards from an older member of her group and held it out pointing it at me like a bludgeon.

"She's a heathen," the auburn haired man yelled again. "She is

Legion — one of many."

And so he was going Biblical upon me. And yet while I was the one in danger, it was my God that was being smeared. The young man was unceremoniously adding more tarnish to the name of Jesus Christ with his deviation of His teachings. No matter if you believed or not, to debase one's own belief system with a distorted viewpoint itself was an appalling transgression.

"Please," I said as I stood up. The woman surprisingly poked me with the edge of the placard she held. Though in panic I was still able to glance at its block lettering: *Cloning is a science of profit.* Prior to being able to slide around the park bench for a quick escape, the group encircled around me in a way that would make it impossible to pass without being molested in some way.

"You are a soulless shell," the auburn haired man yelled out at me from behind.

An older man who blocked my way remarked how in some way I was an example of reckless science. At this point I replayed everything in my mind with a different scenario; as if I hadn't made what now appeared to be a stupid blunder. Unfortunately there wasn't a take back button, was there? And to prove it, I was about to find that out. So my mind already began preparing itself for the inevitable dreadfulness that would be. All I was assured of was that it wasn't going to be anything grand.

At this point I wanted to contemplate something other than the meaning of life. To my extensive understanding, it was the unpredictability of life that really mattered. What would have happened had I simply pulled away in my car when I saw the activists? I could have simply gone to another park bench in neighboring Wilton, New Hampshire to enjoy the sun or simply gone home and sat out on my back deck to read. What if I had instead decided to sleep in or do as the young coed joggers were, such as enjoy a brisk run along the sidewalk in one of those white picket fence neighborhoods? Sadly my mind fished for anything that would make me experience a different elucidation of my prospects. And yet I already knew that it was simply a protective subterfuge for my dire predicament in hopes of ending this foreseeable distress I was feeling.

Then I felt hope, that wonderful feeling that usually led to naught yet kept one's prospects elevated. To my delight, help was on its way. The young coeds came jogging over to this new commotion in the commons. Immediately they protested the actions of the anti-geneticists to leave the young woman alone. It was only after a beat that I was aware that the "young woman" they were referring to was actually me.

Which leads to what happened this very day that would indeed make me get that answer of whether I, being a clone, did incontestably have a soul. Most folks just figure things happen as they do, generally in place, with no arbitrariness. Such an analogy would be returning home and deciding to make dinner. One would think after it is cooked, you'd sit down and eat. But the thing is, what happens if the meal is burnt? You didn't prepare ahead for such a conclusion. You prepared to have that glass of wine with the meal and you'd be done with it and your day continues. But no, sometimes it does burn and as a result it isn't suitable. So instead it goes into the garbage. So instead you either don't have dinner at all or you have to instead order out. Your day changes, though ever so slightly. And that is really how existence truly is. Something unexpected happens and everything changes. A west coast earthquake, a plane crashing, falling from a horse, getting the flu the day before your two week vacation.

As I stood within the middle of a group of hostiles, and my spirits rose as a handful of young coed joggers came to my rescue, life threw at me ... at all of us, *deus ex machina*. One of my rescuers let out a little yelp as she pointed over by the road. A large vehicle came quickly and plowed into the whole lot of us. I saw, though all in a short moment, the horrible sight of the short haired woman's skull be crushed under the wheel of the flatbed truck as it collided into us. My body suddenly flashed with a throbbing as I felt myself propelled away after impact. The large catalpa tree with all of its carved in scribbles by various lovers stopped my progress.

The very loud snapping sound of what I could only believe were my ribs actually brought back my bearings if only for a moment. A larger man in suit and tie jumped out from the driver's side of the vehicle. At first I thought he was there for our aid, having made a grave mistake while thumbing the knobs of the truck's radio or texting foolishly on his mobile phone. The vehicle simply having gone astray due to a misfortune. But instead he pulled out a pistol and began to shoot both activist and jogger while rebuking the anti-geneticists as scum of the earth.

I was on my side laying upon my oddly angled left arm watching as heads jerked back from bullet impact. My only hope was I was not mistaken as an activist and either helped or left for dead already. I could feel a tug in my brain that was unexpected. I figured if I were to die or black out it would be not much unlike simply falling asleep upon my love seat while watching television, not noticing and the slumber simply happening. But my eyes were fading away in a way I was not expecting. Rather than a blackness or darkness, alternately an emptiness seemed to fill what itself was a void. A nothingness overcame me.

Life in all its ways treated me no more kindly than the next person. The pops of the pistol had already passed into the background of my perception. Now the one thing that I always wondered became front and center in my mind which was simply the question of whether I did in fact have a soul. As whatever fate was to happen upon me, I only knew that their were three alternatives. The first was that I would die and I would meet my maker answering the faith of all those fellow parishioners that attended church weekly with me. That I did indeed have a soul, and life appropriately had a meaning; a meaning that the greatest thinkers asked. What is the meaning of life? The second alternative was that I faded into death and all that was waiting was a void. Nothingness. Simply consciousness leaving and I was essentially gone. And yet that would not answer anything for me since I would be dead while those around me who were being shot, would they experience the first alternative as I experienced the second? Or would we all just enter the void? The last alternative was a bit more arbitrary. Was I simply blacking out? That I was not going to die and any answer would wait for me another day? Was I simply going to regain consciousness laying in a hospital bed as my bones and wounds healed? And I would continue on with life for another fifty years or so with the question of whether I had a soul hanging over me. That question leaving me self conscious with a gloomy sorrow.

Well, to be honest, I hope for the last, not knowing and being alive. My concerns and fears probably no different or unequal than any other poor soul struggling to survive in this crazy world. So the pain in my broken body began to overcome me and either death or shock was to come. My fate was no longer within my influence as both my physical being as well as some crazed gunman were to determine my providence. So I slowly let my senses fade away. And whether I lived, was reborn, or faded into the nether, I cared not for I was only human. And being human, all I could ask for was serenity.

Philip C. Perron was born in Lowell, Massachusetts. He is the founder, producer, web designer, editor, and co-host of the Dark Discussions Podcast, which discusses genre film, novels, and all things fantastic. He lives in Amherst, New Hampshire with his wife, Joanna, his daughter, Colette, and his chiweenie dog, Lilly, where he writes fiction. His latest work, Indian Summer, can be found in the horror anthology Chiral Mad 2. You can find Philip on Facebook and at www.darkdiscussions.com.

REDEMPTION
Timothy P. Flynn

every morning a mirror-image
of repetition, blurred eyes attempt
to define an unsure reality — dread
prickles a bony spine, crackles — pop!

blue-gray smoke engulfs congested lungs
outside this second story window; the city is nestled in slumber
the quiet is intoxicating — people are so overrated —
need ice to caress this fevered, racing mind

the pain, consuming and overwhelming
has no precise origin, it radiates within
pouring out — electrified overload
this world's compression — crumbles shoulders to white dust

to be blind, disregard the revulsion of the everyday
envy those bastards that embrace the ignorance
the worker bees, redemption not allowed to
conflict with the routine, passion doused out
 like a candle flame of hope — dimming, dimmer…

addictive personality — not welcome
self indulgent motives to entertain, need to
find another means to achieve the numbness

why is being good so damn hard?

past demons conquered
birth new entities of torment
martyr for an unknown cause
with each new dawn, another battle

the mind's war is never truly over…

Timothy P. Flynn resides in Haverhill, MA. His previous poetry has been in Space and Time magazine Issue # 115, Anthology: Year One, and Anthology: Year Two: Inner Demons Out. Tim is a husband and father of three, a member of the NEHW(New England Horror Writers), and an online student at SNHU studying Creative Writing/English.

GOT YOUR BACK

John McIlveen

RICKY BRIGGS AWOKE TO AN URGENT bladder, but when he tried to get up he realized that pissing was the least of his concerns. He had slept badly on many occasions, often arising to lower back pain or his legs so entirely asleep that his ass felt like a block of wood. A few times, he woke up with such severe cricks in his neck that it took five minutes to move his head at all, but never had he experienced a feeling like he felt now. It wasn't pain and the difficulty to move that worried him, but the lack of pain and the difficulty to move. He knew he was in some serious shit.

He lay prone on his mattress with his face turned to his wife's vacant pillow. His pillow most likely lay on the floor beside his bed, flung overboard during his usual tossing and turning.

Ricky moved his right foot, which responded splendidly, eliciting a resounding snap as he rotated his ankle. His lower legs moved freely, but when he tried to move his whole leg there was a lot of resistance. His wriggled his fingers without difficulty, but his upper arms resisted in a similar way to his legs, and when he tried to move his shoulders… that's when things got real wonky. His ribs felt as if they were traveling with his shoulder blades, swimming around loosely beneath his flesh, and even though it was painless, it was thoroughly disconcerting... but not nearly as troubling as the fact that he couldn't move his head at all. He tried to maneuver his elbows beneath himself in order to lift his torso, but little happened. He was stranded and helpless, which added together equaled scared.

"Melanie!" Ricky hollered. His words were muffled by the press of his cheek against the mattress. He waited about a minute and then called again, "Melanie!"

He thought he heard could hear her talking somewhere downstairs... probably in the kitchen.

"Melanie! For fuck sake! I need help!"

A few moments later he heard her angered pounding as she ascended the stairs to the second floor.

"Jesus Christ, Ricky. I was on the phone with my mother," Melanie complained. "What's so important, already?"

Melanie was twenty years out of Jersey, but the nasally accent still held firm and her penchant for whining only made it worse. Ricky had once considered it cute and endearing, but after fourteen years of marriage it now affected him like a dental drill scraping at his eardrum.

"I can't move," he said, trying to maintain a sense of bravado, but his fear was too strong and it seeped through in his words.

"Whaddya mean you can't move?"

"Just what I said! I can't move! Well, I can move my arms and legs a little, but I can't move my head at all."

"How come?" Melanie asked.

"I don't know," Ricky said. "Maybe my neck fell asleep or something. Help me turn my head your way. Maybe that'll wake it up."

Melanie slid a hand under his cheek and started to turn Ricky's head, but recoiled when she felt the lack of support. Ricky's head rolled on his neck, and then settled at an impossible angle almost directly facing the headboard.

"Oh my God, Ricky! What's wrong with you?" Melanie backed away, twitching and shaking in disgust.

"Oh God. Straighten it! Quick!" Ricky cried. Panic built within him as his arms and legs rebelled in little paroxysms.

"How? I don't want to!" Melanie whined.

"Come on you fuck-tard! Fix it."

"Ricky, don't be an asshole," Melanie said. "I think your neck's broke."

"Okay," he panted. "I'm sorry. I'm just scared. Can you please straighten my head? It's totally freaking me out."

"Me too, Ricky. You should see it. It's weird. It's fucking creepy."

Melanie returned to the bed, gingerly reached out and then retracted her hands as if trying to pet a cobra. She repeated the action three times before quickly nudging Ricky's head into a somewhat normal position.

"I'm calling 9-1-1," she said.

"Yeah. Do that," said Ricky. He was wide-eyed and nearly

hyperventilating as he watched Melanie rush through the bedroom doorway to retrieve her cell phone. She returned in less than a minute with the phone pressed to her ear.

"Yeah. He can't move his head at all. Yeah. Just his arms and legs a tiny bit. Did I try to move him? Yeah. Just his head. It moved really weird." Melanie quivered at the memory. "Okay, I won't move him anymore. Is he in pain? I don't think so. Wait. I'll put you on speaker phone. No? Oh, okay. They're on their way. Good."

Melanie ended the call and put the phone on the nightstand and looked at her husband. "What happened to you, Ricky?" she asked.

"I don't know. I just fucking woke up this way."

"It's probably those ten pounds you gained putting pressure on your spine." Melanie pulled the covers down to expose Ricky's back.

"I weigh a hundred ninety. That's hardly obese for six feet tall," Ricky rebutted, though in truth he recently breached two hundred.

"Just sayin' is all. Your back looks okay." She ran her hand down the center of his back and again pulled back uncertainly. "Wait... Ricky. How come you don't have any of those bumpy things going down your back?"

"What bumpy things?"

"You know... like your backbone bumps."

Melanie poked along Ricky's spine and felt only sponginess and the blunt ends of his ribs where they should have connected to a spinal column.

"Oh my God! I mean it Ricky. You ain't got no backbone."

"That doesn't make sense," Ricky spat. "That's not possible!"

"I don't know, Ricky. There ain't no bones there," Melanie insisted. "It's like some kind of miracle or something."

"A *miracle*! How is *this* a miracle?" Ricky barked.

"What would you call it, then?"

Ricky simmered in place until they heard sound of a diesel engine, followed by a squeak of brakes in the driveway.

"That must be them," Melanie said.

She darted through the doorway, returning a few moments leading a cop and two heavy footed EMTs lugging bags, gear, and cases into the bedroom.

"I'm sure his backbone's still there," the cop was saying to Melanie. "Those don't just disappear overnight."

"Yeah. I hear what you're saying," Melanie replied. "But I'm totally serious. I think his is gone!" She pronounced the last word *goo-wan*.

Ricky recognized two of them. The cop's name was Danny LaCroix—

Ricky had worked with him for the last ten or so years... not directly, but on the same squad—and one of the EMTs was a pretty but severe looking woman named Shelly something-or-other. The second EMT, a young man who didn't look old enough to shave, Ricky had never seen before.

Danny LaCroix squatted beside the bed with the customary palliative cop smile pasted to his face. Ricky recognized the smile because he had used it many times himself. It scared the shit out of him.

"Hey Ricky. What's going on?" asked Danny LaCroix.

"I can't move most of my body... just my extremities."

"Let's have a look," Shelly what's-her-name said. She pulled on a pair of gloves, grasped one of Ricky's hands, and told him to squeeze. He did.

"That seems fine," she said. "So, you can't move your head at all?"

"No. Well, minimally. Not enough to turn my head."

Shelly probed Ricky's back and muttered something under her breath. Ricky didn't hear what she said, but he did manage to catch the shocked look she and Danny LaCroix exchanged in his periphery, and her faint shake of the head.

"What?" Ricky demanded. "I have a backbone, right?

"Hey. Whatever's going on, I'm sure it's minor," Danny said, trying to reassure him. "We'll have you right in no time."

The EMT cautiously lifted and then lowered Ricky's head. Twenty minutes later, Ricky was securely bound to a backboard and heading for Lawrence General Hospital.

Ricky was admitted immediately, only to wait an eternity for X-rays, and then another before being transferred to a private room. Doctors, specialists, technicians, nurses, and—for all Ricky knew—ice cream vendors, filed through the doorway to see the peculiar new patient. An endless progression of pinching, probing, and limb manipulation was followed by even more of the same. Ricky wanted to scream, and he would have run away if he could. After another infinite wait, an MRI, and a CAT scan, they returned Ricky to his room and instructed him to wait for a consult... as if he had a choice.

Melanie sat on a pleather chair to the left of his bed, staring blankly out the window towards the Lawrence mill district. She was conflicted and avoided looking at Ricky, even when he spoke to her.

"Did you hear anything last night?" Ricky asked.

She didn't respond.

"Melanie!" he said louder.

"Huh?" she answered, but she still avoided looking at him.

"Did you hear anything last night?"

"Like what?"

"I don't know... like someone in the house?"

"No. You know me, Ricky. I would have said something if I had. I slept right through until I got up."

"It's no wonder, with you and your fucking sleeping pills."

"Don't give me no shit, Ricky. You didn't wake up either, and it's your spine that got took." She risked a quick glance and returned her gaze to the window. "Anyway, I wouldn't need sleeping pills if you didn't snore like it was D-Day or something."

They wallowed in their uncomfortable silence for forty minutes until Doctor Leiderman returned carrying two x-ray prints. He was a short but sturdy man in his late fifties, with a greying beard and a receding hairline capped with a dark blue yarmulke. Doctor Leiderman clipped the x-rays to a light box mounted on the wall. From his angle strapped to the hospital bed, Ricky could clearly see the prints and that the unmistakable stack of vertebrae was not present.

"To the point, Mr. Briggs," he said. "We are baffled. It's unprecedented. No one here has ever heard of this kind of thing. We've searched high and low and there is nothing that compares to this in any records... not online or even in any database."

Ricky felt reality tilt and his vision took on a purple hue as he fought to stay conscious. "There has to be an explanation. Spines don't just dissolve."

"Not only that," said Doctor Leiderman. He pointed to the upper back on the x-ray image and ran his finger down along the spinal valley. "If they did there would be evidence of a dissolved spine—a residue in your bloodstream. You have no history of spinal damage. There are no traumatic markings anywhere on your body. In fact—and even more perplexing—your nervous system is still completely intact and undamaged. It's mystifying. Normally, many of the gluteal, tibial, and posterior nerves thread through dorsal foramina--these are skeletal holes in the lower lumbar and pelvic region. To remove this part of the spinal base you would have to deconstruct the sacrum. This is not easy. It would entail hours of intense and precise surgery."

"So, what are you saying?" Ricky asked. "Aliens took my spine while I was sleeping?"

Doctor Leiderman offered Ricky a sympathetic glance and shrugged. "Extraordinary occurrence seems as good an explanation as any we can offer. We've had chiropractors, osteopathic physicians, physiatrists, and surgeons here. No one has answers or even speculations… at least for the time being."

"So what's his prognosis?" Melanie asked, pinning Doctor Leiderman with doleful brown eyes. "Is he gonna stay like... like this?"

The doctor weighed his answer before saying, "Unless another event of a similar inexplicable magnitude occurs, I don't see any chance of correction or improvement. You, Mr. Briggs, will most assuredly need to start therapy on your musculature to keep your extremities functioning and to avoid the atrophy that will assuredly occur without exercise. Your skeletal structure has no central support without your spinal column, and your body becomes like a... well..."

"A gummy worm?" Melanie offered.

"Well... uh... yes," agreed doctor Leiderman. "A gummy worm."

"So, I'm going to live the rest of my life as a fucking vegetable, pissing and shitting myself?" Ricky asked. His eyes brimmed as he awaited the doctor's reply. He could feel Melanie's eyes on him as he unsuccessfully willed the tears not to fall.

"Vegetable is a harsh term and not entirely accurate. I'm sure you will be fitted to some form of support system that will secure your back and your head and will allow you to sit and perform minor and moderate arm and leg movements. As for your bodily functions , you are not quadriplegic or even paraplegic, Mr. Briggs. Your nervous system is still functional and so are you abdominal muscles, therefore pissing and shitting yourself is optional. Not pissing and shitting yourself is optional, as well… with assistance."

"It all sounds hopeless," Ricky moaned.

"Never say hopeless, Mister Briggs," said Doctor Leiderman. "Who knows where technology will bring us? As for now, we will send you to Mass General where they are better equipped to deal with spinal situations. Some of the world's best doctors and specialists are there to help you, so do not give up hope. Not yet."

THURSDAY

Ricky arrived at Mass General late the previous evening and checked into the orthopedics ward. He was angry and defiant, so Dr. Chan, the head of the ward, gave Ricky a shot that knocked him out until the next morning.

He awoke early Thursday morning to the sound of the 6 a.m. shift change and an incessant itching along his spine. He was flat on his back and fastened to the bed by cloth straps to prevent him from toppling.

His upper torso was slightly raised and a cervical collar held his head to reduce the possibility of damage to the unprotected nerves of his spinal cord. He was staring at the ceiling, which seemed miles away in the dim glow from the hallway, and at that moment the full brunt of his truth hit him and left him gasping for breath. If things didn't change—which it seemed they wouldn't—everything he saw for the remainder of his life would not be up to him, but to the whim of whoever moved him or positioned him. If they wanted to sit him facing the corner, they could... and there wasn't squat he could do about it.

Goddammit his back itched!

He tried to maneuver his arm between his back and the mattress, but the resistance was too much. He was absolutely helpless and dependent... an infant. Yet, even infants had backbones.

Ricky was just able to see Melanie sleeping on a roll-away cot the hospital had set up for her on the window side of his room. He felt indignant. He wanted to yell at her—demand of her—*How in the hell can you lay there sleeping while I'm lying here like a wad of dough and itching like a case of poison oak?* He bit his words back, which was uncommon for him.

She slept on her belly, her face turned toward his bed and her arms hugging a balled-up pillow beneath her head. Her pouted lips were slightly parted and a swath of honey colored hair partly covered her cheek. The diffused lighting softened her, imparting a childlike purity to her features, and Ricky perceived her in a way he hadn't for... well, possibly years.

My god, she's beautiful, Ricky thought. *When did I stop noticing?*

As if sensing his scrutiny, Melanie opened her eyes and pinned him with soft cocoa irises. She held his gaze, though she was still hazy with sleep's spell and the innocence of the newly awoken.

These were the eyes that had captured him so many years ago, when they had met. He would have leapt through flaming hoops to gain approval in those eyes, but once he had gained it, it seemed the reward wasn't so valuable any longer. Of course, there would no longer be hoop jumping... or jumping of any variety.

But they were the same eyes. What had changed?

He thought of how those eyes had looked at him at first, with love, desire, hope, and lust... even in the not-so-distant past. Ricky knew he was moderately handsome, but he wasn't Ryan Gosling and he'd been no Prince Charming in their fourteen years together. He was nice enough in the beginning, but as time wore on he became increasingly angry, self-righteous, and arrogant. Any love, desire, or lust he had received in, say, the past six years had been gifts from Melanie. He hadn't deserved it, yet he felt it was his entitlement. The understanding that he may never experience it again was an excruciating gash to his soul. He would no longer be looked onto with desire, but instead with sympathy and possibly disgust.

And contempt?

He would never again be able to run his hands over Melanie's body while in the heat of passion or as a soft acknowledgement of her presence. To feel the smoothness of her skin, the rise of her hips, or the heavy swell of her breasts, was all now a thing of the past, and now he felt a powerful yearning he hadn't felt in years. He thought of the times he could have held her and he didn't... and he mourned.

Awareness of time and circumstance set in, and it was clear in Melanie's expression. She turned her waking eyes from Ricky and he almost cried out.

Just a while longer... a little more time!

"Are you okay?" Melanie asked. Although her voice had been hardened by the years, the compassion was still there when you listened—if you took the time to listen.

Ricky closed his eyes. A part of him wanted to ignore Melanie and the rest of creation, and pretend that nothing was wrong. Another part of him wanted to beg her to hold him and comfort him like a child. To promise—to lie to him—that everything would get better.

"My back itches," was all Ricky said.

Melanie pushed her hand beneath him and scratched as well as the position allowed.

"I don't want to move you in case I hurt you," she said. "I'll do it better when they come to help you go to the bathroom."

"It don't matter," Ricky mumbled in humiliation and defeat.

"Don't be going all pity party, Ricky. You're gonna beat this. You just watch."

Ricky closed his eyes.

The remainder of Thursday passed with a continual procession of specialists, much in the same way as Wednesday had. There was a priest, a psychiatrist, a physical therapist, a phlebotomist, and a slew of others digging for answers and offering false assurances. By nine o'clock that evening, Ricky was so exhausted he didn't fall to sleep... he plummeted.

FRIDAY

Ricky awoke in the wee hours just as he had the previous night. He lay in the darkness, his mind whirling without direction, when something triggered his senses. There hadn't been a noise or movement, but a feeling, like knowing that it was raining outside without seeing or hearing evidence. Something had changed.

His bed was slightly elevated beneath his upper torso, and when he focused his eyes into the shadows, he could just make out a figure sitting in the visitor's chair near the foot of his bed. How had the person gotten there without him noticing?

Melanie had left for home earlier that evening. The lure of a shower, a change of clothing, and her own bed was just too appealing after spending a night on the visitor's cot. *Had she changed her mind?*

"Melanie?" Ricky asked hesitantly.

"Not by a long shot," the figure replied.

The voice was deep and eloquent with a mild rasp. Its intonations made Ricky believe it belonged to black man, and even though he'd thought he recognized the voice, he couldn't quite put his finger on from where. *Did it remind him of an actor or a singer?* The memory of it taunted him.

"Who are you?" Ricky asked.

"Who am I?" asked the shadow-man. "Come on, Briggsy. Are you going to lie there and tell me that you don't know who I am?"

Briggsy was his nickname in high school. After high school, only one person called him by that name, but he was...

"Joe?" Ricky asked.

"See that? I knew you remembered me," said the man.

His tone was amiable, but Ricky felt an underlying sense of threat, which only increased since the man didn't move, but only sat silently in the shadows.

Joe Riddick had been Ricky's partner on the force for nearly four years, until Joe got shot during a drug bust about six months earlier. The bullet had ripped through his larynx and shattered two vertebrae in his neck. The EMTs had responded in top notch fashion and had managed to save Joe's life against dire odds, but nothing could be done about his blown out vertebrae and splintered voice box. The last thing Ricky knew, Joe had been laid up at Whittier Rehab, unable to move or even talk. What made it even more traumatic was that Joe's mental functions were still one hundred percent, yet he couldn't communicate with much beyond blinking his eyes. The fact that he was here in Ricky's room was nothing short of astounding.

"You're better?" Ricky asked. "I thought you were in rehab."

"Four months," said Joe Riddick. "You know, a funny thing about rehabs is that when you're quadriplegic and have no voice, not a whole lot of *rehab* happens."

As Joe spoke, he nodded in his familiar and unique Joe Riddick way, where his whole upper body seemed to nod in unison with his head, as if promoting his words.

"I tell you, bro, it sucked bad. All I could do was lie there, with no way to communicate and nothing to do but think and fester."

Joe studied Ricky for a moment and then raised his chin slightly looking as if he were about to impart some profound bit of wisdom. "You know," he said. "You didn't visit me even once... partner."

Ricky had no words, as the guilty often do. Joe Riddick rose and stepped to the end of the bed. He leaned forward and rested his hands atop the footboard. It was definitely Joe Riddick. His face was partially visible in the weak band of light coming from the hallway and Ricky was surprised by how healthy he looked. He was wearing his navy blue duty jacket with his badged pinned above his left breast pocket and *Lawrence PD* patches on the shoulders. His collar was raised as usual, but Ricky could see no evidence of a bullet wound on his throat.

"Wow. You've healed well," Ricky said. "I didn't hear anything about you returning to duty."

Joe raised an eyebrow and then straightened upright. "Don't know why you would have," he said.

The door swung slowly open, spilling light into the room as a CNA entered. She was young—early twentyish—with dark brown shoulder-length hair, prominent freckles, and a pretty and amiable face. According to her badge her name was Kayleigh. Joe stepped back to the wall, and both men watched the nurse approach the apparatus near the head of Ricky's bed. She started slightly when she saw that Ricky's eyes were open and looking at her.

"Oh! You're awake!" she said to Ricky. "You nearly scared the be-poopies out of me."

"Haven't been doing much sleeping lately," Ricky said.

She looked at the monitors and then at Ricky. "In case you were wondering... you're still alive. This thingy says so."

She moved to the foot of the bed and inspected the urine collection, paying no attention to the man standing near her. She gave a satisfied nod and then moved to the foot of the bed. She looked at Ricky and then returned to the side of the bed to nudge his upper body to the right and reposition his pillow behind his head.

"Aren't you going to say hi to Joe?" Ricky asked.

Joe offered a friendly wave and bowed theatrically, but Kayleigh didn't even look his way.

"Joe who?" asked the nurse.

Is she prejudiced? Ricky wondered.

"My partner," Ricky said and pointed at Joe. "We worked on the force together for years."

Kayleigh looked to where Ricky pointed and Joe shrugged.

"Are you telling me you don't see him?" Ricky asked.

"Sorry. Don't see anyone. I think your meds dosage may be too high," she teased.

"I'm not taking any meds."

Kayleigh chuckled. "Then maybe you should. You seem pretty awake. Do you want me to see about getting you a sleeping pill?"

When Ricky didn't respond, Kayleigh said, "Okay. I'll come by in about an hour in case you change your mind." She walked out the door, passing within inches of Joe.

"Have a nice night," Joe said to her, but she clearly had not heard him. He turned to Ricky. "What a sweetheart... and very pleasant. She might appreciate a thank you one of these times."

Ricky closed his eyes, hoping that it was all a hallucination. Maybe Joe would be gone when he looked again.

"I'm not leaving yet, partner," Joe said.

"Go away," said Ricky. "You can't be real."

"Oh, I'm for real, brother."

Ricky opened his eyes and saw that Joe still stood at the foot of his bed.

"Why are you here?" Ricky asked.

"First let me tell you *how* I am here," Joe said. "I think you know the answer to *why*. As to *how*... pneumonia. The curse of the bedridden. When you're flat on your back and can't move—pretty much how you are now—that shit will set up camp in your lungs and you know what? It ain't leaving. You're screwed. It festers inside of you, and even though your body is essentially dead from the neck down, you can still feel it absorbing your life."

Joe walked to the monitors and studied them as if he were profoundly interested. "You know what the biggest bitch of pneumonia is?" he asked.

Ricky looked at him but didn't respond.

"It hides the truth," Joe said. "You have cancer and the big P sets in... guess what? You've died from the complications of pneumonia. AIDS... pneumonia. Remember Christopher Reeves? Busted his neck falling off a horse? Yup... pneumonia got him. It makes mole hills out of mountains. And do you know what else it does?"

Joe moved his face within inches of Ricky's. Again, Ricky said nothing.

"Yeah. You do," Joe said with a nod. "It turns murder into simple misfortune." Joe righted himself, moved to the pleather chair near the windows and sat down. "Six months ago a bullet stole my arms, legs, voice, and in the end, my life. Thanks to four months in rehab and a dance with pneumonia, that bullet was found innocent."

"It wasn't me who shot you," Ricky said defensively.

"You didn't hold the gun, but you pulled the trigger," Joe replied.

...and in the end, my life.

As he absorbed Joe's earlier words, Ricky's expression changed from defiance, to confusion, and then to one of disbelief. Joe's slow smile showed that he noticed, too.

"Are you telling me that you're a ghost?"

"I didn't tell you that. You figured that out yourself."

"When did you... ?" Ricky started to ask.

"Come on, bro," Joe said, as if trying to reason with a stubborn child. "You might be spineless, but don't try to pass off as stupid."

"Wednesday night?" Ricky asked. "Are you the reason I woke up like this?"

"Nope. You're the reason. I did the work," Joe said and crossed his legs. "Other than that, your deduction skills are working well."

"Why would you do this to me?" Ricky asked angrily.

"Did you really just ask that question?" Joe said, staring Ricky down.

"What? I'm not the asshole that shot you!" Ricky snapped.

"You clearly need some time to think about whom you are and what you are. Do a little soul searching," Joe stood and started for the door. "Lucky for you, there's little else you can do."

"Wait!" Ricky said, but Joe had vanished, leaving Ricky alone.

Melanie returned a little before noon carrying a plastic food storage container and a purse that could have packed an Alpine camp. She set both items on the windowsill and kissed Ricky on the forehead.

"How you feeling today?" Melanie asked. "Did you sleep okay?"

"Tired. I slept like shit," Ricky grumbled.

It was clear that Melanie had slept well. The shadows beneath her eyes had faded and she looked refreshed, vivacious, and... well, she looked lovely. Ricky felt as if it was intentional, as if she had purposefully made herself more attractive in defiance of his condition. He knew it was illogical, but so was waking up without a backbone, and it only soured his mood more.

"I made you some hermit cookies... your favorites," Melanie said cheerfully. She retrieved the container from the windowsill, lifted the lid and showed the contents to Ricky. "Do you want some?"

"Not hungry," Ricky said.

"You sure?" Melanie asked. "They're good. I made them this morning."

"I said I don't want any fucking hermit cookies."

"No. You said you weren't hungry," Melanie snapped back. She sighed and put the box of pastries back on the windowsill. "I was just trying to help you feel a little better."

Ricky looked away when he saw the tears forming in Melanie's eyes. He was disgusted with himself. She had treated him with kindness and he had responded with anger and contempt. He knew he was being unpleasant and unfair, but he couldn't seem to help it with Melanie, she just seemed to bring out the worst in him.

"I'm going to the gift shop and get a book to read," Melanie said.

She paused on her way to the door and then walked out of the room. Ricky knew she was going to ask him if he wanted anything, but then had decided against it. He was both relieved and angered that she hadn't asked, but he didn't blame her either. Melanie was still at the gift shop when Doctor Chan entered the room followed by two lab-coated men and a woman. Doctor Chan approached Ricky in a near stutter-step as if expecting to be bitten.

"How you feeling today, Mister Briggs?" greeted the doctor.

Ricky held the doctor's gaze but didn't say anything.

Undeterred, Doctor Chan continued. "I am so happy to introduce to you Doctor Shauna Keating from Harvard. I spoke to her of your situation yesterday, and she immediately called Doctor Kostman. He is Chief of Neurology at John Hopkins University, and this is his associate Doctor Shota Higuchi."

Doctor Higuchi gave a quick bow as Doctor Keating stepped forward to the bedrail. She was a tall and lean woman with a stern face and short, no-nonsense ginger-blonde hair that only strengthened her severity. Looking up into that face, Ricky felt even more diminished.

"Pleased to meet you Mister Briggs," she said. "When Doctor Chan called me yesterday, I must say I was quite captivated by what I heard."

"Glad I could provide you some entertainment," Ricky said.

"I can imagine your anger and distress at such a traumatic event," said Doctor Keating.

"Then how about if you all stop bending, poking, and jabbing me and fix whatever the hell is wrong with me?"

"Which is precisely why I called Doctors Kostman and Higuchi," said

Doctor Keating, unperturbed by Ricky's acerbic manner. "They have seen your X-rays and scans and they are especially interested in your case. So much so, that they flew here overnight to see you."

"So, what do you want to do to me?" Ricky asked. In his peripheral, he saw Melanie enter the room.

"At this point, we're not certain if we can do anything," said Doctor Kostman, stepping closer to the bed. "It depends on a number of conditions being met. At the moment it is speculative, but from what we have seen and heard about you, you may be the perfect subject."

"Are you going to tell me what for, for Christ's sake?" said Ricky, his frustration mounting.

"Are you talking about some kind of procedure or something?" Melanie asked. She moved to the opposite side of the bed and placed a calming hand on Ricky's arm. "It sounds to me like you're asking him to be part of an experiment."

"Not an experiment, per se," said Kostman. He motioned to the Japanese man standing behind him. "My associate Doctor Higuchi has been working with a meritorious team of researchers and scientists in both Sweden and Japan on a neurorobotic prototype. We believe it is of a design that may work for you."

"What are you talking about, some kind of bionic spine?" Melanie asked.

"Pretty close," Kostman said.

"We are working on a titanium skeletal model, researching the prospect of using neurorobotics in severe cases of spinal trauma," Doctor Higuchi explained in clear but choppy English. His silence to this point had had Ricky wondering if he spoke only his mother tongue. "We were focusing on cases where the spinal cord is compromised, replacing the spinal cord not the vertebrae, but when Doctor Keating describe that your spinal cord was fine, but your backbone gone... well, we hadn't considered spinal trauma without neural damage."

"So, you're saying you want to install a titanium backbone in me?" Ricky nearly hollered, but the fear in his eyes downplayed the anger in his voice.

"We'd like to explore the possibility," Kostman said. Doctor Higuchi nodded. "As I mentioned, there are numerous bridges to cross, starting with procurement of financial backing. This would be an undertaking of monumental proportions and we would need support in the form of an investors or grants. Success would also depend on you on two levels... physical and emotional. Your body may not be able to support this in strength or structurally. Both remain to be determined. Last and most important is your compliance. If there is any hope of having your condition rectified, I'm afraid there will have to be an extensive amount of, as you put it, bending, poking, and jabbing. The less resistance we have to contend with, the more effectively we can perform."

"More to the point," said Doctor Keating. "Depression and a level of anger can be expected from anyone in your state, but you are a markedly negative, angry, and aggressive person. If we are to move forward, this will have to change."

"Who says I want to move forward?" Ricky said bitterly.

"Only you can, Mister Briggs," said Doctor Keating. "Do you really want to live like this? It's your move... so to speak."

SATURDAY

Ricky lay in his darkened room staring at the distant lights from the neighboring building he assumed was also a part of Mass General. He knew the place was huge and comprised of numerous buildings, but where he lie in this city within a city, he had no clue. What he did know was that the view sucked and hours of lying on his back and staring at four walls and a sliver of the neighboring building was getting old fast. He was in the habit of sleeping days instead of nights, and without the Ambien, he doubted he'd be sleeping at all. His muscles thrummed with pent up energy and he could literally feel them atrophying from disuse. He tried exercising, but it was fruitless without his central support system.

Melanie had returned to Lawrence for the night at his insistence. He could take only so much of her pampering. He was miserable towards her, and hours of reflection had presented him with the truth that he usually was, and had been for quite a few years. Even when he tried to be civil towards her, his sense of his own inabilities loomed hugely and only managed to piss him off more. Christ! He couldn't even give her a hearty slap on the ass. Instead, he became nasty and lashed out at her verbally. He clucked with self-disgust.

"Yeah... life loses its pretty from that perspective don't it?" said Joe Riddick.

"What the fuck!" Ricky barked. His heart lurched against his ribs as he tried to focus in on the figure sitting in the corner of the room. "Jesus H. Christ, man!"

"I see we're chipper as usual," said Ricky's former workmate.

"What are you doing back here? Why must you come at night?"

"Isn't that when hauntings happen?" Joe asked. "I told you that you needed time to think... so I gave you some. Have you been thinking?"

"I've been doing little else," Ricky shot back.

"No. You've been doing a lot of sniveling and bitching." Joe rose from the chair and walked to Ricky's side. "Let me make something perfectly clear here, brother. The reason you are here, lying like a wad of dough on this bed, is completely your own doing. You are now exactly what you were before—a spineless, self-absorbed, useless bag of bones. And only you can change that."

Ricky glared at him, but Joe laughed it off.

"Are you mad at me? Does your truth piss you off? You can't even swing at me. All you can do is lie there and stew in your anger and hatred and cowardice. When that beautiful woman you've been neglecting for years is finally fed up with your shit and decides to leave—and she will—you won't even be able to run after her to beg her forgiveness."

Ricky averted his eyes from Joe. "I don't mean to treat her like that. Something about her brings out the worst in me."

"No. Only you can bring out the worst in you. She's your target. Isn't it time you stop blaming everything and everyone but yourself for the asshole you are?"

"Why are you doing this to me?" Ricky asked, barely audible.

Joe jumped forward, leaning over the bedrails until their noses were barely an inch apart. His eyes bored into Ricky's, clear down to his soul.

"You know the answer to that you spineless coward!" Joe growled.

As close as they were, Ricky couldn't feel or smell Joe's breath, but he was aware of an energy radiating from the man that felt electric and lethal. He wouldn't have been surprised if his hairs were standing on end.

"When we walked into that ambush... what were the last words you said to me before all that shit went down?" Joe asked him.

"I don't know," said Ricky. Fear invigorated his every nerve ending and his limbs twitched in his desire to flee.

"Well, let's try something new," Joe jeered. "Think."

Ricky's expression changed infinitesimally, but it was enough to show Joe that he remembered. Joe stood upright with a satisfied smile. The night nurse entered the room and walked to the monitors, passing right through Joe.

"Say it," Joe hissed.

Ricky tried to clear his throat to get the nurse's attention, but it felt as if something had lodged inside, pinning his larynx. The nurse didn't even look at Ricky as she turned and left the room.

"Stop being a coward and say it! Repeat what you said to me before our little bust went south."

"I..." Ricky started.

"Come on," Joe urged. "I..."

"I gotcha back."

"I gotcha back," Joe repeated, nodding. "But you didn't. You were too busy covering your own ass."

Ricky was silenced buy the truth.

"Ricky," Joe said. His tone was conspiratorial. Ricky slowly met his eyes.

"Who's got whose back now?" Joe asked, and then he was gone.

Ricky agreed to let Doctors Kostman and Higuchi perform any tests necessary for fitting him with the titanium spine. For the two following days he was flipped, spun, measured, and then probed, prodded and punctured. He spent what had seemed like hours nestled within the donut-hole confines of then MRI machine, its knocking and whirring playing in his memory long after he was back in his room, and then well into his evenings.

Melanie, loyal as ever, stood by Ricky's side and patiently weathered his outbursts. To his credit, they did seem to be tapering off a little. Ricky was becoming more aware of his disposition. Joe's words had shaken him to the core.

When that beautiful woman you've been neglecting for years is finally fed up with your shit and decides to leave—and she will—And she will— And she will— And she will—

It played in his memory on a perpetual spool.

Ricky's parents were both gone. His mother passed away seven years earlier; his father... three. His only sibling, an older sister named Gwen, lived on the west coast. They hadn't spoken since their father died, and before that... when his mother died. He and Melanie had no children, although Melanie had always wanted them. Ricky would always string her along, promising that they would in time, but always *not yet*. Ricky felt children stole all of your time and energy, and he hadn't been willing to make that kind of forfeit. The math was easy. If Melanie left...

And she will—

...it left only him. He would be utterly alone. Who wanted that? He wouldn't even have the ability to kill himself and escape this prison. That was the truth that made it unbearable. Even with all his facilities intact, if Melanie left, the loneliness would be intolerable. His only choice and hope was to undergo the operation—if not for a second chance, then at least as a way out.

WEDNESDAY

"When would the surgery take place?" Ricky asked doctor Higuchi.

Standing near the foot of Ricky's bed, the doctor perused his notebook and then looked at Ricky as if just realizing he was there.

"Many surgery," said the doctor.

"Huh?" asked Ricky. He couldn't remember if Doctor Higuchi was Chinese or Japanese, but whichever it was, his accent was thicker than mud.

"Oh... it take many surgery."

Ricky didn't like the sound of that. Surgery meant pain, and Ricky had always gone to great measures to avoid pain. One surgery scared the shit out of him, and the thought of *many surgeries* put his mind on the fringe of shutting down.

"How many?" he asked.

The doctor pinched Ricky's big toe, which made his left leg spasm. Higuchi gave a brisk, satisfied nod and quickly jotted something in his notebook.

"We would need to do it over time. It is very complex and delicate series of procedures and would involve many hours... too many for one surgery. Surgery of that proportion would be too traumatic for body to endure. The prototype spine would be install in single disc segments. Maybe five discs for each procedure. Each disc has intricate cluster of nerves that weave between it and the next disc. Each disc connect would be performed with extreme carefulness not to damage the spinal cord and nerve bundles. Nerve weaving for sacrum alone take sixteen hour."

Ricky felt as if an eel had coiled in his stomach and was sending jolts of panic from his core outward. When Doctor Keating told him that he had checked out okay to perform the surgery—all systems go—he had felt a level of elation he had not felt since this whole mess started. The funding hadn't come through yet, but they weren't too concerned. A procedure as unique and revolutionary as this one would garner a lot of attention. The funding would come, they had assured him.

Now he wasn't feeling quite so enthusiastic.

The doctor pulled down the blanket and then raised the hem of Ricky's Johnny to expose most of his leg. He withdrew an instrument from his pocket that looked like a metal toothpick with a screwdriver handle and proceeded to poke around Ricky's knees.

"You still haven't told my how many surgeries," Ricky said.

Higuchi gave his left knee a painful jab that made the muscle react such that—spine be damned—Ricky's leg kicked outward and pulled him about two inches lower on the bed.

"Ow! What the hell!"

"Sorry," Doctor Higuchi said and smiled his *life is good* smile. "Maybe five or six surgery. One every two month. Twelve to sixteen hours each."

"Will the surgeries be painful?"

"Oh... very painful. Six time very painful," Doctor Higuchi said and nodded emphatically, that damned smile still pasted to his face. "But you'll be very happy after."

The eel flipped and Ricky vomited across the front of his Johnny.

MONDAY

Ricky's insecurity had been increasingly eating at him. He hadn't seen Joe Riddick since that night, but Joe's words bounced around in his head non-stop and his inability to act on his anxiety only managed to acerbate it.

—and she will.

"I have to work, Ricky," Melanie said. "I'm sorry, but if I'm here all the time, the bills ain't getting paid."

She no longer came right after work. The previous week she showed up at five on all but one day. He wondered if she was having an affair... not that he could do anything about it. She gathered a few stray magazines she had brought in and she set them on the windowsill.

"You get out of work at three-thirty," he said. "It's nearly seven."

"I had to go register the car. You know how long that takes. And I had to do some food shopping 'cause there ain't nothing in the house. Life goes on, Ricky." She took a sip from her *Starbucks* iced coffee and set it down.

"So, is that it? Are you moving on? Did you find someone to screw around with already since I can't anymore?"

He knew he had gone too far, but the words spilled out and it was too late to retract them. Melanie stared at him and he had never seen her looking so cold and empty, and it dawned on him that he had never seen her look at him this way before.

"You know what, Ricky? Fuck you! I've had it. I'm going home."

Dread washed over him. He knew her anger was justified as much as he knew his words were poison, but he had no governor. When shit popped into his head, there was nothing to keep it from sliding out through his mouth.

"Hey. I didn't mean it," Ricky said.

"You wouldn't have said it if you didn't mean it." Large tears pooled in her eyes and dropped heavily to the floor. "I stand by you. I come visit you every day, and you keep hitting me with this shit. I don't deserve this, Ricky. No one does."

"I'm sorry."

"Sorry don't cut it, Ricky. You say those words a lot, but I don't think you even know what they mean. I'm going." Melanie picked up her purse and walked to the door.

"Don't leave, Melanie," he begged. "My first surgery is in two days. I need you."

She looked back at him and the disappointment he saw in her damp eyes rattled him.

"You shoulda thought of that before," she said and walked out of the room.

"Sure!" he yelled after her. "Leave me now that I'm fucking crippled!"

Why can't I just shut the hell up? he silently scolded himself.

Her footsteps paused and then resumed down the corridor.

TUESDAY

"Well," said Joe Riddick from the chair at the foot of the bed. "It appears you've mastered the art of fuck-up. Hell, you've probably earned a PhD by now."

"Leave me alone," Ricky said. He had a feeling Joe would be showing up to rub his face in it.

"Not on your life, brother." Joe rose and walked to Ricky's side. "Not on your death, either. I'm going to ride your ass for eternity."

"Why..."

"Don't even go there," Joe warned.

"How could you do this to me?"

Joe leaned on the bedrails. "*How* was easy. I made a little deal with someone. He's not such a bad guy. Certainly not what everyone makes him out to be." Joe leaned forward and whispered into Ricky's ear. "He punishes the sinners."

He nodded and righted himself. He turned from Ricky, but turned back, a finger raised as if he just remembered something important. "Oh! Buy the way. This revolutionary surgery they're going to give you? It's going to be a colossal failure. It will demolish your spinal cord."

"How can you know this?"

"Because I won't let it succeed," Joe assured him. "How would that benefit you? What lessons would you have learned? You'd still be the same, self-centered, spineless piece of shit."

Ricky gawked at Joe, an incredulous look in his eyes.

"Do you doubt that I can do this... floppy boy?"

"No!" I don't want this!"

"Me either, man. But when I left this little monkey show, my wife was still by my side and still very much in love with me. How're you doing with that? Not so good... you screwed it up even after being forewarned."

Joe walked around the bed to the other side.

"The other night you said something," Ricky said. "You told me that I was a useless bag of bones and that it was my own fault."

"Truth."

"But you also said that only I can change that." Ricky finally looked Joe in the eyes.

"I see you've been thinking things over. I'm impressed and a little surprised."

"Are you saying I can get myself out of this?" Ricky asked.

"Don't know. I supposed that's up to you. Maybe you can say a prayer."

"I tried. He's not taking requests."

Joe chuckled. "It worked for me."

"How? You're dead."

"Which is exactly what I prayed for," Joe said.

"Why didn't you pray to get better?"

"You can bet your ass I did," Joe assured him. "But what put me in that particular place wasn't my doing, it was yours, so it wasn't mine to undo. Maybe if you had visited and said a little prayer of your own, things would have been different."

Ricky tried to think of something repentant to say, but there was nothing that could be said.

Joe waved it away dismissively. "Water under the bridge, now."

"What do I do?" Ricky asked, nearly whining.

"Like I said... don't know. That's up to you. But you can start by not being pathetic. Stop the sniveling. Self-pity ain't attractive to anyone." He quickly clapped his hands as if preparing to leave. "I'm going to do you a huge favor, but it isn't because I want you to succeed. In fact, I hope you figure it out. That way you'll have to live on knowing what you are, and what has happened because of it."

"Will it help me get better?" Ricky asked.

"Don't know. What's *better*?" Joe said. "*Better* is debatable. *Better* is relative. Your better and my better are most likely not the same."

Ricky sighed and seemed to shrink into himself.

"Alright... enough small talk," Joe said. "The first thing I have to say to you is that shit smells. You fall into a pile of shit, you'll smell like shit. If you don't want to smell like shit, you have to get clean. If you clean a little off, you'll still smell like shit. If you clean most of it off, you'll still smell like shit. You get it?"

"Yes," said Ricky.

"Okay. Now, there once was this really smart guy named Albert Einstein. You hear of him?"

"Yes."

"Good," said Joe. "Well, Mister Einstein said *we can't solve problems by using the same kind of thinking we used when we created them.* That's your problem Briggsy. You don't change your way of thinking. So think about it... in a different way."

Joe was gone before Ricky could protest.

It seemed that he had no good direction to go in. Joe said that the surgery would be a disaster, and he had more than enough incentive to believe Joe. Deciding to not go with the surgery was an easy choice for a coward, especially if it meant avoiding *six time very painful*. He realized that admitting he was a coward was a huge step for him. He had always known he was, but he'd avoided the confession. It was easier to keep it hidden.

Not going with the surgery may sidestep a lot of pain, but the outlook wasn't much brighter, and as Joe said, the *big P* would probably get him anyway. As far as he could tell, there was only one direction left, though there seemed little to no promise in it.

But in the end, it was all he had. It was time for Ricky to come clean.

SATURDAY

Melanie walked briskly into the hospital room followed by a short and pretty black woman with guarded, tired eyes. Ricky could see the resolve in Melanie's stance and expression. Her guard was up a mile high and she wasn't going to take any shit.

"I don't like being manipulated, Ricky," Melanie said. "You're driving me crazy."

Ricky had barraged her with an onslaught of telephone calls, convincing each staff nurse to ring her multiple times and stressing the importance of his need to speak to her. As Ricky had expected, Melanie was too softhearted, and her resolve to ignore him broke.

"What's such an emergency? Bothering this poor woman, especially at a time like this in her life?"

"Please, pull up a chair," Ricky said. "Both of you. I promise this won't take long Mrs. Riddick, or for you, Melanie, but I need to tell you something of dire importance. You can choose to leave afterwards, Melanie. For how long is your prerogative, and if you do leave, I promise I will not bother you again."

Melanie dragged the chair at the foot of the bed forward until it was angled to the pleather chair. Her expression was a conflict of emotions. Distrust and annoyance were prevalent, but there was a layer of curiosity she couldn't hide. Dannelle Riddick sat opposite Melanie. It didn't escape Ricky that she chose the seat in which Joe Riddick always appeared. Ricky did know how to start, so after a couple of shaky breaths, he leapt in head first.

"I have a confession to make," he said.

Both woman stared at him expectantly, their expressions unreadable.

"I'm a coward," he continued. "It's not irony that I have no spine. It's fate... a message."

"I know you put off the surgery," Melanie said. "It's only natural to be afraid..."

"Wait!" Ricky interrupted. He closed his eyes and gathered his thoughts with uncommon patience. "Melanie. You've always been too kind-hearted to see the truth. I seldom had to make excuses for my actions because you always did it for me. What you are seeing, my canceling the surgery, is just another level of my spinelessness. It runs so deep it has cost lives."

Both women's brows furrowed and Dannelle Riddick's eyes took on a new intensity. Ricky took another deep breath and released it.

"Dannelle. Mrs. Riddick. There are things you need to know about Joe." Ricky saw a defiant light ignite in Dannelle's eyes and he realized that his words were conveyed wrongly. "Please, don't misinterpret me. Joe is totally honorable. I'm the one who was and is inexcusable. My actions were selfish and, as I said, cowardly."

"Mr. Briggs," Dannelle Riddick said. "I have no idea what you're trying to say."

Ricky held her gaze and had to coerce himself to continue. "The ambush, Mrs. Riddick. It didn't go down the way you heard... the way anyone heard. The real truth—and I'm the only person who knew it until now—is that Joe is the reason I came out of there alive, and I'm the reason Joe was carried out of there."

"Go on," Dannelle said, stiff jawed.

Ricky felt Melanie's stare, but he refrained from looking at her, knowing that whatever he saw there would prevent him from finishing,

"We got a tip that someone was dealing meth in front of a small market on Broadway. We watched him for a few days and learned his pattern, which always brought him back to an apartment on Buswell. I don't think we did very well, because he was just as aware of us as we were of him. When we finally made our move, they were waiting for us. We were fortunate at first. We busted down the door and charged in to see three guns aimed at us from down a hallway... our perp, another man, and a woman who turned out to be the perp's wife. One of them fired. Maybe it was a warning shot, because it somehow missed us. One of the rules in our training is to look for an out as soon as you're in. There was a door on either side of us... a bathroom to the right and a bedroom to the left. I got off one shot before diving into the bedroom. Joe ducked into the bathroom. Turns out it was a lucky shot. I killed the perp. Could you give me some water, please?"

Melanie lifted a glass from the over-bed table and directed the straw into Ricky's mouth.

"Thank you." He paused and closed his eyes for a moment. "In the bedroom, I found a young woman in the corner, hiding between a dresser and the wall. She was the fifteen-year-old student from Lawrence High School."

"I know who you're talking about, Mr. Briggs," said Dannelle Riddick, her words as sharp and hard as a carbon blade. "Her name was Keira Pierce."

Ricky paused. He had never known the young woman's name and had never stopped to consider that she had one at all. It added a personal element to it, and for the first time he thought of her as flesh and blood. He closed his eyes briefly.

"To avoid getting shot, I decided to use her as a decoy."

Melanie's gasp made him pause. *Onward*, he thought.

"Joe was standing in the bathroom on the ready. When he saw me pushing Keira towards the door, he knew what I had in mind. He shook his head and motioned me to stay back, but I ignored him. I pushed Keira into the hallway. I heard Joe yelling at me to stop, and then he did something incredible. He dove in front of her as the girl's mother and the other man opened fire. I ran out of the bedroom shooting blindly, but it was easy to take them down because they had both stopped shooting and were staring at Keira on the floor. This is why they had a hard time putting it together. They finally figured out that the same bullet that got Joe in the throat also passed through Keira Pierce's eye and lodged into her brain. In the end, there were five people dead. As you know, only I walked out of that apartment on Buswell Street."

Ricky chanced meeting Dannelle's eyes, but they were studying the floor with troubled deliberation. Melanie was staring at him with similar intensity.

"If I hadn't acted in that way—using Keira to protect myself—chances are everyone except Eddie Pierce might have gotten out of there unharmed. Joe and Keira would most likely be alive today."

After a minute of total silence, Dannelle Riddick raised her tear-streaked face to Ricky.

"Why are you telling me this now?" she asked.

Ricky wanted to look away, but he knew he could not. He said, "The truth needed to be told."

"For whose benefit?" asked Dannelle. "Do you feel absolved?"

Ricky contemplated this for a moment, wishing that it could be true, but he said, "Less now than ever."

"Good," said Dannelle. "And I speak more for that little girl than for my husband. Joe knew the risks of his job. Keira Pierce's life is your penance, Mr. Briggs. Hopefully there's enough decency in you to carry that pain, but I question that. You took from her what was not yours to take. You've gotten away with murder… twice."

Dannelle rose from her chair and gave Ricky one last hard glare. She set a compassionate hand on Melanie's shoulder and then left the room. Ricky watched her departure and then stared at the open doorway until he felt Melanie's stare. Ricky looked at her but said nothing. Finally Melanie spoke.

"I don't know, Ricky. I can forgive you for pretty much anything… and I have. But this…" her words tapered off into nothingness.

With her silence, her disappointment roared in Ricky's ears. She was miles away from him now, which was a sensation he was not used to. It was clear that he had become content with a nearness that was Melanie's creation and upkeep… he had done little to maintain it, but its undoing was all on his shoulders.

"Anyway, my forgiveness isn't what matters here. Unfortunately, the two people whose forgiveness you need aren't alive anymore. And now look at you."

She lifted her purse from the floor and searched through it until she found her keys. She stood and looked at him with profound sadness.

"God damn you, Ricky," she said, and then left.

Ricky watched her go, saying nothing, as he had promised.

SUNDAY

The itching along his spine was at an all-time high. For the most part he had become accustomed to the itching, but this bout was extreme enough to wake him from a deep sleep. He jammed his hand beneath his back and wriggled on the bed until the burning subsided a bit. The full appreciation of what had just occurred didn't hit him until he started dozing off. Ricky sat up quickly, the movement at once foreign, painful, numb, but glorious.

"Well, look at who finally grew a backbone," said Joe Riddick from within the darkness.

Ricky rotated his arms. They felt weak, but he kept at it. He gingerly moved to the edge of the bed and let his legs drop over the side. The weight of them felt like it might pull the rest of him along for the ride. A sharp pain lit the top of his ass crack, but he reveled in it.

"Did you do this? Gave me my spine back?" Ricky asked.

"May have had something to do with it, but don't sing praises to my generosity before you look at the gift," Joe said. He stood and took a few steps in Ricky's direction and into the light. "There's going to be a lot of raised eyebrows about this one."

Ricky lowered his feet to the floor and started to transfer body weight to them. He pushed himself upright precariously balancing on his unstable legs. Another jolt of pain traveled from his ass, up his spine, and into his neck.

"Hell," Ricky said. "If they can handle a spine disappearing, they surely can handle it coming back."

Joe said nothing, but a shrewd smile spread across his face. Ricky didn't like it at all. He took a hesitant step forward and pain jolted the base of his spine again. He stumbled, but managed to maintain his balance, but as his weight shifted, he felt a pulling sensation where he kept feeling the jolts of pain. He reached behind himself and rubbed from the base of his spine and down to the crack of his ass, and he felt what wasn't right.

"What the fuck?" Ricky said in disbelief. Joe only smiled.

Ricky felt the odd appendage, running his hand to the end of it before its shape took meaning. "A tail? You gave me a fucking tail."

"And a very sensitive one, at that," said Joe. "Let's say it's there as a reminder. Although your confession the other night was mostly sincere, there was a part of you seeking sympathy."

"No... I was..."

"Are you going to deny it?" Joe asked. His voice was heavy under the weight of his challenge. "That tail is there to remind you of what you were, what you still are, and what you could become again... a cowering, spineless dog."

As if in affirmation, Ricky's thick, fleshy tail whipped around his side and struck the over-bed table. He grimaced as a searing flash of pain shot up his spine.

"This tail will always be, if you'll excuse the pun, a pain in your ass… a reminder of how it is to be truly spineless, and of how easily you can go back if you forget. And brother? You don't want to forget. It's time to become a new man… a man of honor… a man of your word."

Joe watched Ricky take a couple more steps and then try to see his tail behind him.

"If you're thinking surgery, it won't work," Joe said. "That tail is special. It's different from most dogs. Its design is unique for you. Besides being jam-packed with nerve endings, your spinal cord runs to the tip and then doubles back… kind of like a hairpin. Any attempt at surgery will cripple you… again. It's yours for the long run, Briggsy."

"Come on, Joe. Is there any way I can… try again?"

"Let's not get greedy. You fared a lot better than a few others who were involved. You blew your chance… which reminds me. How's it going with that pretty woman of yours?"

"As if you didn't know," Ricky said without animosity. "She hasn't called. It's been five days."

"Well, Melanie doesn't seem the type who can carry a grudge for long. If you ask me, she's way too good for the likes of you." Joe looked at Ricky and smiled. "Maybe if you crawl back with your tail between your legs?

Ricky said nothing.

"But maybe not," Joe said. He backed into the shadow and paused.

"Hey Ricky?"

"What?"

"Remember," Joe said. "I Gotcha back."

John M. McIlveen, author of "Inflictions" and "Jerks and Other Tales from a Perfect Man" has had more than fifty stories, poems, and articles published in several anthologies and magazines (including 21st Century Dead, The Monster's Corner, Epitaphs, From the Borderlands) and other such places like Buzzymag.com and Metromoms.com.

John is the father to five daughters and an Electrical and Mechanical Designer and O&M/MEP Coordinator at MIT's Lincoln Laboratory. He lives in Marlborough, MA with a beautiful Italian goddess. He has an affinity for black licorice, whoopie pies, and good tequila (please remember this).

TIM DEAL

Tim Deal is a writer, editor, adjunct professor of writing and a Bram Stoker Award nominee. His work has appeared in a number of published anthologies, magazines, newspapers, and Websites. He is also one of the Four Horsemen, the hosts of the annual Anthology Conference (AnthoCon). He holds an MFA in writing, an MPS in Security & Safety Leadership, and is a combat veteran of the U.S. Army.

ACKNOWLEDGEMENTS

I'd like to thank the writers, artists, and fans of the Anthology Conference (AnthoCon), who have supported the efforts of the Four Horsemen since its inception in 2011.

I'd like to thank my brothers in the Four Horsemen (past and present) who bravely decided to embark on this journey together: Mark, jOhnny, and Danny. Beers are on me at *The Boondock Saints* in NOLA.

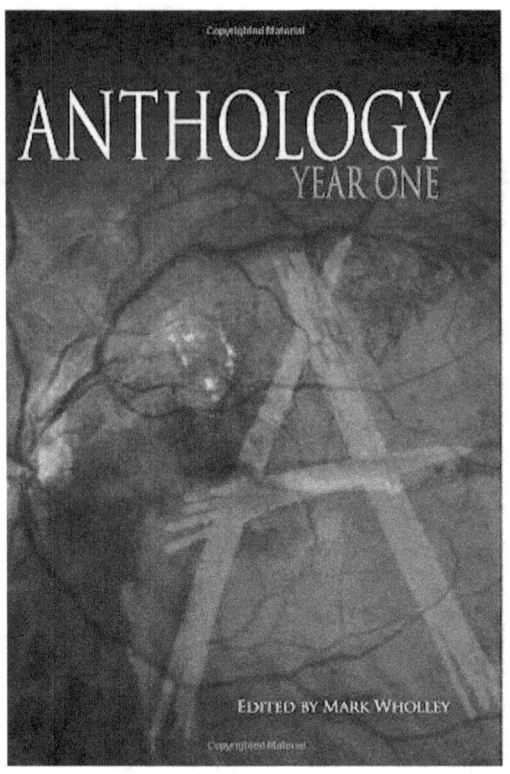

From the minds of guests of the first AnthoCon, Northern New England's only Multi-Genre Literature and Arts Convention, comes a compendium of imaginative prose, poetry and art.

Michael Bailey • David Bernard • Tracy L. Carbone; Scott Christian Carr • Roxanne Dent • Peter N. Dudar; Timothy P. Flynn • Jackie Gamber • Rona Gofstein; John Grover • Marianne Halbert • Dustin LaValley; Stacey Longo • Kevin Lucia • Bracken MacLeod; Gregory L. Norris • Ogmios • Jennifer Allis Provost; Trevor Schubert • Mike J. Smith • Henry Snider; K. Allen Wood • T. T. Zuma.

A thrilling collection of short stories, verse, and art that challenges the boundaries of modern horror, science fiction, fantasy, mystery, and more. Over 250 pages of wildly imaginative creative work.

With Meghan Arcuri • T. G. Arsenault • Michael Bailey • David Bernstein • Tracy L. Carbone • Scott Christian Carr • Victorya Chase • Robert Davies • Mandy DeGeit • Timothy P. Flynn • John Goodrich • Scott T. Goudsward • Marianne Halbert • Stacey Longo • Kevin Lucia • Bracken MacLeod • Michelle Mixell • G. Elmer Munson • Holly Newstein • David North-Martino • Errick A. Nunnally • Craig D. B. Patton • Susan Scofield • B. E. Scully • Julie Stipes • Andrew Wolter • K. Allen Wood • Richard Wright • Candace Yost • T. T. Zuma.

www.ingramcontent.com/pod-product-compliance
Lightning Source LLC
Chambersburg PA
CBHW060901250626
47159CB00008B/2832